VIKING GOLD
ROGUES

A. JAY COLLINS

◆ FriesenPress

One Printers Way
Altona, MB R0G 0B0
Canada

www.friesenpress.com

Copyright © 2024 by A. Jay Collins
First Edition — 2023

This is a work of fiction. Names and characters are either the product of the author's imagination or are used fictitiously, and any resemblance to actual persons, living or dead, is entirely coincidental.

All rights reserved.

No part of this publication may be reproduced in any form, or by any means, electronic or mechanical, including photocopying, recording, or any information browsing, storage, or retrieval system, without permission in writing from FriesenPress.

ISBN
978-1-03-917832-8 (Hardcover)
978-1-03-917831-1 (Paperback)
978-1-03-917833-5 (eBook)

1. FICTION, ACTION & ADVENTURE

Distributed to the trade by The Ingram Book Company

VIKING GOLD - ROGUES

The ORB Chronicles Continued

A. JAY COLLINS

Table of Contents

Cast of Characters vii
Target – Greenland 1
Viking I. 8
Stockman – Can You Help?. 19
Next Victims, Please 28
Black Again. 34
Together Again 40
Rome. 48
Greenland, Here We Come. 65
Nanortalik 81
Nalunaq 84
Big Jim 87
Puerto Banús 95
Hope Brook 104
Ice Man II 106
Loose Lips 123
Phase 1 – Prelims 126
Quest Gold 138
Working With Rogues .148
Phase 2 – The Plan 154
Ria de Aviles 167
The Twist 174
On the Move 182
Where's the Money? 190

St. John's, Newfoundland 197
Money Movers 205
Ghost Barges 215
Money Problems? 223
Emma and the Russian 236
Poor Danes 252
The Sinking of Viking I 258
Poor Roman 268
Time for Truth 273
Until the Next Time 275

Gold Ore Movements

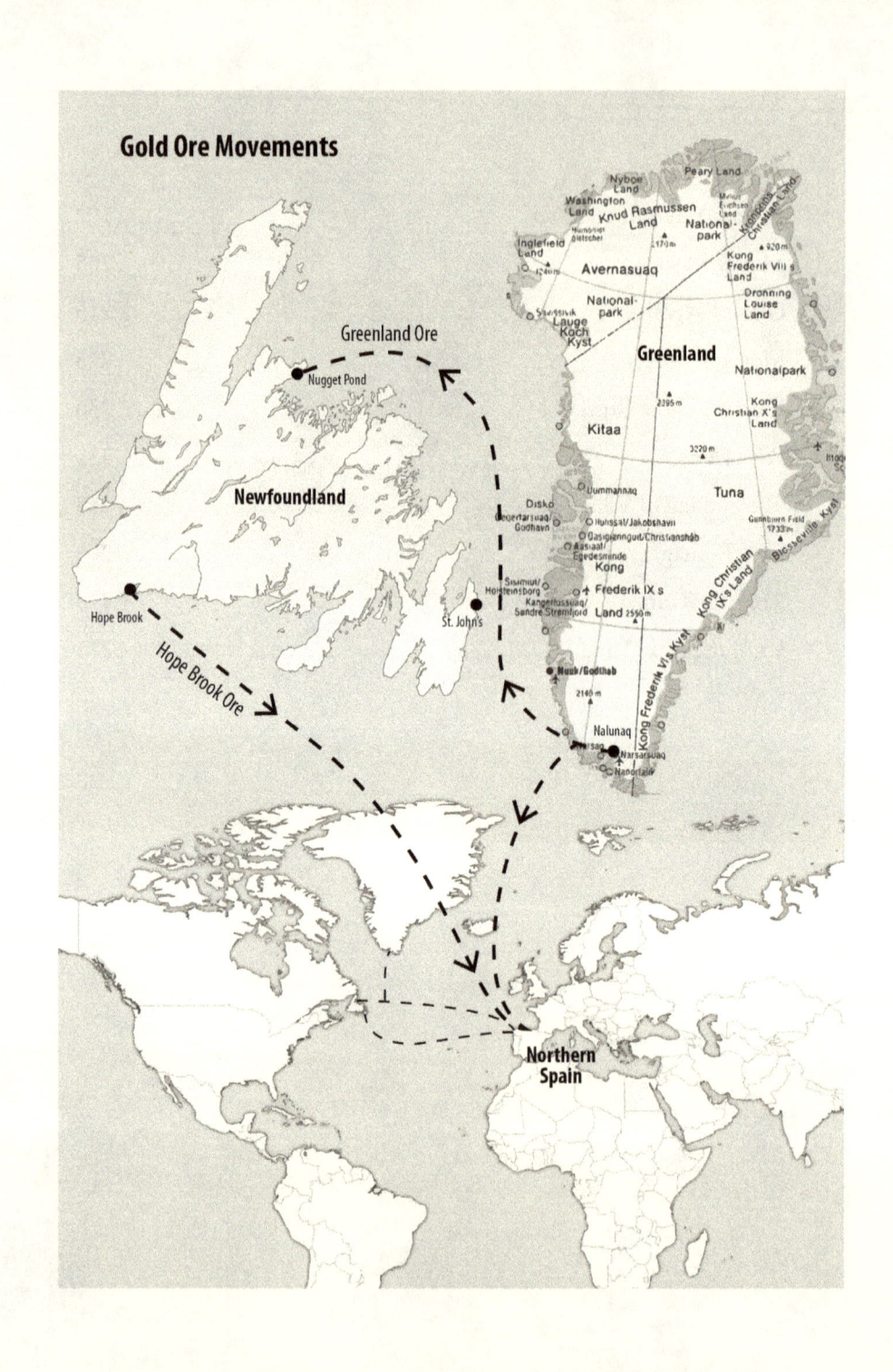

Cast of Characters

ORB Operatives and Associates

Murray Stockman (Stockman) – president of ORB, Organization for Reorganizing Business, and ex-CSIS

Matthew Black – senior field operative for ORB

Lucy Stockman – wife of Murray and an ex-CSIS operative

Emma Stockman – field operative for ORB, and Murray Stockman's daughter; also known as Emma Stone

Colin – ORB operative responsible for IT

Mitch – ORB operative responsible for geology and mining

Alan and Tony – ORB operatives responsible for legal

James Peters – ORB operative based on site as resident engineer in Newfoundland

Plato – ORB operative, international financial expert

Margaret – Plato's wife

Eddie S. Sloan (Sloan) – owns the London-based Sloan employment agency; provides labor as required for ORB

Yanko – member of the GREY group, based in Vancouver, and an ORB informer

Jeff Lewis – financial consultant in London, adviser to ORB

Jules Fortier – ORB operative stationed in Hambros Bank, Gibraltar

The Danes and Their Associates

Finn Hansen – one of the two Danes

Erik Mateus – one of the two Danes

"Big Jim" Garland – owner of CanMine Inc.; underground mining contractor

Gerry, Rich, and Ernie – GREY mining consultant group based in Vancouver

Roman Kerimov – Russian president of Polygold and financing partner

Hans Velder – accountant for the Danes

Vince Taylor – lawyer for the Danes

Others

Henri Blanchette – World Bank

Charlie Tripper – hyperbaric welder supplied through Sloan

Russ Partwick – senior partner at PCW, a funding company

Ed Sleeman – police drone operator in Vancouver

Rudy – Ed Sleeman's superior

Janson, son of Jan – Viking boy from 1,000 years ago

Target – Greenland

Over a thousand years ago, a banished Viking, Erik the Red, accused of murder, set sail from his home in Iceland, headed southwest, and, by chance, landed on the southern tip of Greenland.

Fortunately, it offered what he was searching for: land fertile enough to establish farms along the edge of a fjord.

He returned to Iceland, after his term of banishment expired, to spread the word to his kinsmen, many of whom were unable to acquire agricultural land at home. Most had already been claimed, leaving little for those who wanted an opportunity to establish their own farms.

After assembling a fleet of twenty-five ships laden with over a thousand optimistic farming families, their livestock of cows and sheep, crop seeds, farming tools, and other provisions, Erik the Red led them to Greenland. To him, it seemed an uninhabited island with as much free land as the new settlers could manage.

The fleet fought through a savage storm on their four-hundred-mile voyage, and fourteen ships were lost with their people and cargo. But those who made it through the harrowing seas finally reached what became known as Nanortalik, a small, protected inlet at the southern tip of the island, on the shore of Saqqaa Fjord. When they arrived in the middle of the year, they could see ample farmland, free from snow. The mountains on the north side would provide some shelter from the northerly winter winds as they rushed across the vastness of the interior ice cap.

These first Vikings settled where they landed for a number of years before searching for additional property to be cultivated, farther along the perimeter of the fjord. Some found their way to the Kirkespirdalen—or Church Steeple—Valley about twenty miles northeast of Nanortalik, where they established another settlement with a sufficiency of arable possibilities.

The valley was wide, protected by steep mountains on three sides with shallow but fertile land sweeping up the lower slopes to touch the glaciers feeding an abundance of fresh water to the community.

* * *

Vikings lived in this valley for over three hundred years. When he was just six years old, Janson, son of Jan, and his young Norsemen friends were responsible for tending the community livestock under the shadow of the almost mile-high spike that is Kirkespiret mountain. While keeping their eyes on the cattle and sheep, they would be distracted by their surroundings and, like most youngsters, were inquisitive about everything around them.

Janson was fascinated by one particularly imposing glacier hanging over the saddle between two of the highest mountains. It seemed to threaten an imminent slide into his valley. The ignorance of youth was on his side, and he wasn't afraid. In fact, he often went up to the foot of that glacier, picking up small, misshapen, but smooth rounded stones from the pools of frigid, fresh water as it found its way to the fjord. They were different in color and luster from the other dull gray and black ones and seemed to beckon him.

Each time Janson returned to the glacier outflow, he would collect a pouch of these odd-looking stones, more out of interest than for their usefulness. Unlike other stones, he came to learn by experimentation that these dirty-yellow ones would become somewhat pliable after heating. Janson would lay them out on a flat stone and hold it over the fire under the family's simmering pot of stew until he could see the shapes changing. Once softened, they could be kneaded together to provide larger stones he could pound into a variety of shapes.

Janson made crude rings, molded bracelets, and hammered peculiar-shaped ornaments for his parents and friends, including spear heads and hard tips for their wooden plows. He eventually lost interest in collecting the nuggets and flakes of gold as he got older and went hunting and fishing with the Viking men, leaving the younger ones to tend the livestock.

Over the years, the crudely fashioned shapes would be accidentally discarded or lost and end up on the ground or in the streams flowing across the valley floor. Regardless of the ability to work these stones into shapes when heated, the Viking farmers attached little or no value to what they considered to be only stones—and not very hard ones at that.

This tip of Greenland was home to the Vikings for over four hundred years before they disappeared sometime in the 1400s, with no accounting. Neither Janson nor his community had any idea how valuable his stone collection would become for future generations. Eventually, it came to be thought of as the first gold discovered on this unforgiving island the Vikings named Groenland.

Ten times larger than Great Britain, with a population of only about fifty-seven thousand compared to almost sixty-nine million, Greenland is the largest island in the world but essentially governed by another country: Denmark. The Danes subsidize the construction of buildings, airstrips, and roads, and provide the money and resources to establish and run the schools, clinics, and social services needed to support the many small communities.

Most inhabitants of this island of rock are Inuit, evolved from their Canadian ancestors, whose arrival overlapped the departure of the Vikings. Just like them, they settled primarily on the southwest perimeter for the same reasons, although they were most adept at fishing, which was not a great virtue of their predecessors.

Ninety-five percent of the rest of the island is covered by an uninhabitable ice cap up to two miles deep, gradually melting from the edges, exposing it to a new mineral exploration rush by international mining companies.

While Greenlanders have always lived a rudimentary and simple life and managed to support themselves from what they captured from the sea, or hunted when the seasons were ripe, it wasn't enough anymore. The new age of computers and communications educated the population enough for them to realize they needed more cash inflow if they wanted to improve their quality and style of life, healthcare, education, and social welfare systems as well as creating self-sustaining jobs.

Despite gradually assuming more self-governing roles from the Kingdom of Denmark, Greenland still relied on money from their benefactors to sustain itself. But they knew a new dawn was coming. The development of natural mineral resources, which their country was apparently endowed with, was seen as being able to provide the wealth they needed to become self-governing. The international mining companies extolling those probabilities were welcomed.

Nanortalik is now home to about twelve hundred Inuit, but some remnants of the Viking settlement remain on the edge of town—low, round, stone walls are all that is left of the Viking homes that would have had turf roofs, had they still been visible after a thousand years. As these are such an important part of Greenlandic history, no one dares to mess with what remains.

The town is the tenth largest community in the country and one of a number of Greenlandic towns hosting the newly arrived explorers searching for valuable minerals. Others gather at Narsaq, some sixty miles to the northwest, several fjords and a mountain range away, if they are interested in exploring for rare earth metals—and many are these days—urged on by the stranglehold the Chinese have on the supply of those commodities, and the political usefulness monopolies bring.

The story of the Viking gold discovery never made it into the annals of written history, and any words passed down of such an event faded quickly with their disappearance from Greenland. A little more than a thousand years later, a Vancouver-based mining exploration crew discovered indications of the old Viking encampment in Church Steeple Valley while they were exploring for minerals in the area, based on geological mapping of the country. They found crude gold spearheads, beads, wristbands, and ornaments of various kinds strewn in the gravel where the glacial waters and snow melt had uncovered them over time as the waters shifted. Clearly, there was gold in this valley. The new explorers initially zeroed in on the alluvial gold deposits collecting at the foot of the same glacier where, coincidentally, young Janson had picked out his strange-looking stones all that time ago.

They couldn't explore under the glacier at the time, but they widened their search instead and followed the mineralogical indicators, eventually discovering significant gold resources contained in outcrops of quartz veins high up on the ice-free, south-facing mountainside in what the Greenlanders called Nalunaq— "the place that is hard to find."

Nalunaq is along the Saqqaa Fjord coastline from Nanortalik and sixty miles to the south of the US-military-built Narsarsuaq international airport, having connections to Copenhagen and Reykjavik. Nuuk, the capital of Greenland, has yet to become an international flight hub. The Nalunaq property is bounded by the interior ice cap to the east, the two-mile-deep Saqqaa Fjord to the west, and no-man's-land to the north. There are no connector roads between communities, which have to rely on boats and Sikorsky S-16 helicopters to commute from one town to another.

At the beginning of the twenty-first century, a plan by a Vancouver mining company to develop the Nalunaq property moved forward based on their successful exploration findings. The gold reserve was delineated, and the ensuing study concluded there to be a robust mineralization comprising almost one million tons of one-ounce-per-ton gold. It was considered financially viable, provided the gold ore would be mined using specialized narrow-vein methods to minimize the amount of waste rock that would otherwise be extracted with conventional methods. The more waste rock, the larger and more expensive the processing plant.

The Nalunaq gold was contained in veins that would have to be worked on within a barely mineable width of three feet—the narrowest tunnels can be to accommodate a man and his tools. Specialized equipment would be needed to work within those confines, and there would be several tunnels operating at the same time.

The intent was to extract the gold veins with as little waste rock as possible, then process it at the site. They would ship the ingots out to an offshore location for further refining to increase purity to 99.5 percent gold to be sold to banks. It was a daunting task, but it was the only way the gold could be profitably mined.

The company had spent an enormous amount of borrowed money over twelve years on exploration and studies. It was in the final stage of the Danish government approvals, when the directors and managers were ousted by two of their majority shareholders, Danes. The accusations were based on trumped-up charges knowingly and maliciously released to the market concerning the ethics and behavior of the current board members. Accusations were sufficient for what the two Danish scoundrels were planning—a takeover of a company on the cusp of successfully venturing into a proven world of gold production—without spending one cent of their own money.

The Danes had quite different ideas on how to retrieve the captive gold in a far less expensive way—through high-grading, just taking the best and easiest gold at the lowest possible cost and processing all the ore offshore. Theirs was a short-term solution for garnering an easy and fast billion dollars in profit—a fraction of the potential financial worth of the mine. The alternative long-term solution would be costly but could return billions of dollars, spread over fifteen to twenty years of the mine's life. But these Danes were not patient people, nor were they sympathetic to the Greenlandic cause for self-preservation. They were just visiting.

Unfortunately for everyone involved with them, the Danes were outlandish rogues who, having cut their immoral teeth on the backs of small mining companies, had worked their way up to more brazen accomplishments. In the case of Nulanaq, they conceived an underhanded and fraudulent plan, based on the one developed by the now-ousted directors and management, to build their proposed six-hundred-and-fifty-million-dollar gold processing facility in the valley of the Nalunaq site. It was being touted by the Greenland government as being a major first step for them to become financially independent of Denmark. There would be a new airstrip, instead of having to rely on helicopters. A new road from Nalunaq to Nanortalik (the longest in the country), a transmission line from the Nalunaq diesel generators to bring surplus power to Nanortalik and lots of jobs.

The Danes had convinced the World Bank to finance the project, and they were excited to help with Greenland's move to independence from Denmark and be the primary financiers with a healthy financial return based on production. Meanwhile, according to the Danes, their company's shareholders would guarantee the investment through bonds specially created and backed by Canadian banks. In addition, the Greenland government was to become the long-term recipients of a share in the gold revenue through a five percent NSR—or net smelter return—based on revenues received after all expenses had been paid out. It was a windfall for everyone in what had become the friendliest mining jurisdiction in the world.

But instead of building the facility, with all the associated infrastructure, the mining contractor used by the Danes quickly mined five hundred and thirty million dollars' worth of gold-rich ore and shipped it offshore on barges to points west and south for processing. When they had gone, there was nothing left but debt and hate.

Not only did the Danes dupe the World Bank, their own shareholders, and the Greenlanders, but the proceeds from the gold sales flowed into their pockets as well, with no NSR payout to the Greenlandic government. The Danes' plan had deprived Greenland of a much-needed investment in job creation, infrastructure development, and taxes from the building and operating of a processing plant. It also delayed the prospect of self-rule by years.

While this, in itself, would not normally create a problem so great world powers would become interested, these Danish rogues had pulled, and were still intending to pull, the same trick on other unsuspecting victims.

Something needed to be done to stop them.

* * *

Viking I

It might not be San Tropez, but for some mariners who want to drop in at another hot spot on the Mediterranean coastline, Puerto Banús, a small, chic southern Spanish community located a couple of miles to the west of Marbella, is a popular alternative for those who want to see and be seen, especially if one is part of criminal society.

However, the ultra-rich may still have to drop anchor out in the bay if their boat is longer than a hundred and sixty-five feet, since there is no commercial harbor. That's one problem with overly large yachts—it's really quite a bother to get the tender ready to go ashore, load yourself and your guests into it, remember everything you might need, and take the somewhat bumpy ride to the marina, just for supper and perhaps a spot of shopping.

Hopefully, there will be little to no wind, rain, or even sea spray to struggle with en route to solid ground, otherwise it could dampen everyone's spirits—or worse, spoil the appearances of your guests on arrival, God forbid. Better, perhaps, to wait for fair weather and just stay in the comfort of your floating mansion if everyone prefers, or needs, to make their grand entrance on shore at a calmer time.

Of course, the people already on shore may not give a toss about the arrival of wealthy boat people as they direct their own focus on the colorful display of high-gloss, ultra-clean red, white, and blue Ferraris, Lamborghinis, and the occasional boring, but upscale, Rolls-Royces and Bentleys, cramming the parking lane along the narrow one-way road paralleling the marina and storefronts.

If the boat is shorter than a hundred and sixty-five feet and the owner is lucky, and there's room to accommodate their baby, they could pay up to a mere seventeen hundred dollars extra per night extra to tie up at the marina wall, right across from the shops and restaurants-with-a-view. Here, as they sip their cocktails on the stern deck, they are, likely deliberately, exposed to the passing admiration of those less fortunate on shore, who can only peek with envy as they wander the Malecon, searching for a reasonably priced restaurant or the missing three-for-the-price-of-one beer joint.

Obviously, not all people who visit this free-living, picture-postcard Mediterranean community by the sea fall into any category of impressive wealth just because they are in Puerto Banús. While there are those who are just plain wealthy through "natural" causes and others who wear their wealth like a necklace for all to see—like the nouveau riche and, of course, the wannabes, the eccentric, and, more often than not, the criminal element—most who visit are just simple vacationers who enjoy being in the same personal zone as the wealthy; the good ones as well as the not-so-good. This crowded pot of cultures and backgrounds gives Puerto Banús special status as a condensed cosmopolitan devil-may-care holidaying community and makes it all the more interesting, where everything is accentuated because of the size of the space it takes up—just a mile long and a block wide. Daylight is one thing, nighttime another, and the two don't mix well in the wee hours of the morning. But that's a story for another time.

White Andalusian-style buildings with geometric-shaped clay-tiled roofs line the north side of the marina. Their multi-million-dollar, two-floor, sea-view apartments, with bougainvillea spilling over the patio walls, look out over the roofs of the stores below. Dozens of trendy high-end boutiques, two- and five-star restaurants squeezed in next to each other, bars, and nightclubs wrapping around the corners and spilling over the roofs, and the all-important souvenir shops make the port somewhat overwhelming for fifteen hours of each day.

With all the buildings crowding around the quay and the noise level extra high on summer nights, it is not exactly the place to find some peace and quiet. That is, unless you are one of the lucky ones who not only has a mansion as a boat, but also has it moored at the marina wall. Here, one can shut the world out in an instant by sliding the double-glazed doors separating you from the throng as you find solace in your floating living room.

And so it was, Finn Hansen and his sidekick Erik Mateus, two world-roaming Danish scam artists, relaxed in their spacious stern cabin on their "simple" hundred-and-ten-f00t-long INACE-designed, tri-deck motor yacht,

Viking I, tied to the dock, stern-in, just feet away from shore. Nothing too over the top; just four staterooms, two five-hundred-and-fifty-horsepower diesel engines, a top speed of eighteen knots, and a range of four thousand nautical miles. Enough power, speed, range, and comfort to travel around the Mediterranean ports whenever needed or even take a trip across the Atlantic to North America. It was a home away from home for them both as they ran their business while at sea—or, rather, from a boat, more often than not, docked at some marina or other in the sun. Their land-based office was a post office box in Copenhagen, with the mail being managed by a contracted third party.

Finn stopped what he was reading, swirled the Black Label single malt Scotch around in his Glencairn, took a sip, and placed the tulip-shaped glass back on the coffee table. He took his laptop in both hands, stood, and pushed it toward his friend. Finn was an imposing figure at over six feet, with broad shoulders; a barrel chest; a round, lived-in face but with no laugh lines at the eyes and a hint of cruelty at the corners of his mouth; short, graying, curly hair; and a belly starting to take on the shape of a pot. He stood, legs apart, and waved the laptop at Erik.

"I just got a message from Hans Velder." Finn glanced at Erik, who had sunk into the comfort of his sofa chair and didn't so much as lift an eyebrow in interest. "He's finished the accounts for last year." Even that didn't move Erik into acknowledging what his friend was getting so worked up about. "It seems we did a little better than we thought."

At least this had the effect of Erik raising one eyebrow, which seemed to indicate some level of interest.

"We managed to clear a substantial amount from the Greenland project. It was very, very good." Finn looked down at his laptop and seemed to be going over the details of what Hans had sent.

Erik took both his eyes off the European soccer game he was watching on the sixty-five-inch screen fitted into the cabin wall and looked over at his friend. The TV sound was off so he could think about other things at the same time, and this now included his friend, Finn, who never stopped talking when he was excited. He was excited and Erik knew he was about to be invited to share the enthusiasm. It was just a part of his friend he had come to accept.

"What's the bottom line?" Erik asked without any sign of a spark. He was naturally more of a subdued individual than Finn, perhaps in some part to offset his friend's loudness and excitability. He was also shorter, but more powerfully built than Finn and, unlike his friend, was diet conscious and exercised regularly. Both Finn and Erik were in their late forties. Neither were married, both were womanizers when the time called for them to be, and both had known each other since their Aarhus University days, a lifetime ago, when they both studied economics.

Finn was quite miffed his friend didn't seem to be sharing his own level of enthusiasm. But he carried on regardless, fidgeting with his laptop as he focused on the numbers. "It's a bit of a rough estimate because some of the revenue reports are still coming in, and some expenses have yet to be invoiced, but it's close." He looked up at Erik as he pulled a face and grimaced with his eyebrows pushed up. "It seems as though there is some similarity with unit income and expenses between the projects we've executed so far.

"If I read these numbers correctly," Finn continued, "and I am sure I do, I think Greenland was an extremely successful venture. I like the way Hans has presented the numbers—simple, well-qualified, and described in some detail. We need it as a template for our next venture, don't you think?" He looked for some contribution from Erik.

"Okay, just give me the number, Finn." Erik sounded a little impatient with his friend for not answering his question without the accessorized commentary.

Finn wasn't biting and resisted the temptation to send a sarcastic missile in response to what he considered to be Erik's lackluster attitude. But then, he should be used to Erik's noncommittal manner and subdued responses. That was just him being him.

Finn studied the laptop, poked at something on the screen, looked up at Erik, then down at the screen, and back up at Erik as he took in the details, dragging out the answer Erik was looking for a little further. Finn knew it would annoy him; it was fun, but he succumbed.

"World Bank money plus stock profits plus private funding plus interest plus property sale price, all in about 1.2 billion dollars US. Expenses, including mining, shipping, processing, and permits, about a hundred million.

That leaves us around 1.1 billion, let's say, in income for two years' work. Not bad, eh?" Finn smiled over at his friend.

Now Erik was smiling and turned completely around in his chair to face Finn. "And how many Nalunaqs have we got on the books to date?" Erik knew the answer, but just wanted Finn to remind him so they could enjoy the moment together.

"Four." Finn never turned away. He said it with a fixed smile on his face.

"Enough for a steak tonight?" Erik smiled.

"I think so, my friend. What do you say? Shall we celebrate?" Finn had a broad smile on his face.

There was no need for a response from Erik. He just got up from the couch, poured himself and Finn another Scotch, clinked glasses with him, and raised his in a toast.

"To the next one." They echoed the sentiment together and poured the Scotch back in one gulp. Erik poured another one each.

Their glasses tapped together, and they laughed as both slipped on their loafers, downed the Scotch, and headed out into the warm night air, slightly the worse for wear after an afternoon of drinking.

* * *

El Gaucho de Banús may not be the very best steak house in southern Spain, or even Puerto Banús, but it was Argentinian and served more than acceptable T-bones. Even better, it was only thirty-five steps from the *Viking I*'s slip at the marina. An easy choice for Finn and Erik as they stepped awkwardly onto the sidewalk amidst the vacationing pedestrians, who made a little extra room for them and their obvious need for space as they drifted one step in either direction sideways for every two steps they took going forward.

Making their way across the narrow one-way street, they squeezed between a powder blue Maserati Gran Turismo and a gunmetal gray Bentley Continental GT, both immaculately shiny, and turned to the left.

They were greeted outside the arched brick entrance of El Gaucho by a tall, stunning brunette with lots of hair piled high with strands billowing around her face. She had an equally stunning smile with a set of immaculately white teeth and wore a tight, short red dress with a plunging neckline. She was new to

Finn and Erik and was clearly employed just to titillate customers into the restaurant by standing in a somewhat provocative position to one side of the door, beckoning the "right" people with a wave of the menu. She had a good sense of who to "invite" and who should be left on the street and invited Finn and Erik forward. They followed as though she was the reason they were interested—but she wasn't. They really wanted a steak, but it was fun to tease her.

Finn almost fell into her as he asked, *"¿Tienes una… mesa para… dos de… nosotras… por favor?"*

"Yes, of course," the brunette replied, understanding immediately she was not talking to a particularly fluent Spanish-speaking stranger. But she did recognize money when she saw it, even if it was new. She picked up two menus.

"Please, follow me." She flashed another teeth-filled smile, beckoned them with a finger pointed toward the inner room, and swaggered off with her body seeming to move in several different directions. She showed Finn and Erik to one of the booths lining the restaurant walls, smiled again—or was it the same smile, just lingering? —and gracefully held her hand out to show them they had arrived. They squeezed past her into the booth, being deliberate about trying not to press against her while barely touching a few of her extremes they couldn't avoid, as she whispered, "Enjoy," to each of them.

Clearly, Finn was in love again, and it showed as he took the menu, pecked at the brunette's hand with his lips, and slumped clumsily down into his seat. Erik was not impressed but was used to Finn and his ways. The brunette swaggered off and was replaced at their table by a rather short, round, balding waiter with a somewhat dour face and a thick black mustache, who simply said, "Welcome to El Gauco, gentlemen. Drink?" He had his pencil and notepad at the ready.

They already knew what they wanted, without looking at the menu. Medium-rare sixteen-ounce T-bone, mushrooms on the side, and a two-ounce Scotch straight-up to start with and a couple of pilsners with the meal—each, *por favor.*

As they waited for their steaks and sipped at their Black Labels, their minds started to focus on business again. Finn had picked up his concentration level despite his alcohol level, and Erik was his usual stiff, and slightly intoxicated, Danish self.

"So, what now, my friend?" It was Erik. "We need another Greenland, so let's figure out where we go next."

"I've been thinking about that." Finn slurped at his single malt through pursed lips but seemed to have somehow sobered up enough to be thinking clearly enough. His overly large eyebrows wrinkled as he got lost in his thoughts. "You know, Greenland was an ideal situation, wasn't it?" Finn echoed Erik's sentiment.

"All the studies had been done, and that company out of Vancouver—Summit Gold, wasn't it? —had spent all their own money to get the place up and running before we took it out. It was the smartest move we've ever made. We need to replicate that move with another company." Finn sat back as though the idea had just gelled.

"We were a bit lucky, Finn," Erik reminded his friend. "Let's face it. We're not always going to be able to get board seats and, on top of that, take the company over from the inside."

"I think we can, my friend."

"Oh, do tell me." Erik was intrigued.

The T-bones arrived, and they tucked in, each spiking the steak with a little hot horseradish. Finn was chewing on his third mouthful.

"You see, Erik"—he chewed a few times more and settled the steak into a pocket in the side of his mouth— "we have the money to buy our way in." Finn looked up at his friend with a devilish look in his eyes. "We just have to look for more companies desperate for money, with a good project on their books." He continued to chew, but looked up at his partner in crime as the idea took root.

Erik smiled, chewed, smiled, and chewed some more. "What do you define as a good project for us?" He sounded a little cynical.

"Oh, there are loads of them out there," Finn continued, unruffled by the tone of Erik's question. "Of course, there are also lots of duds. But I think we know enough by now to understand how to spot the good from the bad, don't you think?" He picked away at the meat closest to the bone. That was his favorite.

"And perhaps we need to spread the money around a little further, just for everyone to know there are new guys in town, flush with money and looking at mining companies." Finn settled back to chew at the meat some more.

"Do you remember the mining engineer… John Petersen, from Oslo?" Erik asked without looking up.

"Yes, why?" It was Finn's turn to just keep eating.

"I'm just thinking what we need is a mining professional with us who can help spot the duds." This time, Erik stopped eating and glanced at his friend.

"Not a bad idea, Erik. But maybe we should establish a small team to do the weeding out for us rather than an individual. They each have special skills these days, and I know Petersen was more of a mining engineer with some macro-financing experience—but I don't think that's enough for what we need to do." Finn paused.

"Yes, I think you're right." Erik nodded.

Settling back deep in thought and distracted from further talk, they finished their steaks and washed them back with the last of their pilsners, which had replaced the malt whiskeys. Wiping their lips with napkins, they made satisfied sounds but were still not talking as the table was cleared and the bill arrived. Finn flicked his credit card onto the plate and waved to the waiter for the machine.

As they left the restaurant, they watched the brunette repeat her performance with more potential customers. She looked even more beautiful than when they arrived, or so Finn thought. Erik had to push Finn out onto the sidewalk before he made a fool of both of them. Alcohol didn't seem to affect Erik in the same way it did Finn. But it broke the spell of their more serious thoughts, and their laughing caused the crowd on the sidewalk to shrink back a little to make room as they stumbled forward into a small cigar booth to one side of El Gaucho.

Puffing on reasonable Toro Cuban cigars, clipped and fired up by the proprietor of the place, Finn and Erik laughed at nothing in particular while strolling contentedly past the busy stores and restaurants still open along the marina. They blew their cigar smoke thoughtlessly out into the throng.

Puerto Banús, and its immediate neighbor, Marbella, a stone's throw away, had become a premier destination for the global criminal elite, and the Costa del Sol is considered to be the southern frontier of Europe's organized crime, with multiple criminal groups representing many different nationalities operating out of the area. It was an ideal hideout for the older Finn and Erik, who, having nothing to do with the drug trade, were ignored by the criminal element, who seemed to treat them respectfully, believing they were somehow "connected" but not involved in their business. Also, Puerto Banús was a particularly well-positioned location for the Danes, being only a sixty-minute drive to the British overseas territory of Gibraltar, a tax haven separated from Spain by a fence and passport official.

As midnight approached, the clubs would be full of members of one gang or another, who lived up in the hills and came out to party almost every night. They weren't a particularly classy lot; you could tell by the yelling and shouting going on between them. It got worse as they got liquored up and girls got in the mix. The scariest and most violent were the English and the Russians. They were just too wealthy and well-connected for the local police to stop them without serious consequences for themselves.

* * *

As the night wore on, the number of flashy cars doing the one-way road circuit, looking for marina parking, increased, jamming up the narrow road as the young came out to play. There were nightclubs all around, but most were where the wealthier gangsters hung out and haunted the back streets of Puerto Banús, looking for a little something extra to help them improve on what would otherwise be just fun.

No—the club scene was not a part of who Finn and Erik were. They preferred the comforts and safety of the nearby, more cultured facilities like the Santa Clara and Marbella golf clubs. Not that they were protected against the gang members in those places; it was just the criminals tended to be on their best behavior when in those upscale environments. But Finn and Erik managed to stay away from their action, regardless, and played down their real roles in life, acting as though they were really just wealthy, "retired," middle-aged men who loved this part of the world—and had a nice boat.

They mixed well with the martini and Scotch crowd, organized golf games, charmed the ladies, and got serious with the men as they talked about the world economy, who or what the problems were, and how they would fix them. Idle chitchat for those with little else to do but mingle with like, but empty, minds.

On this particular night of celebration, and as they finished their cigars, they called a local brothel they used frequently and requested their usual girls be sent over to the boat for a few hours of fun. Neither of them was into drugs; alcohol was their pleasure, although the girls came with their own cocaine, just added to the bill.

* * *

It was just past two a.m. and the girls had gone home. Finn and Erik met in the main cabin. Both wearing their shower robes over their naked bodies, they slumped down on the sofas and shared another Scotch.

"I've been thinking, Erik." Finn sipped his drink and stared out of the window at the lights coming through the window from the mega yacht next to them. There wasn't anything else to see; the boats were so close, only the fenders hanging over the sides separated them.

"Give it to me, Finn. I should have known you had other things on your mind as well as drink, food, and the company of ladies."

"Well, yes. I did get a little thinking time between all the moaning and groaning. Hopefully I contributed, but with mine, it doesn't matter. She does all the work." Finn didn't smile. Now he was serious. "I'm thinking we need to create a small group of professionals who can look at projects and let us know what they think. We can provide some links, but with their knowledge, they can add to the pool of possible targets. We just give them some boundaries and let them do the searching."

"What kind of boundaries?" Erik had perked up.

"Things like proximity to tidewater; needs to be gold if we want to get the best bang for our buck; what the financial side of the company needs to look like; what kind of players the management and directors need to be, and so on. We can refine it as we go." Finn drifted off as though that was all there was to say about what was needed. The rest would just follow automatically.

"Are you thinking of anyone in particular?" Erik was on the same wavelength but pushed Finn further.

"I am, actually." Finn didn't look at Erik. He just kept staring at the lights from the boat next to them. "Do you remember those guys we got mixed up with near the end of the Greenland job?" Finn turned to look Erik.

Erik nodded.

"They were just a small group, but they had some good people. Mining, process, financial, project, and they could recruit other resources when needed. They seemed to have some inside knowledge of a lot of companies, don't you think?" Finn looked for some response from his friend, who just nodded again.

Erik didn't want to interrupt Finn's thoughts by tempting him to be sidetracked by his own comments.

Finn continued, buoyed by Erik's apparent agreement so far. "What if we approach them and use their resources for what we need?" Finn's eyebrows went up as he looked for some sign of excitement from Erik. He didn't get any, but then he was used to that. It didn't mean there wasn't some simmering positive thinking. Erik was just reserved. "I thought the same as you," Finn continued, "about just having the one person, I mean. Like Petersen in Norway." Finn flicked an arm out, and then made a circle in the air. "But it's all too big for him and he always wants to get too close to us. We need a small team who doesn't ask a lot of questions. What d'you think?" Finn waited.

Erik was thinking. It took a little time.

"It sounds like a good approach. Why don't you try to make contact tomorrow? Where are they based?" Erik agreed with everything Finn had said.

"Vancouver, I think." Finn sat back, smiling to himself.

Erik shrugged and sidled off to his cabin, with a wave at Finn as he went.

* * *

Stockman – Can You Help?

Murray Stockman—or just Stockman, as everyone called him—and his wife, Lucy, relaxed in the garden of their second home, in Hope Cove, a little seaside town in the southwest of England. Well, it was hardly a town; and only just a village, and two at that. There was an Inner Hope and an Outer Hope, divided by a rise in the cliff between them. On the east side, most of the houses of Inner Hope had thatched roofs and eighteen-inch-thick cob walls and dated back at least two centuries, and likely more. Apparently, it was a favorite with pirates in those early days, but then most coves along the south and north coasts of Devon and Cornwall were favorite destinations for smugglers, who found them to be natural shelters from storms, and replete with sympathizers and distributors of their booty.

Hope Cove was another of those comparatively remote parts of England where time stood still, the permanent population didn't grow, and everyone did their shopping, or went to church, in one of the more populated towns at least thirty minutes away by car via the narrow country lanes bounded by high, centuries-old hedgerows.

Murray and Lucy loved this simple part of the world. Tranquility and beauty all round, with the locals tipping their hats or touching their foreheads to each other as they passed in the village as signs of greeting with an unspoken sentence. Of course, they didn't stand a chance of becoming locals in their lifetimes, even in Outer Hope, but they weren't looking for that. They were looking for a retreat where they could imagine themselves before the time of cell phones and computers.

Stockman was the inventor, and the central pin of ORB—the Organization for Reorganizing Business—an international group of contracted specialists, all cleared for Class 2 Secrecy, one level down from Top Secret, who worked on projects when needed. They were often involved with politics, corporations, or groups that had somehow been wronged and wanted reparation.

Stockman was an inch under six feet tall, powerfully built, sharply intelligent, and devoted to his wife, Lucy. Since his military days, Stockman had been embedded in a security position with some of the most powerful people and groups in the world. ORB became a natural development for Stockman as he brought his skill sets to a focused group who chose their missions and were financially supported by world leaders needing a group like ORB to do work for them they were unable to do.

No one had a permanent position with ORB, other than Stockman. Their mission was to help reputable, trustworthy, and respected industry leaders and government executives' control, manipulate, or monitor situations around the world that had gotten out of hand and needed some "adjusting."

ORB's leadership was guided by the hands of a group of twelve senior industrialists from across five countries, sprinkled with a few permanent government seniors from three countries, who reviewed and approved (or not) projects Stockman brought to the table. Financial support came from the members of the group, or rather, their employers. It was a wealthy, powerful club with a global vision. Stockman had put the group together after his time with CSIS, the Canadian Security Intelligence Service, and after his last appointment as security chief for Domar Oil, which had major oil and gas assets worldwide.

Lucy, Stockman's wife, had also been a member of CSIS, but now played at being Stockman's confidante. Her second sight often anticipated issues before they came to Stockman's attention, and she would offer her words of wisdom before being asked for them. But, more than that, she kept Stockman safe, provided a home, and slipped him his Plymouth Gin and Schweppes tonic, with a slice of fresh lemon and two ice cubes, every evening at exactly six p.m., whenever he was home.

The old dial-tone phone rang in the living room, just through the open French doors from the garden. It was using the forwarded number from Stockman's cell phone. All a part of the façade. It would be impossible for Stockman to be incommunicado to the extent he would really like. That would have to wait until he was thoroughly retired in a few more years.

Lucy left her book on the small side table next to the garden chair and stepped inside the living room to answer the impatient ringing.

"Hello. Stockman residence," Lucy answered the call and paused. "Yes, he is. Who may I say is calling?... Henri Blanchette? With whom?... Oh, the World Bank in Washington? Yes, yes, I'll get him. Give me a minute, would you, please?" Lucy held her hand over the mouthpiece and looked at Stockman. "Did you catch that, dear?"

"Um. The World Bank. Sounds intriguing. Yes, I'll take it." Stockman reached over for the phone. Lucy took her hand off the mouthpiece and handed it to him, then looked at her watch. It was just coming up to six p.m., or one p.m. in Washington, and time for a gin and tonic. She got up and headed to the kitchen, leaving her husband to his business.

"Henri? I don't think we've ever met, have we?" Stockman paused as he thought back over the years. He was very good with names and faces, but Henri's wasn't on his list, although Stockman was well aware of what the World Bank was.

"No, no, we haven't, but I've heard a lot about you and your organization, Mr. Stockman. I'm hoping we can get together to talk about a problem we have that you might be able to help us resolve. Do you have a moment to talk?"

"Yes, of course, and just call me Stockman." It didn't sound to Stockman as though there was space for an idle bit of chitchat before the formalities of business. "Perhaps you can give me a bit of an outline of the issue? I don't want to waste your time if it's not something I can do for you." Stockman paused and waited for Henri. *The World Bank*, he was thinking. *That means something pretty important for them to be calling.*

"Yes, of course." Henri paused for a few moments as he collected his thoughts. "As you probably know, the World Bank finances projects all over the world. Most of them are associated with improving the lives of people by creating jobs and building transmission lines, power plants, wastewater plants, water treatment, and so on and so on." He paused, waiting for Stockman to acknowledge his understanding of what the World Bank was.

"Yes, I'm aware of many of the projects the bank has financed, Henri. Very rewarding work," Stockman offered.

"Good. As you may know, then, we often get involved in industries where we believe there are long-term benefits adding to the social fabric for populations that might not be able to attract private investment for things like oil refineries, mines, manufacturing plants, and so on. In essence, we keep an open mind to investments and often go where corporations don't."

"Yes, I know that, too, Henri." Stockman showed his concern. "I don't generally think about getting involved with the World Bank. One assumes you look after your own business, good or bad. What's happened to make you come to me?"

"A few years ago, we got mixed up with a mining company, Summit Gold, based in Vancouver. They were developing several gold mines, and one was to be located on the southern tip of Greenland—"

"I didn't know there were any mines in Greenland," Stockman interrupted.

"Oh, the country is far richer in minerals than most people think. Of course, a lot of it is supposed to be under the ice cap and can't be economically mined just yet. But there are resources, especially rare earth minerals, on the perimeter of the island where snow and ice melt for about four months of the year." Henri seemed genuinely excited. "You wait until the ice recedes enough through global warming. Then you're going to see a whole lot of mining interest in Greenland. It'll be like the old gold rush days—or worse."

Henri Blanchette had gotten somewhat excited about his prediction, probably by the prospect of more World Bank funding potential than by global warming. *One hoped*, thought Stockman.

"Oh, how about that?" Stockman was genuinely surprised and happy to add another piece of information to his arsenal.

Henri went on.

"I don't know if you know this, Stockman, but Greenland is totally reliant on Denmark for funding, and that's the problem the Greenlanders have with trying to think big. It's not as though there are many people there, but infrastructure and communications desperately need upgrading if they ever want to be self-sustaining. We're not at all sure if the Danish government supports that initiative, you see, but that's where the World Bank comes in..." There was a pause as Henri gave Stockman a second to absorb what he was saying.

Henri sounded more serious. "One day, several months after we had been talking to the same company, but under the original ownership, we got a call from these two Danes, who were the new owners of this Vancouver mining group. I don't remember the details of how they took control, but now they were looking for World Bank funding. Apparently they had the ear of Polygold, the big Russian gold group, who were considering either payrolling them or guaranteeing loans."

"Okay, nothing new so far, eh?" Stockman interrupted.

"Not at all. These two, Finn and Erik something or other—that's not important right now—were looking to develop what turned out to be a very robust underground gold mine. I mean extremely rich by normal standards in these days of generally low-grade gold deposits."

Henri waited for another expression of surprise from Stockman, but it didn't come. Stockman was listening intently to Henri, but still wondering what he could do for the World Bank.

Henri pushed on.

"Oh, they made a lot of promises of employment and everything associated with something like this, including off-site support work, infrastructure construction, taxes, all that stuff, oh, and a share in the gold revenue for the country." Henri was clearly angry. "Can you imagine what the Greenlandic government was thinking, and likely already planning for their future? They were all eyes, ears, and welcoming arms. It was a godsend for them, and I met with their premier and his people in Washington a couple of times. They were very excited at the prospects of mineral development.

"But finding someone prepared to fund them for a mine in Greenland..." Henri paused as Stockman cut in before he had a chance to recover his thoughts and carry on.

"I can understand that, Henri, although these days there are a lot of, let's say, conventional ways of raising funds. If I recall, World Bank funding doesn't come free unless there is a compelling emergency need for support."

Lucy handed Stockman his first gin and tonic of the day and went back to her reading in the soft, high-backed chair in the bay window overlooking the ocean—and listening. Stockman would talk to Lucy later, as he always did, about any project he was considering.

"Of course, you're right, Stockman," Henri continued as Stockman sipped at his G&T. "For something like this, we would expect the return of capital plus a healthy interest as well as a royalty. Not a lot different from other lenders except, perhaps, less restrictions on the repayment period." There was a pause.

"Not all our money comes free, you know." Henri was talking as though he and Stockman were sitting opposite each other in the same room, where eye contact and facial expressions would be important. But all Henri's expressions of anger and frustration, and his own self-recriminations, were in his voice right now. "For many projects, there's not a charitable bone in the body of the World Bank."

Henri waited for a comment from Stockman, but again, none came. "We do finance projects that have difficulties going the more traditional route," he continued, "provided we see a social benefit to the country in which the project will be built, and where we can negotiate a healthy return on our investment so we can finance those that can't."

"Good to know." Stockman was enjoying the discussion but wasn't sure where it was leading to. "And where do you think I come in to all this, Henri?"

"As I said, these Danish boys had approached us and came to visit. They had an impressive portfolio, including everything there was to know about the property that was essentially shovel ready. The studies had been completed and signed off on, the two governments—Denmark, and Greenland—had given their approvals, and even the local fishing population supported them wholeheartedly. All they needed was cash, six hundred and fifty million worth." Stockman could almost see the shocked expression on Henri's face as he blurted out the amount. "And there was no way the Danish government was going to ante up with that kind of money, although we were quite encouraged, believing Polygold could be in the mix.

"It is true Summit was a novice in the world of mine development, but they seemed to have the talent, experience, and, of course, the talk. With cash, they could afford to get the right people in place. There was no doubt about that, at least when it came to running a company; they seemed to be excellent. It took a few months, but in the end, we signed off on a deal with a lot of upside potential for everyone. Frankly, there wasn't a lot of wrangling, which, knowing what we know now, was not surprising." There was a silence. It lasted for thirty seconds.

"And?" Stockman asked. "I get the feeling we are very close to the reason for your call to me. Is that right, Henri?"

"The fact is, they took the money and headed in a different direction," Henri blurted out and stopped.

"Oh. How could they do that with all the controls the World Bank has in place?" Stockman was taken aback, but he was definitely interested now.

"You're right, Stockman. We do have a lot of checks at various points along a project, but most of them are attached to the front end before things really get going in the field. But frankly, this one got away from us." Henri paused as though in deep thought.

"You know that location," he continued, "on the southern tip of Greenland, didn't exactly inspire our guys to do their full due diligence by going to the site after the first visit, and they relied on reporting from the Danes rather than visual checking. Oh, they met in Copenhagen on a regular basis, which was quite an attraction for them. Even the government guys were there, and they all laughed and talked, and laughed some more, but the fact was, yes, there was mining going on, but they didn't end up building a processing plant." Henri waited for Stockman.

"Oh! What did they end up doing, then?" Stockman was genuinely taken aback. He took another sip of his G&T.

"They just shipped the damned ore and had it processed somewhere else. So, on the very few visits our people made to the site—I think two in total—they saw the mining, they saw some kind of port facility, they saw site roads and a power line at the mine, and that's about it. They had been convinced by the property manager that the company was bringing in modular equipment for the crushing and milling." Henri sounded disappointed.

"Our people even talked to the major equipment suppliers, but in the end, it was all smoke and mirrors. There was no equipment purchased, no engineering, there was no employment for the locals, and no repayment of capital. In the end, we lost it all."

"Surely you have the property as collateral?" Stockman offered.

"Not really. We generally don't ask for collateral. Our clients very often don't have any security to put up—that's partly why they come to us. There's really nothing of worth to us if there's a default on payment. We aren't equipped to deal with property development." Henri went quiet for a moment. Stockman didn't want to interrupt Henri's moment and stayed silent.

"Oh, we'll file for restitution," Henri eventually confided, "but those Danes knew what they were doing. They created a shadow company and leased the property from them. In the end, even the property wasn't really theirs. Of course, there could be some shenanigans going on behind the scenes, and I understand they've been able to somehow unload the property to someone else, but at this point, it's a dud for us.

"By the time we caught up with it, they had mined out what they wanted in less than two years and barged most of it to the Rio Narcea plant in northern Spain for processing. All that was left at the property was an underground tunnel and a mess on the surface."

"Incredible, Henri. Two years? You didn't find out for two years?" Stockman was stunned by the admission.

"Listen, Stockman. We're nothing more than a sort of government administrative body, really. The United Nations is a huge, multi-faceted organization owned and supported by a lot of governments, so you might imagine the complexity. Lots of moving parts, you know, and not all of them are in sync.

"By the time we found out at the ground level, it was all over. Payments had been missed, but extensions approved. Reports had been filed but were full of holes we never caught. People moved on to other things and other organizations, et cetera.

"I know it all sounds unfathomable, but believe me, it doesn't really surprise me, and neither is it the only thing we have ever missed. We deal in the billions of dollars, maybe even trillions, so six hundred and fifty million could get lost here or there without anyone really getting nervous for a while."

"Incredible. What about Polygold?" Stockman had paused in shock but recovered quickly.

"There was no Polygold. It was all a part of the scam. Sure, these Danes knew this Kerimov person, the president of Polygold, but when it came down to it, they just kept delaying his involvement. I don't think there was ever an intent by Polygold."

"Then what can I do for you, Henri?"

"Well, there are some things we, as the World Bank, can't do. We can go to court, we can try to locate these guys who took us for a ride, we can try to get our money back, but the fact is, we're not able to go behind the law to do any of it. We need some help. My guess is this is not the first, or only, time these arrogant bastards are going to pull a stunt like this. They're probably planning their next move right now. I suspect they already have some poor schmuck in their sights."

"You're probably right, Henri. It certainly sounds intriguing and would likely fit with what we do. Let me see what we can find out about these guys. Any idea where they are?"

"We lost sight of them a long time ago. But do we know they're Danish—the names Finn Hansen and Erik Mateus have just come to mind—and likely well-known in the business world over there. They've probably gone to ground by now, but you could start over in Copenhagen and see if they turn up at the exchange. I'll send you over some photos of these guys. I understand they have some pretty influential friends there you can talk to. Oh, you could also check with the Greenland government people; they were intimately involved with these people and provided some guarantees, which turned out to be completely useless. You can imagine they aren't too happy with these Danes either, but there's little they can do."

"Sounds good, Henri. Let me think about it and talk to some of my colleagues. If it looks as though we might be able to do something, I'll send over a proposal and an NDA. You need to sign it and get it back to me. In the meantime, let me make some inquiries." Stockman took another sip of his G&T.

"Thank you, Stockman. I appreciate it very much. You may need to come over for a meeting, but I'll leave that up to you to decide."

"Let's see what comes up, Henri. Send me over a message, with your coordinates, to this number. It's my cell number. We can talk later, but I think I've got the story. I need to do some digging." There was a pause before Henri said his goodbyes and Stockman ended the call with a promise to be in touch again soon.

"Sounds interesting." Lucy handed Stockman another gin and tonic, then went over to her favorite chair next to the window and looked over the cliffs to the water below and on, uninterrupted, to the horizon.

"I think it is, Lucy, my dear." Stockman reached for his glass.

* * *

Next Victims, Please

Finn and Erik sat in two of the six luxurious dark gray low-back leather executive chairs at the round, gray quartzite-top table in their floating office located amidships of *Viking I*. They looked very much the part of two well-heeled but casually attired, wealthy individuals, with their files in front of them, laptops open, and pens at the ready, just in case they needed to resort to the pad of paper next to them. A rather large, well-attired steward stood by, immediately outside the door, ready to service anything they needed at the sound of the buzzer on his belt.

When their Zoom call connected, Finn and Erik faced four people crowded around an oval table in some simple, unadorned room in Vancouver. It could have been an office or someone's basement. It didn't matter.

The group called itself GREY, for Gerry, Rich, Ernie, and Yanko (presumed to be short for Yankovich, but who knew?). Formed for the express purpose of working with Finn and Erik, they weren't a registered company and were completely unknown in the industry as GREY. As individuals, however, they had garnered a lot of respect as independent experts. Combined, the underground mining specialist, the process specialist, the mine economist, and the project development person could tell potential investors if the ore could be economically mined, what the best method of processing the ore would be, the estimated costs and returns for the reserve, the environmental sensitivities, and the practicalities of building the mine facilities. These elements, together, would allow Finn and Erik to better understand the economics of what they intended to do.

No one was smiling, but they all said, "Hi." It was enough. Each of the four men gave their first name. Finn and Erik smiled at each but were silent. No other introductions were made.

Finn had contracted GREY to establish a short list of companies that could be of interest to him and Erik as their next target. Gerry's group didn't know what was meant by a "target," but what they did know was what was asked of them in return for a hefty payment: to provide names and briefs on several companies that could be ripe for acquisition and development. The companies needed to be gold companies with an underground mine potential—preferably previously operated but not a high priority, be financially needy, have a less-than-competent board of directors, and the property ideally needed to be somewhere near tidewater.

There were plenty of companies to choose from when it came to their financial inadequacy and management incompetency. Some had gone into development, and even production, before they failed as a consequence of their shortcomings. But the other requirements were just a little more difficult to find in combination with these failings. However, the group came through with a list of potential candidates.

Gerry, who seemed to be GREY's spokesperson on the call, operated his laptop, and the first slide came up on the screen. It was titled "Donegal Mine – Ireland." An aerial shot of the property filled the screen, and he started describing what they were all looking at.

"The Donegal property has been operating as an underground gold mine on and off since 1887 but stopped in 1998 because of new health and safety laws, which would have almost doubled the cost of sinking mine shafts and galleries. Also, changing pollution control legislation would have made the owners liable for the quality of the mine discharge into the Mawddach, had the mine remained open. So, the owners walked away.

"It was purchased in mid-2013, from the Northern Irish government, who had been playing around with reclamation, and was being prepared for operation once again with a substantial increase in proven reserves reported to become the largest gold producer in the United Kingdom. Distance to tidewater is approximately 9.2 miles by established road. All infrastructure is in place, and all permits received. Board of directors comprises four with no legal or financial representation. Trades at around thirty cents on the Vancouver exchange but not a lot of takers and has a weak management structure, consisting of one accountant, two exploration geologists, and one secretary."

Then he flipped to the next slide, which was titled "Gallyantas Gold – N. Ireland." An aerial shot of the property filled the screen.

"A Canadian company has been working on this property in Northern Ireland since 2009, under prospecting licenses. The property would be an underground mine and contains over six million ounces of gold in the reserve category. Unlike zinc, Ireland has been slower in getting its gold industry up and running. But there are several well-respected, interested parties pursuing gold production. A good stake in this company is entirely possible in return for a good position. This property is scheduled to produce upwards of a hundred and sixty-two thousand ounces per year over an eighteen-year mine life and has at least one major backer.

"The property is about seventy-five miles to the west of Belfast, and thirty miles south of Londonderry, both on tidewater. Currently trading at about $1.47 on the TSX with four directors, with somewhat dubious backgrounds, who are attempting to take the company private."

The final slide read "Hope Brook – Newfoundland, Canada," followed by another aerial shot.

"The Hope Brook Gold Project, near Port aux Basques, Newfoundland, is located on the southwest side of the island. The original owner produced more than seven hundred thousand ounces of gold from underground mining until 1997, when the mine closed and the owner declared bankruptcy. There remains significant infrastructure in place, albeit some needing upgrading and repair, including a transmission line with functional power to site, intact site roads, tailings ponds, camp facilities, and a gravel airstrip that can accommodate a DC-3-size plane.

"The property has been acquired several times since closing. Quest bought the property five years ago at a basement bargain price. It claims the gold reserve categories contain seven hundred and fifty thousand ounces left underground, but they don't have the skill sets to convince the market it's still a viable prospect. We think the last owner left a bad taste in the mouths of the financiers, and they just want to stay away from it. This property is only a few miles from tidewater and already has barge ramps in place. That's how the old mine brought their provisions in.

"All the old underground mining equipment is still on site but needs some serious attention. The five-hundred-ton-per-day process plant is still there, but also badly in need of attention, and we think the mill was running off-balance, like a car with three good wheels and one with a bent axle, when the original owners stopped production. Since the mine shut down the first time, an extension of Highway 470 has been constructed from close to the mine site to Port aux Basques to the west, but we still believe the hopper barges are the best solution.

"This is an easy target and likely the least expensive of the three to purchase. Quest is based in Vancouver, and this is their only property not in an early exploration phase. They seem to be out of their depth, have no experience, and can't raise any interest or money. The word on the street is they would like to unload it. Their share price is down at five cents, with nothing going on, and no obvious prospects."

The group went quiet as they waited for Finn or Erik to ask questions. Finn spoke up first.

"Thank you, gentlemen." Finn was slow and deliberate as he thought about the options and whether he had any questions. "Each of them looks interesting, and, clearly, they fit the profile we gave you. Great job." The faces in front of Finn and Erik moved their mouths together in thank-yous. Finn shifted in his chair and leaned toward the camera.

"Now, we need you to provide us with some financial details. I'm sure you have already looked at the preliminary numbers." He paused, waiting for signs of understanding. The faces looked at him, wide-eyed. "They should show the mining of the ore is economically viable, of course; otherwise, we would not be looking at your summaries. Correct?" Finn stopped.

There was a general nodding of heads of those in Vancouver.

"Yes, yes, of course." Gerry looked around at the other three faces. They were all indicating their agreement.

"Well, if that's the case," Finn piped up, "the next step would be for us to get an understanding of the estimated capital needed to get the mines up and operating together, don't you think?"

Again, the four faces all nodded eagerly.

"With their rates of return and long-term economics of each property."

Finn paused for questions. There were none. "Now, I would think the property owners already have those details, but we'd like you to cast your eyes over them and see if there are any deal-breakers, if you know what I mean."

"No problem." It was Gerry again, finding his tongue. "We've already made a start and should have some information in a couple of weeks." All the faces appeared thoughtful.

"Let me help by prioritizing the properties." Finn looked over at Erik, who just nodded.

"Newfoundland first, then Ireland, then Wales. All three need to be assessed." Finn stopped and looked again at Erik, who just did a thumbs-up with purpose.

"Okay, understood," they all echoed.

"Let us know as soon as you finish the first one."

Again, they all nodded together.

"Thanks, everyone. Talk again in two weeks—or earlier." Finn waved at the group, then stopped. "Ah, yes, your money will be wired tomorrow. You've done well."

He exited the Zoom call without waiting for a response. The GREY group members would each receive a substantial sum of money for their services. Far more than they could make in the market, and they knew it. They were ultra-keen to keep working with the Danes.

Finn looked over at Erik, who was still staring at the screen, even though it was blank.

"I guess we can agree the most obvious target is Hope Brook, Erik. It sounds like it could be a repeat of Nalunaq, except the refinery will be a lot closer this time—I hope."

"True, unless they're booked and we have to head over to Spain again." Erik looked away from the screen and over to Finn. "There is something like twice as much gold at this Hope Brook property, so it'll be a big campaign. I hope the refineries can handle it."

"We'll find out, my friend. Let's get things rolling before someone else comes along and muscles in on the action." Finn was clearly enthusiastic and very happy to be getting another venture up and running. As far as he was concerned, the hardest part was over choosing the next target.

"Contact Vince Taylor over at Monroe & Hopkins and have him start digging into this Quest company and see what we have to do to set up a meeting with them. Vince is going to have to put some kind of an offer together, so talk it over with him and see what you can come up with. I want to be able to put it in front of Quest as soon as we can meet them." By this time, Finn was brimming with ideas and scribbling notes on a piece of paper next to him.

Erik just took it all in and lifted his phone out of his pocket. He flipped open his contacts and searched for Vince's number. He was with one of the largest mining-oriented law firms in Toronto, a hub for both majors and juniors in the industry. The Danes also had to look for ways to finance their ambitions. Regardless of having made a small fortune on the last project, there was no way they were going to use their own money.

Obviously, they would propose a new processing plant and emulate the same methods they had used for Nalunaq, with the exception that they wouldn't be able to go back to the World Bank. They had already contacted a Russian oligarch, Roman Kerimov, the president of Polygold. He had surfaced on one of their earlier schemes when Finn and Erik had duped a bunch of mine company shareholders into unwittingly selling all their stock through them and onto the Russian. Once done, the Russian pounced and took the mining company over.

"Yes." Finn was thinking out loud. "I think our Russian friend may be just what we need here, Erik. Don't you think?"

Erik nodded. "I think you're right, Finn. A greedy oligarch with more money than brains and looking for any way to get even richer. Let's make contact."

* * *

Black Again

In the early 1950s, Truman Capote called it "a strangely enchanted place" when he arrived in Foria, on the northwestern side of the idyllic volcanic island of Ischia, in the Bay of Naples, a stone's throw away from Capri. This is where he wrote, swam, and basked in the Mediterranean sun. In those days, Capote stayed in a "pleasant pensione, an interesting bargain, too," as he described in his essay, "Ischia." It was his place away from the madness of New York, where he was forever being tempted away from his passion for writing by the revelry surrounding him. But he and his partner, Jack Dunphy, found their place together on the Mediterranean, at least for long enough to soak in the inspiration and get the writing juices moving again. It was where he wrote parts of some of his best, and most meditative, novels among the "smell of wisteria and of the leaves of lemon."

"What strange place and strangely enchanted is this one" —Truman wrote—"it is an island off the coast of Naples, very primitive, inhabited mostly by winemakers and shepherds." To Cecil Beaton, he wrote: "It's really beautiful and strange... the sun is as hard as diamond." But that was in those days, and times had moved on. Tourists had discovered Ischia, and while much of it is still reminiscent of those days seventy years ago, there came a reckoning as foreigners found their travel feet and explored the four corners of the earth, bringing with them all their expectations in these modern times.

Just minutes from Foria and built on the cliff at the northwest tip of the island, Matthew Black relaxed by the thermal pool, in the grounds of the Mezzatorre Hotel, an old castle. It was one of his favorite places in the world, and he felt the euphoria, and smells, in the air Capote had described. It was all around him, and uniquely tuned by the sulfur and other mineral odors coming off the ground water and carried in the air, permeating every domicile for miles around. The castle, or rather the watchtower, was built between the sixteenth and seventeenth century and eventually became a hotel. It was complete with natural thermal springs, warmed from volcanic activity miles below, oozing mineral waters up through the rocks to soothe the body, only to disappear back into the ground, to circulate over and over again.

Matthew was in his early forties, tallish, reasonably fit, with sharp features and short, thick, curly black hair. He was intelligent, had a quick wit, and was an easy conversationalist. His natural charm, white teeth, and smile disarmed most people. When not relaxing, he was constantly alert to his surroundings and ready to spring forward to react to any threatening situation when needed. Oddly, he had been a welder in his early years after he had finished his mechanical engineering degree. A strange combination but one fitting his lifestyle in his early years, when he was looking for good money and excitement. Now, with ORB, his practical talents were sometimes used for the job, and his understanding of industrial environments was essential.

He had been in Foria now for two weeks and was looking to spend another two weeks relaxing, enjoying occasional visits into town and sightseeing. For an island only twenty miles in circumference, it was rife with interesting sights, sounds, smells, beaches, people, and crazy traffic. If one could only live through the edge-of-the-seat driving through the narrow roads and the speed with which the oncoming vehicles seemed to hunt one down, one would live to do it all again the next day.

For now, Matthew lay back, with a straw hat over his eyes, and took in his surroundings. A glass of carbonated water with lemon sat to one side, and a small bowl of olives sat on the other. His thoughts were lazy, his mood tranquil, as he smiled at his memories and looked forward to seeing Emma. Tomorrow, he would meet her at the Porto d'Ischia and share some time with her roaming the streets, shopping for nothing in particular, tasting the locally grown fruit, eating the freshly caught fish, and sipping the island's famous home grown limoncello, among other things.

The explosive climax of the "1812 Overture"—using brass, percussion, and real cannons on the battlefield of Borodino, west of Moscow, as the French were defeated—played from Matthew's phone. The internationally recognized piece reeked of strength and leadership, which was how

Matthew regarded Stockman. Perhaps not to the same extent as Napoleon was regarded, but there was a remote resemblance of style. Anyway, Matthew liked the tone, had matched it to only Stockman, and answered.

"Hello, Stockman. Great to hear from you. How are things, and how is that beautiful Lucy these days?"

"Well, we're both very well, Matthew. And yourself?"

"Oh, you know, life's a bitch, but someone's got to live it. The sun is too hot, the sea too salty, the food too satisfying, and the music just drones on with a romantically melodic style of love. It's all too much to take." Matthew guffawed and guessed that Stockman was smiling.

"In Italy, are you, Matthew?"

"I am indeed." It always amazed Matthew that Stockman knew where he was at all times. "Settled into a beautiful place hidden from the world on the northern tip of Ischia."

"Sounds very nice. It's raining here, Arsenal just lost again, and there's a rail strike looming—you know, same as usual. Regardless, Lucy and I are thoroughly enjoying ourselves at the cottage in Hope Cove. It's like an oasis. I'd like to say we know nothing, see nothing, and hear nothing—but that would be a lie. News trickles in, no matter what."

"It sounds as though someone has disturbed your world, Stockman. Anything I can help with?" Matthew sounded genuinely concerned.

"Well, now that you ask." Stockman laughed. "There is something that's come up, and I'm just letting it rattle around in my brain before I do anything about it."

"Would you like to use me as a sounding board?"

"I would, actually, Matthew. That's the reason I called." Stockman paused, wondering where to start, but then dove in, regardless, and shared the discussion he'd had with Henri from the World Bank.

"Sounds like quite a scam," Matthew offered. "But maybe it's a one-off. If it is, the question is, do we really want to commit resources to this? These Danish guys are long gone by now and maybe even changed their names if they were even theirs in the first place. Don't get me wrong. We could do it, and maybe even get most of the money back. But is this what you want us to spend our time on, given the other problems we're dealing with, Stockman?

Bigger fish to fry and all that." Matthew paused.

"I hear you, but I have to say, old son, my senses tell me these guys have either done this before, or will be doing it again, or both. The kind of reward would be too great a prize for them to give up after only one haul. They may not try to bamboozle the World Bank again, but you can be sure they'll identify other targets.

"We could leave this one to the World Bank to resolve, I know, but I have a very strong feeling these Danes will try it again and again unless someone puts a stop to it; otherwise, there are going to be one hell of a lot of people, companies, and governments hurt. I also think they've done this before. It all seems too smooth to be a one-off."

"Um, yes, you're probably right." Matthew was coming to the same conclusion. "I don't know what kind of cash haul they got away with in Greenland, but it would certainly include the loan from the World Bank, plus any other cash they accumulated along the way, through other sources. If they barged the product out and processed it offshore, costs would be small compared to processing it all on site, especially considering the prize. Although, you would have to count the mining costs into the equation, of course. Still, it has to be significant." Matthew was trying to calculate as he thought.

"I was doing a little talking with Lucy earlier, Matthew. We came up with a number in excess of one billion dollars. Now that's a prize!"

"Wow. Is there any press on what happened?"

"Not a bit, from what I can tell. The company originally involved was bona fide, respected, and out of Vancouver. Yes, they were about to start on an underground gold mine in southern Greenland. And, yes, they had solid gold results, and they spent a lot on exploration, mine testing, permitting, and all that, but in the end, and this isn't common knowledge, these two Danish scallywags, who were on the board, convinced the rest that the Vancouver-based president was on the take.

"Anyway, the board got rid of him, as well as his Vancouver-based team, and took the project over, delisted the company on the TSE, and re-listed it on the Stockholm exchange. They raised a lot of cash as a new listing and convinced the World Bank that Greenland was in desperate need of a financial boost. Their plan was to get enough money out of the World Bank to finance not just a mine and processing plant, but also a total upgrade of all the support facilities in the community of Nanortalik, which they claimed was going to be the center for the new, and more modern, rare earth mineral mining industry. Well, that was the key to unlocking the World Bank treasury. To finally weaken the Chinese grip on rare earth minerals has been the number one priority for governments around the world, as they edge toward electrifying vehicles."

"You've been busy, Stockman. It sounds as though you have a pretty good grasp, but then what happened?"

"Well, once they re-listed, it left just Danish-speaking leadership who, as far as I can tell, never really grasped what was happening. What with all the reports and press releases being in English and so on, everything went to shit before they could catch on. By then it was too late and they were left with nothing. Meanwhile, the two Danes had organized mining out the gold-rich ore by triple-shifting, and initially barging it all over the north coast of Newfoundland until that went bad. Then they had to ship it all to northern Spain, where they ended up processing it all." Stockman paused as he was thinking.

"That was when gold was hovering around fourteen hundred dollars an ounce, you know." He paused a moment, as though waiting for a reaction from Matthew, but none came, so he finished the thought. "Can you imagine how much greedier they've become since then, with gold now sitting around eighteen hundred and fifty dollars an ounce—about a twenty-five percent increase? Or, to put it another way, two hundred and fifty million more than they would have got away with had that been the market price for the Greenland gold. Not bad, eh?" Stockman emphasized the last two words.

"It's quite a story. Do you have any intel on the guys involved?" Matthew was getting more intrigued by the moment.

"My friends tell me—well, that is, Henri from the World Bank—that a Finn Hansen and Erik Mateus were the main culprits. There are likely others they used to pepper the board of the company once they took over, but I haven't got that far yet. I know the company collapsed and lost its exchange listing. It seems our two friends went to ground somewhere in Europe, but we haven't figured out where just yet. But then, we haven't tried. I'm still in the thinking stage—should we or shouldn't we? And who would be our clients?"

"It's important to find out where they are, Stockman, but perhaps just as important is to know whether they are up to the same tricks somewhere else."

"You're right, Matthew. Now, it's decision time. Do we take this one or not? We do have another problem about to come up for us to deal with, but that one could actually wait a while before we act. Come to think of it, now that I'm saying this out loud, I think I've decided what we'll do. Thank you, my boy. I'll see you soon."

With that, Stockman rang off and left Matthew staring at his phone. He shrugged, smiled, and put the phone back on the table, then picked up the soda to quench his thirst and got up.

"He'll be back," Matthew murmured as he dove into the pool.

* * *

Together Again

Emma arrived at Porto d'Ischia on an early afternoon hydrofoil ferry from Naples. She looked stunning, as usual, in a white short-sleeved blouse with a mandarin-style collar, long black cotton pants with a thin leather belt tied in front, and a pair of white high-tops. Oversized sunglasses gave the impression her head was smaller than it was. Her short black hair poked out from under a broad-rimmed white straw hat, with a black and white polka dot band and matching ribbon tied under her chin to protect against the sun and wind on deck. Regardless, she still had to keep her hand on top of it as the ferry rushed through the Mediterranean Sea air to Ischia, one of three islands in the Bay of Naples.

Emma was not only Matthew's favorite lady, but she also happened to be his preferred co-conspirator, his more-than-occasional lover, and the daughter of his boss, Murray Stockman. They had worked on a couple of projects together; sometimes with Emma just monitoring his predicaments from the shadows in case he needed help, and sometimes more visible at his side. It was whatever the project needed, but Matthew was always in her vision somewhere, somehow.

Emma was single, athletically constructed, fit, a standard 34B, and in her mid-thirties. Most often, she was Emma Stockman, but sometimes Emma Stone. It just depended on the job, where she was, with whom, and who she preferred to be at the time. Her everyday style preference was for short-cropped black hair, cut in a pixie style for easy management, and minimal makeup. Clothing was optional, but her preference was for black jeans, a tucked-in high-collared white shirt, and high-cut ankle boots or, for more casual moments, black Reebok Freestyle His. She could always camouflage herself as a more feminine female any time, but it was not what she was comfortable with, although she was one sexy lady at any time, with no lack of libido.

Matthew met Emma at the end of the gangway once the ferry had pulled into its slip at Porto d'Ischia and its lines were secured. He grabbed her only piece of check-in luggage and wrapped an arm around her waist. She slung her small black leather backpack over her shoulders. They hugged and kissed as he twirled her away from the edge of the quay to the safety of the dock.

"Great to see you, sweetie." Matthew was smiling like a Cheshire cat.

"You too, my man." She smiled broadly. "What has it been—three weeks? Too long!" They laughed. The last time they had been together was at the beginning of the month in Vancouver. He lived on one side of the city near Stanley Park, and she on the other near one of the marinas. They met up quite often, sometimes stayed over, and sometimes played and slept with other friends. It was all so casual, easy, and modern. But they always found each other again, as good friends do.

Matthew had rented a white Fiat 124 Spider soft-top, with just enough room for two, and found a small parking space next to the customs house on the dock. He wasn't sure if he was allowed, but he took the chance. He pushed, twisted, and turned Emma's bag into the pint-sized trunk.

"Hungry?" Matthew watched for Emma's reaction.

"Thank God you asked. I'm famished. I didn't bother eating before I got onto the ferry." Emma suddenly looked starving as she held the palm of one hand against her stomach. "I missed breakfast and thought they might have something onboard, but it was all vending machine stuff." She was smiling in anticipation of what was in store.

"Come on." Matthew held her by the hand and gently pulled. "There's a great little pasta place just over there." He pointed to a row of restaurants, cafés, and stores with barn-like doors lining the east side of the harbor. "We can walk from here."

They ambled over, holding hands through the small tourist groups milling around. The harbor was bustling with visitors looking for boat rides out to the bay, around the Aragonese Castle attached to the island by a short causeway, or just strolling around, taking in the sights or people watching. There were boats for hire, with or without an operator, and those just circling the island or visiting the other nearby islands—Positano and Capri—or further, over to the Amalfi coastline around the corner from Sorrento.

Emma's head seemed to spin as she looked all around her to take in as much as she could of her surroundings while they walked. She stared up at Mount Epomeo, the volcano dormant since the turn of the fourteenth century but providing a beautiful green backdrop of fields and trees above the port town.

The harbor bustled with water traffic moving in all directions; commercial vessels mixed with pleasure boats, and a fishing fleet taking up space at the far north end of the harbor. Children were diving, unattended, for mussels and limpets, from the stone breakwater at the entrance to the harbor, to take home to add to the *vongole* for supper that evening.

A ferry foghorn sounded its warning whenever one arrived or departed, to move the water traffic out of its way and allow it to pass between them. There was so much to take in, it was impossible for Emma to grasp it all, but in those few minutes it took to reach the restaurant, she knew there was something magical about this place, setting it apart from so many of the other places she had visited in the world.

The small restaurant seemed to have been built into the rough stone wall running down the side of the dock. Somehow, small greenery had managed to find a foothold to grow in the cracks of the wall where the crumbling old cement had started to come away.

A waiter welcomed them and pointed to a small, cheap round metal table outside on the uneven stonework that seemed to be a part of the quay. It had no tablecloth, but it did have an equally cheap, seven-foot diameter, red Peroni Beer umbrella poking through a hole in its center. There was no ballast to hold it from spinning in a breeze or toppling over if the wind picked up. But it afforded shade sufficient to protect at least one of the two-fold-up chairs offered. Emma pulled it out from under the table, looked at Matthew, and smiled.

"Do you mind?"

"Not at all. I'm getting used to the sun, as long as I wear this hat, that is." He smiled, touched the rim of his white straw hat with its obligatory wide black band, and Emma winked her approval.

"What's the news?" Emma asked.

"Well…" Matthew started but was interrupted by the waiter. They both ordered the marinara and a Peroni each. The waiter whisked off, not stopping long enough to take the menus back, but with what seemed to be a mildly disdainful demeanor. They both looked at each other and shrugged at the flippancy and briskness of the waiter.

"Maybe we're supposed to sample the *hors d'oeuvres*? He looks a little pissed," Emma wondered out loud.

"Who cares?" Matthew laughed. "Just their temperament. Pay it no attention." They both shrugged it off.

"As I was saying," Matthew started again. "I'd thought this was going to be a somewhat extended break away from the madhouse, but I got a call from your dad yesterday."

"Oops." Emma gave an agonized look at Matthew. "Anything we need to talk about?"

"I'm not sure. I think so. He kind of left the discussion hanging and I'm guessing he's just working things through his brain, but it wouldn't surprise me if he calls again over the next couple of days for us to move out."

"Oh well, let's enjoy things while we can." Emma sat back as the waiter plopped her meal in front of her and quickly backed away to do the same for Matthew.

"Boy, that was fast." Emma looked at the plate of pasta as though expecting to see some sign of fast food. There wasn't. There was just an incredibly inviting aroma licking her nostrils. "Guess they have a pot of it on the stove 24/7." They laughed.

"Parmesan?" Matthew asked as the waiter was trying to get away.

The waiter frowned, stepped back, and pretended to smack the back of his own hand. "No, no, no, no … *pescano, pescano*." He volunteered two hands and the full extent of his arms to the two plates of marinara. "No, *pescano*." He slapped his forehead. "*Turisti!*" With that, he tutted his way back into the restaurant with the fingers on each hand pinched and raised as though they were holding some invisible thing.

"I guess he doesn't want us to have cheese with the fish." Emma looked at Matthew for support.

"I think you're right, and he doesn't look the type you want to piss off twice." They laughed, lifted their beers, and saluted to each other.

The meal was wonderful.

"I don't think it could have possibly been improved by parmesan, do you?" Matthew smiled, and Emma raised her eyebrows as she swallowed the last of her meal and mouthed "no, no, no," then scraped the remnants of the sauce left on the rim of her plate with a tiny piece of bread and sucked it into her mouth. She sighed contentedly and licked her lips, trying to savor any hint of what might be left.

The waiter had clearly been thinking about his earlier, possibly, overdone admonishments of his two patrons, albeit tourists. Perhaps feeling as though he could well miss out on a tip, he decided they deserved a locally made limoncello each, and with a flourish, graciously set two glasses carefully on the table in front of them. The handwritten bill was slid onto the table as the waiter picked up the empty plate and bottles, then humbly retreated to the inside of the restaurant with a shallow bow all the way.

They both laughed softly at the apparent change in the waiter's demeanor, but enjoyed the locally made lemon liqueur, paid the bill with cash and left a sizable tip, then wandered back to their car.

The little Fiat was an almost perfect size for negotiating the narrow, winding island road leading out of town and up toward the old volcano, although a road just six inches wider would have helped.

For many tourist drivers, it would be a heart-stopping experience, meeting coaches, scooters, and old, overloaded trucks coming toward them on the narrow, winding roads that climbed and dropped for much of the way. It could have been a wonderful scenic drive, but for the maniacal driving of much of the traffic insisting on less-experienced drivers having to grip their steering wheels, continually change gears, and hurtle toward each other with eyes straining ahead. Neither oncoming nor following traffic was prepared to slow down for the visiting drivers. There was no moment for a sideways glance at the view over the cliffs for the driver—or the passengers. They were all in it together.

Whether by good luck or overly defensive driving, or both, Matthew and Emma still had fun with the thrill of the experience. They arrived safely at the Mezzatorre Hotel, having climbed up as far as Serrara Fontana before dropping down again to the coast on the north side of the island.

* * *

Matthew and Emma savored the last of their Biancolella wine as they watched the sun set and the lights coming alive on the Italian coastline, miles in the distance. The evening temperature was perfect, the humidity more bearable, and the gentle southeast Mediterranean breeze drifted across the terrace as they talked. The sky was clear, and the soft sounds of a single mandolin reached them from somewhere below the hotel, probably from the nearby village square. It was magical.

"Let's go for a swim." Emma looked expectantly over at Matthew as they lay near the edge of the pool. They were both already in their bathing suits, and it seemed a logical conclusion they would just slide in for a dip before the wine took over completely.

They spent a leisurely twenty minutes in the pool, touching and swimming away from each other without averting their eyes while the mineral vapors lapped at their bodies and infiltrated their heads. It was invigorating, yet relaxing. They finally swam slowly toward each other, embraced, and pushed themselves gently to the edge of the pool.

It was time to get out, dry off, and move on to the next stage of their ritual. They went up the outside spiral staircase from the pool patio to Matthew's room on the second floor, their towels wrapped around their waists and wet footprints tracing their way on the floor tiles. The French doors in his room were still open to the veranda. A classic quarter moon suspended itself in just the right position in the sky, helping create the romantic setting one only reads about in romance novels. The sound of the mandolin filled the air; the aroma of scented flowers wafted through the open windows and mingled with the vapors coming off the pool. Who could resist the passion it represented? No one, unless…

"Hello, old boy. Stockman here," Matthew answered his cell phone before the first cannon blast of the overture announced the caller.

He let out a silent groan, his shoulders slumped, and his eyes caught the look on Emma's face as she was about to get into bed. She smiled and scooted under the sheets, lost for words.

"Oh, hi, Stockman. How are things?"

"Good. Good. You know I was talking to you about those Danish guys yesterday?" It seemed only a few minutes ago when Stockman had last called, and he just picked up the conversation now as though there was no gap between calls.

"Yes, I do, Stockman. Yes, yes, I do." Matthew repeated more to remind himself of what was likely to follow, but not wanting to open his mind to it just at this particular time. But he couldn't help himself. "Have you got any further with that?" Matthew asked almost half-heartedly, but pleasantly, and patiently and bit his lip as though deliberately berating himself for encouraging Stockman who would now assume there was all the time in the world for him to chat about whatever had come into his head. But then, he was the president of ORB, and one had to consider, regardless of what time of day it was, who he was, and what had made him call. It was always important when Stockman called.

"I have, my boy, and we have to get together with some of the group. How about Rome in two days' time? Just a hop, skip, and a jump for you from where you are. You're almost there, and of course, Emma is with you." There was a lingering pause as Stockman waited for confirmation of his assumption.

"Yes, she is, Stockman. Came in from Naples this afternoon."

"Ah, good. So, let's say the Portrait Roma Hotel on Via dei Condotti. Do you remember it from when we last met? "

"I do. What a beautiful hotel." Matthew smiled. He loved that place. Fabulous location. "It will be perfect. Can you make a couple of reservations for Emma and myself and we'll be there on Thursday evening? I'll make our travel arrangements from here to Rome."

"That sounds really good, Matthew. Thanks for the prompt action and tell Emma I'm really looking forward to seeing her. I'll round up a few of the guys."

There was a loud "HELLO, DARLING" from Lucy in the background behind Stockman.

"HELLO, MUMMY," Emma shouted back. "And you, of course, Daddy." There was no point in trying to hide. It seemed as though "Daddy" always knew where his daughter was, along with everyone else in ORB's core.

"Maybe see you both on Thursday evening." Stockman was ready to sign off. "Perhaps we can dine together in the hotel, if you arrive no later than, say, six p.m.? If not, make it nine a.m. on Friday morning in the Via dei Condotti Suite, where I'll be staying, hopefully, if it's not already booked. Breakfast provided, of course." Stockman closed his cell phone.

Matthew and Emma went back to where they left off. Matthew stripped off his almost-dry swimsuit and climbed into bed.

They tossed this way and that, rolled over and back, as their juices rose, and their giggling moved into a phase of grunting and groaning, then moaning and humming. The breeze coming through the open windows kept them cool and brought the aromas of the countryside into the room. They needed the atmosphere of their surroundings to envelop them, to work with them, and lead them through the process of lovemaking, with the magic of the outside looking in. The sky winked, the moon stared and smiled, the air enveloped them, the sound of music encouraged them, and the drink helped them forget ORB for the moment and to dispel any lingering hesitation they might have had after the call from Stockman.

It was glorious, and they both sighed with satisfaction as they rolled onto their backs to their appropriate sides of the bed, drew the covers up, and slipped into a dreamy sleep.

The sound of the "1812 Overture" startled them out of their drifting.

"Hello, Stockman. What's up?" Matthew tried to sound awake and ready.

"I think I know the play they're going to make next, Matthew. Good night, old boy. See you soon." And he was gone. Matthew put his phone down, smiled, shook his head, and lay down.

"Okay, let's try that again." Matthew beat his pillow into submission, pushed an arm under Emma, and closed his eyes.

* * *

Rome

Their fifty-minute commuter flight from Naples touched down at the Leonardo da Vinci International Airport at around three p.m. on Thursday.

Ninety minutes later, Matthew and Emma arrived at the Portrait Roma Hotel, located above the Ferragamo men's flagship clothing store on Via Bocca di Leone, a narrow road in the center of Rome. It was an old city townhouse the Ferrogamo family had converted into a fourteen-room upscale hotel within spitting distance of the Spanish Steps and all the area afforded.

It would be a delight for Matthew and Emma to enjoy the shopping, restaurants, and sauntering through the crowded lanes around the hotel—if they got a chance. There was no harm in wishing, but Matthew didn't hold out a lot of hope.

Stockman sat with Matthew and Emma at a greenery-crowded rail-side table at the hotel's private rooftop terrace under a clear sky with dusk just beginning to fall. Given their afternoon arrival in the city, they had managed to get together before the next day's business.

The lights of the city were starting to twinkle, with the headlights of the unceasing traffic below headed toward and away from them in all directions. Not all the roadway noise reached their ears at this elevation, but there was the constant drone of traffic and the inevitable car horn honking unavoidable in Rome.

In fact, it seemed to be a part of the culture of driving here. Just a cross to bear as traffic in Rome scurried frantically through crossroads and junctions, often paying little attention to traffic lights, warning whistles or arm waving by the *polizia*. Meanwhile, horses pulling carriages clip-clopped with their passengers through the melee, oblivious to the mechanical panic surrounding them.

Stockman and company spent some quality time together catching up as the strains of familiar Italian music, piped up from somewhere in the hotel, remained barely muted by the sounds of traffic below. Somehow the music and the street noise blended into a white noise that didn't distract the conversationalists on the terrace.

Stockman and Emma caught up as a father and daughter would. It was not often they managed to get together, what with Emma living in Vancouver and Stockman and Lucy spending time in Hope Cove and Montreal. But they always found time to catch up, and with Emma working for her father, more access was available to both of them. They often touched base on a personal level as well as on a business one. Emma also regularly talked with her mother, and their efforts to maintain the relationship created a sense of familial normalcy—and it was, despite their not-so-normal lifestyles.

As for Stockman and Matthew, their only real common thread was associated with ORB. Other than that, neither tended to poke their noses into each other's personal business, unless invited—and that was rare—although Matthew was sure Stockman knew a lot more about him than he did about Stockman.

Their meal was relaxed and fluid, with no obvious business overtones and no embarrassing moments of silence. They shared personal stories about the places they had visited, the interesting sights and the sorts of people they had met. Matthew and Emma talked about Vancouver and what they liked, and didn't like, about it. They compared it to the other cities they had visited and stayed for long enough to get a feel for what it might be like to live in those places. Stockman filled them in on what he and Lucy were doing down in the southwest of England and even extended an invitation to them both to visit "any time."

It was all very convivial, as it should be. Stockman was charming, Emma was on her best behavior, and Matthew felt quite comfortable, albeit somewhat suspicious of the unfamiliar personal exchanges. He couldn't help but get the feeling Stockman was just sizing him up. Was it as a potential long-term partner for his daughter? Was it somehow related to ORB? Or, perhaps, it was just to see for himself how he and Emma connected. He didn't know before they dined, or after.

If he was in Stockman's position, he would want to see how the two got along; whether they were cut out to work together for the long-term; whether there were any obvious difficulties that could arise from their relationship; or even whether the father, being the boss, might make things awkward for them both. Matthew would never know the answer and decided, instead, to just enjoy their short time together.

Of course, it could all be just a reason to spend some quality time together away from the "office." But Matthew doubted that. Stockman wasn't the type to do anything without a reason—unless he happened to be with his wife, and even then, her background lent some doubt as to whether there were extraneous motives for what they were both doing in the company of others. Matthew let it go and focused on the pleasantries of dining in the beauty of the moment.

It was still early by Italian time as the three of them made it to the elevator. Stockman said his goodnights as he stepped in and left them standing in the hallway. He was a ten p.m. guy no matter where he was in the world.

"Goodnight, you two. I have to get my beauty sleep, you know." Stockman tapped his finger to the side of his nose in a "you know what I mean" way and winked.

They all smiled and knew Stockman was more likely to be on the phone for the next two hours, covering off some business and talking to Lucy. But no one said anything about that, and Matthew and Emma just volunteered a "Good night—see you in the morning—sleep tight." Emma added "Daddy" to the end of her good night and pecked Stockman on the cheek. Matthew shook his hand.

They watched the elevator door close before heading to the cocktail lounge and settling on a couple of witch hunt cocktails, recommended by the barman, where Scotch and dry vermouth are mixed with just a wetting of Strega liqueur and lemonade. Deliciously summery and typically Italian—and as potent as two ounces of vodka martini. So, they had two and spent the rest of the evening laughing and poking fun at each other. It was eleven thirty p.m. by the time they decided to head up to their rooms. This time they needed to rest and be at their most alert for the morning meeting.

Well, they did get as far as the tenth floor for Emma, but she managed to drag Matthew out of the elevator, without too much of a struggle, and over to her room for a nightcap and some social interaction. They still had lots of time before breakfast.

* * *

By nine a.m. the following morning, the ORB members selected by Stockman for this next assignment had gathered in the Via dei Condetti Suite living room, next to the bedroom where Stockman had slept. They helped themselves to the pastries and fruit set out on the small kitchen countertop with the Nespresso machine nearby.

Stockman had rearranged the two small round tables and extra chairs so the seven ORB team members could fit comfortably. His laptop was set up and he was using it to project the screen onto the wall above the fireplace mantel.

He had already welcomed everyone as they came into his suite, with some shoulder patting, handshakes, and laughs. There was no one new to him, so the greetings were short. A warm hug for Emma, who responded with a peck on his cheek. There were no other signs of their personal relationship, although everyone was aware they were father and daughter.

This was the first time Emma had been present at such a meeting. Most often, she was in the field, tackling issues associated with sabotage, maintaining surveillance, making contacts, or taking the pulse of situations before people like Matthew, the project lead, came in. Once the lead was comfortable, Emma would generally take up more of a supporting role, often keeping well away from the action but close enough to help if needed. That way, she maintained anonymity and kept one step away from the front line of danger.

"Well, let me start by welcoming you all, once again," Stockman started with a smile on his face, as he looked from one to the other, "as we embark on a new mission." He paused. Each member of the team smiled.

"Before I get into the project itself, I'll just go around the table and introduce each of you to your latest task first, for a change. You all know each other, so we can dispense with the formalities. Remember, we have a server at our disposal for you to file all your comments and reports, and I urge every one of you to contribute. It'll become our best way to keep everyone up to date, and you'll all get the password soon. You're welcome to catch up with each other after this meeting." He paused and looked at the faces in front of him and remembered the last time he had worked with each on a project. "I think we'll be in Rome for a few days, so there'll be opportunities for you to get together informally as well as meet if, or when, we need."

Stockman took a moment to fiddle with his laptop and some notes he had made while Matthew and Emma exchanged glances. Their eyebrows raised in anticipation of having some personal time together after all, here in the Eternal City, as the Romans referred to it, in the belief it would last forever, no matter what happened to the rest of the world. Of course, that was before there was traffic and crazy drivers in Rome.

"Let's start with Colin." Everyone turned to look at Colin, nibbling at a croissant. He put the pastry down, wiped his hands on his lap and acknowledged the attention with a silently mouthed "Hi." Colin was a quiet IT geek kind of a guy, but he was always smiling, always had a quick joke to tell. He had a family tucked away somewhere close to the Welsh border, on the English side, where he had a farm of sorts and pretended at being a landowner in his spare time. Tall, gangly, bespectacled, with a tangled mop of curly, graying hair, he had an easygoing outlook for a person who was one of the best there was in the complex world of computers.

"Colin will look after IT again." Stockman looked around at the faces. "I think there's going to be a fair bit for you to do on this one"—he caught Colin's eye— "including more money intercepts and transfers, but we may also need you to break into a couple of personal computers and things like that. We'll likely need some financial background on our targets as well as on their victims. Good to have you back."

Colin just nodded and smiled.

"Oh, by the way, we'll likely need Plato, and maybe even Margaret, with us again, and I know you all worked well together on the Iranian caper, so let's repeat when it comes to financial intercepts, if they're needed." Stockman put two thumbs up at Colin.

"That's great. Plato's just a whiz at the money game." Colin smiled. He didn't know Margaret, Plato's wife, but he had heard good things about her from his other ORB associates, and her international contacts through her father could be a great help on any project they undertook.

Stockman turned his attention to the next one in line, one of the two ORB lawyers, Alan. Tony, the other lawyer, couldn't make the meeting this time around.

"Alan, I think you can handle this one yourself, but don't hesitate to bring Tony in on things if it gets too much. You'll be dealing with stock exchanges and personnel backgrounds and likely a bunch of other things. We'll need information and control, I suspect, on stock transfers and contracts. Nothing you haven't dealt with before."

Stockman smiled at Alan, who nodded back and gave a two-fingered salute. He had been involved in all the projects Stockman brought to the table and was an expert in international law and securities. He was a well-dressed, well-constructed, and well-heeled person who could fit in with the aristocracy of society if needed. Sitting next to Colin, Alan seemed to be Colin's complete opposite and yet they survived and worked well together.

"Mitch," Stockman smiled at his old friend from many years in the field together, "you'll need to look at the underground mining aspects of this project, and there will be some, as well as the mineral economics, if it comes to that. We may have some issues Matthew may need help with."

Mitch smiled and waved to everyone. He was a real all-rounder and a top-notch geologist by profession. When it came to mining projects, both underground and open pit, as well as processing facilities, he could lend his hand at most things to do with the practicalities of a project as well as the economics and was a dab hand at helping create physical problems for the cause when needed. Mitch was a stocky, barrel-chested man in his fifties, with thick arms, strong hands, a lot of laugh lines around his eyes when he smiled, and shaggy black hair.

"Tom, would you look after shipping aspects?" Stockman looked over at Tom, another long-time friend. Tom was ex-Canadian navy, tough as old boots, and had a lined and tanned face to match. He had seen his fair share of shenanigans over the years on both the good and the bad sides of life. But altogether, he was one of the best, and Stockman trusted him implicitly.

"The folks we're dealing with here are going to be working with self-propelled hopper barges and tugs and the like, so we may need your help. As far as I know, they may already have assets on standby in Spain from their last project and may use them for this next one. You need to get a handle on exactly what their hardware looks like, performance and support requirements. Keep your eyes on whatever they have and let us know if anything moves or if any people are there. Matthew can supply you with whatever field guys you need to help but equip yourself as you see fit."

Tom nodded his agreement. After his term in the navy, Tom had become a specialist in offshore tugging and ocean freight, and based himself these days in St. John's, Newfoundland. His company transported loads between the Canadian east coast and northern Europe as well as the eastern US seaboard. He knew everyone in the industry, and they all knew and respected him.

Tom was always on hand when emergencies occurred, other than for ORB, in his part of the world, and they happened all too often around the Grand Banks. The banks were a series of submerged plateaus southeast of Newfoundland where the ocean was relatively shallow and one of the richest fishing grounds in the world. The combination of steep changes in depth, currents coming from a number of directions, and cold inflows meeting warmer ones created all the ingredients needed for shipping catastrophes, especially during the spring fog, which could stick around for weeks.

"No problem," Tom responded and looked serious as he took notes.

"Emma," Stockman turned to face his daughter, "you need to stick with Matthew and take on what you can. Not sure yet what will come up, but from what I understand about some of the people involved, I'm sure there will be special issues for you to manage." He looked over at Emma and smiled a knowing type of smile before glancing across to Matthew.

"I can always do with the help," Matthew offered and looked at Emma.

"All good with me." Emma moved into a more attentive posture as she accepted her role.

"We'll need more ORB operatives as we move along. They'll all have particular parts to play, but that all has to be worked out, so we'll leave them out of it for now." Stockman sipped his coffee.

"Okay, let's move on." The screen on the wall was filled with a map. "This is southern Greenland." Stockman had circled Nanortalik. "This is home to something like fifteen hundred Inuit. All they really have to sustain themselves is the fishing industry, and occasionally hunting. They have reindeer, or caribou if you are a North American, as well as polar bears, whales, seals, and the like. But really, only the fishing brings in any money and it's a huge industry. Walrus tusks used to be valuable, but the ivory quality is not as good as elephant or rhino tusks. Anyway, I digress. You know, Greenland is amazingly interesting, but that's for another day.

"Over the last twenty years or so, geology explorers have discovered substantial amounts of commercially mineable minerals of all types. When gold was discovered in financially viable quantities, just around the corner from Nanortalik, national flags were flown, and the country generally basked in the glow of a potential wealthy future for all. As it happens, there's a lot more to the country in terms of mineral wealth, and as the ice cap melts, so the prospects of exploration and production improve. But we're concerned with just one gold mine."

Stockman flashed another photo up on the screen. It showed a shallow, mile-wide valley strewn with boulders, three miles from the backdrop of a mile-high range of sharp-peaked mountains where ice clung precariously to the slopes and reached just above the valley floor.

"This," Stockman aimed a laser light up at the screen and pinpointed a spot about two thousand feet or so up one of the mountains on the west side of the valley, "is Nalunaq. You can just make out the two portals and the access to each winding its way up." He moved the red laser dot along a streak in the photo ending at black holes—the portals.

"Nalunaq has been explored, studied, and brought to commercial production primarily with the help of World Bank funding. In fact, they provided funds for the entire area to be upgraded. The community needed roads, bridges, an airstrip, school upgrading, utilities, and all the rest that goes to make up what we expect of a comprehensive social system. The expectation was for hundreds, and maybe thousands, more people to invade the place and work the mine properties. But it never panned out—no pun intended." Stockman paused, eyebrows raised, looking at the faces around him, expecting the shoe to drop.

"You see," Stockman continued in a somber tone, "some greedy company shareholders, a couple of Danes, decided to rob the bank, so to speak. They did a company takeover—nasty piece of work, I understand—changed directions, and barged all the high-grade gold ore away from Greenland in super-fast time and processed it elsewhere before anyone really had a chance to fully understand what had happened.

"The World Bank was left substantially out of pocket, the Greenlanders were back to where they started in terms of self-governing, and the governments of both Greenland and Denmark had been completely bamboozled. Meanwhile, the protagonists disappeared with the loot, so to speak." Stockman paused, and Colin took advantage.

"Wow, quite a story, Stockman. Any idea where these folks disappeared?"

"Not quite yet, Colin. But I do happen to have an idea who they might target next."

The audience squirmed and looked at each other.

"Are you telling us they mean to strike again?" Alan clearly seemed concerned.

"I do; and just for the record, it would seem the Nalunaq gold mine was not the first and apparently not the last one to suffer from a similar demise—unless we get there first. There's no doubt these guys have conned their targets out of billions of dollars." There were raised eyebrows and low whistles all round.

"Now listen. I don't know who or what all their previous targets were, right now. I suspect we'll find out over time, depending on whether the ownership wants to declare their embarrassments or not. What I do know is the World Bank would like their money back, and the Greenlandic and Danish governments would like reparation of some kind. I'm sure the other minority investors want these rogues caught as well, or stopped, or both. If it doesn't happen, anyone thinking about investing in Greenland is going to have a tough time getting financing in the future."

"You mentioned you may know what their next target is likely to be. Are you able to share that information?" It was Matthew.

"I can, Matthew. A reliable resource of mine in Vancouver just confirmed it to me." Everyone perked up to listen more intently.

"Let me qualify my resource first. You may need to meet with him." Stockman looked over to Matthew as the others also focused on what he was about to say. "A fellow by the name of Yanko, I won't bother with surnames, contacted me. He's a member of a four-person group—GREY, I believe they call themselves—specializing in the major aspects of mineral development. They assembled specifically at the request of the same Danes as we're about to pursue.

"When they're not working for these Danes, they contract their specialist services out to the industry as individuals. Yanko has done work for us a couple of times before, in fact. Very reliable, and particularly skilled in mathematical modeling of ore bodies for some very high-profile companies. He has a lot of other associated background—I think he's a mining engineer by profession—but mine economics is where he is most effective, and most sought after.

"Now, I've never known Yanko to work for anyone other than reputable organizations, but then, maybe I wouldn't know if he did. But I do trust him. He tells me this group he's associated with has been contracted to research target mine properties around the world. Not unusual, you might say." Stockman had their attention.

"But the interesting thing is all these properties have to have similar characteristics to the Nalunaq property—underground gold, infrastructure in place, permits in hand, shovel ready, hard up for money, near tidewater, and an inexperienced board." Stockman looked around him. His audience had caught on.

"You may think these requirements are all too much to expect, but my intel is there are thousands of mine properties out there, waiting for money. Most don't have a profile similar to Nalunaq, but odds are that out of those thousands, there are going to be a handful fitting the picture."

"Don't keep us in suspense, Stockman. Where is it?" It was Colin again. He was smiling and rubbing his hands together in anticipation of what was to come.

"Well, I understand from our friend, Yanko, there are three properties recommended for consideration at this point. One in Ireland, one in Wales, and one in Newfoundland. "

"I don't suppose the one in Newfoundland is the Hope Brook Mine?" It was Mitch, the mining specialist. The look on his face suggested he thought his guess was a good one. "That property has been on the books since the late nineties. It's a beautiful spot, with everything in place. Provided there is a reserve, it could be mined out really fast."

"You're spot on, Mitch. I think Hope Brook will be their next target. Vancouver-based Quest Gold are the owners, and a sorry bunch they sound, from what I have read about them so far. It also seems as though the other two properties could follow shortly after Hope Brook is fully hooked. My guess is these boys are going to do two or three in quick succession, or perhaps in parallel, if they have the resources. But when, I don't know. My gut is telling me something and it has rarely proved me wrong."

The room of ORB members waited.

"I think they're going to hit it very soon." Stockman stopped and went for a coffee. He turned back to the table as Alan started to ask a question.

"What's the plan?" It was Alan. "This doesn't sound like a normal sabotage job, but I guess we need to stop these folks, and even try to get the money back from at least the Greenland venture."

"Well, first let's find out who and where these rogues are." Stockman finished a mouthful of croissant and washed it down with a gulp of black coffee. "Yanko tells me he knows there are at least two, one called Finn and the other Erik. He doesn't know surnames and isn't even sure the names he was given are correct. But I know their names from my World Bank source.

"They all had a Zoom meeting and from what Yanko could tell, these guys were calling from a boat. There was water outside the cabin, and occasionally he could see, through one of the windows, people wandering by, and other boats moored. He doesn't know where they are, but it's warm and sunny because the people he saw going by were in shorts and T-shirts." Stockman paused for his audience to visualize the scene.

"He said it looked as though they were moored right up close to the main dock and he could just make out some white buildings and some mountains in the background. Doesn't give us much, but it's better than nothing."

"See if Yanko can give me a time when the Zoom call was made, can you?" It was Colin. "I may be able to backtrack and get some information depending on who made the Zoom arrangement. It's a long shot, so I'll need date and time, and make sure it's GMT or, at the very least, tell me what time zone they were in when they made the call."

Stockman nodded and made a note.

"I'll see what my contacts can give me on the Hope Brook property. See if anyone has been approached to sell stock or offer money." It was Mitch.

"Good, Mitch, but don't ask questions about Quest stock just yet. It's too early." Stockman smiled as he watched his friend sit back and grimace his understanding.

"I'll take a visit to Greenland," Tom piped up, "and see who knows anything about tugs and barges being used. I just need to have an idea of the date of the moves."

"Go ahead with tracking the barges, Tom—that would be a great help. As far as I know, the moves were made over the last two years, ending about four months ago. Destinations include Newfoundland and northern Spain. That should narrow things down a little." Stockman paused to see if Mitch or Tom needed anything else right now, but they seemed satisfied, and Stockman looked over at Matthew and Emma.

"Matthew, you and Emma get back to Vancouver after we've finished here in a couple of days. Start poking around the mining community and see what's been happening in the world of finance and whether any juniors have been getting bites from individuals offering big money. Nose around Quest and educate yourself as to who they are and what we might be able to get into there.

"I'll get some legwork going on this Finn and Erik pair and see what our people come up with." Stockman took a sip of coffee. "We'll also need a fix on their money, where it's going, and how to get hold of it, plus get to know if they are just the players for some bigger fish. It's hard to believe it's just a couple of guys out there doing this, but you never know." Stockman seemed to be finished and glanced around for questions or comments.

* * *

There were a lot worse places to spend some time in than Rome. There was little Matthew and Emma could do for the new project just yet, other than some internet research and call back to some contacts in Vancouver. They had enough free time to wander, take in some tourist sights, and spend leisurely meals together in the bustling restaurants of the back streets of the city, where some of the best high-end stores were also located. They didn't leave the city in case they were needed, although they were tempted to take an excursion south—but maybe next time.

There were two short meetings over the next couple of days.

The first meeting was after Colin had managed to track the Zoom call made from Vancouver and booked by Yanko's group. The call was picked up by parties in the Marbella, Spain area. It couldn't be pinpointed any closer than that, but the possibility of there being a boat involved meant a marina, and a quick search located a likely one in Puerto Banús. Matthew or Emma thought they should make a visit there when they were finished in Rome. They weren't sure what they were looking for just yet, but if a boat was involved, it would likely be tied up at the marina. Hopefully they would get a fix on these Danes.

Mitch and Tom got the group together again but this time the discussion concerned the ore shipments from Greenland. Perhaps that would be the basis of the next plan the Danes might have for the Hope Brook property, if that was the next target.

"If I have my numbers right," Tom started, "those Danes double-shifted their operation and mined about four hundred and fifty thousand tons from the Nalunaq underground in just over a year, and then just stopped." He paused and looked to Mitch for confirmation of his information. Mitch nodded, and Tom continued.

"It sounds as though they purchased three fairly hefty sized oceangoing self-propelled hopper barges, with something like ten thousand DWT on average," Tom continued, "with side panels and ramps, and one oceangoing tug, probably leased, but I can't be sure yet. Those barges varied between three hundred and fifty and four hundred feet long and were used to haul six-thousand-ton payloads of ore on each trip a thousand miles or so over to a process plant and refinery in Newfoundland. It would have taken them around six or seven days to do the trip—weather permitting, of course.

"If you're interested in detail, those barges can skip along at up to thirteen knots an hour with their twin eleven hundred-kilowatt diesels apiece, and with the size of payload being about half the dead weight, there was a lot of room for spare diesel fuel and such. Really, the whole exercise would have been quite straightforward. Those barges are equipped with loading and unloading conveyors, so handling the ore at both ends was a pretty simple affair. They sure had it all worked out." Tom looked around and screwed his face up as though he was delivering bad news. He wasn't. It was all fact and all good information.

"Out of interest, what about the ice around Greenland, Tom?" It was Alan. "Problem?"

"Strangely, there are really no great number of troublesome icebergs in southern Greenland as we would normally imagine—I mean by vertical height and diameter, and depth under water—to contend with." Tom perked up and enjoyed passing his knowledge along.

"But there are ice floes ranging anywhere between sixty feet and eight miles across, and they are large packs of flat, floating ice. They can be a real problem for shipping, especially if several of them join together to form even larger masses of drift ice. That's what you see when ships get stuck in the ice, which seems to engulf them until a specially designed icebreaker goes in to get them. Those floes are continually on the move, but a good-size tug, properly equipped, would have no problems keeping the route open for the barges by just going back and forth all the time.

"I took a look at the satellite images in that part of the world, through last winter, and it's really interesting to see the ice sheets forming and moving around the tip of Greenland, with an occasional more traditional-looking iceberg moving along with it. Fascinating. I doubt the fishermen like any kind of ice formations, but my guess is they have ways of coping."

"Good job, Tom. Anything else, anyone?"

"Well, it's clear from reading what I can on the internet, these Danes gave up processing the ore in Newfoundland after a while, for whatever reason, and instead barged the ore down to the north coast of Spain, to the Rio Narcea port facility, then trucked the ore up to the processing site. Quite a chore, by the way. That's quite the trucking route they had to deal with. Things must have gone really badly with the Newfoundland arrangement for them to take on the Rio Narcea option." Tom stopped and raised his eyebrows at the faces before him. "Questions?"

"Do they still have the barges, Tom?" It was Matthew.

"I'm pretty sure all three are tied up in the river estuary at Aviles. That's probably where they stockpiled the ore before loading it into trucks for transporting up to the Rio Narcea processing plant. My guess is they'll be re-using those same barges for this Hope Brook job. They'd be ideal. From what I know, the landing they have at Hope Brook would be perfect for these barges. It has a long landing stage out into the fjord for the trucks and each barge has an onboard crane to get the ore off the deck." As though for confirmation, Tom glanced at Mitch again and sat back.

"Mitch"—it was Matthew— "any clues from your discussions about these guys that were involved? And who did the work?"

"Not yet, Matthew. I was thinking about heading to Nanortalik to talk to a few people about their experience. I'd think these guys would've stayed in one of the hotels in town, and there's only one that would qualify for the likes of us—it's the only place with a bar." They all laughed and agreed he was probably right.

"Good. Matthew, you could tag along…" Stockman suggested.

"I might just do that. Maybe we can head up to Nuuk as well and talk to the premier if you can arrange it. Could you?" Matthew looked at his boss, who nodded.

"Sounds like a plan. As far as I know, he's very amenable to visitors. Let me see what arrangements I can make and give you some options." It was Stockman.

"Thanks, guys." Matthew nodded at both Mitch and Tom.

"Okay, folks. It's a wrap for now. Let's see if anything comes in tomorrow before we head out." Stockman picked up his papers, called out to Alan, and suggested they go to supper together. "You may want to make whatever arrangements you need for the project while you're here in Rome. At least that way we can still touch base with each other if there are any last-minute details we need to work out."

Stockman pulled Matthew to one side as the others left the room.

"Would you call Plato and find out what he's up to? I don't think we have sufficient information on the situation right now to give him any specific instructions but as soon as we establish details of these Danes, we'll get Plato working on their financial history and records, if he comes on board. By the way, I'll leave Quest for you to dig into. See if you can gain their confidence without exposing us; they might think it's weird that an organization like us is taking an interest in their affairs sooner than we want them to."

"Sounds good. Anything else?" Matthew had already started on his research and was ready to contact Yanko in particular.

"I would like you to engage with Sloan on this project, if you need bodies, that is." Stockman eyed Matthew, who just shrugged his understanding.

Sloan ran a discreet employment agency out of London for skilled tradesmen willing and able to go overseas, through his Sloan Agency, to undertake specialist tasks. He had been a center for recruitment for all manner of industrial projects for the last fifteen years. As his reputation grew, so did the different special requests made of him by disassociated parties.

Matthew and Emma spent most of the next day wandering the streets of Rome. The city was not new to either of them, and neither wanted to get lost in the history of the city as much as just spending time being together and sharing some of the new history they were creating. The window displays were filled with gloves, or handbags, or the latest creations in women's wear, eyeglass frames, and shoes. Salamis hung from every inch of the ceiling in the deli, and sandwiches were filled with all manner of cold cuts, with line-ups waiting their turn. Horses with their carts lazily waited for their next customer in the square, and the skyline was framed with majestic spires and cathedral roofs and fountains of such exquisite design one could not help but stop and stare at each one of them. It was never-ending.

Then there was the Trevi Fountain with its' fine spray cooling the crowd. Or the Spanish Steps where they could sit and watch a fashion show before wandering over to an outside café for an espresso and dessert in the mid-afternoon sun. Tourists streamed by in search of something they had never seen before.

* * *

The group had a meal together in the evening on the rooftop terrace of the Portrait Hotel, before they went their own ways to make some last-minute arrangements with each other, or just to say farewell. Mitch and Matthew agreed to visit Greenland as soon as they could and settled on meeting in Copenhagen the following Saturday for flights to Nuuk. That was, provided Stockman could make the arrangements for them to meet with the Greenlandic premier on the Sunday evening, one week from now. That was the beauty of Greenland. It was small enough that everyone in each community knew each other, and it was no different for the premier. He was always open to meeting with his foreign neighbors, always on the lookout for improvements to Greenland's financial position.

The day after the meeting with the premier, arrangements would be made for a charter helicopter to take Matthew and Mitch south to Nanortalik, where they would stay in the Hotel Kap Farval, a twenty-room facility with a bar, on the outskirts of the small community. The helicopter pilot would stay there as well and be ready to transport them over to the Nalunaq mine site and back to Nuuk the next day.

* * *

Greenland, Here We Come

As he always did when he traveled to Copenhagen, Matthew stayed at 71 Nyhavn Hotel. It was a converted two-hundred-year-old warehouse at the port, overlooking the Malmo ferries, at the end of Nyhavn Canal. He loved the feel of the place and the mix of the original re-pointed and new red brickwork, green window shutters, and the heavy original wooden beams with intricate custom carpentry connections that had been cleaned up and recoated. The inside of the hotel had been completely gutted, refurbished, and decorated with modern Danish art and some pieces dating back to the COBRA avant-garde period.

The port area had long recovered from the rough and tumble days of crime when merchant seamen would stumble from one brothel to the next, drinking their way through the port end of the canal. These days, Nyhavn Canal is more of a pedestrian zone for strollers who might be coming from the traffic-free Stroget shopping precinct, in the center of Copenhagen, or just looking for a beer in one of the basement bars at the end of their day.

Whenever he got the opportunity, Matthew enjoyed strolling along the canal, looking at the myriad boat styles, tied up in a row to the quayside, sometimes two abreast, with not a modern mega yacht to be seen. Then there were the colorfully painted fifteenth- and sixteenth-century, five- and six-floor heritage buildings lining each side of the canal and emptying directly onto the quay, where cafes and bars invited passers-by in.

In the evening, Matthew spent a leisurely couple of hours in the hotel's Italian restaurant in what used to be the ground floor and cellar of the old warehouse. It was still a cellar in part, but one that had gone through a substantial upscale overhaul, creating one of the best places to eat in the city with an ambience and wine cellar to match. He spoiled himself and had the rack of lamb with two glasses of a French merlot. He was alone and enjoying a private moment of thoughtfulness. The restaurant was full of Danes and foreign travelers alike, all laughing and enjoying themselves.

The "1812 Overture" crescendo announced Stockman's call just as Matthew closed his mouth over the first forkful of lamb and was about to wallow in the rosemary and garlic sauce that came with it.

"It seems as though Quest is somewhat of a minor player in the industry, Matthew," Stockman announced without introduction. "This fellow, Mah—Stockman had no intention of apologizing to Matthew in the event he had interrupted anything, despite the time, and was clearly just continuing from an earlier conversation— "is the president but doesn't have any pull in the financial world, and their board isn't exactly bursting with expertise. Of course, you can find all that out for yourself when you get back to Vancouver, but in the meantime, I think you need to figure out a way to get in to meet him and let him know what's about to go down."

"I have Emma sniffing around the exchange right now, doing a little legwork before I get there," Matthew responded after swallowing his first mouthful and settling his utensils back on his plate. "I'm going to arrange a meeting with him as soon as I get home."

"Ah." Stockman seemed a little surprised that Matthew had not yet done that, but then he remembered he was heading to Greenland, and recovered quickly. "Thought you would. Just checking, you know. Anything you need me to do?" Stockman sounded a little subservient but silently reveled in the proactivity Matthew was exhibiting.

"Well, perhaps Tony can find out whether any of his lawyer colleagues have been drafting up offers for someone to take over Quest. You never know. If the Danes are going to move, and if they aren't already major shareholders, and Emma confirms they aren't, then I'd bet they're going to look for a way to take Quest over through a hostile takeover or some such vehicle." Matthew seemed quite positive and, again, Stockman was taken a little aback once again.

"Quite. Quite, Matthew. I think you're on to something there. Let me know if you want me to do anything else, but in the meantime, I'll get Tony to snoop around the Toronto legal circuit."

"Great. Anything else?" Matthew sat back in his chair land looked longingly at the meal in front of him.

"No, I don't think so." Stockman sounded a little dubious as to whether he was finished, but he was, for now. "I'll let you get back to your meal. Enjoy." Stockman closed his cell on the other end and left Matthew looking at his own phone as though it was a camera and Stockman was watching.

"How the hell…?" Matthew swung his head around a full three hundred and sixty degrees but didn't pick up on anyone watching. Then he noticed security cameras in the restaurant, with one pointed directly at his table. "Son of a gun…" Matthew smiled and picked up his knife and fork and remembered that even the cameras in restaurants, high-end stores, and offices were often connected to some police control center, where city activities could be monitored, just like the cameras along the roadways and lanes. Those cameras were also rigged to communicate to a number of other crime control groups, company security systems, and government agencies with interest in public oversight, including ORB.

* * *

It was after eleven p.m. when Matthew finally got to his room, after a leisurely stroll along the canal bank with the remaining small clusters of other pedestrians, some coming and going into the cellar bars of the heritage buildings, or just enjoying the fresh air and the colorful lights adorning the boats and buildings. It was a truly beautiful sight made all the better by the warmth of the two ounces of single malt Matthew had sipped at the end of his meal.

"Hi, Emma. It's me." Matthew announced after the first few rings had been ignored and he had slumped down on the bed.

"Yes, I can see it's you, Matthew. Your phone number gave you away." Emma chuckled. "How the hell are you, my weary traveler?"

"Oh, good. Great. Yes, of course." His mind was flitting from one thought to another. "Listen, did you get anything new on Quest?" Mathew quickly recovered.

"They're certainly looking for money." Emma could tell Matthew was tired and just wanted to hear her voice, but she bought into the question. "To cover corporate overhead and pay their salaries, with a little promotion, but there's nothing new in their press releases that I can tell. All sounds a little desperate to me, but then, there are so many junior mining companies in this city traveling the same route, so to speak." Emma paused, waiting for Matthew in the event he wanted to interrupt.

"I don't doubt it, but did you get any intel on their need to raise capital for their Hope Brook project?" Matthew asked patiently.

"No. But I did bump into this guy, Chapson or something like that, in a bit of a seedy but favorite pub-come-restaurant for the mining fraternity in the city." She chuckled at the description she offered. "He seemed a little the worse for wear, if you know what I mean. Big red nose and all that, but he loved talking. Couldn't shut him up. Full of himself and just kept going on and on about what properties he had in his portfolio for sale—he'd gone into the wilds and pegged them himself—and how much of a great deal any of them would make for anyone looking to buy, blah blah blah.

"Anyway, I eventually got him talking about Quest, and he just opened up about what a bunch of idiots he thought they were—I think he thought everyone was an idiot, except himself, of course. Apparently, he told them they had no idea what they were doing. I think he's a shareholder, but he had no time for the directors—all a bunch of amateurs—and if they had done what he'd told them to do at the last GM, they'd be far better off and so on and so on. You know the type. Full of himself and likely carrying a huge load of crap to unload." Emma sounded a little cynical and stopped.

"Okay, but did he know whether they had an offer on the table?"

"He didn't know for sure, but he doubted it. He says that if they did, the news would be all over town, and the stock price would be on its way up—but it wasn't more than a greed blip, as I think they call it. So, I guess there isn't one yet, Matthew. That's good, isn't it?"

"That's very good, Emma. It means we still have time to get to Quest. Listen, I'll be in touch again shortly, but keep your ear to the ground. Maybe you can find a way to bump into Mah, their president. Bye for now, darling." Matthew chuckled.

"I'm sure I can." Emma laughed. "Take care in Greenland and make sure you bring me back a memento—and I don't mean anything to do with seal." They laughed and their lines went dead.

Matthew met Mitch the next morning at Copenhagen's Kastrup airport to take the ten a.m. flight to Kangerlussuaq en route to Nuuk, with almost five hours in the air. Kangerlussuaq was the only airstrip in Greenland capable of accommodating international flights. Like many of the airstrips in remote parts of the world, it was the US military that built the nine-thousand-foot-long airstrip to use in World War II to accommodate their largest aircraft at the time. To this day, many are still used, as aircraft got bigger with time and outgrew what commercial airports could offer.

Unfortunately, Kangerlussuaq was hardly a community, and the majority of people stopping there were just using it as a transfer point to other destinations both within Greenland and offshore. Inevitably, once Nuuk, as the country's capital, extended its airstrip, Kangerlussuaq's status as an international passageway would be abandoned unless new mineral discoveries were made to open up the area for business.

Matthew and Mitch boarded the Dash 8-200 for their short trip to Nuuk, about two hundred miles to the south. As they came in to land at the capital, under the heaviness of overhanging clouds, they got a glimpse of Nuuk's surroundings. Rock, all rock, with only patchy, stubby grass. No trees. No bushes, no flowers to speak of, although strangely, a golf course just south of the airstrip that had, what they came to understand, arctic grass for its nine greens, imported from Iceland. *Very odd*, Matthew thought but didn't linger on it. It was explained to him that any other grass, in and around Nuuk, was a hardy variety that didn't grow very fast in this northern latitude. Matthew had no trouble believing it.

Along the route to the city center, tall, rectangular, concrete apartment buildings with small windows and no balconies had been built. He assumed the reason was so they could minimize utility runs and stay more protected from the harshness of winter. Most were built close together and next to the main roads, giving one the sense the outskirts of Nuuk were just a strip of life on the way to the golf club and airport. But there was more than that around Nuuk, although not much else. He knew there were more traditional colorful, Greenlandic houses with steep roofs out there, but he couldn't see them on the drive into the hotel.

The cab ride into the city displayed a bleak panorama of rock outcrops under heavy skies, and other than the concrete buildings, there seemed to be little else to consider as interesting. Although there was some fascinating history associated with the Viking age and what remained of their tenure on the island, visitors looking for some exciting Viking stories might be somewhat disappointed to discover they only settled in a very small area of the country and were just farmers looking for agricultural land. The romantic and exciting stories of Viking conquests didn't appear to be the case in Greenland. There was no one to conquer at the time, the Inuits having arrived after the Vikings arrived, and they really weren't looking to fight—just to farm.

However, there are some very interesting Viking artifacts that still linger, but what happened to those Vikings, over time? No one seems to know. Maybe they all died in Greenland, although there are believable stories of Vikings heading to Newfoundland. Perhaps it was the walrus tusks they used for trade that were forgotten when the more valuable elephant ivory came on to the market and their revenues dried up; or their doomed-to-failure fishing expertise compared to the Inuit. It could have been a drought, as currently hypothesized by some scientists, or in-fighting that splintered the colony band. While they were quite capable of writing, there weren't any Viking notes, as such, discovered or left behind, and an explanation may never be discovered.

Some of the remnants of their stone homes and churches in settlements remain as reminders of their presence. Perhaps, as most believe, they just kept sailing west, looking for greener pastures on which to settle and farm. Nevertheless, the legends of Erik the Red, still reputed to be the first Norseman to discover and settle in Greenland, hold some mystique for the inquiring mind, especially when some of it is tied to the discovery of gold.

It only took a little less than twenty minutes for their cab to reach the Hotel Hans Egede in what appeared to be the center of town. It was a modern, Danish style building reminiscent of the apartment blocks they had passed on the way from the airport, except the hotel had just a dash of color on the metal strip above the entrance emblazoned with the name of the hotel. But it was comfortable and more than adequate. By the time they arrived, it was too late to get food in the restaurant, and a quick look around the streets showed the place to be almost devoid of traffic and people. Everything seemed to have shut down for the night; after all, it was coming up to eight thirty p.m.

Mitch and Matthew shared a couple of Scotches from the bottle Matthew had picked up en route, while they went over their itinerary for the next day, Sunday. They would be meeting the prime minister, Hans Erikson, in the Hereford Beefstauw restaurant, on the fifth floor of the hotel, in the evening and had the first part of the day to wander the city. They decided on having a lazy breakfast around ten a.m. before taking in the sights—if there were any.

"You'd never guess what I can see from my window, Em." Matthew sounded almost excited when he called Emma on Messenger and could see her face come up on the screen when she answered his call. She looked as though she was heading out and he had just managed to catch her.

"Oh, hello, Matthew," Emma answered almost sarcastically, as in doing so might bring his attention to the fact he didn't even bother to say, "Hello, darling, it's me."

"Oh, hello, darling." Matthew realized he was remiss. "Go on, guess. Go on," he repeated.

"A walrus?" Emma replied glibly.

"A Bang and Olufsen store! You know, the old B & O speakers. Can you believe it? Of all the places in the world. It's right there across the road—not another store around, nothing. Only this speaker store. How can they survive?" Matthew calmed down.

"Well. Who would have guessed? Mind you, if I recall, Denmark is B & O land, isn't it?" Emma was being sarcastic again.

This time Matthew recognized the tone and laughed. "Yeah, I know. But isn't it exciting?"

"Mmmm. How was the trip?" Emma pulled Matthew back to earth.

"Oh. Good, good. It's a bit… how can I say this? Spartan. I mean here in Nuuk. They do have a golf course, though." Matthew pushed himself to sound in good spirits.

"Planning on getting a round in while you're there?" Emma responded, tongue-in-cheek, as she smiled.

"Right. I don't think so." Matthew pretended to sound unamused by Emma's wit.

"What's on the agenda before you head to Nanortalik?" Emma asked, even though she knew broadly what Matthew's itinerary was.

"Supper with the premier in the hotel restaurant. Let's see what he knows about these Danes. Maybe they'll use the same template for Hope Brook. Any word on Mah?"

"I think he eats at a little Greek place around the corner from his office. I followed him there yesterday and they all seem to know him. He seems to have the same table every day and I was planning on slipping into his booth tomorrow, if he turns up alone, and see if he responds to a meeting invitation. Or maybe I can just get him to talk right then."

"Good job, darling. A real pro. Don't tell him about the Danes, though. I'll do that when I get back after I get a few more facts about their modus operandi. Just poke around the edges and see if you can find out how interested Quest are in selling."

"Will do. I have to go but keep in touch." Emma closed her cell phone before Matthew had a chance to talk again.

"See you later, Em—take care." He smiled. Emma was a little quirky sometimes but that was, in part, why he liked her so much. She was never afraid to speak her mind, talk to anyone, and have a laugh at his expense, or her own.

* * *

It was another bleak and overcast day in Nuuk, but warm enough not to have to go out in full winter regalia. Which was just as well, because neither Matthew nor Mitch had anything with them other than a sweater, down jacket, jeans, and a hat. Having had a relaxing and typical Danish-style breakfast of open sandwiches and a beer, rather than a Jägermeister, they spent a while looking out over the view of the fjord and the city. Both seemed to be completely devoid of activity of any kind, but perhaps that was what it was like on Sundays.

They decided to walk down toward the water instead of just wandering the empty streets. A few hundred meters from the hotel, near the water, they found themselves next to a market of sorts that was clearly busy. Venturing in, it was easy to see this was primarily a fish market, with its tables spread out on both sides of what looked like a warehouse. It was, in fact, the old fish market, where both hunters and fisherman could bring their catch to sell.

The place was strewn with fish, as well as meat and birds of all kinds, laid out on tables for the shoppers to choose.

The air was pungent with the smells of raw, fresh everything, and Matthew and Mitch slipped their way around on a floor of slushy ice mixed with blood and water. There were no freezers. The air temperature was cold enough to keep the food fresh. There was cod, catfish, salmon, Acadian fish, trout, halibut, whale blubber, seal, ptarmigan fowl, auk birds, guillemots, and seagulls, as well as eider duck. With the start of the hunting season, there was a choice of fresh musk ox and reindeer meat carved to order. Matthew backed into half a reindeer; the front half, frozen solid with its skin, antlers, and eyelashes still intact and its eyes staring off into space over his shoulder. The other half would have been thawed, skinned, cleaned, and cut into steaks and placed on one of the tables for the customers to consider. There were men and women with sharply curved knives, or ulus, used to slice the thick blubber of seals into bite-sized pieces. There was even some Greenlandic lamb, considered some of the best in the world as a consequence of the clean and pristine conditions in which they were bred.

It was hard not to just stand and stare at the people poking and discussing the foods laid out before them. Their purchases were tossed into plastic bags, weighed, and paid for. Never before had Matthew thought he could just stand and watch the goings-on in a fish market in a place like Nuuk, or any place. But then, there wasn't much else to do in Nuuk on a Sunday for a pedestrian visitor without a set of golf clubs.

A casual walk past a small, well-looked-after church, and a little farther toward the water, brought Matthew and Mitch to a cemetery of sorts. It was clearly ancient and had not been used for any recently deceased clients, from what they could tell. There were some wooden crosses and plastic flowers on what seemed to be scraggy-looking grave sites. There were also a couple of totally dilapidated round stone walls and an old, faded sign in several languages, including English, stuck in the ground, describing the area as a Viking cemetery and an original Norse settlement site. The small area looked out over the fjord, just a few feet farther on. Matthew couldn't help his human nature but to look down at the ground and let his eyes search for relics, while knowing full well it would be pointless.

* * *

Premier Hans Erikson was a small, unsmiling Inuit man who greeted Matthew and Mitch in an unassuming and humble manner as he approached them in the dining room where they had already been seated. They shook hands, and Hans introduced them to a woman named Marianne, who had accompanied him. They weren't sure who she was, or whether she worked with Hans or was a family member or friend. Hans was a quiet man, but fortunately, Marianne could carry a conversation. They both spoke softly as they welcomed their visitors to Nuuk, and to Greenland. There was small talk about where Matthew and Mitch came from, and where Hans and Marianne were raised. He was a native of Nuuk, had not traveled extensively, but spoke English perfectly, as did Marianne, who had been brought up in Denmark where she earned her degrees from Aarhaus University, culminating with an MBA in Social and Political Science.

"Unless you are vegetarian, may I recommend the reindeer? It's in season right now and, when roasted or grilled fresh, is probably better than any beef you may have tasted." Hans looked around the table to see if either Matthew or Mitch were interested.

They were sitting in a spacious semi-circular booth under the watchful eye of a reindeer head. The other walls were adorned with an assortment of hunted Greenlandic animals, and in a number of cases, there were several of one species. In fact, Matthew counted four other reindeer heads within his vision. He wondered how many more heads there were on the walls of Nuuk homes, offices, and workshops.

The restaurant was cast under dim lighting, with heavy dark wood furniture quite unlike the Danish light woods used in the rest of the hotel. There was a bleak feel to the atmosphere, but maybe that came with the dark, low-hanging clouds peering through the windows, or a seeming desire of the patrons to feel as though they were alone. Or perhaps it was normal and had been this way forever. It looked as though it had.

"That sounds fine to me." It was Mitch, and Matthew agreed.

It was unanimous. They all ordered beers and barbecued reindeer steaks—medium rare.

Matthew wasted no time in getting down to business. "I don't know if Stockman mentioned why we're here." Matthew waited for some response. Hans just looked at him. Marianne was silent but attentive.

"Well, we're searching for the people who mined out Nalunaq." Matthew didn't dwell on the discomfort he felt with the lack of verbal response from either Hans or Marianne. "I assume you met them at some point." Matthew tilted his head to the side and stared at both of them.

"We did." It was Marianne who answered. Hans sat quite still and listened. "We remember them well." She paused and watched them both. "Why are you looking for them?" She looked at Matthew blankly, giving no hint of her suspicions.

"In a nutshell, let me say we're very aware of their escapades here in Greenland, and the fact they took a lot of money and left little behind."

"Yes, you're right. But what if you catch them? What do you expect to do with them?" Marianne was the inquisitor again. Hans stayed still.

"I'd like to think we could recover the money they took from the World Bank, as well as whatever they may have taken from yourselves, and others associated with the project. But we'd also really like to stop them from doing this again."

"Oh." It was Hans, who suddenly seemed to be interested.

"Yes," Matthew continued, "we think they have two or three other targets in mind. We want to stop them. What can you tell us about them? Are there just two? Are there more? Where do they come from?" He stopped and waited as their beers arrived. They all sipped at the froth on the top of the amber brew and settled their glasses back down on the table.

Hans fiddled with his, drawing his finger through the condensation on the outside of the glass. He was thinking and the others gave him the time he needed.

"I was the unfortunate one they dealt with most of the time." Hans didn't look up. He just drew more condensation down the beer glass with his finger and turned it a quarter turn to do it all again while trying to keep the glass within the wet circle it made on the table.

"I doubt I will be re-elected after that fiasco, but such is life. People have to have someone to blame, and it's my turn this time." He paused, still looked down at the table, and then, as though a small light flicked on somewhere in his brain, he said, "We were so ecstatic to have new investors that I'm afraid our, my, naivety got the better of us." Hans looked at Matthew and Mitch but avoided Marianne's eyes. Clearly, he was still hurting from the experience, and likely looked forward to the next election so he could lose and go back to the peace and quiet of a normal life, out of any limelight where he would be constantly reminded of what he considered to be his failure. That was, at least, how he would view it.

"Don't feel too bad"—Matthew held his hands up— "you aren't the only ones. We think there were others before you, and now maybe more."

"That's of small comfort, I'm afraid," said Hans sadly. "We've been injured badly and we may not be able to recover for a long time."

"We understand." Matthew wanted to turn the conversation to what he needed. "Can you tell us more about these people?"

It was Marianne who started. "They were Danish; I still can't believe it." Matthew thought he saw tears at the corner of her eyes. "Quite different from the people we dealt with previously—and they were foreigners." She said it with a look of shock and surprise, as though one might expect such criminality from foreigners, but not Danes, who she would consider as being as good as her own kin.

"These two were all business, and continually pushed us to sign off for permits, and then loans, with everyone, including the World Bank. We didn't have to put up any collateral or anything like that—we have nothing to offer, other than land and permits, you see." Marianne looked around with her hands open and palms up in a "you know what I mean" way.

"They offered us a five percent NSR, which is net smelter return—you see." She looked wide-eyed, expecting some sign of surprise on the faces of Matthew and Mitch. Any offer of an NSR was usually reserved for special financiers, but five percent was definitely high. "I don't know if you appreciate what that means," she continued, realizing she wasn't getting a reaction to her announcement, "but it is substantial and far more than anyone else would get from any mine operator under normal conditions—I checked." Marianne suddenly looked tear-free and angry. "That's five percent of the revenue from the sales of the gold, less refining and transportation costs. It was a windfall for Greenland and was likely to continue for a number of years as they discovered more gold—hopefully. As you know, that didn't happen." Her face turned from angry to sad as her eyes shifted from Matthew to Mitch and back.

"Do you happen know who did the mining work on site?" It was Matthew, changing the subject from one that clearly unsettled Marianne and very likely Hans.

"We know it was a contractor based out of Vancouver. CanMine, I think." Marianne recovered her posture, and looked at Hans, who nodded to confirm the name. "We didn't have any interaction with them but occasionally one of the Danes would bring the owner, Big Jim Garland, to our meetings to give us an overview of what was happening on site. Obviously, he had been prepared before the meeting on what to say." Marianne looked sorrowful and cast her eyes down toward the table. "But then, he was only doing his job, and no matter what they were going to ultimately do with the ore, CanMine's job was just to mine it."

"What about the money, the loans and such?" Mitch asked.

"Fortunately, in retrospect, we provided none. It was all coming from the World Bank, a little from the Danish government, and other private financial companies who were following suit, expecting good long-term returns. Our job was only to sign off that the information the World Bank was getting was correct—to the best of our knowledge—and, of course, permits, although the approval was left to the Danish government agencies. We made no promises about the company itself, in terms of their standing with the Stockholm exchange or any other party. That was for others to verify. It seems they passed all the tests." She looked around again, her hands open with palms up. She looked reluctantly accepting.

The reindeer steaks arrived, and they settled in to eat. The first couple of mouthfuls drew sounds of approval as the diners washed the rich, lean red meat down with their beers.

"Oh boy. That's interesting," Matthew commented. "You know, I thought it was going to taste like beef, but it's got a taste of its own, hasn't it, Mitch?"

Mitch nodded his agreement but was too busy with his next mouthful to be verbal.

"When did you first realize things were not going to plan?" Matthew asked abruptly, while the others were still thinking about their steaks.

This time it was Hans who responded. He put his utensils on the table and rested his elbows at the sides of his plate. He clearly needed time to get his thoughts together every time he came to answer a question.

"It was over a year," Hans started as he sat farther back in his chair and forgot about the meal, "after they started to take the ore offshore before we started to wonder. The World Bank wasn't bothered." He grimaced and shook his head. "Their payback would come from revenue, and that wasn't expected until the ore was processed. They didn't know the ore was never going to be processed on site, where the results could be witnessed, and those rogues had been telling them they were going to take some of the ore off-site just to do some sample processing, while they designed and built the plant. Of course, it was all nonsense." Hans paused and wiped his mouth with his napkin.

"We didn't question anything until we started to get uncomfortable with nothing happening on the road connection to Nanortalik." Hans picked up his knife and fork and prepared a piece of meat to eat but didn't. "We sent some people over to the mine site but, to be honest, it was easy for them to be duped into believing everything was on track." He put the meat into his mouth and chewed for a few seconds before continuing.

"Yes, they watched as ore was being trucked to a barge at the shoreline, but they never thought to question it. They assumed it was all going to be tested off-site. In just under two years they were gone, and so was the gold. The rest is history." Hans lowered his head and rested for a moment before he picked up his knife and fork and started to slowly eat again.

"Can you tell us anything about these guys?" Matthew looked from Hans to Marianne.

"Finn Hansen and Erik Mateus. Those were their names. I shall never forget." There was a look of real anger in her eyes as Marianne responded. "They were the ones we saw the most of, although we're sure there were others. I think they coordinated with another group, but I don't know who. Hansen and Mateus were here when they were getting the permits finalized. They needed them before the World Bank would forward the first part of the loan." Marianne seemed to be thinking, pulling the timeline together in her head.

"Then I think they spent time in Nanortalik sorting out their contractor, although I'm quite sure they never got their hands dirty themselves. Hansen is the big, overweight one with short curly hair. Mateus is the fit, shorter one with a crew cut, and doesn't do much talking." Marianne pulled a photo out of her purse. It was a group shot of Hansen and Mateus with Hans, Marianne, and a few others. She handed it to Matthew. "You can have this. I have others."

"That's great, Marianne. Thank you. You've both been a huge help to us and, again, we're truly sorry about what has happened." Matthew looked at Hans and Marianne. They were both the perfect picture of solemnity and just a hint of watering of the eyes. He suspected they would have those feelings many times before they laid it all to rest with little hope of any recompense. Matthew even patted the back of Marianne's hand as a show of sympathy. "I promise we will do our best to stop these people and return some, if not all, the money lost." Matthew paused to let his words sink in. "I suppose, on the bright side, I understand there is a new owner of the property, and they are ready to move forward with a new project. Let's hope they're successful for your sake." He smiled and the faces of the others brightened a little.

They finished their reindeer steaks and beer, and then it was time to leave. Matthew settled the bill, after he had enthused over the steaks to Hans again, and told him it was an excellent choice, and something to always remember.

"Listen, both of you. Again, we are truly sorry for what has happened here." Matthew stood to leave. Mitch pushed his chair away from the table and stood next to him. "Hans, Marianne, many thanks for your help. I hope we will be able to get you some justice and stop these rogues from doing this again to someone else."

They all shook hands. Matthew and Mitch headed out from the restaurant, and when Matthew looked back, he saw Hans and Marianne sit back down at the table, deep in conversation.

Matthew invited Mitch to his room for a Scotch before they turned in, and they talked about what they had heard. There were no real surprises, but at least now they had confirmed the names, a brief description, a photo, and some kind of an understanding that there appeared to be an offshore-based company behind Hansen and Mateus. It was enough information to pass on to Stockman.

"Hello, my boy. Cold enough for you up there?" Stockman chuckled.

"Not as bad as I thought it might be. We spent a pleasant day slipping and sliding about in fish guts, ice slush and blood but, other than that, it's a sight one only needs to see once in a lifetime."

"Sounds very interesting. Taking in the culture, so to speak. How did it go with Hans? Quiet man, isn't he?"

"Yes, he is a little quiet, but fortunately he brought along someone who could speak more. We have an outline description of the two men, their names—Finn Hansen and Erik Mateus—a photo of them, and a note to suggest they were operating through some unknown company or individual. We also have a line on their contactor, CanMine, out of Vancouver. I'll be meeting with them when I get back home. My sense is they are probably going to do the same work at Hope Brook. Not bad for the price of an airline ticket to Greenland and a meal for the premier, eh?"

"Terrific. Great start, Matthew. See if you can take a phone scan of the photo and message it to me. I'll follow up with a search for these guys and see what I can find out about their other contacts. I have an idea, but let's see. Now, you two are off to Nanortalik tomorrow morning?"

"Yep, the crack of dawn," Matthew joked. "The twelve forty-five p.m. chopper flight. Should be there for a couple of days at most. I just want to get confirmation of what kind of an operation these guys had set up and whether they left anything of any use behind they might want to go back for. We'll be at the hotel if you need us."

"I hear they have an interesting bar in Nanortalik, Matthew. Sounds like there's quite a mix of people, a bit like that bar in *Star Wars*, I expect, what with all those oddities of the universe with a common goal—drink." Stockman chuckled again. "Talk to you later and be careful not to upset the locals. I think they've seen enough of us foreigners for a while."

"We go in peace, Stockman. Talk later." Their cells went off.

* * *

Nanortalik

There are only nine seats on a Greenland Air Bell 212 helicopter. It took just over an hour to fly south to Nanortalik from Nuuk, with only this one flight a day. Three of the seats were empty when Matthew and Mitch boarded. Instead of leaving the seats empty, the pilots dragged on more boxes and sacks to take up the space for delivery to Nanortalik and strapped them in. They would be returning on the same helicopter to Nuuk in two days—weather permitting.

Hotel Kap Farval was only minutes from the heliport in Nanortalik, to the west of the diesel tank farm where the winter fuel supply was stored. There were only two taxis in the town, and one of them was at the heliport. It would bundle in everyone who needed a ride, rather than do a return trip. Fortunately, Matthew and Mitch were the only passengers. The others seemed to know where they were going and walked. It appeared everywhere in town was within walking distance, although it could take some time to walk from one end of the development to the other in the snow. But then there was lots of time available and the single snowplow was continually being used to keep the roads open.

The hotel was perched on a mound overlooking the inlet, and presented itself as a box of bedrooms, with a pub doubling as a restaurant hanging on the end. Bedrooms were simple, cramped, with steeply sloped ceilings, but were sufficient, comfortable, and warm enough to weather a storm. The reception desk was the bar, and the manager was the owner, a large, long-gray-bearded man, with a short, stocky wife, who together resembled a wrestling tag team difficult to match. Regardless, they wore ready smiles and welcomed strangers like friends, and they made Matthew and Mitch feel like long-lost cousins as soon as they signed the register and handed over a credit card—the latter being the trigger for more smiling.

It didn't take long to strike up a conversation with the owner. He didn't have a lot of good things to say about the Danish rogues. Yes, they had stayed at the hotel whenever they were in town, and, yes, they had always paid their bills and bought drinks for everyone, but they had left the town hurting badly when they pulled out and took the gold. There was a new property owner now, and while the town was wary, they encouraged them to stay and try their hand at mining. Apparently, there was a good gold resource remaining. The Danes had just cherry-picked the high-grade and didn't want to go any further. It was generally thought if they had stayed longer, their skulduggery would have been exposed for what it was. But such was life.

The first night at the hotel was one long, loud celebration, as it likely was every night after everyone had tucked a few pints of beer away. Clearly, this was a major meeting place for the drinking population of Nanortalik, who all knew each other.

Matthew and Mitch got involved in a number of discussions as they propped a drinker or two up against the bar. One had even brought his collection of Tupilaks, and Matthew chose one that had been carved out of whale bone to depict a small person growing out of another. It was ugly, but apparently brought with it all the myths of the ritualistic chants accompanying the carvings about avenging monsters and witchcraft. Matthew listened, but the storyteller seemed to be sinking farther and farther to the floor as he exhausted himself with the telling. Matthew left him still talking and wandered over to the next person. The night carried on...

In one story, an overly zealous and obviously inebriated local for some reason mentioned a conversation he'd had with one of the Danes, Finn, who had dropped a little gem about his friendship with a Russian he called Roman... something or other, who apparently controlled a large mining company, Poly... something or other. Even in his drunken state, the storyteller thought this Dane was just name-dropping to sound more important than he was, as though he needed to impress, because it was never mentioned again. But the drunk remembered, and so did Matthew.

Matthew and Mitch worked the bar, talking to as many folks as they were able. Some conversations were clearly destined for the trash can with their owners, who only seemed to be partly in touch with reality. However, one interesting topic of discussion was about the contractor used for the underground mining and the fellow they called Big Jim, who owned it. It seemed he was quite a character, although he didn't spend a lot of time in the company of Finn or Erik. He sure liked his drink and often spent at least one night at the hotel. He seemed to stay for part of his time at the site, and some time in town. But, by all accounts, he was just a contractor and didn't appear to know much about who he worked for, or what their strategy was. Although he had mentioned on a couple of occasions the difficulties he had with meeting schedules, and they always seemed to be in a panic to get out of there—for what that information was worth to Matthew. But it was worth it. It confirmed what ORB already knew: CanMine was the contractor but was probably not involved in the scam. Finn and Erik were the front men, some Russian was possibly in the mix somewhere, although not the prime lender, and they all got out as fast as they could once the high-grade ore had been barged away.

* * *

Nalunaq

Early the following morning, with the sky overcast, but with the cloud high enough, the AS-350 helicopter could fly with no weather-related problems, and they made their way along the fjord to Nalunaq. The route went past the landing where the Danes had loaded the barges. There was a pile of ore still sitting nearby, but no other equipment, although the empty fuel barrels were still stacked with a fuel pump sitting close by. The place was a mess, with oil spills unchecked, rusted-out mechanical parts strewn around, unused water and air piping tangled in piles the same way, and wire and cable half submerged, as though discarded at the last minute.

The site itself looked serene, although there were people wandering around. Apparently, the new group that had purchased the property were finalizing their own advanced exploration drilling and were using the site camp that had been left behind. They were going to have to take ownership of the environmental mess if they expected to get permits to mine.

The AS-350 lowered itself carefully onto the helipad, off to one side of the camp, and Matthew and Mitch got out, subconsciously hunched as they walked under the still-rotating blades and strode over to the nearest building. Stockman had made contact with the new owner and someone was there to meet them as they came forward.

"Hey, guys. Glad you could make it." An outstretched hand was offered by a tough-looking, barrel-chested, almost six-foot-tall man in his fifties. Despite the intimidating appearance, his demeanor was pleasant enough. "I'm Bill, Northern Mines. We have the property now and trying to figure out what we have here." He smiled.

Matthew and Mitch shook hands with Bill and immediately made a good connection.

"Thanks for letting us come on to the property, Bill. I guess you know why we're here."

"I do. I don't think that's going to happen again." He looked from Matthew to Mitch and smiled. "Let's go over to the dock and then up to the mine. There really isn't a lot to see, but it'll at least give you a feeling for things."

"Is there anyone here that remembers those guys?" Matthew asked.

"No, I don't think so. They brought in their own miners and truckers. All the equipment came in on barges and they took it all out the same way. No one here was involved in anything they did, and I doubt anyone in Nanortalik was either, from what I hear. It's sad; the locals are a good bunch of people and it's pretty fucked up to think about what happened to them. I mean, the whole country suffered, let alone the World Bank and the shareholders. What a disaster. Anyway, let's get going. Your pilot's being entertained and fed over at the camp, so he'll be ready to go when you are."

They drove to the barge landing area on the shore of Saqqaa Fjord. It looked even more of a mess at ground level than from the air.

The Danes had been frugal with their spending on the jetty and used over-wide pontoons secured to dead-weighted, large-bore pipe to reach out to the barges. It would have been a short, rocky ride for the ore trucks as they crawled over this last section. But it was only about fifty feet to the barges because the steepness of the fjord sides allowed the shallow-drafted vessels to get in close to the shoreline. Regardless, the relentless comings and goings of the ore trucks over the pontoons had certainly done some damage, but maintenance hadn't been part of the plan, so long as it all hung together long enough for what they needed.

They went over to the mine. Once the ore came out from the mine, it had been dumped into a stockpile and loaded onto trucks, where some remained. It was an easy, steady decline all the way to the barge landing. Again, there was nothing much to see at the mine other than the portal, what was left of the air ventilation piping, and a rudimentary power line from the old diesel generator location. The generator was long gone—probably sent out with the equipment when the work was completed—and waste piles had been haphazardly left to contaminate the area.

"They didn't spend a lot on this campaign, did they?" Mitch turned to Matthew.

"It's about as basic as it gets, and I doubt anything met code—including safety. I guess that tells me something about these guys." Matthew looked around him at the mess.

"Oh, what's that?" Mitch asked.

"Once they started, they went like hell."

It only took a couple of hours and a cup of coffee for Matthew and Mitch to conclude there wasn't anything else worth looking at for what they needed. The new owner was going to build a small gold processing plant and had already started to hire local labor and were doing some early work on pecking away at the new road to Nanortalik. They also seemed to think there could be some rare earth minerals to uncover. But these were early days. Proceeds for funding were being raised privately, and with gold in the seventeen-hundred-dollar range, that was not too hard to do. It was really the prospect of the rare earth minerals that had inspired them to claim the property and raise the interest of financiers.

The AS-350 was waiting for them at the camp site, with the pilot already warming up the engine. The helicopter circled the site once before heading east, back to Nanortalik.

Matthew considered the trip well worth it. He had a far better grasp of the practicalities of an operation such as what they thought the Danes were planning again. There was absolutely no reason why it wouldn't be a repeat performance, and the template they had established would work well for any similar property. From what Mitch had concluded from his trip to Greenland, the Hope Brook property would offer much the same potential, except it already had a barge landing. It was a good start.

* * *

Big Jim

As ever, Matthew delighted in returning home to Vancouver and never failed to appreciate the flight approach to the city when there was no cloud cover and he could look out over the mountains, ocean, and islands melded into one landscape. It wasn't always like that, of course, but one had to take the bad with the good and, regardless, he reveled in his good fortune, as he had done many times before, that fate had brought him to this place to live.

Vancouver was truly a beautiful part of the world, relatively free compared to the stresses of other cities and where the air smelled fresh and uplifting as soon as one exited the terminal, unless smoke from summer forest fires, often hundreds of miles away, drifted through the city. You could smell the burning wood, see the veil of gray hiding the sharply exquisite outline of the mountains, and even catch a speck or two of ash in the air.

It was just a thirty-minute ride from the airport to Vancouver's downtown and Matthew's apartment. He had a two-level penthouse perched at the top of a sixteen-story high-rise in the west end, looking out over the beaches and parks—prime real estate. The area was a thriving mass of humanity in the summer, but Matthew had managed to secure a sanctuary from the noise that came with downtown living. It was ideal to have a choice of either reveling in it, just enjoying it, or ignoring it. One would never have to feel alone in Matthew's part of the world, nor would one have to go far to find a peaceful corner.

He tossed his bag on the sofa, walked over to mix a martini, dropped two pitted Sicilian green olives into the glass, took a sip to taste, and stood at the window. He watched in awe as windsurfers fearlessly raced across the bay, fighting with the wind and waves as they skipped from crest to crest. Laser sailing dinghies kept well out of their way as they zipped through the water with their small sails taut, their hulls half out of the water, and their single-handed crew member fighting with all their strength to maintain control and course as they tried to judge where the next rush of wind would come from. Despite the offshore wind, the beaches were calm and littered with sunbathing bodies and eager swimmers. The sidewalks were crowded with scantily clad ladies, guys just dressed in shorts and tattoos, lovers strolling arm in arm while they whispered to each other, couples on their rollerblades zigzagging through the maze of people and vehicles, fast bikes, slow bikes, and people just walking their bikes, and the rest—well, they just took their time and wandered along the promenade in the sun.

Matthew took another sip of his martini and called Emma.

"Hey, Em. Everything good?"

"Everything's great. Sat next to our friend Mah at lunch. I had planned on getting to meet him at his office, but I changed my mind and thought catching him on the hop like that could be better." There was that touch of sarcasm again.

"But we managed to talk and once he got the drift of where I was going with the conversation, he seemed to pick it up a bit. The bottom line is, as he says, they're always looking for a buyer. Full stop." Emma paused and waited or Matthew to ask questions, but before he could, she blurted out, "Oh, how did you get along, by the way?" She suddenly remembered where he had been and didn't want him to think she had forgotten.

"Good, thanks. Actually, I think it went really well."

"Oh. Do tell." Emma was intrigued.

"You know, Greenland is such a wonderfully odd place, but I would still encourage most to avoid it—cold, somewhat forbidding, certainly close to the end of the world, and as boring as hell. I only just got in and am still getting my thoughts together, but I'm sure glad Mitch and I went there. Want to come over to help me think? I've got wine."

The invitation was too good for Emma to refuse, but then she didn't need much persuasion.

"Give me thirty minutes and I'll be there. Are you ordering in, or shall I pick up something on the way?"

"Why don't you get Chinese from the place on the corner here? I'll order and it'll be ready for you as go by."

"Sounds good. See you soon." Emma was gone, and Matthew called the Chinese restaurant and ordered the usual. He reached up for some glasses from the shelf and a bottle of wine from the fridge.

They sat on the terrace overlooking the bay and happily chomped away at the noodles, Mongolian beef, garlic beans, and a few other Chinese tidbits, while they sipped ice-cold pinot grigio and talked about their adventures.

As Matthew recalled his trip, he thought it seemed more interesting now than it had when he was actually there. In fact, as he recollected to Emma, he realized his experience was likely more unusual than almost anyone would have in their lifetime. Iceland, maybe. Greenland, highly unlikely. But then where else would you get a barbecued reindeer steak fresh from a kill and a genuine Tupilak to go? *Yes*, Matthew thought, *it was a nice little adventure that actually contributed a lot to what we were looking for, but I had real concerns as to the depth of distress caused by the Danish rogues to these innocent people.*

They talked for an hour and strategized their next steps. There was an easy flow in the way they talked about their business, and generally agreed as each offered a part of the plan. They finished the bottle, cleaned up the Chinese mess, and settled down with glasses of limoncello, which Matthew had brought back from Ischia, to watch the lights below from the rooftop garden. The sounds from the African drums being played over at Third Beach, a mile or so away, added atmosphere and rhythm to the night. This was life on a typical summer evening in the west end.

It was easy to fuck. They had done it before and knew the ritual, the movements, the sequences, the small talk, and the rewards. It was never boring so much as a path that had been well trodden, and looked forward to being trodden again, and perhaps again. There were passing thoughts that crossed their minds and revealed, without questioning, as each rose to the occasion of listening and responding. Emma played with Matthew both physically and mentally, but in a fun way, and he was no better. There was a fusion and a breakaway. A coming together, and a passing. Each wandered through the other's memory and played on history, the future, and their love. They really loved, and they really remembered, caressing and laughing, caressing and smiling. It was a history of comfort and memory. Of love and adventure. Of moving and pausing, waiting for the other. How could it be so exquisitely memorable? Easy.

* * *

It hadn't been hard for Big Jim to take the bait of a potential project when Matthew had called the previous day. Matthew met him at his offices in the city.

"Call me Big Jim. Everyone does." He had a kind of goofy smile on his face and a bit of a banana-shaped head with a sprig of straight hair sticking up like some cartoon character. While he was not particularly big, as his name implied, he was tall; probably six-two.

They shook hands and settled into comfortable chairs on opposite sides of a round glass table in Big Jim's twenty-fifth-floor office, looking north out over one of the marinas in the city with the mountains providing a magnificent backdrop.

Big Jim was a displaced Aussie with all the markings of one. He was brash, self-confident, and open, with a touch of crudity in the way he talked. His offices were somewhat humble for a person who claimed some notoriety in industry and had clearly undertaken some substantial projects, judging by the few oversized photos on the walls.

As he stared at one of the photos in particular, Matthew claimed he needed help with an underground mining project in the northern reaches of Canada. He noted it was in similar terrain to the one shown in the photo and wanted to know more about CanMine's abilities and how they could best help.

There is something very distracting about a man who sits facing his audience while leaning his chair back on two legs, poking both his hands down the front of his trousers and clearly pushing his testicles from one side to the other, behind a thin screen of material, all the while pretending he was really just tucking his shirt into place, made worse by performing his act under a see-through glass table. It's especially odd if it's an unconscious habit, and the person appears to have no idea he's doing it.

Big Jim was like that, though, and anyone who happened to be in the same room at the same time would have great difficulty concentrating on what he was saying as they silently tried to guess which side of his trousers held the greater amount of testicle paraphernalia at any one time. Sometimes it seemed as though Big Jim could actually balance his penis and testicles in the center with his hands hidden by the material of his trousers. It seemed he could juggle it all into position, balancing for just a few seconds and then releasing, just to repeat the cycle. Then, he would be off again, invigorated by more conversation, tossing from side to side, until there was a reason for one of his hands to come out to daylight. All the while, he would be talking business without any apparent hint of what he was doing or care that anyone could see his performance.

Matthew listened to Big Jim describe his accomplishments, and tried to focus on what he was saying, rather than what he was doing. It was difficult, but the young lady who brought Big Jim his coffee was clearly indifferent to his activity; she just left the tray, turned, and walked back out of the office with a shudder of her eyes. That in itself was strange, but she seemed to accept Big Jim for what he was: odd. Women were like that. Somehow accepting of even the strangest of men despite them sometimes being a little weird, as long as they were respectful and good to them.

Big Jim was clearly proud of his achievements and explained the specialty nature of his work on narrow-vein mining. Matthew feigned interest and urged him on to talk about some of his most memorable projects. Naturally, Big Jim talked about his most recent job in Greenland, and that led to Finn and Erik.

It seemed Big Jim had originally met Finn on one of the Dane's visits to Vancouver while he was looking to wind up some business dealings with a mining company in the city. He was searching for a specialized underground mining contractor for the Greenland project. They met, connected, and set up an agreement where Big Jim would provide the resources to mine the gold ore at Nalunaq.

Big Jim's company was one of the few underground mining companies in the world that could expertly mine out a narrow vein just under three feet wide, dramatically reducing the amount of waste rock. That was the secret to successfully high-grading the Nalunaq deposit, where the vast amount of waste that would otherwise come with conventional underground mining would have substantially diluted the gold percentage. That would have made the whole venture much more costly, and possibly not make the mine financially viable at all.

Big Jim had a big ear-to-ear smile on his face as he let Matthew know he was going to do another job with Finn very soon. In fact, he was going to visit him in Marbella at the end of the week to discuss another project that was, apparently, very similar to the Greenland venture. Matthew's ears pricked up.

"Oh?" Matthew looked suitably surprised.

"Do you know that area?" Big Jim asked innocently. "Never been there before, but it sounds crazy good."

"I've visited there a few times and had a place on the beach just next to the Hotel Don Pepe Gran Meliá for a while. You should stay there. It's a really good boutique-style hotel."

"Great. That sounds great. Thanks for the recommendation." Big Jim was enthused.

"Don't thank me until after you've stayed there." They both laughed. "How long are you going to be there?" Matthew was trying to avoid looking at Jim's jostling in his pants as he thought of his answer.

"A few days, I think. It just depends on what we have to talk about." Jim finally pocketed the last ball as his hands came up on to the table to clutch at his coffee.

"Where's the project, Jim?" Matthew asked with an innocent look.

"I'm pretty sure this one's going to be in Newfoundland."

A piece of the jigsaw fell into place for Matthew and confirmed what Stockman had thought.

"A little out of your way, isn't it?" Matthew asked, as though he didn't already know.

"Yes, it is, but we happened to be involved with a project over there years ago, and I guess they came back to us for our experience. For all I know, it might be the same property. I think it's going to be Hope Brook. Do you know it?"

"I don't, but good luck." Matthew paused and then turned the conversation back to his own business. He managed to describe what he was looking for, albeit fantasy, but it was good enough to hold Big Jim's attention, and they spent the next thirty minutes talking through the commercial points of a business dealing, as well as the timing and resources needed. Matthew learned about CanMine's resources and people, asked if Big Jim was capable of handling more than one project at a time if he had to. Big Jim wasn't sure what the Newfoundland schedule was just yet. Nor did Matthew offer any dates for what he might expect for his mythical project, but Big Jim seemed quite confident in CanMine's ability to handle two or three jobs at the same time. It was difficult for Matthew to know if that was true, but he took it at face value.

That was enough for Matthew. He had closed the circle for locating the Danes, with what Yanko had told Stockman, and now Big Jim had let their approximate location be known. He had confirmed CanMine was the Nalunaq mining contractor and was most likely going to do the same at the Hope Brook property. As the contractor, he wasn't the one responsible for the outcome—just the mining—and Matthew had to be careful not to let anything slip about the immorality of the Greenland caper. Big Jim would probably have no clue about the other side of that business.

Matthew couldn't stand to watch as Big Jim started his trouser routine again, as though everything had spilled out of place. He got up, satisfied he had enough information for now, and started to make his way out of the office with handshakes, nods, and laughing.

Matthew turned back. "Oh, who are you flying with, Jim?"

"BA to London and Iberia down to Malaga. I have to pick up a rental and drive down to Marbella from there."

"Well. Enjoy yourself and try to come back in one piece. The partying down there can be intense. And don't forget the Meliá. I think you'll like it. We'll talk when you get back." Matthew gave a final wave over his shoulder and into the elevator.

Matthew called Emma as he stepped onto the sidewalk outside Big Jim's office building.

"Can you come over, Em?"

"When? Now?"

"Just finished with Big Jim. I'll be home in about fifteen minutes. We need to do a little planning, and you need to do a little traveling."

"Got it. On my way." Emma closed off her cell phone before Matthew had a chance to suggest she didn't have to rush, but then that was Emma: keen, ever ready, and ahead of the game.

*   *   *

"Okay, Em." Matthew let her in through the apartment door. She already had a key fob for the building. They walked over to the living room and relaxed as Matthew poured a couple of glasses of pinot grigio. "I just had a very interesting meeting with this Big Jim Garland fellow, the owner of CanMine."

Emma raised her eyebrows in expectation, took a sip of her drink, and waited.

Matthew laid out what he and Big Jim had talked about; the link between him and the Danes; the upcoming meeting with the three of them in Marbella. Big Jim was heading there at the end of the week, and Emma needed to pack a bag and get over there as well. Her job was to keep an eye on him and find out anything she could about his meetings with the Danes.

"No problem, Matthew. I'll book tickets on the same flights if I can get hold of his Iberian flight number. Do you want me to get friendly with him?"

"I think that'd be wonderful, Emma." Matthew clinked his glass to Emma's. "You may even get to actually meet Finn and Erik. And who knows where we go from there?" They smiled at each other. It was quite a coup to get into the lion's den so easily and quickly. Hopefully, it would pay dividends, but Matthew was already ninety-nine percent sure the next target was the Hope Brook Mine in Newfoundland, from what Big Jim had told him. Now they needed to better understand the timing.

"While you're over there, I think I'll take a trip to Newfoundland with Mitch and get a lay of the land."

"Sounds like a plan. What if they're planning on others at the same time?"

"Good question. I think Stockman and Yanko may be able to figure that out. You may also be able to get some additional information while you're down in Spain with Jim."

They drank their way through the rest of the bottle of pinot grigio and went over the details of what they thought she needed to do if she got the chance while in Marbella.

*   *   *

Puerto Banús

It wasn't hard for Emma to spot Big Jim in the priority departure lounge in Vancouver while they waited for their flight to Heathrow, although she deliberately avoided his attention. All in good time. Fortunately, once they boarded the flight, she had a business class seat at the back of the section and on the opposite side of the aircraft to him, while Big Jim was up at the bulkhead. She looked up occasionally, as though just to make sure he was still there. He had become engrossed in some conversation with the person sitting next to him and she felt somewhat relieved to be able to relax for the duration of the flight. She planned on connecting with him while they waited for their Iberia flight to Malaga.

There was no Iberian business class and no VIP lounge in Malaga. Emma "accidentally" bumped into Big Jim as they hung around the counter, waiting for an agent.

"Weren't you on the flight from Vancouver?" Emma looked at Big Jim with cautiously surprised eyes, pretending she could have made a mistake.

"Yes. I recognize you, too. From the lounge. Do you live in the city?" It was very idle chitchat, but Big Jim was obviously interested. Emma looked interested enough to respond.

"Yes. Yes, I do. Over on the north side near the marina. And you?"

"I have a place in the Terminal City Club." Big Jim seemed buoyed by the opportunity to chat with a beautiful lady while he was away from home.

"Very convenient. Do you like it there?" Emma seemed interested, but she already knew this.

"Yes. I've been there for about five years. Works for me. Where are you heading?" Big Jim sounded more and more friendly as he got into his stride.

"Marbella."

"Me too! You there on business or pleasure?" Big Jim liked where this was going.

"I've always wanted to visit the area and head up into the mountains. See a few villages. Take in the culture. You know." Emma could see Big Jim was focusing on her intently. "What about you?"

"A little business, a little R and R. Whatever I can fit into a five-day spree away from home base. Where are you staying?"

"Over at the Meliá in Marbella. I've heard it's really good and right on the Med."

"Well, I'll be damned. Me too. How about that? How are you getting there from the airport?" Big Jim looked surprised. He seemed to be an open book, or at least that's what his gawky face told her.

"I'll get a rental so I can do some sightseeing." Emma shrugged.

"Me too. I'd like to suggest we share, but I guess we both need to be mobile." Big Jim showed his disappointment on his face, but he was right. Neither could afford to be without wheels.

"Yes, I think that'd be best. But we could hook up sometime to exchange notes." Emma played it coolly, blinking as though shy.

"How about dinner tonight at the hotel? Just get to know each other a little more and maybe we can take a trip into those mountains together?" Big Jim looked keen.

Emma was a little taken aback by Jim's forwardness, but she recovered without a hint of hesitation and appreciated the ease with which it was coming together. "Sounds good. Let's meet in the lobby at, say, eight thirty."

For some reason, she looked at her watch, while Big Jim broke into a face-splitting smile at Emma's reaction and, like all men, he was expecting far more than he thought he was promised by the look she gave him. "In the meantime, I just want to do a little window shopping in the stores here."

"No problemo. See you at the gate." Big Jim was content and strolled off, hands in pockets, with that smile still on his face.

Emma turned and strolled away, quite happy with the arrangement.

* * *

Emma sidled up to Big Jim in the Meliá that evening as he was eyeing up everyone in the lobby of the Don Meliá. He looked like a fish out of water in his Hawaiian shirt and shorts, but that was the man and, well, it was warm out.

"Hey." Emma tapped Big Jim on the shoulder, and he swung around, almost bowling her off her feet.

"Hey, you. Wanna eat?" Big Jim looked eager and happy.

"Reception told me there's a great restaurant just at the end of the hotel grounds, right next to the beach. Want to try it?" Emma looked eager.

"Sure. Let's do it." Big Jim followed Emma through the lobby to the gardens and pool area and down to the gate at the far end. She pushed it open and checked to make sure she had her room key to get back through the security lock on their return.

"Boy, I don't know about you, but I'm bushed. Long day." Big Jim caught up to Emma and pulled alongside her.

"I closed my eyes for an hour before coming out," Emma commented. "It's really tough sleeping or getting any rest on a plane, don't you think? That's why I never drink and fly. It just makes it a whole lot worse."

Emma bounced off down the steps, through the bushes, and out onto the pathway along the beachfront. The air was fresh and the sea calm. The wonderful smell of cooking was coming from a small, yellow-painted restaurant with Mediterranean-blue shutters and awnings less than a hundred feet farther along to the west. Big Jim was in tow, a foot behind Emma and talking all the way.

The restaurant was furnished in a simple Spanish style with solid, dark wood furnishings, blue and white checked tablecloths, ocean-themed ornaments decorating the walls and shelves, fish trophies and photos, and the inevitable fishing nets hanging from the ceilings with cork floats attached to the edges.

They picked at a tapas-style appetizer, local unpitted olives, and freshly baked bread, matched with a fresh, young white wine from the Bodegas Bentomiz vineyards to the east of Malaga. Both ordered the oven-roasted mackerel and watched as two restaurant staff members in black pants and white shirts stood on the illuminated beach close to the water's edge outside the restaurant, with fishing lines straining against the pull of the current. Clearly, the fish served in the restaurant was as fresh as it could be. Emma had a passing thought that perhaps some visitors even had to wait while their particular fish was caught.

"What kind of business brings you here, to the south coast of Spain, Jim?" Emma asked, as though she didn't know.

"Ah, yes." Jim's attention turned away from watching the fishermen and over to Emma. "I run a small underground mining company. We do jobs the big boys don't want to do or can't do. Or maybe the jobs are too small. I don't know. Sometimes it takes specialized equipment they don't have, but we do. I don't want to bore you with the details, but we specialize in what we call narrow-vein mining, where we use our custom equipment to carefully extract underground gold veins without taking out a lot of the surrounding rock. It's a bit of an art, really. Boring, eh?" Big Jim smiled but avoided poking his hands down the front of his pants. Somehow, he knew it wasn't appropriate when he was out with a lady—not that it ever was.

"No, it's interesting. Is that why you're here?" Emma asked.

"I'm going to meet some guys tomorrow who I worked with before, and I guess they want me to do the same thing as last time, but this time on the south coast of Newfoundland. We were there a couple of years ago, doing some work for another group, so we know the area quite well." Big Jim seemed proud of what he did.

"Where did you go the last time they called you?" Emma anticipated the response, ready to guard against telling him anything about why she was really in Marbella.

"You'd never guess." Big Jim's eyebrows arched. "Greenland. Can you believe it? Right on the southern tip of the biggest island in the world!" Clearly, Big Jim was still in some shock at where he had worked and how much he had made. "What a job that was." He popped another olive in his mouth, sucked at it for a second, bit at the flesh from around the pit, then squeezed the stone out of his mouth into his hand. Emma just watched and waited for him to finish. He was smiling the whole time.

"We worked like hell," Big Jim continued as he picked out another olive, but resisted popping it into his mouth, "three shifts a day, underground, for just under a year, and we took out about four hundred and fifty thousand tons of ore. They barged it all off to some place offshore for processing."

"Wow. That sounds like a big job." Emma looked suitably surprised.

"It's not a lot by comparison to most mining operations, which could go on for years until the resource is exhausted, but for the time we had to complete the job, it was pretty big. It would have been a darned sight bigger an operation if we went in with conventional underground mining and had to excavate the gold with all the waste rock that would come with it. That would have turned into a huge event, not to mention the money having to be spent on barging all that useless rock offshore. Probably ten times more than we handled for the same amount of gold in the end." Big Jim was clearly enthusiastic, but stopped when he was realized he was likely boring Emma.

"Anyway, enough about my world. What about you? What's your th-th-th-thing?" Big Jim accentuated the question and looked expectantly at Emma.

The waiter placed the mackerel in front of them, with a second bottle of wine, as though fully anticipating they would expect it, and left them alone as he took away the empty appetizer dishes.

As they tucked into the meal, made the obligatory satisfied sounds of taste and presentation, then toasted each other with a third glass of wine, Emma described the non-existent drudgery of her make-believe work, the daily chore of a pretend life, the occasional highs, but all in all, nothing Big Jim could possibly find interesting. In fact, he learned nothing at all about her other than she lived in Vancouver. But then he already knew that.

"What are you doing tomorrow?" Big Jim asked after they were getting ready to leave the restaurant.

"I was planning on driving up into the hills, to a place called Ronda. It's supposed to be an old Moorish town, with this massive gorge and beautiful views. A friend of mine told me about the hand-carved olive-wood pieces they sell at a small place nearby. There's also a great restaurant built into the side of the gorge that serves a particularly good roasted suckling pig I'd like to try." Emma's eyes were wide open with excitement at the prospect as she acted out her role.

"Oh. Sounds good, but why don't you come with me and you can do that trip later? I'd appreciate some company and you might find it interesting." Big Jim looked excited by the prospect.

"Aren't you doing some business?" Emma wondered out loud.

"Yes, but it's on their boat. It's huge and docked at the Puerto Banús marina, so perhaps we'll get a ride." Big Jim looked like a kid just finding out he was about to get a new toy, as he rubbed his hands together in anticipation.

"Well, okay, if you think your business partners won't be put out." Emma wasn't going to argue with an invitation that would put her right into the lion's den.

"Oh, hell, if they don't like it, too bad. If you get bored, you can always go wandering around the place. I hear it's very high end. Are you coming?" He sounded as though he was top dog, but really had no clue as to what to expect. He was just hoping things would work out.

They made their way back up through the bushes, through the security gate, and into the hotel grounds. Jim was still encouraging her to go with him the next day. There were a few people silently swimming in the illuminated pool and enjoying the peacefulness of the warm, clear, moonlit night.

Emma appeared half-heartedly to agree to go with Big Jim the next morning, although, in truth, she was ecstatic at her good fortune. They would drive their own cars to Puerto Banús in case the meeting went on longer than Big Jim expected. In which case, Emma could head out to do whatever she wanted.

* * *

Emma called Matthew from the hotel at eleven thirty p.m. local time. It was around two thirty p.m. in Vancouver.

"Hi, Em. How's it going in the land of the rich and famous—oh, and not to forget the criminals?" Matthew joked.

"Ha, ha. You may laugh, but I happen to be in a beautiful hotel on the Mediterranean coast, with all the good-looking people, vino aplenty, and only time to spare." It was Emma's turn to laugh.

"I assume you arrived safely?" Matthew asked.

"I did, and I contacted your friend, Big Jim. In fact, we had supper together this evening in a lovely little restaurant right next to the beach." Emma sounded smug.

"Okay." Matthew was impressed but held his comments back. "What's happening tomorrow?" He turned to more serious matters.

"Big Jim's heading down to the marina for some business talks with these Finn and Erik guys, just as we expected. I'm tagging along." Emma hadn't taken a breath before Matthew cut in.

"What? No, no, no. You can't do that, Emma. What's to say you won't be discovered and everything we are supposed to be working for falls apart? What if something happens you can't do anything about? What...?"

"Listen, Matthew," Emma interrupted, "it's all cool. Big Jim seems innocent in all this. All he does is the underground mining. He's quite a simple guy, really. I don't think he knows what the Danes are up to at all."

"I'm not a hundred percent sure he's as innocent as he appears." Matthew sounded concerned.

"Well, this could be exactly what we need." Emma sounded excited. "They're going to be talking about the mine in Newfoundland. I'm just going to pretend to be an uninterested date for Big Jim and keep out of the way until he's finished. I'll just look pretty and sit on the deck in the sun. Of course, I might overhear some interesting things. If not, well, there's always Big Jim, who I'm sure will spill the beans over supper tomorrow evening, with a little prompting.

"And I'd really like to take a close look at the Danes. What harm can it do?" Emma paused and waited for Matthew to chastise her further, unless he had already thought better of it, given the circumstances.

"Okay. Okay." He knew he wasn't going to convince Emma, and a part of him really liked the idea of having someone so close to the Danes. "Take care, Em... and make sure you call me as soon as you get on land again."

"Will do." Emma could tell from Matthew's voice he was unsure about this turn of events, but she ignored it with a flippant, "Call you tomorrow, sweetie." She hung up.

Matthew hated to be called "sweetie." It seemed so condescending, but then, that's what he often called Emma. He shrugged it off and reached for his wine glass.

* * *

Emma and Big Jim met at the hotel reception the following morning and walked out to their respective vehicles together. Emma followed him to Puerto Banús, a few miles west, and they parked a couple of spaces away from each other at the marina.

They were met by Finn and Erik at the Iberian café just as Big Jim had arranged, and while the Danes were very polite, they were also clearly disturbed by Big Jim bringing someone else along to what they thought was going to be a private meeting. But too late. The introductions were made and the four of them made their way over to a yacht, moored up against the sea wall of the marina, with the adventurous name of *Viking I* in strikingly large gold letters emblazoned across the stern and up the port side. They stepped aboard, brushed past two hefty crew members, who watched in silence as the four went through the sliding doors into the air-conditioned aft cabin.

The cabin was spacious, with long, butter-yellow leather sofas and armchairs marking out the limits of the talking area. A large Oriental rug was spread out between the chairs, and a heavy-looking glass-topped coffee table stretched from one sofa to the other with enough leg room between for guests to sit comfortably but still reach their drinks.

Comfort was uncompromised, with all modern conveniences nestled around the room, including a sixty-five-inch flat screen television set into a wall, a well-stocked bar, side tables, lamps, and a very high-end music system with Wi-Fi speakers in at least six places in the room Emma could spot.

She also noted cameras positioned over all entryways, as well as on the rear deck, and noted the monitor set up in a corner of the cabin showing all camera views. The walls were adorned with artwork—mostly paintings of sailboats thrusting their way through turbulent waters. None were calming.

The access to the upper bridge deck was through the aft cabin and up one of two walkways, one on each side of the room. Access to the hallways led forward on both the port and starboard sides of the yacht, through doorways behind the bridge deck stairs. Emma could just make out other doorways off the two passages she assumed would access sleeping quarters, washroom facilities, and other areas. She couldn't see far enough forward to tell what there might be at the far end of the hallways, but she guessed it was likely to be the master suite and perhaps another way up to the control bridge.

"Do make yourself comfortable, Emma." Erik pointed with an open hand, palm up, to one of the sofas. He looked over at Big Jim, flicked his wrist, and pointed to one of the sofas for him to do the same.

"What brings you to Marbella, Emma?" Erik asked, as though interested.

They spent a fairly cordial, if not entirely focused, thirty minutes talking about Puerto Banús, the beauty of the Mediterranean, the restaurants, and the clubs that seemed to be everywhere. They touched on the criminal element, but only in passing, and no one dwelled on the subject. Clearly, neither Big Jim nor Emma was particularly knowledgeable about the notoriety of the town.

"Emma"—Finn had come to some point in the conversation when he felt he needed to move on— "perhaps you'd like to spend some sunshine time on the deck, while we talk business with Jim." It wasn't said as an invitation so much as a suggestion, and Emma got the hint and obliged. She rose from her armchair and collected her belongings.

"There are magazines and a small bar on the aft deck, as well as suntan lotions, towels, and the like. Please help yourself, but we may be a while." Erik smiled at Emma and made his way over to take her by the hand and lead her out into the fresh air. "If you need anything, just press the buzzer and one of the stewards will be happy to help." He pointed to the buzzer on the table between two of the loungers.

"That's very nice of you, Erik. Sorry to be a bother, but Big Jim really wanted us to spend some time together today and maybe head up into the mountains after you're all finished." Emma put on her innocent tourist face and looked up at Erik.

"Our pleasure, I can assure you. Perhaps you'll still be able to make it up to Ronda after our meeting—I assume that's where you will want to visit? Everyone does."

"Yes, it is. Thanks again." Emma fluttered her eyelashes, cocked her head to one side, and the thought of how he really knew her plans flashed through her mind.

Erik gave a slight bow and closed the sliding doors behind him as he went back through into the aft cabin. Emma opened the bar freezer nestled between a marble sink top and what appeared to be a small dishwasher. She examined the contents of the cooling cabinet for chilled glasses, drinks, and accompaniments, and made herself an ice-cold vodka tonic in a highball glass, then added two squeezed slices of lime before settling herself onto one of the loungers she had pulled closer to the sliding doors. She slipped her sunglasses down over her eyes, placed a small white straw hat on her head with the brim pulled down to eye level, and flicked open one of the magazines from the side table.

* * *

Hope Brook

By the time Matthew and Mitch landed in their chartered Bell 407 helicopter on the site of the Hope Brook Mine, it was clear this place was almost a duplicate of what the Nalunaq mine site offered in terms of an underground mine and tidewater within two miles. The only difference was the deserted and dilapidated mill at Hope Brook, as well as a large but uninhabited modular camp. Clearly, the old mine had been abandoned with no regard for an environmental cleanup campaign, and the tailing pond dikes had breached as the Newfoundland storms added to the volume contained. The contaminated overflow had found its way south, over land and streams, to the ocean.

It was a wild and desolate location with nothing but the occasional moose, marmot, or red fox making this their home. There was no one within at least a hundred miles of the site, and once the mining had stopped and the workers went home, human life was unlikely to return, not even to hunt.

The land was barren, treeless, and bare of vegetation. Rock outcrops dominated the landscape except for the remnants of what the mine operators had left behind: a network of gravel roads, spoil tips, a tailings pond, pole lines, and rusted mining equipment strewn around in haphazard fashion. The old mill building creaked and groaned in the wind as loose steel wall sheeting continuously grated against itself and the building steel. Spare parts, piping, old crates, and shipping containers littered the area. The pre-built camp seemed to have been secured with plywood, leaving doorways, but not all the windows. Some had been broken, likely by flying debris, leaving the weather free to create havoc and damage inside the accommodations.

Matthew and Mitch weren't interested in the mill or camp and flew over to the underground mine. The portal appeared to be intact, but the mine equipment had rusted out and rested where their operators had left it all before they went home.

They flew over the barge landing site where the supplies would be delivered. An old tractor and a few trailers were still there, but, again, they were rusted out and had been discarded once they were no longer needed. An old barge was still tied up to the pilings but had been badly beaten up by the storms that often lashed the coast. It had been a self-propelled unit, but clearly the pilot house had been wrecked by nature and had come apart. The jetty seemed to be intact, although beaten up through wear and tear. The surfacing would likely need to be replaced, but the structure appeared to be sound, at least from a visual overview.

It was a thoroughly sad sight but gave Matthew and Mitch a good understanding of what they believed the Danes would be dealing with and what they would need to do to get the mine back up and operating. The campaign would be very similar to the one at Nalunaq: mine in three shifts a day and get the bulk ore down to the barges. The difference here would be the distance between the Hope Brook landing and the offshore processing plant. If it was available, it would not be as far from Hope Brook to the north coast of Newfoundland as it had been from Nalunaq to the same processing facilities. It was just a logistics issue Matthew appreciated. But what if the more local processing plant couldn't, or wouldn't, take the Hope Brook ore because of other commitments, or it had to be shut down for maintenance or whatever? Maybe they would have to ship it all the way to northern Spain again.

These were thoughts Matthew mulled over that had to be built into the ORB plan.

* * *

Ice Man II

As Finn, Erik, and Big Jim sat down with their coffees in the aft cabin of *Viking I* to chat, the vessel engines came to life with a throb that settled to a purr, and once the crew released the bow and stern lines, she moved gracefully away from the Puerto Banús marina.

Big Jim looked surprised, but he wasn't going to be getting any answers from either Finn or Erik other than a casual comment from Finn, who mentioned they were going to meet their "business acquaintance" so "don't worry."

Instead, they started talking about projects as though there was nothing untoward happening, discussing the Greenland job and how happy they were with Jim's performance. He was not entirely convinced of their sincerity now that they were pulling away from shore for no apparent reason and without telling him why. He needed to hear their plan and what was expected of him. His gut told him it smelled a rat, although how big the rat was remained to be seen.

Jim's initial surprise at the yacht's departure from the marina turned to anxiety that increased as they headed farther out into the Mediterranean, leaving Puerto Banús behind them and heading toward some unseen point. In Jim's mind, leaving the relative security of the marina with no mention of where they were going, or what was in store, increased his nervousness as the realization sank in that no one back home knew where he was, when he was due back in Vancouver, or who he was meeting. No one, anywhere, knew anything that could help them locate him should they get concerned if he didn't eventually turn up at the office in a week or so. He was starting to worry about what he was really becoming involved with. Providing resources to these guys was one thing, but for some reason, it all seemed more convoluted this time around as they powered farther from the marina. What was he really getting involved in?

The Danes sounded somehow more dominating than when he had done the first job for them. He just wasn't sure, but even their body language seemed just a little different, and they still weren't telling him, or Emma, where they were going.

Was he just imagining it all, or was the fact the boat was putting out into open waters, with the coast disappearing, making him hypersensitive? What the fuck? Where the hell were they going? Clearly, it was almost out into international waters by now—but why? Perhaps he was being overly suspicious, but then, perhaps he needed to be. He didn't really know these guys, but as he got to know them more, he had a feeling they were a little odd—or, worse, criminals. He tried closing his mind to negativity as he realized they were going farther out to sea and he was losing sight of land altogether. By this time, he had no option but to go along with them. He would play dumb. That should be easy—if his anxiety didn't overtake him, or he said something that riled them.

Three miles from shore was sufficient to evade the onshore eyes of anyone who cared to watch as, thirty minutes after leaving the marina, *Viking I* used its thrusters to move over to the stern deck of *Ice Man II*—a yacht almost one and a half times its own length. Two crew members from each vessel rafted them together. Clearly, the boats were well out of range of any shore-based scopes, but they could be identified and positioned by satellite.

Big Jim nervously wondered why they were so far away from prying eyes and who would care what had happened to him. Little did he know, or could he even imagine, that anyone could know the course and exact position of any boat equipped with a radar detection system, as *Viking I* and *Ice Man II* were. But then, he had never heard of ORB, and they were tracking them both.

By now, Jim's mind was whirling with different thoughts, although he noticed Emma hadn't moved from the lounger and appeared content to just stretch out and sip at her drink. She didn't appear to be bothered at all by the fact they had left the marina, and she never asked. He didn't realize she was also concerned and was focusing on maintaining her cool so as not to give anything away. After all, as far as Finn and Erik were concerned, Emma should have no worries about going for a little boat ride.

A large, smiling, robust man in a baggy, short-sleeved yellow shirt, huge azure-blue shorts, flip-flops, and a large, tanned, well-lived-in face that seemed to have been beaten up a number of times, was standing on the lower deck. His blond hair was cropped short, his huge hands outstretched, his arm tattoos exhibiting what seemed to be foreign words, and he was clearly in charge as he invited his guests aboard at the stern, where two of his crew reached out to help each of the guests onto the deck.

"Welcome. I am Roman… the Russian… Roman Kerimov." He introduced himself as though adding his country of birth was part of his name. But he was magnanimous in his greetings, slapped Finn and Erik on their backs, vigorously shook hands with Big Jim and Emma, and invited them all to join him in the lounge. They followed his hulking calves, thick swinging arms, and large head as he talked idly about the sea air, the beauty of the Mediterranean, how pleased he was they had come out to meet him, and how much he was looking forward to the visit. Big Jim was beginning to relax.

As they lounged about in the even more luxurious cabin than *Viking I*, and indulged in continuing idle chitchat, Kerimov sauntered over to where Finn and Erik sat, bent down, and whispered something to them, and then fixed his sights on Jim.

"So, Jim, you are our underground mining contractor again. *Da?*"

Big Jim nodded, smiled, and seemed much more subdued and humbler than he had been previously. To Emma, the statement confirmed that Kerimov was at least one person up the ladder from Finn and Erik, and a part of the conspiracies. Or perhaps he would just be involved in this one.

"Looking forward to working with you all." Big Jim nodded and smiled. "Just here to figure out some details with Finn and Erik, and then I'm on my way back to Vancouver as soon as I can get there to get things organized." He seemed somewhat sheepish and eager to get business out of the way and go home. But his anxiety settled down a little now that it seemed Kerimov was some kind of a "friendly."

"Ah, good. Well, I am sure Finn and Erik will look after you, and now that you will be spending my money, I will be taking a great interest in seeing how you perform. *Da?*"

They all laughed and a round of drinks made its way through the room. No one had asked for anything in particular, but, obviously, vodka was the chosen refreshment.

Now Big Jim realized why they were here. Kerimov was the money Finn and Erik needed, and Kerimov wanted to meet the man who was going to be actually doing the work in the field. He didn't know if or where Kerimov fit in on the Greenland project, but because he hadn't met him before that one started, Big Jim guessed he might not have been the financial muscle. Oh well, it'd all come out in the wash.

It wasn't long before the attention of the conversation among them turned to Emma. She pretended to be jolted out of her own thoughts and looked up at the three men. She didn't struggle to hold her own. The questions were easy to negotiate with intelligent responses. Then, suddenly, Kerimov turned to her.

"So, Emma, Murray Stockman is your father?"

Emma was struck by her inability to move or respond immediately. It took only a second but felt much longer before she could regain some composure. She looked over at Kerimov, took a sip of her vodka, fluttered her eyelids, and responded.

"What made you ask that?" Emma seemed comfortable in her skin and with her response. No one else in the cabin made a move other than Kerimov.

"Well, Stockman and I go back a long way, and I always remembered he had a daughter called Emma, and as I look at you, I can see your father." He gave nothing away, but neither did Emma.

"Oh. When did you get to know him, Mr. Kerimov?" She didn't blink.

"I think it was as far back as when he was with CSIS, assigned to the Canadian interests in the Balkan States. Just a young man with a beautiful wife… Lucy, if I remember correctly. Do I?"

"Yes, you do, Mr. Kerimov. My father has been around, shall we say, but he and I don't travel in the same circles anymore." Emma held her vodka glass close to her lips, ready to sip. It was replenished without her invitation, and she relaxed back in her chair.

"How long have you known our friend Jim here?" Kerimov held a hand out toward Jim, but still held his gaze on Emma. The others sat tight, waiting for the response.

"Jim? This Jim?" Emma pointed awkwardly at Big Jim sitting next to her on the sofa. Kerimov just stared at her, a very slight smile on his face as he waited for her response. "All of two days… if that." Emma made a sucking sound as a sign of nonchalance.

"So, Emma, why are you here in Spain? Isn't this just supposed to be a little break for you away from the 'office,' so to speak?" Kerimov obviously knew more about her than the others and she suddenly felt exposed.

"Odd question, Mr. Kerimov." Emma eyed him suspiciously and squirmed just a little, hoping the movement didn't give anything away that could be misconstrued. "But since you ask, I'm taking a short break in Puerto Banús to clear the cobwebs away, then I met Jim, or Big Jim, as everyone seems to call him.

"Another Vancouverite, you see, and he was kind enough to ask if I would like to come along with him for the possibility of a boat ride with Finn and Erik—and here we are." Emma gazed out to sea. "I didn't particularly want to, but I took a liking to my fellow West Coaster, and he seemed like he could do with some company. So here I am." Emma smiled and held a hand up as though to say *voilà*. "If I'd known there would be so many questions, maybe I would've just driven up into the mountains like I'd originally planned. But, hey, I can do that tomorrow, and Big Jim needed some company today." She smiled broadly at Kerimov, who stood motionless and just stared at her.

Big Jim smiled a broad, ear-splitting grin and poked his hands down the front of his trousers. He started the ritual of moving his junk from side to side.

"What are you doing?" Kerimov was abrupt as he questioned Big Jim and let his eyes drop to Big Jim's crotch and back up to his eyes, Kerimov's hands held palms up and pointing in the direction of the problem as his shoulders hunched as if asking a question.

"Whhhat?" was all Big Jim could respond.

"I would prefer to talk to you without wondering what is going on with…" Roman waved a hand at Jim's crotch.

"Whhhhat? Oh… Okay. I get you." Big Jim was caught off guard, but not embarrassed. "Just my strange way of saying I'm comfortable with what's going on, you know." He was trying to splutter something else but decided it would be better just to stop talking and stop playing with himself. Now was clearly not the time.

Kerimov got out of his seat, looked away from Big Jim, and started to walk toward one of the passageways going forward.

"Would you excuse us while we talk a little business?" Kerimov nodded to Finn and Erik. Big Jim didn't seem concerned the three of them were leaving.

"Of course." It was Emma. "Would you like us to go somewhere else?"

"No, no. Stay here or go out to the deck if you would like. I have another room where Finn, Erik, and I will talk." Kerimov didn't wait for a response. He just walked down the hall to the other end of the boat. Finn and Erik followed.

Emma had no intention of staying with Big Jim while Kerimov went off to discuss the next venture with Finn and Erik. She left him leaning over the railing on the aft deck. He seemed content enough to stay out of harm's way and wait for his employers to return.

"Just going to the bathroom," Emma called over at him as she walked down the corridor in the direction in which Kerimov had gone. Big Jim heard her, acknowledged with a small wave of his hand over his shoulder, and drifted back to watching the small waves curling around the boat.

Emma listened at each door as she made her way toward the bow. She could hear talking coming from one of the rooms near the end of the corridor and tried the handle of the door next to that room. It opened, and she glanced cautiously inside, established it was a vacant bedroom, and slipped inside. She wasted no time in putting her ear to the adjoining wall and made out Kerimov talking to Finn and Erik as she kept nervously glancing back at the cabin door. She had locked it but wasn't sure it was enough to dissuade anyone from coming in—especially if they had a key.

"Do you two know who this Emma is?" It was Kerimov. He sounded relaxed but firm.

"Not a clue." Finn spoke up. "She just tagged along with Big Jim. We never thought anything of it, other than we could have done without the complication." They both stared wide-eyed at Kerimov, knowing they had done something wrong, but not knowing what.

"She is the daughter of Murray Stockman, the head of ORB." Kerimov stared at both of them and waited for some response. They shrugged at him, looked at each other, and shrugged again.

"Is that an issue?" This time, it was Erik. "Are we supposed to know her?"

Before Kerimov could respond, his phone pinged an incoming message and he looked down as it lay face-up on the table in front of him. He scowled and pushed himself up out of his chair.

"Give me a minute." Kerimov was out of the door before his Danish partners could respond.

Kerimov turned several corners and headed to a remote part of the vessel one level down. He put his palm on a security panel next to a door and it slid open. The communications room was manned by two men staring at a number of monitors capturing activities and sounds in every room of the boat, as well as incoming signals from news media and stock markets from around the world. One of the men motioned to Kerimov to watch over his shoulder at a monitor showing Emma listening at the adjoining wall to his meeting room. Kerimov smiled wryly and nodded.

"I should have known." Kerimov mumbled to no-one in particular as he left the room, headed to the aft deck, and exchanged pleasantries with Big Jim for ten minutes, confirming he was an innocent in all this.

Meanwhile, Finn and Erik had been left to consider the situation.

"What do you think?" Finn looked over at Erik.

"I don't know who this Emma or her father is, but if Kerimov is concerned then we need to pay attention" Erik blinked at his friend.

"From what I can tell," Finn continued, "I assume getting rid of her will raise some serious flags with this ORB group and if Kerimov knows them, we don't need the attention. Let's just wait and see what she gets up to with Big Jim in Marbella. We'll finish our business alone with him, let them spend a couple of days together, and then make sure they leave." Finn looked grim as he said it. "What do you think?"

"Okay." Erik shrugged but seemed perturbed.

"What?"

Erik shrugged and shook a hand to indicate his hesitation and lack of confidence in Finn's flimsy plan.

"I think we need to tighten things up." Erik was serious. He was thinking on the run. "Let's talk about it with Kerimov.

Emma had heard everything that went on in the meeting room and realized her presence on the boat had thrown a wrench into ORB plans. Matthew had been right to warn her off. But it was too late and they would have to make the best of it.

Emma continued to listen against the partition wall when Kerimov blustered back into the room. She had no idea where he had been, nor did she suspect anything might be amiss.

"Okay, gentlemen," Kerimov's voice boomed at Finn and Erik, "I have some business to attend to so let's take a break." He put his fingers to his lips to let them know there were unwanted ears in the vicinity. Finn and Erik froze. "We'll meet up in the bridge cabin and finish our discussion in an hour or so." Kerimov smacked his hands together and signaled the others to follow him back to the aft deck for refreshments. "Let's go. We need some fuel for our brains."

Finn and Erik were a little taken aback by the sudden decision but didn't argue. Clearly, there was a good reason for Kerimov to make this move, especially given the sign he had given for them to be quiet.

The moment Kerimov had said, "Let's take a break," Emma scooted out from her hiding place and along the corridor to where Big Jim was sitting in the aft cabin, playing with his phone. She made it just in time before she heard the door close as Kerimov and the others stepped into the passageway and headed her way.

"Where have you been all this time?" Big Jim looked a little put out by her abandoning him.

"Oh, I was on the upper deck talking to some of the crew," Emma offered, with no other details.

"Oh," was all Big Jim could manage.

Kerimov strode toward Emma and Big Jim, with Finn and Erik in tow.

"Well, everyone, how about a little lunch on the deck outside?" He was back to the same magnanimous hulk who had greeted them when they first arrived. There was no hint of his knowledge of Emma listening in on the meeting nor did it appear he had any additional business to attend to that he claimed had interrupted their meeting. But no-one said anything.

They spent some time in idle chitchat as they served themselves from the buffet set up on the aft deck. The stewards hovered around with wine bottles and coffee on hand and made sure everything needed was provided. Neither Big Jim nor Emma felt much like eating, but they managed a few mouthfuls, as they sat under the shade of an oversized umbrella stretched out over the table that could seat twelve.

They listened to stories from Kerimov, laughed when needed, nodded when the conversation prompted, and made suitable knowing noises at the times that were appropriate.

The meal ended with Kerimov tossing his napkin on the table, pushing his chair back, and announcing he had a little more business with Finn and Erik, who dropped their napkins, rose from the table, and followed him up the port-side staircase to the bridge deck. The two body-building stewards stood silently blocking access from the aft deck, but acting as though they were simply watching out for the needs of the guests. Emma pretended not to notice, and Big Jim didn't. She was nervous her movements would be prevented if she tried to go up to the bridge.

Kerimov closed both doors to the bridge - and locked them. He turned to face his accomplices.

"Stockman, Emma' father, is the leader of a group known as ORB, and ORB have a habit of poking their noses into business that generally does not concern them." Kerimov waited again for some reaction. He got none other than some protruding lips, palms held out and up, and shrugs as they displayed their lack of understanding the significance.

"Oh." It was Finn. "Is that a problem for us, do you think?"

"I don't know yet, but it is too much of a coincidence his daughter has turned up where we are meeting to discuss the types of projects ORB might take an interest in."

"Okay. And Big Jim?" Erik asked.

"Big Jim is just a schmuck who wants a job. It's Emma who is the risk for us, and whether the risk is real or not, we need to make sure we have a plan in place to deal with her before they leave us." Kerimov looked grim as he watched Finn and Erik adjust themselves to this new situation. Kerimov was quite used to making difficult decisions like these, where people were threatening his security, but the Danes were not. Their natural reaction to personal threats was more likely to hide from them. Criminals they were, but only to a point.

"You mean... get rid of her?" Finn and Erik looked stricken at the prospect. Both were criminals, but they weren't murderers.

"No. That would bring ORB down on us. We need to use her to our advantage." Kerimov waited.

"How? Do you think she may actually be able to help us on the next job?"

"No, but she may be able to provide a distraction while we execute."

"Execute?... Oh, you mean the project?" Finn went quiet, happy to realize there wasn't going to be any bloodshed—at least not in his presence.

"Let's just say she needs to be educated a little about what we are not going to do. Feed her false information through the schmuck. If she is really working with ORB and passes the information you feed her onto them, it will lead them in the wrong direction. What do you guys think? Can you do that?"

"Let's think on it. Maybe get back to you before we leave." It was Finn who was already deep in thought.

Kerimov looked grim, head bowed down, hands together and thumbs circling each other. Finn and Erik watched him but didn't say anything. "She heard everything we talked about in our meeting." Roman looked up at the two faces staring at him in disbelief.

"What? How do you know? What happened?" Finn started to perspire. Erik went rigid, his mouth open.

"Let's say I know everything that happens on this ship." Kerimov looked smug. "Emma was listening in the room next to ours while we were meeting," he admitted.

"There is no doubt in my mind now she is working for ORB, and that spells serious trouble for us." Kerimov sat back in his chair and placed his open hands on the table. "So, what now? Do we get rid of her, or play her?" He stared at the two shocked faces in front of him.

The three men were silent for a few minutes as each gathered their thoughts. It was Finn who broke the silence.

"I say we play her. This could turn out to our advantage. Let them go." Finn looked at the other two. "Keep our eyes and ears on Emma; stick to her like glue and find out who she meets, what she talks about, what she eats, and where she sleeps. We keep Big Jim involved and tell him, when we meet in a few minutes, that we're changing the project location because of problems with the permits and delaying the mining by a year until we get our planning done. He reports back to Emma over the next couple of days, and we should listen in to make sure. Emma reports back to ORB and we should hear that call. Hopefully, they'll lay low if all goes well for us. Are you with me?" Finn watched for some signs of agreement from the other two.

The others nodded their understanding and waited for Finn to continue.

"Someone"—Finn looked over at Erik— "makes a visit to Big Jim as soon as he gets back to Vancouver and lets him know, with a few threats, we don't think it's cool to be talking to Emma. Once we're sure ORB has got the message, we revert to the original plan to get going as soon as we can and let Big Jim know."

"Why don't we just get rid of him?" It was Kerimov.

"Because CanMine needs him. They're all his people and they aren't going anywhere unless he tells them." Finn stared at Kerimov, who just shrugged his big shoulders, grimaced with acknowledgment, and sat back.

"If he doesn't fall in line, for whatever reason, then we'll do something about him. Maybe buy him out and replace him, or worse—but only once his men are on site and working." Finn was on a roll. He loved these kinds of manipulative puzzles. "We can always replace him, especially if we want his company for ourselves to do other jobs." He paused. The others were thinking.

"There's nothing unique about Big Jim." Finn was trying to get the others comfortable with his plan if they had to get rid of Big Jim in any way. "Only his equipment, and we can get someone else to operate it. As long as he stays quiet, Emma and her ORB friends will have no one to communicate with on the inside. They won't know what's happening." Finn sat back with a crafty smile on his face.

"What are the other project options?" It was Kerimov. "Perhaps we set ORB on to one of those we know something about or, even better, on to one we have no intention of ever pursuing?"

"What if we're looking at this all wrong?" It was Finn, and he had their attention again. "What if they aren't interested in the asset at all? What if they're only interested in following the money?" Finn looked smug.

"You could be right." It was Erik. "Maybe they know about Greenland, and maybe the other projects? That would mean they know about the scam."

He didn't mince words, but it was the truth. It was just a huge scam. It wasn't so much the property. Anyone could have owned and mined the gold, but it was the funding that was the problem. The fact governments, financial institutions, unsuspecting mine owners, and investors were all being taken for a ride meant it was just one big scam.

"Okay," said Finn, "let's assume ORB aren't interested in the property, but in the financing. Then we're just going to have to be extra careful with where the money comes from and goes to. Can that be done?" He looked at Kerimov.

"It won't be easy." Kerimov sat forward in his club chair, put one of his enormous hands through his hair, and slapped his thigh. "But it can be done!" He wasn't convinced, despite his demonstration of bravado. As far as he was concerned, his money was safely hidden in a number of accounts around the world under secret identities. No, it was the property and the gold they'd be after to protect, if they were really interested at all. It was worth billions in the hands of the right mining company. And that was where he was most focused. But he wasn't sharing that thought with the others just yet. The fact was, he didn't feel in the least bit threatened by whatever ORB was up to. Any focus would be on the Danes, and they needed to look after themselves.

"Well, I think we still have a project." Finn smiled. "Now, let's make it tough for ORB to follow the trail of not only the money but also the project. We need to keep a careful watch on Emma and tell Big Jim only what we want him to tell her. Let Big Jim carry on, but on a different timeline than what Emma will be led to believe, then bring everything forward and start immediately. Do you have the funds on hand for that?" Finn stared at Kerimov.

"I'll use my own money for us to get started." Kerimov beat his chest with one hand. "Let's get this done, gentlemen. Start as soon as you can. I also suggest we still buy out Jim's company. We may need it one day to build our own team to operate equipment if we continue to work together."

They talked over more details, but seemed content with their plans, with handshakes all round. Finn and Erik would go over things with Big Jim after this meeting. For now, they would put any possibility of getting rid of Big Jim on ice and avoid purchasing his company unless they really had to—or at the most, buy the company out once work on site had started and the workers were committed.

They intended to go ahead with the purchase of Quest as soon as they could and without Big Jim knowing. It never crossed their minds that ORB might be poking around Quest, but then neither did any of them know what ORB was capable of, including Kerimov.

When Roman left the meeting room, Erik walked down the passageway and invited Big Jim to come back to meet with him and Finn. They explained to him the latest plan to change the project location for various reasons and assured him his company would not be out of pocket as a consequence. Plus, they gave him approval to buy equipment and special supplies he would need for the project early, in the event the dramatic price increases they had been warned about would happen. Big Jim was oblivious to any looming escalation, but he was quite happy to agree with the purchasing strategy.

They also talked about compensation for mining, and all seemed satisfied with the cost-plus arrangement that came with a substantial fee once the work was completed. Big Jim was happy despite the delay. Finn and Erik were being more than fair—or so he thought.

Kerimov watched as the four stepped from the aft deck of *Ice Man II* onto *Viking I*. He presented each one with a small silver bracelet inscribed with "Ice Man II." He hoped they would wear them. It would make things so much easier to monitor their movements.

"Please accept this little gift to remind you of our meeting here, my dear. Oh, and give my regards to your father, Emma. Perhaps we will meet again one day." Kerimov smiled and waved as they left, as though there were no concerns.

"Will do, Mr. Kerimov, and many thanks for your hospitality." Emma waved and smiled as innocently as she could, knowing some of the secrets these three men were guarding—or thought they were.

Big Jim relaxed a little more once they were back on *Viking I* and heading back to shore. Emma maintained her composure and oohed and aahed, like a typical googly-eyed tourist, at the sights of power boats and yachts and sailing boats around them, with the backdrop of the Spanish coastline edging closer.

Once they were tied up at the marina, Emma made excuses to head back to the hotel and she left Big Jim standing by his car, not quite knowing what to do.

"Can we meet for supper?" he called after her.

"How about seven thirty at reception?" Emma called out over her shoulder as she squeezed into her car. She didn't wait for an answer, assuming he would agree. She wanted to get away to report her findings. As she pulled away from her parking spot, a small gray Mercedes C230 pulled out of a nearby parking spot and followed her. The occupant had already put a tracer under the front wheel well of her car in case they lost her in the traffic. The "little gift" from Kerimov had found a hiding place in the bottom of her handbag and transmitted the sounds of her car radio to the listening post on *Ice Man II*.

* * *

Back at the hotel, Emma called Matthew and updated him, including the fact Kerimov knew who she was and had met her father before. Kerimov had not let on whether he knew Stockman was an ORB person, not that she thought he would know who or what ORB was. Nothing had ever been mentioned, and Emma had played dumb. While she hadn't overheard any details of their project she was sure she would be able to get some information from Big Jim that evening. After all, there was no reason for him to suspect anything, other than good business.

Matthew was concerned but happy she had listened in on the meeting and could likely confirm their target from Big Jim later that day.

"Oh, I'm sure he'll tell me what he knows. He has no reason not to. As far as he knows, everything is legitimate now that he's met Kerimov and understands where the money is coming from. I think he believes Kerimov just wanted to look him in the eye before investing if that's what you would call it. But I didn't get any details on how Kerimov intends to raise the funds, nor how Finn and Erik intend to get ownership of the property. All that information is still up for grabs." Emma paused and waited for Matthew.

"Boy, that's a great start, Em. Let's hope this guy, Kerimov, doesn't know about your father and ORB; otherwise, it could mean your cover's blown and we have to rethink things." Matthew sounded a little anxious.

"I didn't get any sense of any of them, including Big Jim, having any suspicions, Matthew, but I'll keep my eyes and ears open and see if Big Jim knows anything this evening."

"Okay, but give me a call again after your supper. When are you coming back?"

"You know, I might actually go and see this place, Ronda, while I'm here. May as well make the most of it, and there's nothing I can do right now on the case." Emma chuckled.

"Got it. Have a great time, but stay in touch, Em."

Their cell phones went dead, but *Ice Man II* had picked up Emma's side of the conversation very well. So far, so good—for everyone.

Matthew checked in with Stockman.

"We had eyes on Emma the whole time, Matthew. Satellites are a marvelous invention, if they're used like they're supposed to be, and Emma knows better than to go gallivanting off on her own without a tracking device hidden somewhere on her body." Stockman was pleased with what he had heard from Matthew, although he was a little concerned to be getting involved with Kerimov again. The Russian was an old adversary from years ago. They weren't in direct conflict, but CSIS had followed him for a couple of years. They couldn't catch him red-handed in anything serious and had eventually dropped him to focus on someone else.

"It may not come to anything, but we just have to be a little extra cautious. Now we know Kerimov is involved, we need to get Plato up to speed and see what he can come up with on Kerimov's financials and contacts. We'll need to trace his calls and find out where he's getting the money. It doesn't sound as though he was involved in the previous projects, but we don't know that for sure. Maybe he provided a little seed money just to dip his toe in the water, so to speak? So, somewhere or other, he may have some payback from the Nalunaq venture." Matthew waited for Stockman to respond.

"You contact Plato, and I'm going to see what I can find out about their next target. Let's be in touch again soon, or we may have to meet." Stockman paused. "Okay?"

"Yes. I think that's it for now. Emma will be back shortly, so we may call you when we're together."

"Good job. Talk soon." Stockman ended the conversation, and the line went dead.

* * *

Emma and Big Jim wandered up the street, away from the hotel to the main road that went west to Puerto Banús, and on toward Gibraltar, and east toward the town center and on to Malaga. There was a large, open-air pizza place at the junction and, after the day they'd had, they decided it would be far enough.

There was very little Big Jim could tell Emma about his meeting on *Ice Man II*, and she was cautious about being overly inquisitive. But she did discover there was a change in plans and another property had been identified. There would also be a year delay in the timing of that project while the Danes got things organized, and that seemed to be the extent of what she hadn't known already.

"I was a little nervous about this guy, Kerimov, at first," Big Jim confided as he bit off a mouthful of pizza and let the tomato sauce ooze over his chin. Emma pointed it out to him, and he grinned at her as he jabbed at the mess with his napkin. "But I think he's okay. Just had to check me out, I guess. But it's a long way to come just for that, eh?" He took another bite but managed to keep most of it in his mouth this time.

"He's certainly a powerhouse. What does he do?" Emma nibbled at her caper and tomato pizza.

"I don't know. Some big shot in Russia, I think. All I know is he's responsible for getting the financing organized for the job, so Finn and Erik sit up and listen." Big Jim was really going at it with his pizza, and Emma would rather have just let him gorge than try to make conversation. She waited until he was finishing up and licking at his fingers while scooping up whatever had dropped to the plate.

"Oh. I thought he was using his own money for the project."

"Noooo." Big Jim had a scornful expression on his face. "He's the guy who's going to get the money. I don't know who from, but I do know he doesn't use his own." Big Jim turned his head away and looked absently ahead of him at the night traffic.

Emma pretended a laugh, as though to show she didn't really care. But she did, and a major part of the puzzle dropped into place. Kerimov wasn't going to use his own money. It was going to be someone else's—just like the Greenland job, when the World Bank funded the project and lost it to the Danes.

Once they had chugged down a couple of beers, they decided to head back to the hotel and said their goodnights in the lobby. They hadn't arranged anything for the next day and while Emma would really have liked a day trip to Ronda, she knew Big Jim would be calling her. But that was okay. She had what she wanted.

* * *

Kerimov listened in on the conversation between Emma and Big Jim with mild interest at first. There didn't seem to be anything discussed that was compromising, and at least Emma now knew about the changes. The first part of the ruse was complete. Now to wait for her to pass on the information to ORB.

But as he thought about it more, he started to get nervous about Big Jim confirming to Emma that he, Kerimov, was the money behind the new venture.

But then, he remembered, it might have been himself who raised that issue when they were altogether on the boat. Now he wished he had told Finn not to mention it when he and Erik met with Big Jim. But, more importantly, he wished he hadn't bragged about it originally, if his memory served him right. That could have been a mistake if ORB was involved. In fact, it definitely was a mistake.

Kerimov listened as Emma put a call in to Stockman, just as he thought she would. He knew what ORB was and what they did with Stockman at the head—although he really did not appreciate their full strength and versatility. But they did have a penchant for poking into the business of others, and his business was a complex world of subversive activities that would be of high interest to international criminal investigators. No, now he thought about it, he didn't like it at all. Maybe it was him they were after, and not the project after all. Kerimov tucked his concerns away for now and focused on his next move toward getting money for the Newfoundland project.

* * *

Loose Lips

A couple of days after returning to Vancouver from Marbella, Big Jim lounged at the bar, finishing up his third Grey Goose and tonic, with a touch of lime cordial and an ice cube, lustfully staring at any female who went by him. They got more good-looking and inviting the more Grey Goose he had. His coat covered the stool next to him, saving the space in case one of them showed an interest in being bought a drink. None ever did, but that didn't dampen his spirit of hope.

As he was consoling himself for having to drink solo again, someone slipped up behind him, touched him on the shoulder, and pointed to his coat on the stool, then signaled with a movement of his thumb over his shoulder for Big Jim to get rid of it. He didn't use words, just gesticulated, but Big Jim knew what he wanted. It was quiet but sarcastic enough in the way it was done for him to swing around with some intent to look at this stranger, who was plainly being disrespectful.

He stopped at the sight of a broad-shouldered, square-jawed body of a man with close-cropped hair that seemed to cast a shadow completely over him. The body came with company. An equally large, if not larger, version. Only this one seemed to bristle with some kind of unprovoked rage as he stared Big Jim in the eyes. Fortunately, the first body was a little smoother and smiled with a tooth-filled mouth that seemed to be as broad as his shoulders and shrugged. His eyebrows raised in question as he pointed at the jacket on the stool once more.

"Oh, of course. Excuse me." Big Jim acquiesced to the intimidation by quickly settling back, grabbing his jacket, and slinging it over the back of his own stool, while he wore a smarmy smile that said, "No problem," but really meant, "Fuck you."

One of the two big boys sat down, while the other stood at his shoulder and next to Big Jim.

"Another, please, Andy." Big Jim turned back to the bar and signaled to the bartender. They knew each other from the numerous visits Big Jim had made to the same dark watering hole in the basement of a restaurant at the edge of the seawall over the past twelve years. Anyone could find him there, propped up at the bar, after six every weekday when he was in town, where he would sit thinking about life for a couple of hours before heading home to his Terminal City Club apartment. He was always looking for someone to talk to at the bar, and often found a body who needed the same thing. Usually, another lonely business guy in his fifties, who had nowhere special to go after work, or was away from home, and needed to drink his life away.

"You guys tourists?" Once he had settled down, Big Jim opened a line of small talk to the big boys next to him, who were still staring.

"*Nyet*." That was the full extent of the response from the smiley one. Neither was drinking. Both were staring at him with intimidating expressions that implied they were never going to be friends.

"Oh. Business in the city?" Another attempt by Big Jim, who leaned back on his stool and picked up his refreshed drink.

"*Da*. You know Kerimov?" Smiley asked as he raised his eyebrows and lowered his face into Big Jim's.

Big Jim visibly gulped air. His eyes widened and his hand grabbed the GG, slowly bringing it to his mouth. He sipped without tasting, trying to buy a little time to think before responding, and turned his head to Smiley.

"Yeeeeeessss."

"We have message for you." Smiley looked serious now. The smile had disappeared.

"Oh. A message, eh?"

"*Da*. No more *eto* Emma."

"What? What does *eto* mean?" Big Jim was, and looked, puzzled. His Grey Goose lingered at his bottom lip, waiting to be sipped, or knocked back, depending on what happened next.

"No more this Emma. You no more talk to this Emma. You understand?" Smiley was deadly serious, and the spare seemed to hug in closer and passed him a piece of paper.

Big Jim's eyes looked up at an angle at the ceiling with his pupils in the corners and the rest of his face a question mark.

"Ohhhhkay." It was as much as he could get out.

The big boys turned to go. Smiley put a hand on Big Jim's shoulder and, using his other hand, waved an index finger slowly in his face.

"*Nyet, nyet, nyet* Emma—okay?" Smiley was smiling again, but this time it was threatening as his finger prodded Big Jim's chest. They left as quietly as they had arrived, leaving Big Jim still sitting with the GG glass touching his bottom lip.

"Who the fuck were those two?" Andy put his cloth to one side and leaned over the bar to Big Jim. "They were the biggest fuckers I think I've ever seen. Russian, too, I'm guessing."

"Friends." Big Jim whimpered as he swallowed the last of the third Grey Goose, asked for a double, and opened the piece of paper: "Schedule revised—start moving." It was signed "Finn" and dated the day before.

"This one's on me, my friend. I need one after that." Andy poured the double and one for himself, but without the tonic.

* * *

Phase 1 – Prelims

"Hey, Plato. It's Matthew. How the hell are you?" Matthew sat in the comfort of his lounge and looked out over the park as he made his call.

"Hello, my friend. Where are you?" Plato was as enthusiastic as always as he answered his cell. He was somewhere in the Greek Islands with his wife, Margaret, enjoying the sun, beaches, and Mediterranean food.

"I'm in Vancouver. Not a lot of sun, though, other than the liquid kind." They both laughed. "How's that darling wife of yours?"

"You mean Margaret?" They laughed again.

"She's wonderful, thank you. Living in a bikini, enjoying sun, white Greek wine—can you believe it? —beaches, and wandering the village streets. You know, the usual. Are you and Emma still a thing?"

"Absolutely—she would be doing the same thing as Margaret, given the chance, but it's a little cool for that here—and, of course, she's working." Matthew laughed.

"Great. Give her our love when you see her next—she's quite a lady, and beautiful, at that. When are you coming to see us?"

"I think it's going to be a while yet, my friend. Which brings me to the reason for the call."

"Oh." Plato was ready.

"I need some help again. Are you free for a few months?"

"Is this an ORB project, Matthew?"

"What else would it be, Plato? That's all I seem to do these days. What about you?"

"We had a few projects with the American embassy, through Margaret's father—you remember him?"

"Yes, I do. He was a great help on the Iranian caper come the end, when we had to get the word out to the Chinese and Russians about the problems with their Iranian oil plan."

"That's it," Plato acknowledged. "Our latest work for the Americans was, or should I say still is, related to their financial conundrums, having imposed all those sanctions around the world. It's tough for them to keep up with monitoring and controlling it all, especially when it gets right down to individuals." Plato paused. "Sanctioning trade is one thing, but sanctioning people is quite another. Anyway, we're in on your latest project, whatever you have."

"Great. Can you come over to London to meet with Stockman and myself?"

"Sure. When?"

* * *

Matthew called Stockman to update him and find out if there was any news from his end.

"Hello, Matthew. So soon?"

"I think we should meet, Stockman. But this time with Plato. I need to give him the project details, and I would rather have you with me when I do. It'll likely need some of your back room help. Can you make a meeting in London for later this week?"

"Of course, my boy. Of course. Just tell me the time and place and I'll be there." Stockman was being far more accommodating than normal. It wasn't that he wasn't usually. It was just it was more often he who was giving the direction and organizing meetings. But he appreciated Matthew taking the initiative to get this one organized.

"Let's say Club Quarters, the Chart Room, at ten a.m. Friday morning?" Matthew proposed.

"Sounds good, Matthew. I'll get Lucy to make my arrangements and reserve the meeting room. You had better arrange your own accommodations and travel—you know what you need. Tell Plato to do the same. It'll be easier that way."

"No problem. I'll send Plato a text. Let's both think of how to weave Plato into this before we meet on Friday. I have some ideas, but I'd really appreciate your input." Matthew waited for Stockman.

"Sounds good. Let me think on it. We have my friend, the Russian, the Danes, and perhaps others to consider."

"We also have to think about Quest and how to bring them in. There's also an underground mining contractor the Danes use—a company out of Vancouver, CanMine. We may have to do something there as well." Matthew was thinking on the fly.

"Okay. I'll see you on Friday."

Their cell phones shut off.

* * *

The Air Canada flight from Vancouver arrived at Heathrow on time at ten thirty a.m. London time on Thursday. The cab ride to the Club Quarters, just around the corner from Trafalgar Square, seemed to take almost as long as the flight but it was a favorite business spot for ORB people to meet in the anonymity of a small hotel with good facilities in a central city location. It was easy to get to and from, as well as being out of the limelight of larger hotels where their group could be spotted by someone they didn't want to be seen by.

Matthew had the remainder of the day and evening to himself and wondered when the other guys would arrive. They'd likely be staying at other hotels in the area rather than the same hotel. Stockman was probably staying around the corner at the Clermont near Charing Cross station. Plato would likely choose the Grand overlooking the square. It didn't matter. They would all get together in the morning. In the meantime, Matthew took a stroll around, had supper, had a nightcap in the hotel bar, and headed to his room, suitably exhausted from the day. He wished he had brought Emma for the company, and maybe other things.

* * *

"I guess we could have done all this through Zoom." Matthew waved a hand at Stockman and Plato. "The problem is I don't always trust the internet. I'd rather have a secure line, and even then, I'm not sure."

"I agree." It was Stockman. "Better to spend a little extra money for the comfort of security, Matthew. You know my feeling on these things. I'd rather meet face-to-face, if at all possible, rather than be concerned about being phone-tapped, but I suspect we are going to have to succumb to the pull of Zoom sooner or later." Stockman looked over at Plato.

"Totally agreed on face-to-faces," Plato added. "Although a warmer climate would have been nice."

They all chuckled.

"Okay, Matthew. Tell us where you are with things."

Matthew went back over the story of how they came to be here in this meeting room, more for the benefit of Plato than for Stockman, who already knew most of the story.

"Plato, would you reach out to Colin? He has the background on what we're up to, and you two worked really well on the Iranian caper. This is going to be much the same in terms of looking into the bank accounts of the targets, although it's likely going to be more difficult with a man like Kerimov—being Russian, and not an ordinary one, if there is such a thing. He's an experienced international businessman, so he really knows his way around the underbelly of the financial web."

Plato nodded, took some notes, then sat back to listen.

"Okay, first things first." Stockman turned their attention. "Let's talk about the next target, or targets, for these Danish scoundrels." The others nodded. "Get yourself into the Quest offices, Matthew. Find out what they know. Have they been approached yet and, if so, by whom? What's the angle the Danes will use? I suspect it will be financial again. From what I understand, Quest is broke and in need of some private funding.

"The government isn't going to help on this one. I also hear their management is not only thin on the ground, but they also don't have the experience to get a mine back up and running. I don't know why they aren't searching for the right people, but I suspect they're no different from the other juniors in that space… they just don't want to share, but they can't do it alone." Stockman paused for the others to join in.

"I've done a little research on Quest." It was Matthew. "Seems their president, Paul Mah, is a bit of an OCD victim; likes to dabble in minutiae and gets lost in the trenches. That's likely why he can never get anything started or finished—can't see the big picture.

"He's bounced around some in the industry and landed at Quest a couple of years ago when an associate of his, some guy called Bogdown, used his influence as payback after Mah got them out of some trouble with another company.

"Seems they drove that one into the ground, spent all the capital on the wrong things, and pushed the company into bankruptcy. They both managed to jump off the sinking ship and left it to the rest of the crew to tidy things up with the creditors." Matthew shrugged. "Nothing new there, I'm afraid. The industry is rife with amateurs like that."

"Okay, I hear you." Stockman nodded, then looked away from Matthew and changed the subject. "Plato, you'll need to really clue in on this Russian and see if you and Colin can unscramble this banking. We may need to pay his accounts a visit. I'd like to know how many of these kinds of ventures he's financed, if any. Also, let's get a better understanding of how these Danes are intending to operate. I'm not sure where they bank just yet, but it should be easy to find out compared to the Russian.

"On the Greenland project, we know the Danes wrestled control from the mine owners through some pretty slippery maneuvering with the TSE and delisted the company before transferring the listing to the Stockholm exchange. That kind of thing isn't likely to happen here, I don't think, but let's try to figure out their game plan.

"From what Emma has told us, it seems Kerimov is handling the financing this time around, but we have no idea how he's going to be doing that. I have to assume he's not using his own money, so that means he's on the search for financing, and that's one of the parts of their plan we need to control." Stockman paused to take a gulp of coffee. He got up and strode around the room as he thought. The others were engaged in their own thoughts.

"I don't know if you know this," Plato spoke up, "but any US-dollar transfers anywhere in the world, even within countries other than the US, are automatically recorded by one of the US clearing banks in Manhattan. It only takes a subpoena to get the records of specific transactions if we want to find out more about the money trail. The US authorities are extremely sensitive to the wrongful use of their dollar, so getting approval for a subpoena isn't very difficult. Perhaps you could get that set up through your contacts,

Stockman? I'll get you the names of the banks I'd like to begin with." Plato looked over at his boss.

"I remember us having to do that once before, Plato. Good thinking. My guess is most of the transactions of the Russian are in the millions, so that will reduce the number you will have to track. Let's see where it leads." Stockman nodded to Plato and turned to Matthew.

"Now, let's get hold of James Peters—Stockman changed the subject away from Kerimov— "our man from Iran, and see what he's up to. He may be an ideal candidate to get on the books of the contractor to keep an eye open for us and maybe even head up a little sabotage if we need it."

"Good thought." Mathew liked James. They had worked well together. He was sharp, communicative, and a real hustler who took timelines seriously. "I'll contact him. It shouldn't be too hard to get him with Big Jim's group."

"Okay." Stockman held a hand up. "Let's take a break for an hour." He looked at his watch. "Let's meet back here at eleven and I'll get some lunch brought in, or we can go eat in the lobby restaurant."

* * *

Matthew made his way to a quiet room, where people could make private calls, a few doors down the hall. It was windowless, dimly lit, with just a small coffee table and two wing-backed chairs facing the door. A couple of paintings adorned the walls, and it seemed a perfect place for some discreet conversations. Matthew had brought a coffee with him and placed it on the coffee table. He took out his notebook, smoothed it open to the pages where he had made notes from the meeting, and made his first call.

"Mr. Mah, you don't know me, but my name is Matthew Black."

"I don't know who you are or where you are, but you do know it's the middle of the night where I am. And how did you get my private number?"

Matthew had forgotten the time difference, not that it ever bothered him. He traveled through so many time zones, it was sometimes difficult to keep track, and he just did what he needed to do, regardless.

"Oh, my apologies, but this is urgent. We need to talk before you head in to your office on Monday." Before Mah could respond, Matthew pushed on. "This is a matter of some urgency that seriously affects Quest…" He tried not to sound overly anxious as he listened for Mah's response.

"Oh. Okay, well, go on. I'm awake now." Mah had calmed down quickly.

"You're going to get a visit fairly soon from some people claiming to be interested in the Hope Brook property."

"Well, I like that idea. Is that a problem?" Mah still didn't sound concerned.

"Yes. They're crooks, and I represent a company that's going to help you through the scam. Can we meet?" There was a pause as the suddenness of the statement and the lack of detail took Mah aback.

"Sure. When? I assume you're in Vancouver right now." Mah was suddenly eager to get to the bottom of what Matthew was talking about.

"No, but I'll be there tomorrow by around noon. I'll make a reservation for eight p.m. at Hy's under my name, Black. I'll be in the corner booth at the back of the restaurant nearest the kitchen. Is that good for you?"

"See you there." Mah put his cell phone back on the nightstand, got out of bed, and wandered down to his kitchen, trying to imagine what was coming down the line. There had been no movement on the exchange, no press releases that might trigger interest, no board members to be concerned about. No, this was all very odd. He took a slug of Scotch and went back upstairs, not knowing what to believe.

Matthew was already making his next call, this one to the last number he had for James a couple of years ago.

The party answered after only one ring.

"'Ello. James here."

"Hello, my friend," Matthew responded to the familiar voice.

"Well, well, well. If it isn't my long-lost buddy, Matthew. How the hell have you been? And where have you been?" James was his usual chipper self.

"Where are you these days, James?" Matthew asked.

"We're in Guildford, down the road a bit from London; and you?"

"In London, doing some plotting and planning with the group. Would you like to join us?"

"Is it dangerous?" James wondered.

"Same as usual, you know. It comes with the territory."

"I'm in. Shall I come up to London?"

"I'm heading out this afternoon, but we can Zoom each other on Monday, if that works," Matthew suggested. He still had to build a strategy where James could not only fit in with Big Jim's group but also know what he had to look for.

"Sounds good. Make it Monday afternoon, though—say two p.m.? I'm doing a job in the morning."

"I'll send the link. Talk then, James."

The call ended and Matthew looked over his notes. He didn't want to call Emma. It would either be too early or too late, but whatever it would be, it wasn't worth disturbing her just yet, although he was wondering whether she had been in contact with Big Jim to confirm the start date for mining at Hope Brook.

Matthew closed his eyes for what seemed like a moment before his phone rang.

"Hey, Matthew. It's your favorite woman." It was Emma, sounding as though she was wide awake and still ready for some fun.

"Hi, Em. A little late, or should I say early, for you?"

"I just got back in from a date with friends over at the island. Nothing much, but good fun anyway. What's happening?"

"Well, we've had the first of our meetings and got some things sorted out. I'll be back in Vancouver by around noon tomorrow, and meeting with Quest tomorrow evening to start poking around. Oh, and Plato sends his regards. He's here with us now; and I've got James Peters back in the mix, so that should be fun. Any news from your end?" Matthew perked up to be chatting with Emma. She was always cheerful and positive.

"Well, from what Big Jim tells me—we had a supper date the other evening in Marbella, as I mentioned to you in my message—it sounds as though the project has changed to an unknown location just yet, and it's all off anyway for a year while they get themselves organized. They hadn't talked about that when we were on Kerimov's boat." Emma paused.

"Wow, that's a surprise. We thought they were getting prepared to move quickly on Hope Brook." Matthew was taken aback for a moment.

"I don't think they ever actually said that, Matthew, although Jim was pretty sure that's where he was heading, and right away. I know we all thought Hope Brook was the next target, but perhaps we were just getting ahead of ourselves a little." Emma waited for Matthew.

"I don't know, Em. It sounds really strange to me that they would go through all this trouble and not get moving right away on Hope Brook. It's the obvious choice—at least to us. But, you know something? Kerimov's not the patient type, and I'm guessing the Danes aren't either. Let me look into it. Maybe we can even get James involved."

"Sounds like a plan, Matthew. I think James is just the man to get close to Big Jim. They talk the same construction-type language and I'm not sure how much I'm going to be seeing him anymore. I contacted him yesterday just to say hi, and thanks for spending some time together, but he seemed a little cool, so I left it at that. We didn't make any arrangements to get together. Very strange."

"Do you suspect anything? I mean, Big Jim doesn't seem the type to just give up on a good-looking lady."

"Thanks for that, Matthew, but all I can say is what I felt. He was definitely cool and not looking for any get-together, at least not in the near future, as far as I could tell. He wasn't rude, he just seemed to have lost interest, if you know what I mean. Typical guy!" Emma laughed.

"Yes. Yes, I do, Em. Let me think on it and I'll talk to James. I also have to talk to Big Jim anyway, to get James on the CanMine payroll."

"Okay. You're back in Vancouver tomorrow? Do you want me to pick you up at the airport?" Emma always asked, and Matthew always declined, but it was the thought that counted.

"No, I'll be fine. I guess we should be careful about where we meet, with Big Jim within six blocks of where we each live. At least until I figure out what these guys are up to. I'll call you soon.".

"You bet. Okay. Let's talk tomorrow. Have a safe trip." Emma was deep in thought, wondering if Big Jim was deliberately avoiding her. She wouldn't mind if it weren't for the project and her need to know what was going on. Big Jim had been her way in.

"Bye, Em. Take care and stay out of trouble." It was something Matthew said to her when they weren't together. They signed off.

The hour was almost up when Matthew wandered back into the room with Stockman and Plato not far behind. He updated them on his discussions with Mah, James Peters, and Emma. Plato had called Colin, and they were discussing the Russian banking system and trying to figure out how best to get the information they needed, whatever that might be. But all in good time. Stockman knew they would figure things out, and he was happy Matthew was going to be meeting with Mah the next evening.

However, they were all somewhat perplexed by the change in venue and the timing Big Jim had provided to Emma. It didn't sit right with any of them, and someone needed to verify what they had been told. It could be real, but it could be a red herring.

"Mitch, can you get hold of your contacts at Rio Narcea and see if you can confirm the timing for them to process the next shipment of ore from the Danes?" Matthew was thinking of other ways to confirm what Big Jim was indicating, but he would wait and see what Mitch could turn up first before he tried another approach.

Mitch nodded his understanding.

Their session ended and Matthew headed to Heathrow. Plato had a flight back to Athens that evening, and Stockman had a four-hour drive ahead of him to get back down to Devon. No schedule was set for a follow-up meeting, although each knew it would happen sooner than later. Each promised to stay in touch if even the most trivial thing turned up. Naturally, Stockman would see to it they didn't stay out of touch too long, regardless.

* * *

"Hi, big fella." Matthew had a problem with calling him Big Jim. It just didn't sound right. "It's Matthew here. Matthew Black, remember?" Matthew had put a call in to Big Jim Garland about an hour before they landed at Vancouver.

"Hey, Matthew. How's it going? Anything new?" Big Jim was his usual cheerful self.

"Not much. Just wanted to let you know we were planning on starting preliminary earthworks up north in about six months. Is that good for you?" Matthew lied.

"Sure. It sounds as though we're going to mobilize to Newfoundland any day." Big Jim never gave a thought to letting that information out to Matthew. All he had been told was not to talk to Emma and had no idea Matthew and Emma were working together.

"Oh. Oh, well, it's all good work." Matthew sounded enthused but silently puzzled by the timeline that didn't support what Big Jim had told Emma. "I guess things went okay in Marbella?" Matthew patiently went through his questions and answers now that he had reconfirmed the Hope Brook timing. Everything that Emma had been told was garbage.

"Yeah. Really well. Kind of an odd lot, but they pay well and the work's good."

"Jim, I was wondering if you could do me a favor and have a good friend of mine put on your payroll as a site guy." Matthew sounded a little pleading.

"What's the deal? Is he any good? Does he have a resume?" Big Jim brightened up a little at the prospect of getting someone from an associate rather than off the street.

"He's one of my guys, but I'd like him to get some experience with your guys before he heads up north. Perfect field man. Great as a site admin guy, as well as being an engineer. I'll send his resume over."

"Well, we could always use a good site hand. Let's see his resume." Big Jim really needed help on site management.

"Sounds great. Are you in town?" Matthew asked.

"Yes. Shall we do lunch?"

"I can bring this fellow over to meet you and we can all go for lunch. How about Thursday?"

Big Jim checked his calendar and confirmed the arrangement for noon at his office.

"Sounds good. See you then, Matthew."

"Oh, one more thing—have you got a geologist on board yet?" asked Matthew as an afterthought, but it had just come to him that having Mitch buried in with CanMine might also be very useful.

"I don't." Big Jim was obviously interested. Good underground geologists were hard to come by. "I was going to contract someone out when we got on the ground in St. John's." A mining contractor generally did not have a geologist on the payroll. That was a person the owner or site inspector would normally provide, but in this case, CanMine was doing it all. There was no owner looking over their shoulder all the time. All they had to do was mine, but they would need a geologist to consider the ground conditions and lead them in following the gold.

"Maybe I can help." Matthew went on to explain that an associate of his, Mitch, had just sprung free from a project in Northern Ontario and was looking for a change. Big Jim jumped at the opportunity. Just the resume was fine.

Their call ended and Matthew sat back in his seat, took a gulp of water, closed his eyes, and relaxed for the last hour of the flight. He had no doubt James and Mitch would make the grade. Now he needed to get trumped-up resumes together for them both.

* * *

Quest Gold

Matthew arrived in Vancouver to an overcast and rain-threatening day. He had missed his favorite view as the plane came out of the low cloud and thumped onto the runway half an hour ahead of schedule.

His hired limo dropped him off at home, where he spent a leisurely afternoon freshening up and preparing himself for his evening meeting with Mah. A call to Emma didn't result in anything new other than for him to report his safe arrival back in the city. She was happy, and they arranged to get together for brunch the next day, Sunday, over in Yaletown, where they would have an opportunity to catch up on Matthew's meeting with Mah. Whatever was agreed between them would help set the scene for ORB's strategy moving forward.

Matthew parked himself in one of the booths near the back of Hy's and ordered an Aberlour single malt, no ice. He was fifteen minutes early and had reserved this table specially to watch everyone entering the sitting area of the restaurant as they arrived. While he had seen an internet version of Mah, people could look a lot different in person. Often the web photo would be an old one taken when the subject was younger and looked more vital. But Mah was very identifiable as he arrived and came toward Matthew with his recognizable, disheveled black hair and sagging eyes. Despite the uncertainty of what this meeting might bring for him, he at least put on the appearance of looking happy to meet Matthew as they shook hands and sat opposite each other.

"This is intriguing." Mah opened the dialogue and pressed his hands together on the table. He ordered a gin and tonic without worrying about brand names and smiled over at Matthew. The waitress dropped a couple of menus on the table and left them alone.

Matthew filled Mah in on the situation, starting with the involvement of the Danes in the Greenland scam, and how ORB had gotten involved. Mah needed to know Hope Brook was most likely the next victim through an imminent purchase attempt of Quest by the Danes. Further, Matthew explained, Quest would never see the money that might be agreed to if ORB was not involved. Mah seemed to perk up at hearing all might not be lost.

Matthew explained that Quest should sell the property to the Danes at as good a price as Mah could negotiate. It would attract them into a trap set by ORB to catch them and have the full transaction money paid out from the offshore bank accounts of the Danes, as well as whatever money had been scammed from others.

Mah seemed to take it all in his stride and had a strangely cynical smile on his face. "Why are you doing all this?" he wondered out loud. His drink arrived, and he scanned the menu. "Having anything? I'm starved."

They both stopped talking for a few moments while they considered the menus and ordered.

Matthew carried on from where he left off. "Let's just say we heard from a reliable source these guys have done the same thing before to some other unsuspecting folks. It seems they're looking for their next targets." Matthew stared at Mah, who had his mouth open as he listened. Mah couldn't believe what he was hearing. It all sounded so... surreal.

"Quest is the first on their list, from what we've learned." Matthew sat back and watched Mah's face as he took it all in. The cynical look had long since disappeared and the look of concern replaced it as it dawned on him he could lose everything he and Quest had invested if ORB was not successful. But then he remembered what he had heard about ORB, and he relaxed a little.

"Okay, what do you think I should do?" Mah was seriously asking. He was dumbfounded and lost.

They spent the next two hours dining and discussing a strategy to deal with the Danes should they approach Quest. Mah became more comfortable in Matthew's company after he had explained the outline of a plan and he was clearly in awe of ORB as Matthew described the kind of work they had done over the years. ORB's intent now was to put a stop to the scams being pulled by the Danes, but Mah had to play his part. If ORB was successful, Quest would be paid out from the funds recovered from the bank accounts of Finn and Erik. But Matthew was careful not to go into detail about how that would happen—after all, he wasn't absolutely sure yet they could do it. The details were evolving as Matthew and the other members of ORB learned more about the targets.

* * *

Finn and Erik arrived in Vancouver a week earlier than Matthew and settled into the Pacific Rim Hotel, a five-star, down close to the water, and far enough from the inner-city noise that the area was a joy to walk around, relax on a bench on the marina walkway, or just sit and plot and plan. Not that the Danes needed tranquility. They were people of action with a need to move, no matter what. Peace didn't really suit them, but it was still good not to be surrounded by distractions, and they often were.

They refreshed their memories of the past stock charts for Quest Gold, the company they were about to visit, the owners of the Hope Gold mine in Newfoundland, and re-educated themselves as to who the senior management and directors were. Their research of each of their backgrounds concluded that not one of them, either from management or on the board, had actually executed a project, let alone had a background of any significance in the world of mining. In fact, even their backgrounds in high-level business were suspect and identified nothing of consequence.

There was a smattering of accountant types; one rather youthful, and likely inexperienced lawyer with no mining industry experience, although he did look the sharpest dressed of them all; two fairly old corporate farts who were clearly nearing their capacity as credible thinkers but did manage to hold a smile of well-capped teeth; one metallurgical engineer in a flak-type jacket, with the distinctive look of having just come out from the bush; one project-type person who seemed to have garnered some experience as an environmental tree-hugger when it came to mining; and a president, who lay claim to be some kind of fund manager who could develop a financial spreadsheet but who had little experience with the practicalities of running an operation, let alone building one. And these people represented the entire upper level of Quest Gold.

The company was trading on the TSX for eight cents a share and going nowhere. It had a market value of only four million dollars, with around fifty million shares outstanding. Lots of room for an expansion of share volume and very little appetite in the market to purchase them.

Quest Gold press releases were not exciting and brought no great news, other than announcements of yet more field exploration, and revised tables of what they announced were gold reserves and possibilities. There were more releases associated with the filing of the necessary securities forms, the announcements of what they considered to be substantive information, but really only referenced the continual revisions to the previous studies. All of it intended to poke the stock and try to make it grow by just enough to fund corporate expenses for the year. It wasn't working, and neither were their attempts to get financial help—from any source—to get Hope Brook back up and running. There was barely enough raised to keep the doors open.

The work GREY had done on the property, even since their Zoom meeting, was significant and they knew how to make a mine financially attractive—provided the gold was there. GREY had concluded the only way Hope Brook could work out financially, with little risk, was if the ore was extracted, just like at Nalunaq, and shipped offshore. While this was not the same kind of narrow-vein underground project, the same mining method could be used to high-grade the Hope Brook deposit. But it needed an expert underground mining geologist to precisely delineate the higher-grade gold veins as they disappeared through the rock in various directions.

The fact was, the Hope Brook mine had already had much of its easily extracted gold assets plundered in the first phase of mining activity under the management of the original owner. It was now on a care and maintenance program, more for the benefit of environmental stewardship than for any other reason. But there was still gold there.

The original owner had effectively mined using conventional methods, taking large volumes of waste with it and putting it all through an over-strained processing plant. In the end, they had just walked away from the property when they had completed what they intended to do. They left it in the hands of the courts and the province to manage the cleanup. They'd taken all they could, had run the mining and processing equipment into the ground, and then stopped paying their bills. There was no money for reclamation, no money for care and maintenance, and they'd frittered away all the company investments intended to provide pensions for the miners. There was nothing left of value when they departed, and neither did the pitiful sale of what remained of the property include for the transfer of debt to the new owner.

While Quest Gold were the most recent owners of the property, others had tried before them but failed to make the property successful. They had all got themselves into more financial problems when the industry suffered a global recession. Quest had purchased the asset five years ago through an auction after the last owner had also declared bankruptcy, as did the first.

It was clear Quest had not consolidated the multitude of property reports, going back some thirty years, which would have shown Hope Brook could still be a financially viable venture, provided the mining method changed with the way the gold was disseminated in the ore. It took GREY, as a team of independent experts, to pull it all together to see it for what it could be. Quest was not skilled in thinking outside of the box. They had no such specialized knowledge themselves and had to employ consultants, who could only review and interpret the information provided to them and draw their conclusions based on what was an incomplete file. Quest, themselves, had no sense of the worth of the old studies and rather than hand everything over for a full evaluation, they skimped on what they gave the consultant, to keep study costs down.

That led to a narrow vision through which the consultant could only see what was directly in front of them, and it wasn't a pretty picture. It wasn't that the mine was exhausted of gold; it was just that the costs of mining and processing meant payback was unattractive to potential financiers, who looked for a minimum of a twenty-five percent return on investment. Hope Brook would never make that using tunnel vision, traditional mining methods, and an inexperienced owner.

All indications to the financiers in the know, as well as other mining companies familiar with the management and directors, showed that Quest was out of money. They were simply looking for a new owner to take on the property and the debt. Perhaps the next owner could make Hope Brook work, or just use it as a tax loss to provide personal income.

Finn and Erik had talked with Vince, their Toronto lawyer, before leaving from Puerto Banús. He had drawn up several purchase options for the takeover of Quest and had emailed them to Finn.

The preferred option was a simple enough proposal that comprised the purchase of shares held by the company officers amounting to fifty-eight percent of the outstanding stock at a price of four cents a share—half of their value on the exchange. That amounted to just over a million dollars to be paid in five tranches of two hundred thousand dollars per tranche over two years. It was a gutsy move, purposely intended to shock the major shareholders. But they were prepared to take on the debt as a part of the deal. That was the most attractive part of the offer, and one that would certainly get the attention of Quest's board.

Finn and Erik were prepared to negotiate, but their final offer would be no more than six cents per share, still with an initial payment of two hundred thousand dollars but with the balance payable over three years instead of two.

Once Finn and Erik settled into their hotel in Vancouver, they met with the GREY group and sat with Gerry, Rick, Ernie, and Yanko around a conference table two floors below their room. Gerry had brought his laptop, rented a screen from the hotel, and put the latest figures for the Hope Brook mine on display.

It didn't take a genius to see from the presentation the seven hundred and fifty thousand ounces of gold waiting to be mined. It would mean about 2.4 million tons of ore would have to be moved because the gold represented only 0.3 ounces of each ton mined. Not bad by industry standards these days, but still a lot to consider by the methods Finn and Erik were planning. They wanted to barge all the ore to be processed elsewhere, and the last thing they wanted was to barge waste rock—or, at the very least, the smallest amount possible.

The crux of the matter to Finn and Erik was the degree of certainty GREY attached to the reporting over some thirty years of exploration and reporting. The major plus in all this was that the original explorer was still one of the major mining companies, which concluded the high worth of the mine but discarded it only because it was too small to fit with their portfolio of major properties around the world. They weren't underground miners and preferred the large, open-pit prospects.

The answer from GREY was loud and clear. They had a high confidence level in the quantity and quality of gold remaining underground. The question now was whether there were consistent runs of high-grade that could be extracted without having to move huge volumes of waste rock.

It was Gerry who answered.

"There is about one million tons available from the, let's say, low-hanging gold. The veins are quite wide, and about 0.8 ounces per ton—or about eight hundred thousand ounces. You can do the math on that, but if you can mine it at about six thousand tons per day, with absolutely minimal waste, you could campaign it over about a hundred and seventy days—or, say six months—and keep stockpiling it near the barge landing site while you go back and forth to the refinery."

There was a pause for his clients to take in the numbers.

"That would slow things down some. It takes about forty days for a return cycle for each barge if you use Rio Narcea—meaning around a hundred and seventy barge trips, depending on how much you load into them and what capacity the refinery can take. As far as we know, you can't take it to Baie Verte, up in northern Newfoundland, again. If you thought it was too small before, there's no way it can handle the load from Hope Brook.

"The good thing is the higher value veins are quite continuous and you could drive several small tunnels with side drifts and that would be it. I don't know how the original owners didn't figure that out, but then they had their own low-hanging fruit to go for, I guess." Gerry took a breath. Finn and Erik looked him over as though trying to decide if he was telling the truth, and if he was, how technically reliable he was. But in the end, they were satisfied with what he was saying.

Now was not the time to dwell on the negativity. GREY had had enough time to do the research and had apparently concluded that the other four previous owners had not discovered the key to the mine. If only they had done a deep dive into the archives. But they hadn't. It was a story Finn and Erik found to be common among junior miners, in particular, who were short on money and thin on motivation and knowledge. Most worked to just get themselves paid through sporadic stock sales.

Once the GREY people had left, Finn and Erik sat back, pulled out their laptops, and started to plug numbers into a spreadsheet.

"Too bad about Baie Verte," Finn said absently as he kept entering numbers.

"Yeah, it would have been really good to just have to barge the ore around the west side of Newfoundland and up to the plant, but we knew it couldn't last without a substantial plant retrofit." They carried on with their calculations and put the Baie Verte news to the back of their minds.

The one million tons of most easily available high-grade gold ore would be worth about one and a half billion dollars at nineteen hundred dollars per ounce of gold. The historical information they had accumulated from other projects told them what the escalated costs for mining, freight, and offshore processing cost could be, as an order of magnitude. If they focused on just the higher-grade, they could well achieve a profit in the order of $1.2 billion. As for the payments to Quest, well, after the initial payment, they would of course stop paying. By the time they had mined out and shipped the ore, they would know whether to continue mining the slightly lower grade ore or stop, get out, and move on to the next "client." Any additional ore they mined would be just cream on the cake—but not worth any risk at all.

* * *

Finn and Erik had been in Vancouver now for six days. Most of that time had been spent either on the phone with Vince Taylor, their lawyers, or over at GREY. They were fine-tuning their thinking, and querying Gerry in particular about the potential to process some of the ore at site using the existing facilities. He was the metallurgist in the group. But Gerry soon talked them out of that.

It didn't take much convincing, but they just wanted to be sure they had asked the right questions. The equipment was beaten up, the mill had been run eccentrically and was wearing out the bearings, the plant had not been cleaned out when the original owners had left, so all the piping and equipment was still plugged with slurry, and none of the motors had been turned now for some fifteen years, so flat spots would be a problem to deal with on the shafts. No, it was better to ignore the existing facilities altogether. It would cost a fortune to replace it and years to construct. There was no way the Danes intended to do that.

The best strategy was to ship the minimum amount of gold-rich ore off-site, which was the answer they were looking for. After a few more deliberations, everyone agreed.

Neither Gerry nor his associates at GREY knew about the skulduggery intended by Finn and Erik. So, they went along, naively believing it was all a legitimate business deal that required all their technical know-how—and that's what they gave.

Finn and Erik were happy with their plan and Vince had arranged for a meeting with Paul Mah, the president of Quest at eleven a.m. the following Monday morning at his office in downtown Vancouver. He had outlined a brief, albeit deceptive, description of why they were interested in pursuing Quest. Mah seemed effusive, hoping they were real financially interested parties rather than the scam artists Matthew suggested. But, of course, they were just that.

On the morning of the meeting, Mah met Finn and Erik with a limp handshake, a scrawny mustache that just managed to hang on to his upper lip, and a trace of Asian heritage in his smooth face. He wore an ill-fitting suit that seemed to scream, "I'm all done." His tie was twisted, his shoes were scuffed, and he presented the perfect picture of a person in desperate need.

Finn and Erik, on the other hand, were dressed as typical New York brokers. Strong handshakes, deceptively warm smiles, impeccable manners, manicured fingernails, and suits to match. The only things missing were ties—they didn't want to intimidate Mah, who they knew was somewhat broke.

Mah took them into the company boardroom. It sadly lacked any illustration of success, but did have a white board screwed to the end wall with some felt pens hanging on strings next to it, and an aerial view of the Hope Brook property. Mah constantly smoothed his straight black hair away from his face and looked furtively from one face to the other as he tried to guess what was coming.

"Gentlemen. Thank you for coming. You probably know a lot about us already." Mah looked from Finn to Erik in case either of them wanted some additional information. They didn't appear to. "We could be open to a partnership or just straight financing. I think you are aware of the potential value of the Hope Brook mine, and I trust whatever you are considering takes that value into account."

Mah paused and waited for a response. He looked nervous, and rightly so. The property had not been well researched by any of the previous owners, and Quest was no exception. Mah only knew it had potential, but that's all it was.

It was Finn. "I think we know all there is to know, Mr. Mah. Not much, but enough for us to consider this property as a part of our investment portfolio. We are not interested in a partnership."

"Okay." Mah seemed encouraged, although wary. "Do you have something in mind?"

"Well, both you and I know Quest is going nowhere with this property." Finn didn't pull any punches, but then, he never did. "You don't have the money, or the resources, to improve the prospect further. From what we can tell from the records, there is nothing suggesting there is any guaranteed viability with the mine." He paused as he lied, lowered his head a little, raised his eyebrows, and looked over at Mah. "You know this, don't you?"

"Well, there is a lot of potential there," Mah said almost apologetically. "All we need is the financing to do more exploratory work." He looked up nervously. He knew the property was not commercially attractive with the current plan; otherwise, the share price would be much higher. He couldn't afford to issue more stock and reduce the share price further. No one other than gamblers would be interested in a share price at eight cents, let alone less.

"I don't think we're interested in sinking more money into the property and leaving it in your hands, I'm afraid, Mr. Mah. No, no. That wouldn't do." Finn looked over at Erik, who grimaced and shook his head.

"So, what do you propose?" Mah looked dejected as he realized this was, perhaps, the moment when his curtain would fall.

"We have a proposal for you, Mr. Mah. Hopefully, you will realize it may be your only way out of this mess. Let's say we meet again in forty-eight hours to see where we are, shall we?" There was a touch of theatrics as Finn laid an envelope on the table and pushed it slowly toward Mah. "Please—take a serious look." Finn and Erik got up from their chairs, stared at Mah, and walked toward the door.

* * *

Working With Rogues

Mah led Finn and Erik to the lobby door of his offices and out to the elevators. He shook their hands politely, pressed the elevator button, and ushered them in as the door slid open to an empty car. The door closed slowly, and Mah watched the floor numbers reducing as the elevator went down to ground. He turned, went back into the office, and locked the door behind him.

Matthew was waiting in the doorway of Mah's office at the end of the corridor. They disappeared inside and closed the door.

"I think we managed to record everything we need. They baited the hook and threw it in the pond. Now they'll wait for your response over the next couple of days, so we need to be prepared." Matthew paused and looked up at Mah. "Are you okay? Are you up to this?"

"I'm okay, I guess." Mah looked nervous.

"Hey, look, it's better to know who these guys are and what they're up to; otherwise, you'd end up on the dead end of a deal that isn't really a deal. Understand?" Matthew tried to sound empathetic, but at the same time, business was business, and his job was to ferret Finn and Erik out and figure out where the money was going.

"Nah. I'm okay. I was just thinking this could've been my easy way out of here, but then I remember it's all a scam." Mah slumped down in a chair.

"Look. It's not all bad. Let's face it, if they buy down the debt, make an offer you could live with, scam or not, then we just need to do our part to expose them, and you get your money back with no debt attached. Voilà." Matthew smiled and held his arms up in a gesture of success.

"Now, here's what you do." Matthew sat next to Mah, a glass of water in one hand, a pen in the other, and a plain piece of paper on the tabletop between them. "Meet with the board in the morning." Matthew wrote the first item on the paper and continued to make a list. "Lay out the offer and the terms. Accentuate the debt transfer. Push for six cents a share. Two hundred thousand dollars up front as an act of good faith. Another three hundred thousand on signing. The rest spread over three years. And don't forget, debt transfer." The list was complete. "Tell them this has to happen. You may not get all that, but you have to close a deal of some kind. The fact you're even considering their offer will send a signal as to how serious Quest is. Good?" Matthew watched Mah's face as he stared intently at the list.

"Yeah. Okay, I get it." Mah sounded determined as he considered what needed to be done with his company. "Where do you think things will end up?" He was still a little stunned by all that was happening, which was a lot more than had happened with the company for quite some time.

"Well, we think they'll likely negotiate and settle on five cents, but you need to push for the terms. If you're all going to get out of Quest, at least leave with some cash." Matthew paused and waited for Mah, but he went quiet and was clearly thinking about his options. "What do you think the board will do?"

"I think they'll go along with it. They just want to get out and get on with their other interests. Quest is going nowhere for them, and they know it. If we don't go for this opportunity, the next move would be to reduce the board to a bare minimum, and each of us would take on a management role. It wouldn't be a good place for anyone to work. If needed, we would declare bankruptcy, and there's always someone out there ready to take on something like this, even for tax breaks and government loans." Mah continued to stare at his hands, but then he smiled. "Let's just get on and do this." He smiled and smacked the table with both hands.

* * *

The board of directors didn't need much convincing to go along with the sale, although the details of what the Danes or ORB were planning were kept from them. The board were, however, very vocal in their support of the up-front payment Mah had proposed as well as the debt transfer. They didn't want to wash their hands of Quest without something to show for it right away. After all, the deal was going to be based on a value below the current stock price. Sure, the other shareholders wouldn't be happy, but most were very small gambler investors who spread their money all over the industry. And, who knew, maybe the reduced stock value would increase dramatically if the property was in the hands of some other company?

* * *

Mah led Finn and Erik back into his boardroom two days after their initial meeting. There were the usual pleasantries, coffees all round, and a lot of smiling and hand waving before things settled down to the business at hand.

"Well,"—it was Finn who turned the discussion to what they really wanted to know— "have you come to a decision, Mr. Mah?" Finn had a strange way of using the formal method of addressing people when there was a serious business matter being discussed. "I think our offer was fair and matches the real value of the Quest shares you and your board hold, don't you think?" He looked at Erik and over to Mah, an exaggerated smile on his face. "Well?"

Over the last two days, Mah had been talking back and forth with Matthew as he absorbed the positive energy and got himself ready to respond to Finn. He had reconciled the situation; his directors supported him and now it was time to move on.

"We've considered your proposal." Mah paused and looked over at Finn and then to Erik and back again. "We think there is a deal to be done, but not on the terms you proposed."

"Oh, and what terms would you propose, Mr. Mah?" There it was again. The formality with a touch of sarcasm.

"Six cents, two hundred thousand up front as a good-will gesture payable within one week from now. Three hundred thousand when the final transfer papers are signed, and the balance of $1.2 million payable in equal annual amounts over three years from the date of signing." Mah looked Finn in the eyes to show his resolve. "And, of course, the debt transfer."

Finn shrugged. "Okay. Okay. So, you've thought about this a lot, and this is what the board thinks its share of the company is worth. Am I right, Mr. Mah?" Finn continued to look Mah in the eyes, and both held fast.

"I do. Yes, I do." That was all Mah had to say.

"It seems to me our offer has been rejected, then. Is that so?" Finn stated the obvious as he was thinking.

"It is. Yes, it is. But then, you expected that, didn't you?" Mah sounded terse.

"Yes, I did." It was Finn's turn to be short. There was an awkward pause as both considered the situation.

"Okay. Okay. Perhaps there is some room to move, Mr. Mah. What would you say to six cents and the same payment terms as in our proposal?" Finn didn't waste time on asking for a break to consider the counteroffer. He just wanted to get on with business.

"No, Finn. But we are prepared to move to five cents with our payment terms for the balance." Mah sounded firm and persistent, and both Finn and Erik took note. Now Finn asked for a thirty-minute break.

"Of course. I'm going nowhere for the next hour." Mah looked at his watch.

"Good, good. We'll be in the café opposite." Finn waved a hand in the general direction of the outside of the building, although totally opposite to where he was referring. Mah just shrugged and didn't get up to see them out. They knew the way.

* * *

Finn and Erik wandered back into Mah's office forty minutes later and strolled into the conference room. Mah was sitting in the same chair as he had been when they left. He was engrossed in something on his phone. It was a game, and he was playing it as well, but they didn't know that. He looked up as they sat down. There was an air of dismissiveness about him—or so they thought.

"Okay, okay." Finn was getting irritated, although he was really just faking it, for appearance's sake. "You drive a hard bargain, Mr. Mah, but I think we can get this done. Five cents and your terms for the balance. As soon as you provide us an LOI—a letter of intent, I mean—we'll write a check for two hundred thousand. The moment we sign the final agreement, and it must be within a month, we'll write you another check for three hundred thousand. The next time we pay will be in one year's time, from the time we sign the agreement, for an amount of three hundred thousand; then the same the following year, and three hundred and fifty thousand on the third anniversary. We will assume the debt immediately upon signing of the LOI. Do we have a deal?"

Mah slowly got out of his chair and walked around the table to where Finn and Erik still stood.

"I'll have the LOI ready by two tomorrow afternoon. Come back then with a check for the first two hundred thousand and we will sign the deal." He didn't smile. He just held his hand out to shake theirs.

"That's a little tight, Mr. Mah..." Finn was about to make an excuse for not getting the money on time, but he was pre-empted by Mah.

"I am sure you will find a way, gentlemen." Mah sounded confident. "After all, it seems you are in a hurry to get this all finished, so..." It was his turn to just drift off.

"Yes, you're right. We'll be here at two tomorrow." Finn and Erik stared at Mah, then turned and left. Mah didn't show them out this time, either.

* * *

"Roman. Roman, are you there?" Finn put a call in to Kerimov as soon as they had left Quest and were standing in a discreet corner of the lobby, well away from any foot traffic.

"Yes, I'm here, Finn. What do you have?" Kerimov sounded as though he was on one of the phones on his boat. Finn could just make out the quiet throb of the engines.

"We have a deal with Quest, but you have to wire us two hundred thousand overnight. We'll sign the letter of intent tomorrow afternoon, and the company will be ours." Finn sounded more excited than usual, but perhaps it was because a new venture was moving to the next step. There was a lot to do.

"I'll have the money wired to the same bank as last time." Kerimov didn't need any time to think about the request. "It'll be there in the morning and then I'll call my friends to arrange for them to loan us the funds we need for this project."

Kerimov didn't seem to be interested in the details of the Quest deal, only the fact it was done. After all, he had no intention of paying Quest any more money, regardless of the agreement. And as for the debt he was supposed to take on—well, forget that. Once the gold had been taken from Hope Brook, the company Kerimov invented for the takeover of Quest would declare bankruptcy.

Kerimov was going to be the controlling shareholder of Quest the day after the signing of the LOI and the Danes were going to have to drive the company until they could fill a few of the spots with their own people. There would be an interim CEO established in place of Mah to take care of the day-to-day business, but Quest would be essentially neutralized. Kerimov wasn't going to buy out the other shareholders, either. They were just going to have to be the victims of the venture when what remained of the mine was totally devoid of easy gold. Such was life in the world of business criminals.

* * *

Phase 2 – The Plan

It had only been a few weeks since the last ORB meeting in London, but Matthew wanted the team to get together again. This time, each of the group would have more of the story to tell that would help Matthew bring his strategy into better focus.

Matthew had met with Stockman the evening before, when they dined at Fumo's, one of the San Carlo Group's Italian restaurants in Covent Garden, not far from the Club Quarters Hotel where they had all met together previously. They were there to discuss Matthew's thoughts for moving forward. Additionally, from past experience, he knew there was always some kind of backstory with Stockman involved in a project, and while Matthew rarely knew what it was, his plans would need to be aligned with any specifics Stockman might need to bring to the table.

"Anything I need to know before we meet with the team?" Matthew opened the conversation as they settled themselves into a corner booth at Fumo's.

"I don't know if this is anything we should be concerned with, but it seems the Danes have been quite the pair over the last ten years or so." Stockman ordered a Caol Ila single malt, straight.

Matthew nodded as the waiter held up two fingers while his facial expression was asking whether Matthew wanted one as well. He flicked his eyes to say "yes," and the waiter nodded his understanding and disappeared to the bar.

"Oh, do tell." Matthew looked smug as he settled back to listen to his friend. *Here it comes*, he thought. There was always a trove of interesting stories Stockman had in his arsenal of tales, usually as asides to the project they were working on as he dug into his research and trove of personal knowledge.

"Before their very recent activities," Stockman started with a wicked smile on his face, "it seems the Danes once operated an investment company purposely designed to steal mines from the equity investors as a business strategy." He raised his eyebrows and curled his lips down as he watched Matthew take the bait and lean forward to hear more.

"They invested in, or acquired, what we call distressed assets and companies, including several publicly traded companies we know of. In most instances, they funded, and sometimes over-funded, companies ultimately beyond their repayment ability, forcing the companies into bankruptcy where, in many instances, the Danes would submit an offer to acquire the assets."

It was Stockman's turn to look smug as he picked up his whiskey, sniffed at it, rolled the amber liquid around the bottom of his glass between thumb and forefinger, and took a sip. He paused for the moment and sighed with satisfaction and appreciation.

"How did they manage to influence the directors?" Matthew was a little taken aback by what he was hearing.

"They used associates with undisclosed connections to them, who were placed on boards of directors and positions of authority and used those positions to assist in the death spirals of the companies. They also purposely vended the assets into an LLC, which has no disclosure obligations, while they, shall I say, sterilized corporate records." Stockman stopped, picked up his menu, and tried to focus on the two pages of appetizers, *primis*, and *secondis*, while Matthew sat with his brain working overtime and limply holding his menu in both hands.

"Okay, what do you think we should do with that knowledge—anything?" Matthew couldn't quite focus on the menu.

"At this point—nothing." Stockman looked over at Matthew as they both considered the menu. "What are you having?" he asked, as though he had been just chatting about nothing in particular.

Matthew shrugged and stared at the menu. "I think all it does is confirm we're dealing with criminals"—he was ignoring Stockman's question about the menu— "not just scoundrels, and we need to somehow dispose of them once we get what we need—don't you think?"

Stockman was quite matter of fact as he glanced at the waiter who had stealthily appeared at his side and ordered the catch of the day with no appetizer and only a side dish of cold kale with a smattering of olive oil, a pinch of garlic, and the juice of a quarter fresh lemon—nothing special. The waiter nodded, jotted his note, and looked to Matthew.

"I'll have the same, *grazie*." He held the menu out to be taken and put his elbows on the table. He was relieved not to have to waste time searching the menu. All he wanted was to hear where Stockman's story might take them. "Anything else?" Matthew didn't expect an encore, but Stockman wasn't going to let it go at that.

"Since you ask, let me tell you about the even earlier shenanigans of the Danes, back when they were spreading their wings with the mid-size miners and pulling some pretty crazy stuff. "

"I'm all ears." Matthew was beginning to enjoy himself as he learned more about the people he would be dealing with.

"As their strategy evolved, one of their early ventures involved an opportunity to take over a mine by driving it into bankruptcy. They pushed it along by purposefully suppressing the value of the property to support their submissions to the bankruptcy court that the mine could not turn a profit—and they were prepared to buy it out at a fair but discounted price since, as they put it, no one else would be interested in it. The court agreed and so the Danes had their first taste of blood." Stockman stopped, took another sip of his Scotch, and watched the bewildered face of Matthew.

"Okay, so how did they suppress the value and hide it from the court?" Matthew wondered.

"Ahh, the truth eventually came out when one of the new plant operators got loose-lipped at the local bar where most of the off-shift personnel visited. As it happened, two of the original mine owners who still lived in town were sat together at the bar next to the loose-lipped guy." Stockman looked at Matthew with a devilish look in his eyes, as though he was the bad guy in the tale.

"The story goes that once the Danes got seats on the board and placed some of their own people in operational management positions, they had them continuously return the gold from the carbon processing circuit directly back to the holding pond and just let it accumulate there. They didn't process it all the way through the plant, you see. Instead, they managed to keep recirculating it through the pond, even as it picked up more and more gold in the process and hid something like fifty million dollars there while they filed for bankruptcy, claiming the plant was incapable of working properly.

"Once the sale was complete, they started to take the gold out of the pond and send it out for processing at another plant." Stockman paused as his food was placed in front of him and waited for the waiter to finish his work at the table before he carried on.

"As far as we know, they repeated the same kind of fraud quite a number of times before they turned to what we believe is their current line of work, so to speak. That is, still getting control of companies but trumping up gold production plans, seducing capital loans, and raising stock cash only to turn around and whisk the gold-rich ore off to process elsewhere. All the while, they pocketed the money that had been raised to build full-scale production facilities—that never happened.

"Genius work if you can get away with it!" Stockman tucked into the red snapper and made appreciative sounds as he sampled the spinach.

"I think you're right, my friend. We need to get rid of them." Matthew forked some fish into his mouth, while looking at Stockman as both sets of eyebrows raised, and from that look, they knew they agreed.

* * *

Matthew opened the meeting. "Thanks, everyone, for coming on such short notice."

This time it was attended by all eight major ORB players in the project. Each had made their own way to the same venue as previous in London after a simple call to regroup from Matthew just a few days before. All other arrangements were left in their hands. Stockman had driven up from southwest England; Matthew and Emma flew in from Vancouver; Plato arrived from Athens; Colin had driven across from his farm on the border with Wales; Mitch flew in from St. John's; Tom was already in London, and James drove up from Southampton. Only the lawyers were absent, although Tony was on the conference line just in case he was needed.

"Let's get down to business." Matthew considered the expectant faces before him. "I want us all to leave here with the framework of a plan. It can't be as comprehensive as we may like, but we'll flesh it out as you all get more details and feed them back to me." He paused in case there were questions. There weren't.

"At this point, we understand the Danes planted a story on Emma that suggested they had changed venues and were going to delay any work until next year. Now, that came from the owner of CanMine, Big Jim Garland." Matthew paused to look around the room. "I happen to know from the same source that it was just a story. Probably deliberately put out to confuse us if they believe ORB is somehow in the picture. He tells me they are gearing up to make a start fairly soon." He looked over at Emma who just looked at him quizzically.

"Let's start with you, Emma. What do you know that perhaps we don't know already?" Matthew sat back and sipped at his coffee as Emma stood and walked the room.

"From what Big Jim Garland told me before he went dark, and as Matthew said, he thought Hope Brook was off the table and they were headed in another direction. But it seems now that isn't the case." She spoke thoughtfully and carefully. "I can only tell you what he told me, and now he's not telling me anything. Ever since we got back to Vancouver, he's been avoiding me. That means Matthew has the latest from him."

"From what I can tell, Big Jim has gone cold as a contact for me." Emma looked down at the table and shook her head. "Maybe he has no interest in pursuing my friendship, but I find that extremely odd." Emma's face gave her "disappointment" away. "Also, I'm pretty sure I have, or had, a tail on me." She looked at her audience as eyebrows raised. "I thought someone was following me in Puerto Banús, and then in Vancouver. I had a sweep of my apartment for listening devices, and they found the brooch Kerimov gave me when I met him in Puerto Banús, as well as a GPS disc on the underside of my car. I assume they did the same in Puerto Banús. So, we know they know who I am and that I'm involved in some kind of move against them. I would suggest each of you have a sweep done." Emma paused. The team members nodded.

"Good idea, Emma. Thanks. I guess that might answer the question we would have about why they were supposedly changing plans. They must have realized someone was on to them. Anything else?" It was Matthew.

"Well, without Big Jim on a string, I can't get anything else, so I'm available." Emma's eyebrows went up as she looked at the others.

"Oh, I'm sure there are going to be a number of things to keep you occupied, not least of which will be included in the framework I'm going to lay out in a little while." Matthew winked at Emma. "Do you think you gave anything away while they were listening or following?"

"Well, there was that conversation you and I had when I got back to my hotel after the meeting on the boat with the Danes." Emma looked at Matthew and they both squirmed as they remembered.

"Do you recall what we talked about?" It was Matthew.

"I told you Kerimov had met my father before." Emma squirmed a little more. "But he didn't let on if he knew Stockman was an ORB person, not that I know if he knows who, or what, ORB is. They also know Big Jim and I talk—or did talk, I should say. Oh, and we talked about the fact that neither Big Jim nor I knew where Kerimov was getting the funding, nor how Finn and Erik intended to get ownership of the Quest property."

Emma waited for Matthew, who was deep in thought.

"Oh, and they also know you made a visit to Greenland." Emma stopped and put her hands on the back of a chair as she waited for Matthew's response, and likely from Stockman. Their eyes were popping out as they stared at her and wondered whether there was anything else. "I think that's it." Emma shrugged. "Now what?"

"Well," Matthew puffed his cheeks and blew the air slowly out of his mouth. "I guess the cat's out of the bag." He looked down at the floor. "Kerimov knows who you are"—he looked up at Emma— "he knows Stockman, he knows you talk to Big Jim, he knows you're interested in where he's getting his financing, and he knows we were in Greenland. I'm sure he's figured out why that would be." Matthew paused and caught Stockman's eye. They both looked grim at the news from Emma.

"I think that all adds up to him knowing a lot more than I had hoped. But now that's done, let's expect this guy Kerimov will connect your father to ORB, and when he does, I'm sure he'll realize we're watching him." Matthew believed Big Jim had probably been pressed by Kerimov to pass on incorrect information on the project changes. But he didn't dwell on it just yet. Perhaps James could help.

"We have to assume they're on to us." Stockman stood and walked around the table. "The facts are there and I'm sure he has contacts who can educate him about ORB and my involvement. The question now is whether they will move forward, select an alternative location, or abandon everything."

"We need to carry on and assume they haven't figured it all out just yet. The fact is they have no idea what our plans are, and my guess is they're too greedy to give this opportunity up. Of course, they may change projects, but it's a chance we have to take." Matthew looked over at Stockman.

"I agree." Stockman walked over to his chair and plonked down. "I'll contact Yanko and see if he has any indication of a change in their target priorities."

Matthew nodded in agreement.

"And I'll keep trying to make contact with Big Jim in case he drops his guard and starts talking." Emma sat down.

"Good idea," was all Matthew could think of saying to her. A few moments went by before he seemed to pull himself together.

"Your turn, Mitch." Matthew turned to look at his friend.

"Matthew and I visited Greenland." Mitch remained sitting as he addressed the group. "We met the premier, then we went to the scene of the crime, so to speak. I think we confirmed what we all know, including how they executed the work. Naturally, there are no signs they were ever there, except for the missing ore and the additional environmental mess. A new owner has just started some prelim work. They seem pretty reputable, but I think I'll check them out before I commit that to paper." Mitch stopped and smiled. "You never know." He shrugged. There were a few laughs in the room.

"I'll fill all of you in on our meeting with the premier in my notes filed to the server. There's no point in rehashing here unless someone wants me to." Matthew looked around, but no one seemed anxious to hear all the details.

"We also went to Newfoundland and looked at the lay of the land," Mitch carried on. "It's much the same as the Greenland site, and we're pretty sure the Danes will put on a repeat performance if they stick to the original plan for Hope Brook and barge the ore out. Other than that, there's nothing much to report. I'm going to look over the mining reports for Hope Brook next and try to figure out how they'll mine this one out." Mitch stopped.

"Oh, and one last thing. With James on the CanMine payroll, he knows to stay in touch with me as his first point of contact when it comes to the actual work." Mitch pointed over to James, who silently acknowledged the mention of his name with a wave all around. "I'll let James introduce himself, but he was with the team on the Iranian caper, so he knows who we are." Mitch smiled at James.

Matthew nodded. "That sounds good, Mitch. Any questions from anyone?" Heads shook all round.

"Great. Tom, would you fill us in on what you have?" All eyes were on Tom. He didn't get up from his chair and just stared at the notes in front of him.

"I did a little research," Tom started as he thumbed through his notes and looked up, "and contacted a blast from my past who's working at the Rio Narcea operation. That's where the Danes took the ore from Greenland for processing after they had to abort their initial plan to use the plant on the north coast of Newfoundland. That plant just didn't have the horsepower to process the amount of ore being sent to them. An old associate of mine confirmed the three barges belonging to the Danes are still moored in the Aviles estuary in northern Spain, the last time he heard." Tom looked around then continued.

"I asked him whether there were any communications with plant operations about another substantial contract shipment for processing, and he confirmed there was, although he couldn't give me the timing right now. They're still waiting to hear when it's going to happen." Tom gestured with his hands as though to say, "That's about it."

"Thanks, Tom. I think you had better get over to the Aviles site and get your sights set on those barges and be ready if there's any activity. Regardless of which property the Danes pick, those barges are going to be the first things to move in." Matthew caught Tom's eye before he had a chance to take another sip of his coffee. "Do you know if the tug is there as well, Tom?"

"Not sure. I only asked my contact about the barges. I assumed the tug was a lease, but I could be wrong, and if that's the case, it wouldn't be there until they need it." Tom grimaced with his response and turned his hands down on to the table.

"You can check it out when you get there." Matthew paused as he looked around at the faces. "Okay, James, any comments?"

"Not really. Just getting settled into the office. Big Jim is using me for logistics for now, so that means the movement of mining manpower and equipment. I'm responsible for getting all the materials needed for the job as well as everything for the camp. There are also a couple of projects wrapping up, and he's using me on them." James was quite comfortable in the ORB surroundings, having met some of the people before, including Matthew, Emma, and Plato. They had worked together in northern Iran.

"Are you able to confirm any project changes, James?" Matthew's question was to the point and probably the most important question raised at the meeting.

James thought for a few seconds, rubbed his chin, scratched his head with one hand, and responded. "Well,"—he pulled at one of his ears— "from all the sudden movement that's happening, it seems CanMine are really moving forward right now. That supports what Matthew has been telling us, and what Emma was told was just bullshit."

There was quiet in the room. Matthew looked over at Emma, who pouted at the attempted deception by the Big Jim.

"Can you get closer to Big Jim, or perhaps the CanMine person who organizes the equipment, and try to get some exact dates? Also, if what we were told about the location was also BS? This is really important to us, of course." Matthew was hoping James could establish the identity of the new target as soon as possible. A lot was riding on it.

"Okay, James. Let's hope you get stationed at the site." Matthew's brow was furrowed as he was thinking.

"You bet. I'll be one of the first people on site. The plans seem to be in a state of flux right now, given what I understand of the latest timeline, but they'll come together so we can mobilize as quickly as possible when the time comes. Big Jim seems to be an easy guy to work with and seems to appreciate you sending me his way, Matthew."

"That's good. Keep in touch with Mitch on day-to-day things but plug me in as soon as things start to happen." Matthew strolled over to get coffee. "Oh, James, do me a favor and find out about gold processing facilities in Newfoundland. It seems a very likely spot for our targets to want to take the ore. That's where they processed it for at least a short period when they were raping Greenland. But I don't know what made them change to northern

Spain." Matthew nodded at James.

James was quick to respond. "Oh, I already know about that, Matthew."

Matthew looked at him wide-eyed, and even Stockman looked surprised. "And?" was all Matthew could say.

"And… they can't use the plant in Newfoundland… not big enough. I guess that was their problem the last time. The plant is too small to handle the load the Danes wanted to put through it on a daily basis, and it costs too much to upgrade it to increase throughput." James' mouth turned down and his eyebrows went up. He shrugged.

"Wow. I guess we should have known that before. After all, they did abandon the idea during the Greenland activity. One day they were taking their product there, and the next day it was heading to Rio Narcea. I would think it would have made some news somewhere. Where did you hear it, James?" Matthew wondered.

"Big Jim. He was talking to a couple of the guys in the canteen, and the subject came up. No one was interested, but I found the information interesting enough that I did a little research and read about the Nugget Pond facility, just for my own education. That's the name of the plant they used in Newfoundland. And here we are." James had a big grin on his face.

"Great job, James. Saves us a lot of guesswork, and now we can focus on Aviles and the Rio Narcea processing option." Matthew turned toward Tom, who put two thumbs up.

"Okay, thanks, James. Your turn, Plato." Matthew turned to face his friend—the money man, as Stockman called him.

Plato nodded to Colin as though to get his approval to speak on behalf of them both. Colin smiled and shrugged.

"Colin and I have been working on the financial trail of this fellow, Kerimov, although we haven't got very far right now. Like all Russian oligarchs, his money is likely spread all over the place, including through dummy companies and bank accounts. Our first step is to separate his Polygold dealings from his personal finances, and I think we have that just about sorted. The Polygold finances are somewhat more transparent since they are listed on a few international stock exchanges and file annual reports, so I very much doubt they are involved in any shenanigans as a company. I think we are almost ready to focus on Kerimov over the next week or so." Plato glanced at Colin, who nodded his agreement.

"As for the Danes, Matthew has dispatched some people to Puerto Banús to keep their eyes on them whenever they're around, and they seem to be there most of the time." Plato paused. "Maybe we'll catch them going to a bank, or maybe we'll have to figure out a way to get into their personal files… just considering the options."

Matthew turned to Stockman. "Any comments so far, sir?"

"I think everything's going to plan, but we will have to assume James' senses are correct and their timeline has been brought forward, or should I say, is still the same as we thought originally. We also should continue with our focus on Hope Brook. It may be a risk, but we need to head in one direction or another, and my senses tell me that if they messed us around with the timeline, then they likely also did with the location." Stockman smiled, looked at his notes, and turned his head. "Plato, let me know as soon as you need those bank subpoenas. Matthew, I'm running down more information about this Kerimov. I remember him from way back, but I don't remember whether he played any kind of influential role in those days or who he worked for." Stockman stared at Matthew and gave a shrug.

"Great." Matthew got up and walked around the table as he was thinking and talking. "We need to understand the financing. Where the money goes and where the financing comes from. Plato, you and Colin are in the hot seat there. Let's get a grip on Kerimov and find out what his plans are to raise capital. It's likely going to lead us to another schmuck! Let's get ahead of it and see if we can redirect the money. We also need to know what proceeds he's made on these deals and get that money back. That goes for the Danes as well." Matthew paused, stopped circling the group, and sat down. "But we have to be on the ground. James, make sure we know every move CanMine makes. Mitch, I want you to figure out what we can do to delay mining by as much as we can once it gets going. Whether that means damaging the equipment or creating problems underground—no one gets killed.

"We need to drag everything out for as long as it takes to recoup the money and then get those Danes behind bars. That will take some messing with their shareholdings and the exchanges, but I'll have Tony working on some plans from a legal perspective. I want this done right and aboveboard, but at the same time, make it come as a shock to the Danes.

"Tom, I think we'll both go down to Aviles. We have to disable those barges and the tug. I don't want them all out at the same time; we'll string the problems out. I was thinking we could start by messing with the cathodic protection and do something like welding some stainless-steel anodes to replace the zincs and have the hulls corrode out over a few months. We only need to puncture a few holes for the barges to take on water. We could also mess with the props or engines, but that may be going overboard—so to speak."

They all chuckled at the pun.

"Let's also think about how to disable that tug." Matthew paused and watched the faces as they took it all in.

Matthew was going to use his expertise with welding to get the job done on the tug and the barges.

"We could place a couple of radio-controlled limpet mines on the tug rudders—I think there'll be two of them on the size of tug they're going to need—and blast them off by remote control if we need." Tom sat back, thinking over the details of what he'd suggested.

Matthew had a surprised but cruel smile on his face as he thought about the idea. "I like it, Tom. Can you get it organized for us, and we'll pick up the stuff we need once we're down in Aviles?" Matthew and Tom looked at each other and smiled. *Great idea* thought Matthew.

He turned to Emma.

"Emma, you're going after Kerimov. Once we get his money, he has to go; otherwise, he'll be back with a vengeance." Matthew paused, waiting for a reaction from either Emma or Stockman. Emma just shrugged, and Stockman just continued to watch Matthew. "We'll work on a plan together, Emma, and I'm sure Stockman will be able to help in keeping an eye on where Kerimov is all the time." Both Matthew and Emma glanced over at Stockman.

"We have eyes on his whereabouts permanently right now, so I'm sure we can all pitch in together to make sure we put a stop to his games when the time comes. Any thoughts, Matthew?" Stockman waited for a response.

"Well…" Matthew stood still with his hands on the back of one of the empty chairs. "As I said, we need Kerimov's money before we make our move.

I doubt the full extent of the financing will be made available at one time, so we can expect tranches to be wired based on a timetable. Perhaps James can help us get hold of some kind of schedule once he can confirm the start date." Matthew got a nod of understanding from James. "Once we get that, we can estimate when money might be transferred to pay for the project.

"Let's get into Kerimov's bank accounts as soon as we can and identify if any amounts were deposited from previous projects, and what comes in from the latest financing. We'll remove all of it and send it back to the people that were duped. Same for the Danes. Once all that happens and we stop the barging, we can lower the boom on all of them. Kerimov and the Danes should be neutralized by then. Any questions?" Matthew looked around the room.

"Any thoughts on how we get rid of Kerimov and neutralize the Danes?" It was Emma.

"We'll talk about Kerimov later, Emma, but I'm not talking about anything as drastic as killing him. We just want to take him out of this game and make sure he goes back to Russia.

"As for the Danes, I want to take their companies over and get rid of those two rogues. Once that's done, we'll put them on the streets, where they belong, or better, in jail. I'll work on it with Stockman, and our lawyers." Matthew stopped and looked around. "Everyone clear on what has to happen?"

There were nods and smiles.

"Emma, would you go back down to Puerto Banús and keep your eyes on the Danes with our other agents? Don't let the Danes see you and keep us up to date on any movements of their boat away from the marina. We'll put a satellite on it if they move." Matthew's juices were flowing.

Emma nodded her understanding of what was expected of her.

"Okay, everyone, let's keep communicating with each other. I'm going to hang around here for one more day if anyone wants to discuss their part of the plan. I would suggest you all do the same and take advantage of us all being in the same place at the same time." Matthew looked over at Stockman. "Supper?"

* * *

Ria de Aviles

Now that ORB had confirmed the fleet of three barges remained secured in the Aviles estuary, Matthew and Tom made their plans to sabotage them. ORB intel had reported that only a port night watchman had been patrolling the wharf, and sometimes he never made it far enough along the quay to the barges.

While there could still be a window of time available until the fleet was needed at Hope Brook, Matthew didn't want to wait until the last moment. No, he wanted a practice run to work out any kinks. Nothing was to be left to chance. Everything needed to be planned in detail, right down to the actual welding. In Matthew's opinion, they probably had three or four weeks, once CanMine mobilized, before the barges would have to leave for Newfoundland.

As soon as the Danes moved the fleet and CanMine mobilized, the first tranche of financing could be expected to be dispatched. Plato and Colin had to figure out how to access the funds and siphon the money from the accounts of the Danes and the Russian. It could take weeks or months to identify and access those accounts, and they continued to sift through the myriad of complexities associated with the twisted banking methods that were likely involved.

It was imperative that obstacles be put in the way of the Hope Brook progress to slow it down to give Plato and Colin the time they needed. It meant the barges had to spring leaks, the mine geology had to be manipulated, the tug had to be crippled, and only then could ORB finally move in to deal with the criminals. Nothing could stop the rogues unless their money was accessed.

Theoretically, sabotaging the barges was a simple exercise, but the cause was not to be easily traceable. Replacing the existing zinc anodes that protected the barges' rudders and hulls with stainless steel—a metal of lower electrical conductivity than the carbon steel to which they would be attached—would reverse the order of corrosion precedence. The sabotage would be relatively slow, undetectable, and crippling.

The carbon steel would start rusting out immediately, but after a few months, the rust would turn to layers of scale and gradually fall away, leaving pinholes in the carbon steel that would turn to larger holes. The rudders of the barges would eventually become less responsive, and the barges would take on water through their hulls, which were likely only half an inch thick. It was not clear how long the corrosion process would take, but Tom had estimated that problems could develop within three to six months if the hulls and rudders were constantly in contact with salt water—and they would be.

For the dummy run, they would grind, or knock off, several of the zinc anodes on one of the barges and replace them with stainless-steel plates, tack welded into position. It would give them an idea of the time they'd need for the complete exercise. But Matthew had already concluded he would need help, and while in London, he had contacted Sloan to request an underwater welder to help him.

The individual from Sloan would have to be proficient in hyperbaric welding stainless-steel plates to carbon steel using stick welding—in seawater, at night, and at a depth where one would have to use flashlights. There was no written procedure. The method depended entirely on the experience of the welders.

Sloan produced a well-experienced welder, Charlie Tripper, within a few days. Charlie was an expert welder above and below water and had been a submariner in the Royal Navy. He was fit, forty-five, single, tattooed, and had worked for Sloan for a number of years on a variety of projects. His current contract involved welding a large-diameter carbon steel gas line from Iran to Oman under the waters of the Gulf of Oman. He would travel with Matthew and Tom to Aviles.

Tom had arranged for a local procurement agency in Aviles to gather the materials they would need. The list included high-quality E309 sticks for the stainless to carbon weld filler, two welding machines, fuel, all the cables and wet gear, a thirty-foot-long black rubber dinghy for him to operate during the exercise, and all the personnel gear for diving. Everything they would need for the complete job, when the time came, would be bought now and stored in a building where Tom could acquire it close to where the work was to be undertaken.

This wouldn't be a difficult welding operation for proficient hyperbaric welders, since they were operating in only a few feet of water, albeit having to rely on lights. But that was a normal part of submerged work, especially when divers more often had to work at depth. The hull grinding was a secondary consideration as the welder worked his way to the next spot and stopped for the few seconds it needed to make contact between the grinder and the hull.

It would be a nighttime operation, with Tom skippering the dinghy to deliver the two welders to the side of the barges away from the quayside, lower the stainless plates to each welder, operate the welding machines on the boat deck, and feed the cables to the submerged hulls of the barges.

The dummy run should only take one night, two at the most, but from the practice, they would have a reasonable idea of how long the whole operation would take. It had been a source of critical conversation for them as they went back and forth, putting time estimates for all activities.

Each barge was about three hundred and fifty feet long, with an underwater surface area of something like thirty-five hundred square feet. Generally, anodes would represent about one to two percent of the surface area they were protecting, so each barge had at least forty square feet of zinc anode material—or twenty square feet per side. Ship anodes were more often small, manageable-sized plates—probably no more than twelve inches by twelve inches, or one square foot. That meant there were likely fifteen to twenty zinc plates on each side of a barge hull under the water. Each zinc would be attached to the hull with a bolted bracket or a tack weld, where only a fraction of two plate edges secured it. They would be easy to knock off with a percussion hammer.

Using these estimates for the ultimate exercise, once the project was a *go*, Charlie calculated it would take four hours per barge to knock off the zincs, eight hours to grind the carbon steel surfaces, and about sixteen hours to fit and tack weld the stainless plates into position. The zincs would be dropped to the floor of the estuary, and the stainless-steel plates lowered in groups of two from the dinghy winch. The estimated total number of hours to complete the task would be forty-two hours for each welder, not including some kind of contingency. Charlie added a day to each welder, making it a six-day job for each welder, assuming they could work six hours a day.

Without knowing how much time they would have before the barges left port, the test was imperative if they wanted to identify where they might shave some time off. Perhaps they needed one or two more divers, or they would have to stay underwater longer. On the other hand, maybe there were fewer zincs to be replaced. They would only know once they made the first dive.

* * *

"I think we're ready to go, sir." Matthew had put a call in to Stockman. "Everything's lined up. The only thing we aren't sure of yet is whether Hope Brook is still their target, but that won't stop us sabotaging their fleet."

"Yanko assures me there's no change of plan, Matthew. I just finished talking to him an hour ago. The Danes asked for the latest mine plan, and there was no mention of an alternative. That could be a ruse, of course, but they would need more information on another target if that was the way they were moving. I think we have to say ninety-nine percent sure to Hope Brook and go from there." Stockman paused.

"Agreed. If there happens to be a last-minute change, we'll just have to follow it, but the fact is we have everything just about ready to go, regardless of where they move."

"You're right, Matthew. Keep moving forward, and good luck in Aviles. I think Plato and Colin are having some luck on their end, although it sounds as though Kerimov's finances are going to be hard to crack—but we knew that coming in."

"If anyone can get into the accounts, it's Plato. Talk soon. I'd better get going."

"Good luck, Matthew."

Their call ended and Matthew put the last few things he needed for his trip into a carry-on for the flights and waited.

* * *

As soon as confirmation arrived that the materials were waiting in the procurement company's yard, Matthew, Tom, and Charlie headed to Aviles. Tom had arranged for the lease of a small building on the wharf and took the materials to lay them out on the floor. Matthew and Charlie examined everything, gave Tom a shortlist of more items needed, and set about trying on the wetsuits and fitting the oxygen tanks. Tom collected the dinghy from the procurement dock, fitted the outboard on the mounting, poured the diesel into the holding tank, and fired up the engine to test for noise and exhaust fumes. He added his own version of vibration dampening and exhaust muffling, using neoprene pads tied on with stainless-steel wire, and took the dinghy for a spin around the estuary. It was perfect for what they wanted. They hoisted it back into the building and closed the doors.

They spent most of the day loading the dinghy with their supplies and arranging the coils of hoisting rope to avoid tangling before heading back up to the Hotel Don Pedro, over on the west bank of the estuary.

First thing the next morning, they would take the dinghy out and scout the area close to the barges.

* * *

Matthew, Tom, and Charlie gathered in the small hotel restaurant early the next morning before heading out to the docks.

"Any questions so far?" Matthew looked around. There were none. "Okay, let's go."

They made their way back over to the dinghy, opened the end doors of the building, and pushed it out on a monorail. Once it was lowered into the water, the three climbed down and adjusted themselves in the boat. Tom fired up the outboard and steered across the estuary to the barges. There was no one around, but they kept their eyes open for any movement further away in case someone, or something, appeared coming toward them. The traffic in the estuary was relatively light, but they would still have to be careful in case their movements were spotted.

The three barges were strung out along the length of the quayside, making it easy for the dinghy to hide on the blind side from any eyes on the dock. There were no other boats tied immediately in front or behind the barges, and clearly, the tug hadn't arrived. It was probably too early in the program for that to happen. Matthew was happy with the reconnoiter, and they returned to the building, where they winched the dinghy back up and into the warehouse.

Matthew decided they would practice at night, just as they would have to operate when it came to the actual job. River traffic would be minimal, and they could hide themselves in the darkness of their own surroundings. Practicing in daylight with diving equipment would very likely raise alarms with nosy neighbors.

They were ready for the first dive that night.

Tom had purchased six battery-powered dive lights to Charlie's specifications. Each incorporated a toggle to change from a high-lumen narrow beam, which could focus on the work directly in front of the diver and pierce through the murky water, and a lower-lumen floodlight for swimming to and from the targets. The battery life was only sixty to seventy minutes at the higher lumen, which was what they would be using most of the time. Each diver would take two spare charged units on their dives. As one would lose its charge, it would be pulled to the surface, and Tom would recharge it. The lights were secured in a custom-made head harness. It was difficult working in murky water, and that was what they had to do in the Ria de Aviles, as it brought sediment down from higher elevations, so it was essential to have both hands free to move. Fortunately, there had been little rain over the past few weeks in northern Spain, so surface water run-off was minimal and the river volumes slower moving.

While they had been going over the plan for sabotaging the barges, Tom had also been thinking about how he could cripple the tug. He decided the best was for him to focus only on the rudders. He could have them blown off and render the boat useless without raising a lot of suspicion. After all, it could have hit partially submerged rocks around the shores of Newfoundland. In any event, after consulting with his naval friends, he decided to assemble a Clam Mine Mk. III fitted with a number 9 "L" Delay MK I Fuse. Once the pin was remotely activated by someone onshore, it would be three hours before detonation.

The clam mine was a marvelously simple piece of mechanics. It had a Bakelite casing, with a hollow steel "pin" pushed into it and secured by a steel clip. The pin included a lead break or string that would literally separate once it reached the pre-set temperature. It would release a tension spring with a striker that would hit a percussion cap and detonate the eight ounces of TNT/Tetryl 55/45 packed into the casing. The whole assembly weighed only half a pound and could be fitted to a steel surface with magnets. The unit could fit into the pocket of a windbreaker jacket. Tom decided to use two, one on each rudder, although one per rudder would probably be enough to do the job.

* * *

The Twist

Project Capital Wealth—or PCW, as it was generally referred to in the industry—was a successful but small private financial resource group based in Denver, Colorado. Over the last ten years, they had invested several billion dollars in mineral properties around the world on behalf of their clients, generally Midwestern businesses and individuals looking for rewards outside their normal area of expertise. PCW looked for prospects that flew under the radar of the larger, more commonly used, financial institutions, and trusted their luck and intuition more than any high technical appraisals to help in the selection process guiding their investments. It had seemed to pay dividends for them on eighty percent of the prospects they engaged in. Those failing to return value were primarily the victims of bad geology, changing governments at all levels, or force majeure events, including civil strife.

The PCW hierarchy was, more often than not, pugnacious, haughty, and cowboy-like in their dealings. After all, they invested money that mostly came from high-flying landowners, who still had the cavalier attitude of the early pioneers, gambling for their future. Sure, they wanted good returns, but they knew that didn't come without risk. They preferred high risk and high rewards.

Russ Partwick was one of three managing partners of PCW. He was the most senior, and whatever he put his hand on, the rest followed. He rarely failed. His specific geographical area of responsibility included mining in the Americas. There wasn't anything of interest there that escaped his attention. He had ears to the ground all over, from bona-fide mining companies to sellers of "confidential information." That information could be concerned with the private lives of the controllers of mining companies, to the latest information on mineral assay work that was not released to the public, to the possible responses to environmental applications that were, theoretically, still months away from publication.

Partwick, a nondescript, medium-height, medium-build, curly ginger-haired character with pink-rimmed eyes hidden by an overly large pair of heavy, black-rimmed spectacles, was an ambitious, greedy, and often crafty man working in that gray area close to the edge of legality. He had a hawkish look about him and was constantly on the search for deals where he could manipulate, bully, and strong-arm weak and needy companies into accepting investments from PCW and getting positions on their boards, all with the approval of the securities commissions.

PCW's financial offers would be filled with caveats that were almost impossible to fulfill, which would mean the financed company would constantly be breaching its agreement with PCW. The penalties were severe and eventually tended to push the sponsored company into the waiting arms and control of PCW. In the end, PCW would be in a majority control position and add one more company notch to its belt of conquests.

Sometimes the investment paid off, and sometimes it didn't. Sometimes the returns came quickly, and sometimes they took years to mature. Sometimes PCW would cash in their positions and sell them at huge profits, or just get rid of them to some mining cowboys looking for a money shelter where they could write off their expenses and avoid paying taxes.

Partwick was also an associate of high-placed people with other under-the-radar financial organizations, including Roman Kerimov, a Russian oligarch and close associate of Vladimir Putin. It was Putin who had given the mining slice of the new Russia to Kerimov, who now controlled the largest gold producer in Russia, Polygold. Kerimov was also an avid follower of global opportunities in the mining industry outside Russia, and he and Partwick often dined together when in the same city. Sometimes Kerimov co-signed a financial note for investment through Partwick, but only when he saw the end result would be to his great advantage.

In the 2000s, Kerimov had obtained billions of dollars in loans from big Russian state-owned banks, such as Sberbank, and invested heavily with Morgan Stanley, Goldman Sachs, Deutsche Bank, Credit Suisse, and other financial institutions. Through these loans, he became a major stakeholder in Gazprom, Uralkali, and Polygold, as well as Sberbank, with the support of Putin.

As markets around the world began to tighten in 2007, Kerimov and his associates expected Russia would suffer more than the West from the impending economic crisis. He made a concerted effort to build closer ties with Western banks and corporations. Kerimov decreased his stakes in Gazprom and other Russian companies and approached Wall Street, proposing to invest the vast majority of his fortune in defending the institutions from short sellers. In return, it was expected Kerimov would receive favorable lending terms for future loans. He also became a prime contact for alternative investments in the Americas, particularly in the mining sector. That really attracted Partwick, and he and Kerimov struck up a friendly business relationship where both could profit. Kerimov had shifted his investment strategy to buying stakes large enough to influence the strategies of Western companies he invested in and looked to Partwick for advice.

Partwick saw the opportunity to get Kerimov involved in financing projects PCW was also interested in, except that, unbeknownst to Partwick, Kerimov was not a person who played by the rules—ever.

Once Roman Kerimov had been introduced to an easy way to make a very healthy profit from mining by using funds provided by others and then reneging on repayments, he realized he had found a winner.

Through contacts, Kerimov found Finn and Erik wandering the murky depths of mining prospects, where they were hustling shares from unwitting investors and looking to sell them in bulk to Kerimov so he could take over the company. They discovered common goals and soon began to discuss the possibilities Finn and Erik had been mulling over for several years. What if they could appropriate, or outright own, the rights to a mine worthy of development? And, what if they could raise the finances to extract the gold-rich ore, and rather than process it at the site of the mine and incur all the capital and operating debt that would attract, send it offshore to be processed instead—but not let the financiers know that was the plan?

It was a bold thought and not one that could last forever. But it could work on a number of projects over a few years before the scam would be discovered. Kerimov was very interested.

And so it was that Kerimov became a minor lender "in name" for the Greenland project Finn and Erik brought to him. His name, through Polygold, would attract major financing for the projects—in that case, the World Bank. Little would the financiers know Polygold's involvement with the development of any project would only be a paper one. There would be no money behind it other than an initial amount to get the project off the ground. Polygold's only financial commitment would be for the purchase of any initial stock, or position, needed to take control of the company in distress and a small amount of engineering mobilization money. Of course, any advance payment would be returned to Polygold, with interest, from the proceeds from the prime financiers of the venture, together with a share of the profits.

When Finn and Erik brought the Hope Gold property to Kerimov, he decided to act as the prime financier and approach PCW, through Partwick, to have them contribute at least six hundred million dollars to the project while Polygold would "provide" the balance of whatever was needed. In fact, Kerimov really planned to have PCW unwittingly pay for everything needed, including the advances made by him, in the name of Polygold. That would mean falsification of invoices, contrived cost estimates, and misstatements about project progress—all well within the ability of Kerimov's people. Polygold had, in fact, nothing to do with the conspiracy, and their board remained totally ignorant of what their president was doing behind their backs.

Kerimov never intended to advance any money for the project without recovering it through the financiers. It was simply a maneuver to help convince the market, and PCW, the property was more valuable than previously thought. After all, why would both Polygold and PCW be so interested? Especially since Polygold would theoretically be a majority shareholder in Quest. Their perceived participation in the company and the project would provoke other financial groups to invest, if the newly purchased Quest asked. And they might, if all went according to plan. The fact was, though, Kerimov had used Polygold as a lever before he transitioned Quest to a spin-off of one of his own numbered corporations. That way, Polygold could never be accused of being complicit, and Kerimov could disassociate himself from his numbered corporation any time he wanted.

* * *

"How much are you thinking of, Roman?" Russ Partwick asked. He had just come back from another two-hour lunch and was planning on leaving the office early for a golf game that afternoon when the call from Kerimov came in. Kerimov operated from his floating office on *Ice Man II*, this time located in Cyprus, where Kerimov did most of his personal business. He explained to Partwick about his impending takeover of Quest and the studies collected, and those recently commissioned, on the Hope Brook property. It was a relatively known entity to Partwick, who was aware of the history of the property but not the current status. The property had dropped off his radar once it became dormant when the last owner abandoned it.

Kerimov would send Partwick the Hope Brook reports the next day. His covering note mentioned the project consultants, a major engineering talent in the industry who had estimated it could cost in the order of $1.2 billion, plus or minus fifteen percent, to get the project back up and running. That cost would include the purchase of the property and the immediate need for environmental cleanup. The cleanup was essential to getting their permit, but as far as Roman was concerned, or so he told Partwick, he would post a more than sufficient bond to avoid any delay with the approval. Of course, he told Partwick, it also meant a little money going into the pockets of the Newfoundland technocrats, and one or two politicians who mattered. Kerimov almost believed his lies but had no intention of following through on any environmental cleanup, posting a bond, or applying for permits. He wouldn't tell Partwick all this, and neither did he tell Finn or Erik, in case it spooked them. Any invoices for costs associated with such things would be falsified and flow through Kerimov's dummy company system to PCW.

"Oh, I think you should start at, say, six hundred million." Kerimov let that number hang in the air for a few seconds. "It may be more once we get started and the real costs come in but, for now, that'll be good. Of course, Polygold will be contributing about the same amount. In fact, we have already signed off for equipment worth nearly two hundred million," he lied. The fact was, Kerimov had no intention of buying any mine equipment. He was looking at sending some of his old Polygold fleet over to the project, all painted up to look new, with Quest company logos plastered on the sides, so it appeared things were happening and money was being spent. But Polygold's fleet would only be used for the surface grading, road building and access ramp reconstruction, then sit to one side since all mining was going to be undertaken by a contractor, who would provide what they needed. PCW wasn't to know that. But then, PCW wasn't about to know much about the project. The fact Polygold was invested was enough for Partwick.

"I think I can swing that, Roman." Looking smug, Partwick relaxed back in his chair, the tip of his pen in his mouth and a few notes in front of him. "Give me a few days to caucus with my colleagues once I get your paperwork." They both nodded at the end of their phones as though they could see each other. It was an automatic reflex. "You had better drum up a proposed term sheet as well." Partwick thought he heard a kind of moan at the other end of the line.

Kerimov just hunched his shoulders and let out a sigh, followed by a one-word response. "Tomorrow." He grimaced again.

"Any chance we can get you to provide Polygold guarantees?" Partwick knew he was pushing his luck, but it was expected of him, and he would undoubtedly face questions from his board if he didn't get any.

"I don't think so, Russ." Kerimov was quick off the mark with his response, having anticipated the question. "It would take forever for the Poly directors to sign off, and I really want to get this project started right away to take advantage of the gold price. I'm looking to sell as much gold forward as I can." Kerimov was nonchalant and showed no signs of concern in his voice.

"Understood," Partwick acknowledged, but didn't want to pursue the matter further in case he alienated Kerimov. Business with Polygold was far too important to get hung up on a piece of paper. He moved on without further comment on the subject. "We have a new fund maturing for about two billion shortly, and this project will be the first of the investments for that fund." He waited for Kerimov.

"That's good. Very good." Kerimov let a thin smile crease his face. "Make sure you get this signed one up as soon as you can." The smile faded quickly as he got back to business. "We want to begin work. This is an old operating mine, and it has a huge potential, but it needs a new processing plant, and we have to take care of the tailings' disposal. The one they were using is completely full." Kerimov paused after his lies.

"I'll call you in a couple of days and get the paperwork over to you once I take a look at what you send." Partwick was excited at reeling in a global player, especially a Russian, and being in at the beginning of the venture with apparently no competition was a real feather in his cap.

But then, Kerimov would know the PCW terms had to be reasonable and not the same as other companies would have to endure. On the other hand, did he really care?

No.

PCW would never be paid back, and it would be impossible for them to make demands on Polygold, a company protected by Russian borders and laws, and not those of the rest of the world.

* * *

It took ten working days for the papers to flow to Kerimov from PCW for his signature and return. The deal was done, and the wiring information was sent over to Partwick. The first tranche of funding would be deposited within three days in accordance with the schedule of estimated expenditures provided to Kerimov by Finn and Erik. Partwick was unaware of who the Danes were. His only contact was Kerimov, and they had agreed to limit any press releases or company information on the basis that Polygold wasn't keen to raise their profile outside of Russia—for whatever reason. Partwick said he understood but didn't. Not that it mattered.

"Gentlemen, you'll be free to start your spending when the money reaches me," Kerimov blasted down his phone at Finn and Erik. "I'll set up a funding account for you to make your withdrawals, but I expect you to do all the accounting necessary and report to me each month. Clear?"

"Sounds good, Roman." Finn was very pleased and ready to contract the work at Hope Brook out immediately. "Oh, by the way, do we have the permits?"

"Don't worry about that. It has all been taken care of." Roman was his usual confident self. The fact was, for all the authorities would know, the site owners were just performing their duty and cleaning the place up. After all, there was no building going on and the old mill would stay in its current state of disrepair. By the time anyone took a second look, the campaign would be over, and the new "Quest" would have disappeared.

"Great. We'll get Big Jim's people mobilized." Finn was eager to get moving. "Oh, what about ORB? Where are you with them?"

"Nowhere new. As far as I know, they still think we've delayed things by a year and selected an alternative site. I don't have any reason to believe they think otherwise." Kerimov paused in case Finn and Erik wanted to comment.

"Yes, that's the information we gave Big Jim, and as far as we know, he passed it on to Emma." Finn was pleased with himself.

"And I know she passed it on to Stockman." Kerimov didn't want to divulge how he had listened to the conversations between Emma and Big Jim, and then Emma and Stockman. But he was sure the word had been passed on and the problem neutralized.

"That's good." It was Kerimov. "As we discussed, Big Jim is now quite aware of the real schedule and the importance of not keeping in touch with Emma. He is also quite aware of what could happen if he doesn't do as we ask. By the time ORB finds out, we should be almost complete." He sounded smug, content things were under control, or so he assumed.

It was spring and there was no better time of year to begin mining than now. They finished their call.

* * *

On the Move

"They're on the move," James Peters hissed to Matthew on his cell phone from CanMine's office in Vancouver, clearly excited. It was after normal business hours, and there was no one else around, but he still kept his voice low.

"What do you mean?" Matthew was a little stunned. He had just been spending time with the others on preparing for their dummy run on sabotaging the barges. Now, suddenly, things had changed. He tried to remain calm.

"I guess Big Jim got the word to get going, but I think he already knew it was imminent but didn't tell anyone other than his equipment manager, Lee.

"Lee's been a busy boy and already had the equipment serviced and ready to go when Big Jim called him. He had it all marshaled, ready to be loaded onto trucks headed to St. John's as soon as he got the word. I'm pretty sure I was one of the last to be told, but I don't know why Big Jim was playing this so close to his chest." James paused, waiting for a response from Matthew.

"I can guess, James. But let's leave that to another time. The fact is, they've mobilized. Are you heading out?"

"Next week, by the sounds of it. I have to be in St. John's to help make sure the equipment is loaded onto the barges once they arrive from Spain."

"Keep me in the loop." Matthew signed off.

* * *

It really came as no big surprise when Matthew heard from James that CanMine was mobilizing, but he was still hoping to get time for a dummy run on the barge sabotage.

From an overall perspective, and regardless of the immediacy of CanMine's mobilization, ORB already had their people positioned where needed, with James on the CanMine payroll, Emma and a couple of agents in Puerto

Banús to keep watch on *Viking I*, Matthew in Aviles with Tom and now Charlie, and Stockman keeping watch on *Ice Man II*.

The latest information from Emma supported what James was reporting. *Viking I* had left its mooring in Puerto Banús and headed out through the Strait of Gibraltar before turning north into the Bay of Biscay, undoubtedly bound for Aviles.

The day after receiving the news from Emma, James, Matthew, and Charlie were going back over the details of the work they intended to do that night. As Matthew glanced over to the barges, he spotted movement around one of the pilothouses. Tom had seen it as well and handed him a pair of binoculars, then lifted another pair off the table to his own eyes. Charlie looked over and squinted at the movement. They watched as a person appeared on each of the barges and disappeared into the pilot houses.

Matthew called Stockman.

"Looks as though we have company down here." Matthew held the binoculars to his eyes with one hand and his cell phone to his ear with the other.

"Oh. It seems plans have really changed, Matthew," Stockman responded. "I thought something was about to happen," he snipped. "By the way, *Viking I* just tied up west of you further down the estuary on the north side, so I think we can safely assume they're getting ready to move, but I can't tell exactly when that's going to be. Although," he added, almost as an afterthought, "I did hear from Mitch fifteen minutes ago, and he was fairly sure Rio Narcea was getting ready for a major shutdown and waiting for a new supply of ore." Stockman paused. "I'm sure he'll call you. Have you figured out what to do now you can't get a dummy run in?"

Matthew didn't hesitate. "We're going in tonight. No time to waste. I don't know how fast those guys can mobilize, but they're going to have to check out the barges first. Wait." He stopped, and a few moments went by.

"Are you still there?" Stockman voiced his concern.

"I'm here. I think their tug has just arrived. One of the group is signaling it to dock ahead of the barges."

"Okay. I understand James is heading over to Newfoundland in a couple of days to wait for the mine equipment to arrive."

"Any news on the financial front?" Matthew wondered.

"Too early. We haven't got access yet, and it'll take a while to dig in, so we're going to have to let the Danes start work." Stockman sighed. He would have liked this to have been a really simple operation. Get the money away from the Russian and the Danes and close them down before they actually started any work at the new site. But nothing was that easy.

"Okay. Let's let this play out and hope we can collapse them sooner than later. Meanwhile, we'll put some real obstacles in their way." Matthew sounded eager to get on with things.

"Let's go." Stockman closed his cell phone and settled back in his chair.

Matthew sent Tom over to keep a closer eye on the new group and find out where they were staying. From there, they would be able to access the guest register, get the names, and send them over to Stockman to get dossiers organized on each of them in the event they were needed.

That evening, Tom reported the new group were staying at the Apartamentos La Tata and had four self-catered suites up on the hill on the west side of the estuary. It was unlikely they would all bump into each other. There were eight in the group, a mix of Danes and Norwegians, given their home addresses on file in the hotel registry—if they could be believed. It was easy for Tom to get the names and it seemed the spokesperson for the group was a fellow by the name of Sven. Matthew sent the list to Stockman for profiling and asked him to call Sloan and immediately get another welder down to Aviles to help out. He didn't know how long they would have to sabotage the barges, but he was fairly sure it wouldn't be any longer than a week by the time the barges had been checked over—unless they needed a replacement for a critical part.

At this point, Matthew had no accurate idea of the sabotage scope he had to deal with, having not had the opportunity to inspect the barge hulls under water. How many zincs, where they were exactly located on the barge hulls, how difficult it might be to get to the dock side of the barges, or even whether they had enough room on that side to maneuver. Regardless, tonight was the night they needed to get started.

As soon as the new group headed to their hotel, Matthew, Tom, and Charlie headed over to their building, did a final check to make sure everything was in the dinghy, donned their diving equipment, checked the flashlights, and tested the grinders. The building doors were pushed open at eleven p.m., and the jib crane lifted the dinghy with its load over and into the water. Matthew, Tom, and Charlie lowered themselves down to the boat; Tom undid the turnbuckles on the jib crane and left them to swing free for when they returned.

The engine was surprisingly quiet with the temporary noise suppressant shroud and, using minimal throttle, they glided the hundred feet almost silently across the current to the first of the barges, clamped a magnetic anchor onto the hull, and secured the dinghy. Matthew and Charlie wasted no time in putting on their flippers and goggles, strapping their oxygen cylinders to their backs, and dropping over the side. Their battery-powered percussion hammers were secured to their waists with nylon rope. The noise of them operating would be suppressed by the water.

They would scout the hull of the first barge together and establish where the first set of zincs was located. Fortunately, the zincs had not been painted the same color as the hull and protruded about an inch from the steel surface they were protecting. The wide beams of the flashlights picked up the pattern of the zincs along the hull surface. They were bolted to the hull with steel clips. Matthew hammered the first zinc away using only the half-strength setting on his percussion hammer, and it gently fell away in the current. He signaled Charlie to work his way to the other side of the barge and start knocking the zincs off.

The water was murky, but not as bad as Matthew had originally thought it would be. The flashlight beams really cut through the silt as it streamed by on the way to the river delta.

Matthew felt a tap on his shoulder as he was knocking the last few zincs off their mountings. Charlie had worked fastest and returned to Matthew's side before he finished. It had taken them just over an hour to strip the zincs from the barge. Now for the grinding. They surfaced, replaced their percussion hammers with grinders, and wasted no time diving again, with Charlie taking the far side of the barge without being asked. This was the pattern they would adopt for the other two barges.

The grinding was minimal because the stainless-steel plates would only need to be tack welded, but they ground a few inches beyond to remove the paint down to bare carbon steel. These areas would be the first to corrode. Each plate was twelve inches long, to be tack welded with a single one-inch-long tack and only at the ends. Grinding these areas meant just passing the grinder over two spots a foot apart. The action took less than five minutes before the two welders worked forward to the next location. Again, Charlie made it back to Matthew's side before Matthew had finished. But it was a matter of minutes and they surfaced simultaneously, three hours after they had started.

They had been working underwater now for four hours, changing their cylinders every hour. Their original schedule didn't allow for the stainless-steel plates to be secured to the first barge until the second night, but they had developed a cushion of time such that they could get a few plates in place before they would need to rest, and Matthew was anxious to get a good fix on total time needed.

Tom already had two of the steel plates in the net, ready to sink. He had also positioned the dinghy to the starting point for the divers. He would move the boat forward as they signaled for the next two plates. Each plate weighed a little over twenty pounds, easily manageable while they were tied off, and just had to be pushed into place as the welder tacked it into place. After the first two attempts, each of the divers figured out an efficient system to get their job done. It had taken each of them sixteen minutes from the time of receiving the plate, performing the two tack welds, and repositioning themselves to the next location.

It had been a great night's work. But after six hours, they were exhausted and needed some rest, but not before collapsing in the bar at the hotel, ordering up some food and beer, and going over their first run.

"Okay, guys, correct me if I'm wrong anywhere here, but this is what I made of the timing." Matthew paused as a beer was put in front of him and he couldn't wait to take a chug. He wiped his lips of the froth and took out a notepad and pen.

"Say one hour and fifteen minutes to get the zincs off, three hours to grind the locations, and two hours to get stainless plates tacked. That's about sixteen minutes a plate, so it'll take about nine hours per barge for the full scope—if they're all the same." Matthew sat back, pleased with himself and his teammates.

"We may get this all done and cleaned up in less than thirty hours." It was Tom. "Six days should do it." He smiled.

That is, if they had that amount of time. Matthew was thinking about what would happen if they ran out of time.

"Okay, guys. It doesn't look as though we're going to get that other welder from Sloan in time, so this is how we're going to arrange things in case we run out of time." Matthew looked from Charlie to Tom. "Forget the rest of barge one and do the blind sides of barges two and three first. Then, if there's time and we don't see evidence of barge movement, we'll go back and finish barge two, then barge three. If there's still time after that, we'll go back to the first barge." His eyebrows raised, hands out with palms up, waiting for a comment from the others.

"Sounds like a plan." It was Tom, and Charlie just nodded in agreement.

"What about the tug?" Charlie asked. He was getting into this.

"Leave it for now. We may need to do something mechanical to it if we have the time. If not, then we'll leave it alone."

The others nodded their agreement.

* * *

Finn and Erik had covered the chart table in the cabin of *Viking I* with notes, lists, and maps. The yacht was neatly tied up to the southern side of the terminal in the estuary at Astellerios Ria de Aviles, where the workshops and a dry dock were located for ships needing to be serviced or overhauled. It was a great viewing location for when the barges passed as they headed out.

Finn and Erik used the same team as they had for the Greenland project barging, led by their crew boss, Sven Thorsen. They had mobilized in anticipation of the word being given by Kerimov to service the self-propelled barges while they were tied up to the dockside for safekeeping at the port. Now all they needed was the green light and the down payment and, provided the equipment was all in good order, they could get moving.

Once Kerimov gave the word to the Danes the finances had been put in place, Finn or Erik would put in a call into Sven, who was with the barges farther up the Aviles estuary, to get moving.

The day after his arrival, Sven called Finn to let him know the barge controls and engines were being checked, belts replaced, and oil and oil filters renewed. There were some minor repairs and supplies to gather for the trip to Newfoundland. They needed safety equipment, clothing in the event of storms, radios, batteries, and spare parts for the engines.

"How long do you need?" Finn asked, somewhat impatiently.

"Seven days." Sven was monotonal in his response.

"You have five." Finn was sullen, but he was expecting word from Kerimov the next morning, and he wanted to move as quickly as he could afterward.

* * *

Five days later, well ahead of schedule, when all the zincs had been replaced and the clam mines had been attached to the rudders of the tug, Tom watched as Sven jumped onto the tug, signaled to the fleet to free their lines, and the fleet moved into the center of the Ria de Aviles channel and started the slow progress out to the Atlantic as they anxiously waited to increase speed away from the restricted waterway. Tom put a call in to Matthew at the hotel and confirmed what he was seeing.

"Follow them out past the lighthouse, would you, Tom?" Matthew wanted to make sure they were truly on their way.

As the tug and barges passed *Viking I*, Finn and Erik gave a wave to Sven, leaning out of the pilot house of the tug. Sven waved back with both arms in the air. It was a 2,260-mile trip across the ocean and would take something like twenty days to get to St. John's, Newfoundland, where they would coordinate with the truck deliveries of the mine construction equipment and supplies. Sven was a part of the three-man oceangoing tug crew supporting the barges if needed. He was in constant communication with the fleet as they made their way to Newfoundland. All his men had worked together on special projects for a number of years now and had grown accustomed to each other's strengths and weaknesses. There were few, if any, weaknesses. They were a tough bunch and really knew how to handle the equipment. While Sven spoke English well, none of his crew did.

Tom headed over to the north end of the estuary and up on to the hill, looking over the mouth of the river and the ocean beyond. On the way, he passed the works yard and saw *Viking I* at dock. He put another call in to Matthew.

"They waved to each other, Matthew. It must be the real thing." Tom sounded excited.

"Okay, let's get our things together and get out of here."

It was time for Tom to head over to Newfoundland. Matthew headed back to Vancouver, and Charlie went back to his contract work.

* * *

Meanwhile, James and the rest of the CanMine group were being mobilized to St. John's with all their personal effects. The self-contained camp trailers were shipped across the country with the mining and construction equipment on low-bed truck trailers or flat-beds, and the bulk materials and consumables on truck-hauled containers. It would take between seventeen and twenty days for the equipment to reach St. John's, Newfoundland, where James would meet the convoy and supervise the loading onto the re-mobilized barges for the journey around the south coast to the Hope Brook site. It was a perfect time for the work to start.

* * *

Where's the Money?

Plato and Colin wasted no time after their meetings with Stockman and Matthew in London, and had never intended to delay their activities, even if the Danes had delayed the project. But now that they knew there was no delay, it was imperative they moved quickly and effectively if they were to manipulate the financial picture of both the Danes and the Russian before Hope Brook progressed too far.

They were making headway with first tracking down the financial trail of Finn and Erik. It wasn't difficult. While *Viking I* had been moored in the marina in Puerto Banús, every move and conversation by Finn and Erik was carefully monitored by Emma and the other ORB agents. One had followed Erik across the Spanish–Gibraltar border several times and trailed him to the Hambros Bank each time. The operative reported back to Plato, who called Matthew. It was a bit of a gamble, but they decided Hambros was probably the primary bank where the Danes held accounts, given its convenience. While they searched for other possibilities, it was just plain luck in the long run that this really was the one and only bank used by Finn and Erik for their business dealings.

While not considered to be included as one of the standard top ten tax havens in the world, Finn and Erik preferred a Mediterranean bank location and Gibraltar was perfect as a protectorate of Great Britain, even as a tax haven. It provided an easily accessible, proven location for their banking needs, with no corporate tax for any non-resident-based companies, and no questions asked.

They had built a good relationship with senior members of the bank, originally used in Anglo-Scandinavian business and originally the sole banker to the Scandinavian kingdoms for many years. That was, in part, what sentimentally drew Finn and Erik to it initially, if such was permitted in business. These days, clients came from all over the world.

Plato opened an account with Hambros Bank in Gibraltar as soon as confirmation was received and cleared with Stockman and Matthew. Once Plato became a client of Hambros, he secured a password and account number. From there, it became fairly straightforward for Colin to access the bank's client list and confirm Finn and Erik were indeed customers. More effort was needed to access their accounts. They needed someone on the inside at the Hambros Bank.

* * *

Jeff Lewis, a financial wizard based in London, was a previous associate of Stockman and had helped on an ORB mission a few years ago. It was time to put in another call. Jeff's position in the banking world could help now with getting someone placed on the Hambros payroll in Gibraltar.

"Hello, Jeff. Stockman here. How are you these days, old chap?" Stockman started, once he got through the human shield protecting Jeff from casual inquirers. It hadn't taken much once Stockman announced his name.

"Hello, Stockman. How the hell are you?" Jeff had an infectiously happy voice and sounded genuinely pleased to hear from his old friend. "What can I do for you?" Clearly, he knew Stockman never called just for a chat.

"I'm doing fine, Jeff, and from what I read in the newspapers, you seem to be heading up in the world of financing, as I always knew you would." Stockman paused.

Jeff was a financial consultant to governments and international banks. He didn't take to being an employee and preferred the relative freedom of contracting his services. His small team, based in London, sat on quite a number of boards to advise on corporate financial matters and security declarations each year, as they were required. Of course, there were things that were to be divulged in those declarations and others to be avoided. That's where Jeff's group shined.

"Thanks, Stockman. Always good to hear from you. Are you still in the business?" Jeff didn't need to elaborate on what that business was. ORB was Stockman's life, and anyone who knew him knew it.

"I am, Jeff. Can we talk?"

"Of course. I've got a few minutes." Jeff chuckled and shut the door to his office. "Maybe longer, for you."

Stockman described what he needed and listened to how Jeff was quite familiar with Hambros in London, as he was with most banks in the city. Their head offices were in St. James Square, just around the corner from Jeff's offices. They still had a considerable portfolio of clients and some influence in the financial world. In fact, Jeff knew a couple of the Hambros board members and a smattering of executives on their corporate management floor. He would try his best to secure some help for Stockman.

* * *

Two days later, Jeff contacted Stockman.

"I have a good man scheduled to begin in the Hambros Gibraltar offices this coming Monday. With your blessing, of course. I used the fellow on our last venture, but I don't think you ever met. You need to get in touch with him and let him know what you want him to do. He has a very broad mandate over there, and he's here in London right now, so better be quick." It was just that short a conversation.

"Thanks, Jeff. We owe you one."

Jeff gave Stockman the contact details for Jules Fortier, his new player, and they hung up after promising lunch in the city as soon as both could make it.

Stockman wasted no time and contacted Matthew.

"I think we have our man for Hambros, Matthew. Do you want to talk to him, or shall I just go ahead? He's due to start at the Gibraltar office on Monday."

"You'd be doing me a favor if you could do a face-to-face, Stockman. I'm a little busy right now. I'll catch up to the fellow once he gets into the bank, if you could send me over his contact details."

"Will do, Matthew. I'll file a report on the server with contact information. Plato and Colin will also need to make contact, so you should talk to them once I finish up and I'll leave it to you guys after that. Take care." Stockman signed off first.

Stockman punched in the number given to him by Jeff for Fortier.

"Hello, Jules? Jules Fortier?" Stockman hesitated just to make sure he had contacted the right person.

"Yes. Stockman?"

"It is. Can we talk? Or better, let's have dinner tonight," suggested Stockman.

Le Gavroche was quite local and would provide an impressive introduction for Fortier since he was French and would hopefully appreciate this particular restaurant. Plus, it was a favorite with Stockman—and that was more important.

They met inside the dining room lobby of Le Gavroche at seven p.m. and shook hands. Stockman had already commissioned a small corner booth, watched over by the painting of Albert Roux, one of the original owners of the restaurant. It always drew the attention of first-time diners to Le Gavroche, once they had read a little of the history of the restaurant, if they didn't know it already.

Stockman and Fortier spent the pre-eating time talking about themselves by way of introduction and sipping at a Balvenie—French oak whiskey—before tucking into the veal loin for Stockman and the lamb cutlets for Fortier. They hadn't bothered with hors d'oeuvres.

The conversation flowed easily. Fortier spoke six languages, including Spanish, French, and English, lived in Monaco most of the year to avoid French taxes, and had a forty-year list of accomplishments in the banking profession. He was suave, persuasive, and well-polished. Stockman liked him.

Fortier understood exactly what was required of him by ORB while he was in Gibraltar, although he was not privy to the reasons. But then, he knew of ORB and their reputation, as well as Stockman, whom he had spent a little time researching before their meeting. He also knew better than to ask too many questions, in the event he was caught and was faced with betraying ORB. After all, he was not a permanent member of the group, but was just a contractor performing a specific task—no questions asked.

As a cover, he would be acting as a consultant on behalf of Jeff's company, working for UK Finance to audit credit compliance records, payment-related services, banking methods, markets, and disclosures, as well as to take on a few clients for the bank to ease the load on the other managers. UK Finance had an overarching responsibility to ensure any banks registered to do business under its umbrella conformed to a strict set of rules both in the United Kingdom as well as overseas. It was a well-planned cover for Fortier to reach into the Hambros banking records, searching for transactions associated with Finn and Erik—and anyone else ORB might be interested in. Stockman didn't think ORB would discover anything associated with Kerimov—but he wasn't going to waste this opportunity to take a look, just in case.

It would take a little while for Fortier to extract the records of Finn and Erik without raising the eyebrows of the employees who were guarding such files. After all, the examination of personal files was not really a part of his primary mandate for the bank. As he worked through the records, he nibbled at the odd bits of personal information that came up but didn't take any interest. It would likely be a couple of weeks before he secured what he needed—the account numbers, mobile accounting passwords, and any usernames Finn and Erik used. But it would come.

Plato and Colin were quite content with how Fortier conducted himself and reported back.

* * *

The task for Plato and Colin was more complex for those accounts associated with Kerimov. He seemed to fit the profile of the usual oligarchs, who moved their money around through dummy accounts and shell companies using a variety of bank brands around the world. Some oligarchs were known to have over a thousand shell companies.

Fortunately for Plato and Colin, Kerimov was not extreme, but he was careful and there was one thing in common Plato was looking for in any of his accounts—the US dollar—and that's where he focused. It was logical to assume any financial dealings Kerimov would have with the Danish scams would be by way of US currency, and that meant the money transfers would be traceable.

Plato was not particularly interested in tracking other denominations from all Kerimov's dealings. It would be an almost impossible task, although the US government often went deep when financially sanctioning individuals. There was always the possibility Kerimov would move some of his money into non-US banks once the US dollars cleared the ones in Manhattan. In those cases, it would be impossible to penetrate them, and ORB would have to be satisfied with balancing off any deficit with money coming from other Kerimov sources where the money stayed in the US.

The banks in Manhattan had to record every transaction, via the SWIFT system, anywhere in the world, made in US dollars, even though it might only be for a fleeting moment as the financial trail passed through one of them on its way to some other bank Kerimov used—whether in the US or offshore.

The oversight of SWIFT is based on a special arrangement agreed upon by the central banks of the G-10 countries. SWIFT is the most widely used payment service provider worldwide. As the main carrier for payment information, its message types, formats, and technical infrastructure set a kind of benchmark for the processing of payments. Average daily traffic through SWIFT is in the order of ten million messages per day, with an estimated value of over ten trillion US dollars, and both those numbers are likely on the short side.

It was up to Stockman to subpoena the Manhattan-based bank records of Kerimov's US-dollar transactions. He couldn't cover all of them at the same time, so he and Plato came up with a shortlist of those who managed the lion's share of transactions and hoped somewhere in their records would be Kerimov's vapor trail. Stockman started with JP Morgan Chase (Chase Bank), Citigroup, Goldman Sachs, and Morgan Stanley. Colin developed an algorithm to quickly sort through the records and shortlist them into manageable files. He had started the algorithm to begin searching one month previous. If nothing came up, he would open the date to two months previous, and so on. If there was nothing over the past year, Plato would ask Stockman to subpoena four more banks and they would start the process again.

Plato decided to focus on Chase Bank first. The fact was the cloud of suspicion continued to hang over the bank after the fiascos over the previous twenty years. Clearly, they no longer maintained the kind of respectability they had worked on for so many years, up to the nineties. After that, it was all downhill for the bank in terms of trustworthiness, although they still maintained a position as the most powerful and influential bank in Manhattan—and the US, and just about the whole world. But they had plenty of skeletons in their closets. Investors of, say, a more dubious nature would tend to choose Chase because they were known to "bend the rules" when they considered it appropriate for the good of their most-valued clients. Plato put Kerimov into that slot—a "most-valued client."

It took less than a week before smatterings of Kerimov transactions began to appear from the Chase Bank archives. Plato widened the timeline for the search, having had the luck to land on some Kerimov dealings so soon. They didn't stop with Chase and followed up in parallel with the other banks, although nothing appeared with Kerimov's name attached during the early stages. While he might have been hiding his identity behind a number of false bank accounts tagged to fictitious corporations, the initial US-dollar transactions would be all Plato needed for his ORB work.

As they uncovered more information from the bank files, they found notes included in the files from a senior bank executive indicating Kerimov was a "suspect" foreign client, who had millions stashed in various accounts at the bank. It seemed he was making questionable cash transfers and concealing who actually owned certain accounts. It also appeared he had falsified financial statements for one of his companies, none of them Polygold, and he'd been involved in the unexplained "disappearance" of millions of dollars in merchandise in another venture. The notes indicated Kerimov might be involved in fraud and money laundering. But the trail ended there.

The challenge would take some time for Plato and Colin to unravel.

* * *

St. John's, Newfoundland

Despite being a few weeks into spring, there was a miserable dampness in the air and a threat of rain when James arrived in St. John's. But regardless of the bleakness, rows of colorful wooden houses greeted him as smiles of hope against the gray background.

This was more than just a fishing port. It was also a cruise ship stopover, a major ferry terminal for points north and south, and home to one of the largest coast guard fleets in Canada.

It was often a stopover for merchant ships heading east across the ocean or south along the Atlantic seaboard to the Americas. While the port was alive with activity, there was a coziness about the adjacent downtown area, stretching along the north side of the harbor.

People with rosy cheeks and smiles on their faces wandered the streets, stopping to pass the time of day with each other, waving at an acquaintance across the way, or tipping an imaginary hat with a finger of acknowledgment. They were used to heavy rain, storms, and the bone-chilling fog that often rolled in from the Atlantic in the spring and fall.

James didn't spend any time admiring or taking any particular interest in his surroundings other than the port and marshaling areas. His head was full of everything he had to get organized for when the barges and trucks arrived. He needed a lay-down area for the arriving trucks to unload, transfer trucks to move the equipment to the barges, a loading slip and crane, barge moorage, hotel accommodations for everyone, and a small control office for a local person, or two, to pick up supplies for the site, including food. Computer equipment and phone lines had to be arranged.

He had about fifteen days before the first of the barges was expected and while he wasn't a professional loadmaster, he would need to make sure the barge loads were evenly spread over the decks and through the fleet.

Mitch lived in St. John's and met James at the JAG Hotel on George Street, close to the harbor in the center of town. James made reservations for all his crew and more reservations at the Sandman on Team Gushue Highway, just off the Trans-Canada Highway, for the truckers. It would be an ideal location for a marshaling area for CanMine, and a convenient location for the drivers to rest up before taking the long drive back across Canada.

The next day, James met with the St. John's Port Authority and got permission to land the barges adjacent to Southside Road, opposite where the majority of the port loading and unloading operations were carried out on a commercial basis. He secured the services of two operated heavy-duty forklifts, a twenty-five-ton mobile crane, pallets, and protective covers. The port authority helped him get the use of a small unused office on the wharf. James went shopping online for supplies and office equipment and arranged for power and telephone services.

Mitch and James spent a couple of days working on getting things organized and discussing the project, including the best points for sabotage potential if, or when, it was needed, before Matthew called them. It was as if he had been listening in on their discussions.

"Listen, guys. Start thinking about how you can create some havoc with the mining. Nothing dangerous; just enough to delay things. We need to stretch things out a little to give Plato a chance to break into the bank accounts." Matthew paused. "Thoughts, Mitch?"

"Well, we could cause all kinds of problems, Matthew, especially at a remote site like Hope Brook." Mitch looked up at James. "We've been talking, and we think we can mess with the equipment if needed, but we can do a lot better by messing with the geology. Get them to waste their time heading in the wrong direction underground. Know what I mean?" Mitch was still thinking.

"Boy, sounds like a great idea, Mitch. But don't they have another geologist besides you that might catch a problem?" Matthew liked the idea but wondered.

"They do, but he's on day shift and doesn't follow the vein. His job is to follow the structure and look for danger areas and flooding. As far as they're concerned, I'm the vein guy, so to speak, so it's my job to plot gold direction." Mitch chuckled. Matthew laughed. James guffawed.

"I'll leave it in your capable hands, gentlemen." Matthew ended the call.

* * *

It was early May when the barge fleet moved out from Aviles. It had been at sea for a full day, heading to St. John's, when *Viking I* left its mooring and started its own journey across the ocean to the same destination. It was well within its range and would take about a hundred and fifty hours—or about eight days at two-thirds their top speed.

North Atlantic weather in May was generally good for sea traffic, but their route would still take them just to the north of the Grand Banks. It was one of the most notorious ocean locations in the world, where huge storms and hurricanes could rage, causing heavy seas and tremendously high waves, often too much for the commercial fishermen to handle.

To make matters worse, the fog generated by the cold Labrador current meeting the warm Gulf Stream at this time of year meant extremely low visibility for the crews—and it could linger for weeks.

As long as the rough seas weren't too extreme, there were only dollar signs in their eyes as Finn and Erik thought about their latest prospect and didn't give a thought to whatever, or whoever, ORB was. Kerimov would take care of them if there was anything to take care of. Their thoughts had been taken up with the acquisition of Quest, the financing, contracting with Rio Narcea for the ore processing, and keeping the Newfoundland government at bay—all of which now seemed to be under control.

It was now a matter of moving the mining as fast as possible—three shifts per day—to get the gold-rich ore away for processing. Revenues would be immediate, as the financial tranches from the PCW loans would begin to flow into their accounts through Kerimov—after he deducted his "fees." Quest's stock price would rise based on optimistic expectations, and Kerimov would slowly leach his stockholdings onto the market while the price was high. Yes, this was a very satisfying and straightforward project—just like the last one.

The plan was for *Viking I* to tie up in St. John's Harbour, wait for the barges, and Finn and Erik would watch them being loaded with CanMine's equipment before following them over to Hope Brook to witness the unloading and mobilization to site.

Finn wanted to use the three men they'd had in Greenland overseeing the contractor, and he had arranged for them to meet in St. John's and travel to Hope Brook on *Viking I* as they talked about what was expected from them. While Sven was their manager of the transportation, Niels and two of his hand-picked men, Lars and Peter, were their choice as their eyes at site. They weren't underground mining types, but they weren't naive. They were all ex-army and came with substantial experience in construction and security. It would be their job on a daily basis to ensure the contractor was working as well as he was expected to.

* * *

All went well for the Danes as the equipment arrived in St. John's and was loaded onto the barges. There was more than enough room for everything, and the fleet set off from St. John's Harbour, out through the Narrows, into the ocean and south, then west, to Hope Brook, one barge after the other, with the tug shepherding them out into open water and through the various islands en route.

The Hope Brook barge landing at West Arm was about four hundred miles from St. John's. It would take over forty hours for each barge to travel that distance, and the pilots were careful to keep their speed down to ten knots and stay away from the rocky shoreline and islands that dotted the route. There was Black Rock, Bob Rock, the Tinker Rocks, Shag Island, Wreck Island, Comber Islands, and more. Not quite the mostly habitable island jewels littering the waters of Georgia Strait on the Pacific Coast, but more deadly with the specks of rocks peeking out from the ocean's surface, threatening amateur seagoers.

The first barge arrived at the West Arm barge landing site, near Rose Blanche, during daylight. It had been used by a number of previous owners of the Hope Brook property and was still in reasonable shape. CanMine would need to tidy up the approach and repair parts of the jetty, but it was still a good roll-on/roll-off landing.

In emergencies, it was possible to use the recently completed Highway 470 that had been extended to Rose Blanche to connect a number of small communities on the south coast, and passed close to West Arm, where a very small community had been established. The *MV Challenge One* provided a daily passenger and freight ferry service from the West Arm location to the closest community, La Poile.

Viking I arrived and tied up to the government pier—the only one capable of taking that length of a boat. The other one was for the ferry and the recreational boats starting to operate now the weather was warmer.

Mitch had arrived with James and had all his survey and geological equipment with him. He and James had been assigned one site vehicle between them. The day geologist had another vehicle. The crew would travel the site as needed using a crummy—a converted five-ton truck with seats and windows. It doubled as an ambulance and clinic as well as a freight-hauling vehicle for consumables. Another truck had been armored and acted as an explosive magazine to be parked away from the mine. Enough supplies had been imported to last three months.

The camp trailers were easy to set up at the old camp site, up near the dilapidated mill building. There was power from the grid available and well water flowing through what seemed to be an operating potable water plant, although it was forbidden to be used for drinking without the filters. Enough bottled water had been brought in to last three months and the well water would only be used for fresh water needs in the mine, showers, toilets, and for non-potable requirements in the kitchen.

It took five days to unload the barges, install the camps, grade the roads, and move whatever equipment was needed up to the mine portal, ready for the first crew to head underground. The conveyor sections for the mine were plug-and-play. The conveyor belt was not continuous, and slip plates needed to be used at the ends of each section of the conveyor for the product to be pushed forward to the next belt.

Meanwhile, Mitch had been busy marking out the underground geology to trace the gold veins ready for the miners. For now, the markings were as accurate as they could be. He would wait for instructions from Matthew before he led the miners astray.

James was busy organizing everything and getting power hooked up, pumping fresh water to the mine, and rigging the fuel tanks with feed transfer nozzles and manifold piping. He wanted everything that was possible to sabotage, apart from the mining, at his fingertips in the event the situation called for it. James was armed with the control device for the clam mines attached to the tug rudders. It was his responsibility to time the explosions correctly once Matthew gave him the go-ahead.

Finn and Erik wandered around, asking questions, and generally getting on everyone's nerves. None of the men at the site knew who these two were, but they did understand them to be the people who paid the bills. Only Big Jim had met them, and he wasn't there.

Finn wanted to go into the mine. Erik didn't.

Finn went in through the portal with Mitch. The tunnel had two rails embedded in the floor for the old mine cars parked outside, but they wouldn't be needed for what the Danes were doing. The conveyor would do the work faster and lighting was strung along the roof of the tunnel and had yet to be energized. Flexible ventilation ducting ran the full length of the tunnel with air outlets and returns every fifty feet or so. A three-inch-diameter, high-density polyethylene water line was strung and anchored to the side of the tunnel with taps for hoses every hundred feet or so.

The tunnel narrowed as they neared the end and, while their helmets were equipped with headlamps, Mitch used a strong, wide-beam flashlight to show all the details of the tunnel walls and roof. He illuminated a gold vein in the side wall that disappeared into the solid rock in front of them. That was where he would start. The miners weren't interested in the disseminated gold that would mean mining out too much waste on each side of the vein, although some of it had to be mined out to provide enough room to work. While it would be economically justifiable for a bulk underground mine operation if there was a mill on site to process the ore, the intent of the Danes was to take as little ore as they could—and that meant narrow mining the veins wherever possible. The nature of the veins at Hope Brook was such that using the same mining techniques as at Nalunaq was not possible. The veins at Hope Brook were closer together but spread over a width greater than the minimum three feet. At Nalunaq, the veins were distinct and much farther apart, requiring separate narrow headings.

Finn looked smug as he stared at the gold vein with bulging eyes and watched Mitch work.

Mitch chalked arrows along the vein he saw first and looked for others with his trained eyes, as Finn watched. Despite there being veins of gold, they were still difficult to identify in the mafic of a variety of rock colors. He identified two others fairly close, and he chalked them as well. As the miners advanced in the direction of the arrows Mitch had made, he would follow in at night and mark the next section. The day geologist would be at hand if needed, but his task was to monitor ground conditions more than gold veins.

The miners would blast their way carefully forward in widths just enough for them to fit. They would muck out the blasted ore with the veins and feed it onto the conveyor. The conveyor would discharge directly into a control hopper and into the forty-ton capacity trucks that would haul their loads down to the barge landing area a few miles away, dump directly onto the barge until it was full, and return to the mine for the next load. They targeted two thousand tons of mined high-grade ore per day and the only way to do that was by using a conveyor out from the mine. For a relatively narrow-vein underground mine, the production rate was comparable to other mines with similar equipment, using the same technique—except here, they were working three shifts, seven days per week.

It would take three days to load one barge. One truck cycle would take a little less than two hours to load, transport, unload onto a barge, and make the return journey to the mine portal. They had six trucks and one spare. In a single eight-hour shift, one truck could make four trips, or move a hundred and sixty tons. Six would move nine hundred and sixty tons per shift, or just under three thousand tons per one full day—at most. The better assumption was they could average two thousand tons per twenty-four hours for three days. That would allow a good contingency and match the processing capacity at the facility in northern Spain.

Finn and Erik had arranged for two more equally large barges to be leased. They would arrive in a few weeks from Nuuk with their own pilots. The initial campaign would involve the barging of six thousand tons per barge. It would take fifteen days to load the five barges. During the time the barges were all away from Hope Brook at once, or fifteen days per month, the trucks would stockpile the ore at the barge loading area. Once the barges returned, future campaigns meant the barges would be loaded to an average of twelve thousand tons—still within the dead weight allowance for each.

* * *

Once the underground mine conveyor had been installed, mining began immediately. It had taken a little longer than Finn and Erik wanted, but within a few weeks, the gold-rich ore came off the head end of the conveyor and bounced into the back of a truck.

The hopper closed as the first truck moved away to the barge loading area, and the next truck took its place. Six trucks were a perfect match for the loading, transporting, and unloading sequence. A truck was always available at the hopper when needed. If there was any truck delay, the miners would rest and the conveyor would run empty until a truck arrived.

Three months after the mining started, the Danes had established a well-oiled system. The barges had been filled, sailed to Aviles, conveyed their loads ashore, and journeyed back to Hope Brook—all according to plan. The mine operation was simple, and everyone knew what they had to do. Big Jim had visited the site a couple of times, but only stayed a few days. Enough to make sure sufficient resources were in place and the team were happy campers.

Preliminary revenues from the sale of the processed gold at the plant were being wired to the bank of Kerimov's choice and the distributions made to cover all expenses, including those for the processing plant operations, payroll for the miners and support staff, all indirect costs including catering, remote payment allowances, and freight, as well as the cut for Finn and Erik.

So far, no one from the provincial or federal governments was asking any questions about the mining and none had visited the mine site. For all they knew, the site was being cleaned up.

The payments from the PCW funding, triggered by reports from Kerimov on project development, were being received on time. If PCW chose to visit the site, there would be little to see. But they hadn't bothered and weren't likely to. Hope Brook was in a god-forsaken location, as far as they were concerned, and not easy to access. It would take anyone from PCW two days of travel to reach there and two days back—no, it wasn't worth the bother. It was enough to rely on the reports and an occasional photograph. They trusted Kerimov—after all, he was the president of Polygold.

* * *

Money Movers

Jules Fortier had been ensconced at Hambros Bank in Gibraltar for just over four months and reported back to Matthew on a regular basis. There had been nothing of relevance to report during that time, although he had become a respected member of the bank's management team and a trusted employee to manage the accounts of a dozen wealthy clients on a personal level after working there for just two months. None of them were Finn or Erik's. That was where he was going to have to be especially cautious, knowing full well any access to the accounts of anyone other than his own clients would be immediately known to, and questioned by, the client manager. If something went wrong with a client's account, investments, funding, or complaints, it would all fall on the shoulders of just the manager. He needed their account numbers, passwords, usernames, and bank user codes provided to wealthy clients who wanted additional security. This was going to be more difficult than he had hoped.

Then one day, Alex Pritchard, the Hambros Bank consultant for Finn and Erik, left for a four-week vacation with his family to some place in Asia. A couple of weeks before he left, he had consulted with the bank manager, and they had divided Alex's client list up between two other senior consultants. It appeared to be a stroke of luck. Fortier was the receiver of the accounts belonging to Finn and Erik, as well as four others. All accounts transferred temporarily were issued new user access codes, but the account usernames and passwords remained the same.

Before Pritchard had left, he had personally notified Finn and Erik of his plans, provided them with the temporary access code, and given them Fortier's name and contact numbers, and assured them of his superior abilities and utmost discretion. The Danes didn't argue or comment one way or the other.

Fortier decided to play it safe and wait for one of the account holders, Finn or Erik, to visit the bank. He knew one or the other made the trip to Gibraltar at least once a month. That way, he would have a legitimate reason to look at the files, although he was aware of the timeline of ORB's project and the need to treat this matter with some sense of urgency. However, no one at ORB was prepared to take shortcuts, even though they all knew none of the other project operatives were going to move forward with the rest of their plan until ORB had access to the money.

Fortier didn't know the details of the ORB plans, but his discussions with Matthew left him to put some pieces together about what was being planned once he had unlocked the details to the accounts of the Danes. He wondered, without asking Matthew for any details, whether there was one or more other ORB agents in the bank he was not aware of. Perhaps they were even watching him, and while he didn't notice anyone being obvious, he still wondered if anyone was following him back to his apartment in the evening. But he couldn't be one hundred percent sure. Not that it really mattered to him. He knew what he had to do and would do it as soon as an opportunity arose.

As it happened, Erik strolled into the bank two weeks into Pritchard's vacation. He asked for Fortier, gave his name, and received a smiling acknowledgment from the receptionist at the client services desk, who picked up her phone, tapped two numbers, spoke silently to whoever answered, placed the receiver back down, looked up at Erik, and said, "Mr. Fortier will be with you in just a moment, Mr. Mateus. Would you like something to drink?" She gestured to the sitting area.

Erik shook his head, strolled over, and dropped into a lush sofa chair. He picked up *USA Today* and was about to read the headlines when a hand stretched out toward him.

"Mr. Mateus? I am Mr. Fortier, but please call me Jules." Fortier smiled as wide a welcoming smile as he could. "My apologies for the absence of Mr. Pritchard, but rest assured, I am completely at your service." That smile again. It was almost gushing, but Erik just shrugged.

"No problem... Jules. I just want to check on some transfers and get a read out on our investments." Erik wasn't sparing any time for formalities.

"But of course, Mr. Mateus. Please follow me."

Erik followed Fortier down a corridor and into an office with his name displayed on the door—gold on an oak plaque, in keeping with the general decor throughout the bank. The whole place reeked of wealth, secrecy, and serenity, designed to provide a client with positive feelings about who was looking after their money. Doors along the corridor were all closed. There were no windows looking over the banking floors, and assistants were neatly tucked into discreet corners so as not to be easily seen by visitors.

Fortier's overly large desk was double-sided. He sat on one side with a computer screen facing him, and the client, or in this case Erik, sat on the other side with another computer screen facing him. Both sides had a keyboard, both were connected to one CPU, and the intent was that a client could see everything showing up associated with his accounts as their manager keyed in his information. They were also able to tap in their password and access code without the banker, or anyone else, seeing. It worked well and gave clients confidence there was nothing hidden, and they were able to point and ask questions about any detail they saw.

Fortier pressed a few keys, spelling Erik's name, and five account numbers showed up. Erik watched his own screen as the information appeared.

"Would you like to see each of them, Mr. Mateus?"

"Let's just do the investment account." Erik looked serious and didn't waste words. He wasn't rude, he was just to the point. He entered his password and access code when prompted. They appeared as asterisks on Fortier's screen, but a small camera hidden in the desk lamp lighting Erik's side of the table captured both secrets in a video.

"I think you can see the deposited amounts made over the last month on the right-hand side of the ledger, Mr. Mateus. Are they what you expected? If I am correct, there is 23,000,480 US dollars deposited over three tranches, and 4,620,000 US dollars shown as debits. The debit payments all have the names to whom the payments were made if you just click on each of them. Of course, all US-dollar transactions have been dutifully processed according to international regulations." Fortier was all business and looked to Erik for any further instructions.

Erik studied the numbers in front of him and had a puzzled look on his face. He had to assume Kerimov had deducted his fee accurately, but he couldn't tell if that was correct from what he was seeing. It was something they had to clear up the next time they talked to him. Ideally, Finn and Erik should know the gross revenue before deductions.

"Is there anything wrong, Mr. Mateus?" Fortier noted the look of concern on Erik's face.

Erik hesitated, not wanting to share any details with anyone he didn't have to.

"No, I don't think so. I just think there should have been larger amounts. But that's not your worry. I have to go back to my people."

Erik stood, thanked Fortier, and made his way out of the bank, leaving the banker somewhat amused by the lack of discussion and the hurried departure of his client. He read nothing into it. Many clients were tight-lipped and wanted only minimal interaction. There were no paper trails between the bank and their clients. No emails, statements, or reports. No visible sign there was any business at all, except behind passwords and details held by the bank.

Clients and their bank managers communicated by phone or met on the bank premises. Money was wired in accordance with the client's instructions, and never without them. That was a fundamental and unspoken rule. It was a relationship based largely on trust.

Fortier went back to his office, closed the door, glanced over at the desk lamp, sat in front of his computer, and opened the remote camera icon. The whole session with Erik had been recorded in 2560p Ultra HD resolution with audio on a pinhole camera embedded in the cap of the lamp shade. It had a sixty-degree viewing angle and communicated through Wi-Fi. The unit had been wired into the AC feed to the lamp but operated by remote control from Fortier's location.

The details of Erik's password and account code were clear from the video, and Fortier wasted no time in accessing the files of the Danes who shared the accounts and had joint signing authority where needed. Fortier worked his way backward in dates through the current account first. There were actually four of them, excluding the investment account, and at first Fortier wasn't sure why that would be, until he saw a capital letter as a heading on the first page of each account. He guessed it was a label of sorts for the contents of the file. The latest recorded date was assigned to an account with the letter H.

Fortier didn't know what it meant, but it was information he needed to pass back to Matthew. He made note of the capital letter headings of the other three accounts and surmised the investment account to be an amalgamation of assets using the funds from the other four accounts.

"I think I'm in, Matthew." Fortier had put the call in to Matthew when he returned to his apartment. He sounded almost matter of fact, but then he wasn't caught up in the full ORB picture and had no knowledge of what could actually happen once he had completed his task. All he knew for now was his task had just started.

"Great. Have you had a chance to look over any details?" Matthew was excited but fairly sure he didn't sound it. He wanted to keep calm and let nothing slip, not even to another ORB operative.

"Just an overview. There are five accounts, four of which are labeled with a capital letter. The latest has a capital H—do you know what that could mean?" Fortier paused, waiting for Matthew, although he wasn't sure he would get an answer.

"I think I do. It's the initial of their current project. Does there happen to be an account with a capital N?"

"Yes, there is. The dates of the transactions were up to the end of last year, so the one before the file with the capital H." Fortier was intrigued, and he couldn't help himself. "What do they mean, Matthew?"

"Those letters are related to projects the Danes are carrying out or have already carried out. It's useful information but doesn't affect what we are doing… but keep them separated, would you? I'm not sure why right now, and it may never be important, but one never knows."

"Right you are, Matthew. I intend to collate the information and transfer it to Plato over the next few days. I have to be very careful with the use of the Wi-Fi here in the bank. It's private for the bank, but who knows who has access? I think that may be the first thing I have to determine, and if it's a problem, I may have to bring things out from the bank on memory sticks—we'll just have to see. Oh—by the way, there seems to be nothing associated with the Russian, Roman Kerimov, although you can appreciate it is hard to tell when most of the oligarchs use dummy names, companies, and accounts." Fortier was finished with his reporting and waited for Matthew in case he had any comments or instructions. He didn't.

"Good job, Jules. I think we have a line of the Russian, so unless you come across anything, I don't think you need to spend any effort looking for something. Let me know if either of the Danes shows up again, and especially if they're acting, let's say, jittery."

"I will, Matthew. Oh, but that reminds me. Mr. Mateus seemed a little unsettled when he was here. He mentioned he thought the numbers were low, but he would need to follow up with others. I have no idea what all that was about." Fortier waited.

"Thanks again, Jules. I don't know what it means either." Matthew had a good idea of what was going on, although he didn't know why at this time. Maybe it was Kerimov doing a little cheating on the side.

"Okay. Take care and give my regards to Stockman." Fortier clicked his cell phone off.

* * *

Plato had been slowly trying to follow the financial trails Kerimov had made in the world of banking. Occasionally they seemed to wind through Polygold, sometimes through his personal life, and often through somewhat anonymous dealings, whether business or not, but never associated with Polygold. Some seemed to be tied to his family in Russia, some were tied to various companies where Kerimov had large holdings personally, but most were not self-descriptive and gave nothing away in their file names to anything Plato, or ORB, were looking for, at least at first glance.

Plato's search had increased in tempo after Matthew let him know the project had been brought forward by almost a year, to where they thought it would have been originally. In fact, Matthew let Plato and Colin know they should be also looking for any very recent transactions. They could be indicative of capital being raised or expenditures starting to flow, in both the Russians' accounts and the Danes', that could be associated with activities in Newfoundland. That would be the Hope Brook project Matthew knew was currently underway.

Meanwhile, Colin had never slowed his pace at all, since he didn't know how complex the problem might be. He had been working his way through the algorithm he had devised to sort the US-dollar transactions Kerimov had made internationally, but which were governed by their need to touch base with the Manhattan banks. Plato wanted to focus on Chase first. Colin discovered smatterings of Kerimov activities during his search before Plato widened the timelines and asked his friend to start looking at other banks, with JP Morgan next.

There was an absence of Kerimov's name in the other bank files, but the notes appearing in some of the Chase files indicated he had interests in other companies or, perhaps, dummy ones that had been named or numbered. It was enough for Colin to hunt down the names and numbers of the entities mentioned in the Chase files when he searched the other banks' databases. Sure enough, a couple of them were peppered with accounts and transactions belonging to those "companies." Now Colin just had to match them to when the Greenland gold project occurred in the timeframe established by ORB.

While Plato and Colin only had the dates available during which the Greenland project was executed, it was sufficient to match US-dollar transactions to approximate dates, and those transactions were identified by whoever the sender was. But all in all, the amounts were not huge, and nothing like what would be expected from a gold project revenue stream.

After Matthew's call, Colin changed some of the parameters of his algorithm and applied it to the Chase transactions, looking for anything from or to anyone or anything associated with Hope Brook. Both Plato and Colin spent a few days working with the new algorithm and fine-tuning it to their latest needs. They were matching company names from the Chase files, deposits to depositors, and dates to dates when the first sign of a credit payment made to Kerimov moved through the Chase system. It came through an account with the prefix "HB" followed by a series of numbers appearing to be random—likely a dummy incorporated company. The money stayed in the account for several minutes before being split and sent out to other parties—all in US-dollar amounts. The credit payment had come in from PWC, a US company and one associated with financing mine developments. Clearly, Plato and Colin were on to something, but they didn't know what relationship there might be between the two entities.

* * *

"Hello, my boy. How are things going?" Stockman seemed almost cheerful as he answered the phone to Matthew.

"I think they're going fairly well," Matthew responded with as cheerful a sound as he could muster to match Stockman's, knowing he didn't have all the answers just yet.

"Yes, that's what I hear." Stockman sounded smug, but happy.

"Oh, who else is reporting?"

"Well, we can't let Fortier look after half the farm, can we now? We don't really know him."

"Ah, I see." But Matthew didn't.

"I don't know if you have ever met a gentleman by the name of Alex Pritchard?" Stockman paused.

"I've never met him, but that was the name of the guy Fortier is subbing for at the bank... you can't mean...?"

"I do mean, Matthew. How do you think Fortier managed to take over the Danes' accounts? Let's just say Pritchard is an ORB sympathizer. In any event, he needed a vacation and was only too glad to help us out."

"Well, I'll be. Good job. But I doubt you know the latest with Plato and Colin." It was Matthew's turn to sound a little smug.

"No, I don't. How are things going with the Kerimov accounts?"

Matthew described where things were with the Kerimov finances. Plato had a line on Kerimov's involvement with the Greenland project, which appeared to be minimal, and where things were on the Hope Book Project. Plato had claimed to have gained a participant control over the account they had identified so far and was ready to test it with a small transfer in and out. As for the accounts for the Danes, Fortier was in full control of that situation. He had copied the files, rather than send them through the internet, and couriered them to Plato, who was now in a controlling position on the accounts and could hack in at any time. Again, he was ready to run a test.

"Good, Matthew. Very good." Stockman was deep in thought.

"I'm thinking about running a test that might compromise their friendship—the one between the Russian and the Danes, I mean."

"Oh?" Stockman sat with furrowed eyebrows and a quirky smile on his lips.

"It sounds to me as though the Russian is using PCW money to fund this project. When the tranches come in through his account, he takes a cut and sends the balance on to the Danes. They have to pay the contractors and suppliers but, from what Fortier tells me, he thinks the Danes may be concerned they don't know the gross revenue, so they don't know what the Russian is really getting from PCW. Follow?" Matthew waited.

"I can see where you're going with this, but why?" Stockman was a little perplexed by the additional layer of sabotage.

"I want to drive a wedge between the Danes and Kerimov, so they start to distrust each other. Maybe that way we'll be able to gain access more easily to their funds before they discover the problems aren't with them, they're with someone else. And by then, we'll likely be gone, or close to it."

"Well, play it your way, Matthew. I can't disagree with your thinking, but I hope adding an extra layer to the plan doesn't cause us problems we can't prepare for."

"My sense about this is good, Stockman. I think we have the right guys to make this happen, and while we're messing around with the minds of the Russian and the Danes, we can be messing with everything else. And they probably won't notice until it's all over."

"My guess on this, Matthew, is that you really want to get these guys and hang them completely out to dry. Am I right?" Stockman chuckled.

"I do. I really do. They've ruined a lot of lives, not just some of the big boys but a lot of the street investors. They have zero scruples and it's time they faced their maker." There was a pause before Matthew laughed out loud. "Makes me sound a little angry, doesn't it?"

"Just a little. But then we have to be angry to be in this business in the first place—don't you think?"

"Talk later." Matthew finished his call and put his cell phone back in his pocket.

* * *

Matthew put a call in to Plato, who had temporarily relocated to London with his wife while he and Colin worked together on the project. It was a good central location to everywhere they wanted to reach in the northern hemisphere. The communications were excellent and, of course, access to financial institutions was beyond reproach should he need help. He also anticipated further meetings with the team, and this was as convenient a location as it got.

Matthew started the call. "Plato, let's play some financial games with our friends, shall we?"

"I like the sound of that already, Matthew. What're you thinking?"

"Try changing the transfer amount from Kerimov to the Danes. Make it substantially less than the Danes would expect, so both parties will notice immediately. But make sure Fortier knows so he can try to prompt his clients into making some comments on their shortfall. I would expect it will look like a simple oversight at first, so the next one needs to follow quickly and also be substantial, but this time make it the other way around and transfer way too much from the Russian to the Danes. I would like to see what the Russian will do." Matthew was pleased with himself, but his brain was already moving on to the next moves.

"While you're doing that, start siphoning money from the accounts of both the Russian and the Danes and transfer it over to an account Stockman will provide for you. Start low and gradually build it. I would like us to be taking some physical action in the field at the same time."

"Such as?" Plato thought he knew, but just needed some clarification.

"I think it's time we reduced their revenues." They both laughed.

* * *

Ghost Barges

Curtis was on the midnight to eight underground shift. He liked it that way. It let him enjoy some daylight hours in the brush, hunting hares, marmots, and maybe even a red fox if he spotted one, just some fun to while away the time doing something he liked, and it distracted him from the time he was spending away from family. He could also avoid the confines of the camp and the monotony of just watching movies or playing pool.

He only used a pellet gun for hunting; just enough to pop his prey in the butt to make them jump and scoot off. Killing animals for fun was not Curtis' thing. But he would spend an awful lot of time hunting those little creatures, and it led him to all kinds of other interesting things that often became his local hobbies, like collecting small rocks and trying to make some sense as to what they were and where they might have come from.

Curtis was no geologist, but he had been an underground miner since he was eighteen and had come to understand and feel his surroundings in that domain pretty well. A thin, wiry guy, well able to fit into the crevices, he could tell if the ground was competent, whether there were faults that might cause trouble, if the drill blast holes were hitting ground that was too soft, or if there was too much water and more effort was needed to get it under control.

He could smell the air and tell if there was something in it that shouldn't be, or if it was too stale to breathe, or if it wasn't circulating efficiently. He also had a good eye for spotting mineral chips in the rocks around him and could often spot gold and silver even in disseminated surroundings, so long as he was shining a pit helmet light on the mine wall. It was a lot easier to see the gold and silver in veins when they were there, and a lot of times they weren't. But at Hope Brook, it was easy. The veins generally stood out from the grayness of the mafic—the native rock that held the gold—at least for him. Others had trouble following the gold as it lost itself in the matrix of some underground rock colors.

But it took Curtis several weeks before he realized they weren't following the gold veins any longer. That feeling was increasing as they mined in farther, but he hadn't said anything in case he was wrong—and he could be. Now and again, they would cross a vein, but didn't seem to stay the course. But then, not all gold veins were clearly visible. Some had somewhat disseminated gold, where the specks of gold strung together in clusters such that the geologists called them veins. But now he was feeling really uncomfortable. They hadn't picked up a solid strand of gold particles for a while. It was time to raise the alarm with his crew boss.

* * *

Theoretically, one might assume each ten thousand tons of high-grade ore barged to Rio Narcea, at 0.8 ounces of gold per ton, could eventually be worth twelve million dollars or so, after the seventy-five to eighty percent crude gold doré bars poured at the processing plant refinery were further refined at a certified facility. That is, if there was no waste rock included—but, of course, there always was. The final product would have to be a 99.5 percent authentically stamped pure gold doré that banks would be interested in purchasing for resale.

Initial payments from the processing plant to the mine owner for the contained gold in the ten thousand tons of ore processed are only preliminary, based on assay results from the first stage of refining. Technically, it could be something like two-thirds of the final anticipated value in the order of, say, eight million dollars payable by the processor as the crude doré is shipped off for the final refining. Meanwhile, all expenses have to be paid by the mine property owner for mining, freight, processing, and the like.

But worse, even narrow-vein gold mining includes waste. The equipment used specifically to mine narrow veins is incapable of only extracting the gold, so the immediately surrounding rock has to be extracted at the same time as the vein and is referred to as waste. It's processed together to separate out the gold. That means the gold ounces per ton is actually less than advertised. So, the ten thousand tons of ore in the barge could be, say, only 0.5 or 0.6 ounces per ton, meaning it could really be worth only 7.5 to nine million dollars after the final refining, or just five million as a preliminary payment. But all expenses would remain the same, no matter what the gold grade. It costs as much to mine and process a ton of one hundred percent waste as it does to mine and process a ton of 0.8 ounces per ton of gold ore.

In the case of the ghost barge loads, the waste ore the miners had been extracting when the gold veins disappeared was the largest component of the barge loads. There were only trace amounts of disseminated gold. So, while all the expenses remained the same, no matter how much gold was contained in the ore, the revenue was millions of dollars less than expected after assaying the crude doré.

It only took Kerimov one look at the revenue from the first ghost barge for him to sound the alarm. It was less than two hundred thousand dollars after expenses were paid for; the balance of even the preliminary proceeds would be negative. Needless to say, Kerimov was livid, as his eyes bulged while he stared at the wire information in his hands. His head seemed to increase in size as his blood pressure rose, his desk shook as his fists pounded it, and his whole body quivered as he attempted to stand but slumped back. Four more barges to go, at least, until they could figure out what was happening. That was a potential loss of over fifty million dollars by the time the dust settled on the final assays. It had to stop. The returning barges must not be loaded with waste ore for a return journey to Aviles.

"What the fuck are you guys doing over there?" Kerimov screamed down the line to Finn and Erik as they relaxed on *Viking I*, in its Puerto Banús moorage, completely oblivious to what was happening with the ore. They were speechless and stayed that way for a few telling seconds while Kerimov screamed at them again. "What the fuck is going on?" he demanded.

Finn recovered first. "With what?" he asked mildly, thinking Kerimov must be close to having a heart attack by now. "What do you mean?"

"The ore. The fucking ore. It's no good. We just had ten thousand tons of crap processed and lost millions." Kerimov let the information sink in.

Finn and Erik stared at the phone like deer caught in headlights.

"What do you mean, crap?" This time, it was Erik. They could hear that

Kerimov was uncontrollable and would probably have shot both of them had he been in the same room.

Kerimov explained, with a number of expletives thrown in for good measure, what he thought had happened with the first barge of ore. Without stopping for a breath, he let them know what was very likely going to happen to the next four already en route to Spain—each loaded with ten thousand tons of "crap" ore, not to mention the ore accumulating in the stockpile at the barge landing site. He didn't have any details. Didn't know the reasons, who was to blame, or why they were at this point. He just knew these Danes were the target of his anger, and the fuck-up had to stop.

"What the fuck!" Finn and Erik shrieked in unison. Then they shrieked three more times, interrupted only by Kerimov, who shrieked the same words at the same time. It was like a chorus of despair and a cacophony of "fucks," as none of them could figure out what could possibly have happened. What if the entire geology was wrong? Or they were mining in the wrong direction? Or the high-grade had been hijacked? What if, what if…? There were too many what-ifs to focus on.

"Call that fuck-up, Big Jim, and find out what the fuck is going on," Kerimov shouted as his purple face turned an even deeper color. "They're probably still mining and stockpiling fucking garbage down at the dock—what a fucking waste of fucking money." Kerimov couldn't seem to stop his onslaught of Russian-accented foul language.

Finn was already on the phone and calling Big Jim Garland in Vancouver. He didn't care what time of day or night it was.

* * *

Mitch had figured out the barge cycles and when the first of the waste ore loads would reach the refinery in northern Spain, get processed, revenues calculated and paid out, and the barges return to Hope Brook for reloading. Allowing for some delay in the processing of the payment for the gold, the first of what he called the "ghost" barges should arrive back any day. He knew all hell would break loose as soon as the news of the reduced payments reached the Danes. What hell that would be, he wasn't sure, but it was time for him to leave. They had mined out about a hundred thousand tons of gold-starved ore, lost the vein direction, and got themselves tangled up in bad ground. Mitch figured it would take the Danes a few months to get things back on track, what with having to deal with the ground conditions as well.

By the time Big Jim called James and spoke to the lead hands at Hope Brook, Mitch was long gone, together with any evidence of how he had left things. It was a catastrophe that seemed impossible to worsen. But it did.

* * *

The construction of a hopper barge incorporates a double hull as standard practice. The outer shell would gradually corrode when the anode-reversals did their work and the carbon steel became the target of oxidation.

Once corrosion had penetrated the outer hull, seawater would gradually fill the spaces between the two hulls. The center of gravity of the barge would lower to a point where it would sink. And if the water was somehow not evenly distributed through the hull, the barge would capsize in the direction where most of the water had accumulated. All this would happen without the crew knowing until it was too late.

Of course, it was entirely possible a crew member would realize the barge was getting lower and lower in the water, but it would be so gradual as to potentially not be flagged as critical at the time when something could have been done to salvage the mess.

Left too late, whatever sump pumps were installed to control minor leaks between the hulls would be overcome with the continuous, and increasing, volume of water pouring in, and they would not be able to keep up.

And so it was, the first of the ghost barges to start its journey back to Hope Brook began to take on water two thousand miles west of Aviles, halfway across the North Atlantic—or about halfway home and five months after the zinc anodes had been changed out for stainless steel by Matthew and Charlie, with a little help from Tom. The other two ghost barges would likely suffer the same fate around the same time. Then there would only be the two leased barges making those trips back and forth. The potential was it would take a dramatically longer time for the ore to be moved than what the Danes had planned unless they could access more leased barges. And that would take time and money.

Ten- to fifteen-foot-high rolling waves washed through the vessel and slammed the barge into the troughs, only to do it over and over again. The wildness was relentless. It was impossible to see the barge sinking in those conditions. Dark gray, rain-laden storm clouds persistently shed their loads over the pilothouse windows to the point where the windshield wipers couldn't keep up to provide the navigator a clear view of what was out front of the barge or get any sense of whether it might be listing to one side, or from one end to the other.

The first pinholes in the hull, caused by the corrosion, had enlarged, encouraged by the continuous pounding of the barge in the heavy seas. The seawater pressure on the thinning holes weakened the hull further, and more water poured in to fill the space between the hulls. By the time the crew realized their dilemma, it was too late to do anything about it.

"Mayday, mayday, mayday!" one of the crew yelled into his radio and waited for a reply. He repeated his alarm three more times before another voice crackled over the receiver.

The crewman yelled out the name of his vessel as Barge Number 1 and its call sign—even barges had them. He knew his automatic identification system, or AIS, was broadcasting, so other ships would know his exact position already. But better to be safe than sorry, so he provided coordinates. They were incredibly lucky to get help as fast as they did and be transferred off the barge deck before it sank.

The first ghost barge sank three thousand miles west of Aviles after a complete collapse of the outer shell of the double hull.

The barge crew watched it sinking from the deck of the ship that had saved them and wondered what the hell had happened. They just couldn't fathom what could have caused such a catastrophe, but decided the barge hull must have been breached before they left on the mission. It was just a matter of time before the barge would take on water. There was no way they could have known, but they silently blamed themselves for not sending a diver down to check the hulls before they had first left Aviles. An inspection would have taken less than a day and could have been carried out while Sven and his men serviced the motors. "Damn stupid," one of the crew hissed and promised to let Sven know to have the rest of the barges checked out at Hope

Brook or taken into St. John's, where there would be competent divers.

The rescuing vessel was a container ship making its way to Montreal via the St. Lawrence River. While it had not intended to visit St. John's, it was barely out of their way. They would lay anchor in the Narrows and ferry the barge's crew ashore.

The second ghost barge sank close to Aviles as it was heading into the estuary to be unloaded. A ten-thousand-ton load of ore helped it on its way down, but the crew managed to climb aboard passing boats around the estuary. The third sank quickly on its way from Aviles, and the crew were picked up by the fourth, still-seaworthy barge, which powered on to the unloading dock. It had been a difficult crossing with high winds, deep troughs, and pounding waves almost the whole way over from Newfoundland.

By the time the news of the other two barges got to Sven, he was in St. John's. He was still apoplectic with rage, angry with conspiracy theories, violent with the thought of retribution, but happy all his men had survived. That was a miracle in itself, and he figuratively patted himself on the back at having at least had the good sense to keep to the commercial shipping lanes as the barges crossed the North Atlantic. A more direct route could well have meant their demise, with little to no ocean traffic in the vicinity of their distress.

* * *

Sven's call with the Danes was not a pleasant experience. While they could lay little blame on Sven for the quality of the ore, they did blame him for not servicing the barges completely in the first instance, despite the time constraints set by them. While they would never know what happened to cause the sinking, they had concluded it was far too much of a coincidence for all three barges to sink at almost the same time, while the two leased barges remained intact. No, there was something more to all this than they really wanted to admit. The word "sabotage" crept into their conversations, although it remained a mystery as to who, what, or why.

Kerimov was not lost for thoughts. Once he had calmed down from his intense anger that came with a lot of exclamations of "fuck," it didn't take him long to conclude there was a very strong potential ORB was somehow involved in the shenanigans. But he had no idea how, who, or even where to find out, although he was fairly sure this Emma Stockman, or Stone, or whatever the fuck she called herself, was somehow wrapped up in all this. For Kerimov, the final straw was the discovery that some of his personal funds had somehow been diverted to the Danes.

* * *

Money Problems?

It was bad enough losing over fifty million dollars on processing the waste ore, but now money was disappearing from Kerimov's accounts and reappearing in the bank accounts belonging to the Danes. So far, there had been something close to eight million transferred by parties unknown. Kerimov's banks denied any wrongdoing; the Danes claimed innocence and returned the money to Kerimov, but the problem continued. Every few days, money would be wired out of Kerimov's accounts and over to the Danes. Each time there was a transfer to or from Kerimov's account, a small amount would be deducted and wired elsewhere—location unknown—except to ORB.

The frustration Kerimov felt was beyond anything he had felt before, and he desperately wanted to blame someone. The Danes were the focus of his bad intentions for rectitude, although he couldn't prove anything. But then, when was the last time he needed to prove anything when he was looking for retribution? His gut told him everything he needed to know.

As he pondered how to handle the situation with the Danes, it dawned on him that it just didn't make sense for them to be implicated in financial shenanigans with him. They had too much to lose.

As he rationalized the situation, he began to move his focus away from the Danes, and something else started to take shape in his thoughts. ORB had been in the back of his mind ever since his encounter with Stockman's daughter aboard *Ice Man II*. It couldn't have been an innocent coincidence that Stockman's daughter appeared on his yacht with Big Jim at the same time he was planning an off-the-books hijack of a mining company and their property. She was certainly suspect, but he thought he had put a stop to any potential for ORB involvement by planting false stories. But now... well, perhaps they had somehow caught on and were back on his trail; that is, if they ever left. It was hard to believe Big Jim would have said anything about the revised schedule after being threatened, so it had to be someone else—but who? Regardless, in Kerimov's mind, it was still ORB behind the problems, no matter who alerted them.

Yes, he thought, *it could all be caused by ORB—and not the Danes*. He was sure that son of a bitch Stockman had a hand in the sinking of the barges, so why couldn't it be him and this ORB group of his who were also messing with his money—another coincidence?

He was convincing himself that, for whatever reason, they were after him because he still couldn't come to terms with ORB having any interest in a small remote mine in Newfoundland. So, what the hell were they after?

Somehow, he had to get to the bottom of things. And then it came to him—if it was Stockman and that company of his, the fastest way to the truth and the solution to his problems would be through his daughter, Emma. She was the key, and while he knew little about her, he did know she lived in Vancouver.

Kerimov wasted no time in putting a call into his contacts. He wanted that bitch on *Ice Man II* right now!

* * *

Even though they couldn't watch them, Plato and Colin were having fun driving the Russian and the Danes crazy with their financial antics. They had everything they needed to manipulate the accounts of both parties—unless they changed their accounts or, worse still, their banks. While they were diverting funds from one to the other, they took a cut and sent it on to ORB to start the fund for repayment to those that had lost at the hands of these culprits. It would be impossible to track down those responsible for the transfers, and even Fortier was no longer managing the accounts of the Danes at their bank in Gibraltar. In fact, he would shortly be moving on to other endeavors, where he would fall out of sight of anyone who might come looking for him.

The money from PSW was arriving on the fifteenth of each month, so apparently not using a milestone schedule. That was even easier for Plato and Colin to deal with since they were so regular. They intercepted the funds as they passed through the Chase Bank to others, all within a few minutes, and repackaged the wires to the Danes by increasing the amounts from the Russian, reducing the payments to Kerimov, but leaving the payments for expenses intact—for now. They could follow the transfers back from the Danes to the Russian within a few days as the repayments came through the Chase Bank as well. Of course, Plato siphoned off a "little" fee for ORB's troubles from those amounts as well.

Plato waited for Matthew to give further instructions.

* * *

Mitch was three thousand miles from Hope Brook, out of reach of the Danes who, by now, would know he had led the underground mining crews away from the gold veins. He had done enough unless ORB wanted him for anything else, and only Matthew had his contact information, if that should be the case.

The Danes engaged two new underground geologists from the west coast of Canada and shipped them over to Hope Brook. After seducing them with hefty sign-on bonuses and promises of even heftier completion packages, they transferred to the Hope Brook site a week after the offer was made. It took them a couple of weeks to redirect the crews back to the gold veins, and within a month, mining was underway again at full speed in the right direction. The three sunken barges had been replaced by ones from Denmark and the stockpile of waste ore down at the barge landing had been dozed into a useful profile to provide a better access for the mine trucks bringing ore into the landing.

All in all, ORB had only temporarily interrupted the activities at Hope Brook to this point, but they had been successful in scuttling the barges, wasting some three months, reducing the revenues to the Russian by over fifty million dollars, and causing chaos between the Russian and the Danes over the money transfer issues. The whole exercise to date likely cost Kerimov, Finn, and Erik almost a hundred million dollars, but it would come straight out of the financing loans from PCW. For all that, though, it was still just an irritant to the rogues while ORB tested its abilities to manipulate both financial and physical matters. By now, they had enough information and the ability to go in for the kill. Stop the mining altogether, siphon the funds, and ruin the Russian and the Danes. The key to putting an end to the rogues was through their money.

* * *

"My name is Stockman, Murray Stockman, president of ORB." Stockman had put a call into PCW and, after several attempts by two intermediaries to pry out of him his reason for calling, managed to get through to Russ Partwick. He didn't know Partwick, although he did know he was on top of the pile of the PCW Americas group, and that's where Stockman wanted to start—after all, he was fairly sure Newfoundland fell into that domain.

"What can I do for you, Mr. Stockman?" Partwick had heard of ORB but had never had cause to use them. What he did know about them was quite intriguing, and this Stockman fellow had a solid reputation with institutions Partwick had dealt with and was still dealing with.

"Just Stockman will do. May I call you Russ?"

"Sure. What can I do for you... Stockman?"

"Have you heard of my company, ORB?"

"I have, not often, but enough to know your reputation and the type of business you are involved in. I have to say this is all very... mysterious." Partwick chuckled. Stockman didn't.

"Perhaps you also know Roman Kerimov?" Stockman stopped short of saying more until Partwick responded. Stockman knew it would be a shock for Partwick to hear that name coming from someone associated with ORB.

There was a long silence before Partwick coughed. "Kerimov? You mean the Polygold president?" Partwick was stalling and suddenly not looking forward to this conversation. Something unpleasant was in the wind, and he didn't like the feeling welling up inside him.

"Yes, that's the man." Stockman didn't like this conversation either. He had no ax to grind with Partwick—at least as far as he knew. "Well, it seems as though he is up to no good—and PCW is funding it."

"What do you mean?"

"Apparently he has you financing a fraud, I'm afraid. And for an awful lot of money."

"What? How? Fraud?" Clearly, Partwick was taken aback by what Stockman was telling him. "I'm astounded by your accusations, Stockman, and I have to say, somewhat dubious about your intent with all this."

Stockman could imagine Partwick squirming and wishing this conversation wasn't happening.

"My relationship with Kerimov is based on his excellent standing as the president of Polygold and is a powerful and well-respected one." Partwick wasn't lost for words in defending Kerimov. At this point, he refused to consider it any other way, seeing as the Russian had so much of the money PCW had already wired and, if what this person, Stockman, suggested was true, it would all turn into a nightmare.

"PCW have been doing business with Polygold for years. Yes, they're Russian, but they have never given us any reason to doubt their trustworthiness..." Partwick would have continued had Stockman not interrupted him, and his deep, resonating tone trumped the shrillness of Partwick's shocked one.

"Ah," Stockman stopped Partwick mid-sentence as the word rumbled from his mouth, "but we're not talking about Polygold here, now, are we, Russ? Your agreement is directly with Kerimov, and any Polygold guarantee is worthless. I think you know that." Stockman stopped to let Partwick digest what he was hearing.

"How do you know all this?" There was an edge of panic in Partwick's voice.

"Let me tell you a story, and you can decide whether you think I am right." Stockman started from the beginning: Greenland. It was not really the very beginning, but it was a sufficient place to start for his purpose here with Partwick. He didn't need to dredge up all the sordid details of everything the Danes had done in the past, nor all the dubious sideline projects Kerimov had undertaken to improve his personal wealth over the years.

Partwick didn't interrupt. He listened attentively. Grunted here and there. Voiced his concern with a discernible "those bastards" or a "fuck me," but all in all, he kept his thoughts to himself until Stockman had essentially brought him up to date.

"Christ, what do we do now? What the fuck do I do now?" Partwick almost whimpered as he thought out loud. "We're something like four hundred million into this project, with more being sent through the pipeline any day, and you're saying there's nothing there?"

"That's right. That's their modus operandi, and Kerimov has arranged to finance it all—and a lot more. I'm afraid you've been suckered into believing there'll be some capital assets in place at the end of all this, but I'm here to tell you there won't be. It's all smoke and mirrors." Stockman could hear Partwick breathing heavily and swearing under his breath.

"You may want to check with the prime minister of Greenland, who I am sure will tell you the sad story about his being duped in much the same way. Oh, and don't forget to contact the World Bank. I believe they lost more than you on their Greenland venture in a similar way. What you need to do right now is stop any more payments."

"But what about what we've already paid?" Partwick could hardly grasp the situation and was not at all constructive in developing any kind of plan to catch Kerimov.

"Listen, we'll get your money back, minus a fee for our services, of course, but you have to stop payment immediately and throw up some believable reason to Kerimov for doing so. ORB has some work to do yet to recover the funds they've received to date and neutralize him and his accomplices. Can you do that?"

"Yes, yes, of course. Right now. I think there's another hundred million due to be transferred this week." Partwick stopped while he was thinking of the mechanics of how to stop payment and confront Kerimov with some made-up story.

"Good luck. I'll send you a number where you can contact me. Whatever you do, don't give the game away or you won't get any money back, and Kerimov will be off doing the same thing to some other poor soul."

The conversation ended, and Stockman sat back thoughtfully in his comfortable sofa chair by the window, looking out over the bay. It was six p.m., and Lucy handed him a gin and tonic, patted him on the head, dragged her hand slowly and lovingly across his shoulder, took her own glass to the chair opposite him, and stared at the same view. He hardly noticed.

* * *

Matthew and Emma were in Vancouver, enjoying a warm spring evening in Matthew's penthouse garden. They were hidden from the prying eyes of apartment dwellers in the high-rise apartment building opposite, up to about the sixteenth floor, by dense bushes clinging to the perimeter railings, tumbling over the top, and spilling down the other side. The flower buds were busting to display themselves as the sun drew them out of their hibernation. Matthew and Emma drank cold pinot grigio, stretched out half-naked on loungers, and talked about how they might deal with Kerimov.

Their discussion started out seriously, but as the wine flowed, it became more outlandish with another glass or two. Still, they did settle on the framework of a plan to somehow get aboard *Ice Man II* and sabotage the machine room to sink the boat. The only problem was finding out where it was and how to get aboard without being seen.

Fortunately, Kerimov's crew kept their AIS system active, and the radar ORB used to follow *Ice Man II* showed it had been sailing between Malta and the Cayman Islands, two secretive banking havens where the global ultra-rich often parked their wealth. It had also taken a trip to the Bosporus in Turkey—gateway to the Black Sea and the southern Russian ports of Sochi and Novorossiysk. Now they appeared to be heading toward the Panama Canal, and Stockman wondered whether they intended to head north up the Pacific coastline for some reason. ORB were not tracking the reasons for the visits, only its movements. They never lost sight of *Ice Man II*.

Reports on the movements of *Ice Man II* were intermittently transmitted to Stockman, who, in turn, sent the information on to Matthew. Now Matthew shared it with Emma as they pored over the details, trying to come up with some way to deal with Kerimov and disable his ability to keep playing his games at the expense of innocent people.

Matthew's cell phone played the ringtone of the "1812 Overture."

"Matthew, I think your problem may be solved." There was a smugness about the way Stockman made that statement.

"Oh, and how's that?" Matthew was amused by the prospect of some interesting banter.

"Well, it seems our Russian is about to dock in Vancouver."

"What! What do you think is going on?"

"Nothing good, you can be sure. We have no intel yet on what he's planning, but it's most likely meetings between Polygold and the big gold players in the city. They do share a few mutually interesting properties in South America, and he tends to sail in to meet with them every eighteen months or so. He ties up over at the Weyerhaeuser Terminal on the north side of the harbor, and they all go over to him. No one has ever seen him actually come into the city, but you never know."

"Okay, let me know when he arrives. I think this would be an ideal time to set something in motion to deal with him when we've finished our job."

"Any ideas?" Stockman was having some fun.

"If we want to scuttle *Ice Man II*, we may have to use explosives, although I would prefer not to. Anything else would need one, or more, of us to actually be on the boat—and that could be very dangerous. I would prefer to have something go wrong with the boat from the inside, but I'm not sure that's feasible. Any thoughts?" Matthew waited a few seconds for Stockman to speak.

"I would expect them to have some maintenance carried out while they're docked in Vancouver. Maybe we can get one or two of our techies in there to mess with their control system and autopilot. Perhaps they could install remote actuators, and we can wait until they hit a storm or rough coastline before activating them." Stockman paused. He wasn't very enthused about his own plan. Too complex and too reliant on stealth, with all those Russians on board keeping their eyes out for problems.

"Wishful thinking, Stockman." Matthew wasn't keen on the idea either. "Too risky. That boat is going to be heavy with security, and impossible to get anyone to find their way to the control center, and then have the space and time to work without being discovered.

"No, I think we have to work on the outside of the boat, underwater. Maybe use the same mines as we installed on the tug—clams. Small, difficult to spot, and able to be remotely detonated. No waiting for a storm or a rocky coastline—just the right time dictated by us. And don't forget, these days, the modern mega yacht is resplendent with layer upon layer of safety systems. One controller goes down, and the next one takes over, if you know what I mean."

"I do, Matthew. I think you've got it. Let's make it happen." Stockman was happy. Things seemed to be going ORB's way.

They signed off, and Matthew went back to his pinot grigio with Emma. She had heard the conversation between Matthew and her father but hadn't wanted to barge in on the call. There was no need.

They talked about the arrival of *Ice Man II* at the Vancouver harbor. It was a real stroke of luck, although Matthew had a bit of an uncomfortable feeling nagging at him about how much of a coincidence it was. He ignored it and turned his attention back to Emma.

"Why don't you get ahold of Tom and have him organize a few of those clam mines for us to use here? You should probably prepare yourself for a dive under the Russian's boat to place the mines. I think one on each of the propellor housings up against the hull and one in the bow thruster tunnel should do it. Both places are going to be difficult to examine by anyone just doing a check on the zincs if that happens," Matthew suggested.

"Are the mines magnetized, or will I have to weld them on?" Emma asked.

"Magnets. Just got to find the right spot and set them against the hull. Nothing needs to be done to the control mechanism. They'll already be programmed by Tom. All we have to do is set them off when the time comes."

"Sounds simple." Emma held both hands in the air, palms up, and had a happy frown on her face. "Voilà—I guess." They both smiled, shrugged their shoulders, and headed indoors. Time to open another bottle.

It didn't take much for them to make it to the bedroom, after grabbing another bottle from the bar fridge, with a couple of fresh glasses, and luxuriating in the comfort of air-conditioning and a king-size bed.

* * *

Unbeknownst to Matthew, Stockman had arranged for two ORB agents to stay in a leased apartment on the twenty-third floor of the high-rise kitty-corner to Matthew's apartment building. They could look down to where Matthew and Emma were now tossing and turning in bed, although the details remained obscured. Armed with military-grade scopes and listening devices, they were able to keep eyes and ears on two of their most senior people, but particularly on the daughter of their president. That was Stockman's primary concern. He had an unsettled feeling now that he knew Kerimov was coming to Vancouver.

The ORB agents could also watch the two casually clad, crewcut heavies who sat at a window seat in the ground-level coffee bar across the road from them. They had been easy to spot, as they initially checked out the entrance of Matthew's apartment building and turned back to check out the rear access gate. Now the crewcuts' eyes glanced from one entrance to the other as though they were waiting for someone to come out of either one.

Matthew half-expected the Russian would plan on kidnapping Emma to use as leverage against Stockman and ORB. It was the best move Kerimov could make, since he clearly knew ORB was on to him. While neither Matthew nor Stockman knew the extent of the Russian's knowledge of what ORB was up to, they did know he would be extremely nervous and looking to create a back door.

Matthew hadn't discussed his thoughts with Stockman, but as soon as Stockman had told him the Russian was heading to Vancouver, Matthew's brain lit up with suspicion, and he admitted his concerns.

"Already thought about that, my boy." Stockman was serious. "I have two agents watching from across the road. Apparently, they've spotted a couple of Kerimov's heavies already. They know what to do."

"Are you thinking what I'm thinking?" Matthew asked.

"You mean they're likely going to grab Emma and take her back to Kerimov?" Stockman's voice was filled with concern.

"Yes," Matthew said slowly.

"Let them do it. Emma can take care of herself, and we need her on that boat. Our guys will be on their heels the whole time. If anyone threatens her, it'll be their last threat." Stockman paused.

"I think I'm going to head out after she's gone, just to keep an extra pair of eyes on things."

"Take care, and go easily, Matthew. Nothing can go wrong. Once she's on the boat, we'll take care of Kerimov. Talk later." Stockman signed off.

If Emma came out by car, the heavies would follow her to her apartment in their own car. If she came out and walked, they would follow her on foot toward her apartment. The fact was, she wasn't going to make it to her building elevator. Either way, she was heading back to *Ice Man II*. What the heavies didn't know was they were being watched by ORB agents.

* * *

It had been an exhausting two months for the Danes as they set about repairing the damage caused by Mitch, the geologist they had used at the recommendation of Matthew. They wondered about that but didn't have the time to dwell on it while being so concerned with correcting the problems.

It was Yanko who had made the recommendation for a couple of local BC geologists, who dealt with narrow-vein mining, to replace Mitch. Yanko had really seemed to have come through for the Danes and sent resumes as well as arranging for the geologists to leave their current contracts and head over to Hope Brook.

Yanko's recommendation appeared to be good. The new geologists made great headway and directed the underground miners back to the gold vein at a record pace. Niels and his men took a deeper interest in what was happening after the ghost ship catastrophe. No more mistakes—security tightened, and they watched every movement, listened to conversations, and visited the mine right up to the active faces as often as they could. They watched over the shoulders of the new geologists and asked questions whenever new markings on the mine walls were made. There seemed to be little room for more subterfuge.

The Danes never knew Yanko was really a double agent of sorts. He had contacted Matthew as soon as he had located the replacement geologists and was ready to arrange their travel to St. John's. Yanko was not concerned with what Matthew did with that information, but he did assure him no photos of the replacements had been transmitted to the Danes. He always referred to them as Stoner 1 and Stoner 2—suggesting they were just nicknames for their profession. The Danes didn't seem to care.

Matthew had Mitch find two contract geologists from Northern Ontario and ship them to St. John's with the promise of substantial sign-on and completion bonuses. Then he had Tom meet Yanko's geologists, load them with money, and pack them off to northern Ontario to take the place of the ones Mitch had found, with contract close-out bonuses after six months and airfare back to British Columbia. The geologists were all content.

* * *

Sven and his crews coddled the barges as though they were babies. They examined every inch of the five barges above and below water, every time they were docked, whether at Hope Brook or at Aviles. No chances were taken—then the tug sank.

No one could fathom what had happened to it. As always, it guided one of the barges out from the Hope Brook landing over to the southeast corner of Newfoundland where they were to see it off across the Atlantic.

The captain had come about to begin the journey back to the mine. Without warning, there were two pops and one of the two twelve-foot-long steel rudders partially rose at an angle out of the sea and smashed back down ten feet away onto the rough ocean surface and sank. It had brought with it part of one of the propeller housings that would normally sit immediately ahead of it. The housing had brought with it a section of the hull, torn away from its weld. And that was it.

Seawater taken on over the stern rose rapidly to flood the engine room, and then the lower deck. The two Cummins five-thousand-horsepower diesel engines spluttered noisily, creaked, and belched steam, filling the living quarters and up into the pilothouse. They came to an unceremonious halt with a final gasp as the flood of seawater engulfing them turned to steam as it hit the hot surfaces and cracked parts of the metal shrouds with the sudden dramatic change in temperature.

The tug rapidly disappeared below the waves, with barely enough time for the captain and his crew members to scramble around for some precious personal effects, get the life raft into the water, and jump in. Their pitiful "Mayday, mayday, mayday" was quickly picked up by several ships going back and forth through the St. John's Harbour Narrows. It had taken just fifteen minutes from the time of the pop to the sinking. The crew were in shock and stayed that way for some time. But they were safe and lived to tell the tale to Sven as soon as they landed in port.

Meanwhile, James had constantly been checking his watch from the mine site, waiting for an hour to go by before he figured the tug had made it to where it was supposed to be when he detonated the clams. One would have done the job—but two were better.

* * *

The Danes were mortified by the turn of events. First the mining, then Kerimov and his money woes, and now the tug. Surely nothing else could go wrong. Thank God for *Viking I*, which was moored near the barge site and afforded them a comfortable, if not luxurious, place to chill while they arranged to keep the mine running smoothly. At least that was going well, and they thanked Yanko for his enthusiastic and speedy attention to the details of getting the replacement geologists in place.

Work at the site continued in earnest, with the new barges hauling back and forth to Aviles with no serious interruptions until Kerimov called Finn two months later.

"Are you guys fucking me again?"

It was a repeat of the last problem with the geology. Somehow, the gold vein had disappeared once more, and the miners were off-track yet again. They were fifty thousand tons of ore into waste, and nothing showed up until the process plant operations team wired Kerimov a measly three hundred and sixty thousand dollars for the disseminated gold particles that dropped out of the treatment. It wasn't even enough to pay the bills.

The geologists claimed innocence on the basis the gold vein had temporarily disappeared, and they were frantically searching for where it continued, but in the meantime, they had to remove the ore that was essentially in the way. They were still searching. Their excuses seemed logical to most.

"Why the fuck didn't they stop it from being taken to the process plant? Why didn't they just dump it at the portal?" Kerimov was livid, especially when he didn't get a reasonable answer. Even Niels and his men were lost for words, having no experience in the world of mining. Unfortunately, the Danes had been absent at the time; otherwise, things might have been different.

By the time the gold vein was re-established, more time and money had been lost, but at least they still had geologists and the barges, unlike the time before, and the work began again in earnest.

* * *

Emma and the Russian

What Kerimov didn't know, before his arrival in Vancouver, was that ORB had monitored the movement and location of *Ice Man II* using their AIS since his meeting in Puerto Banús. Most times, it was the only piece of equipment that could accurately pinpoint the location of a boat anywhere in the world—and especially useful if that vessel needed help.

Kerimov hadn't seriously thought about being watched until now. But the combination of the mining incident, the money issues, and now the tug fiasco were all too coincidental to be believed as merely "accidents." While the mishap with the tug was a somewhat trivial occurrence compared to the mining and money episodes, it was still another irritant Kerimov convinced himself had been designed by someone who wanted to mess with him. Now he was convinced he was being watched, but he didn't understand how, since he was always on the move and always on his boat. Not being a nautical aficionado, Kerimov was somewhat ignorant of what an AIS was, and didn't know his boat was equipped with such a device. If he had known, he would have had it deactivated years ago and only activated it had his boat run into problems while at sea.

It wasn't hard for Kerimov to feel insecure when surrounded by unexplained phenomena that touched his life. But then, as a narcissist, he always thought of himself as a victim in these kinds of circumstances and the center of someone else's attention. But now, he was even more convinced ORB were the ones behind all these problems and must, therefore, be interested in the Hope Brook venture. Although why that would titillate their interest, he still didn't understand—or didn't want to. Surely it wasn't a big enough fish for them to go hunting.

With *Ice Man II* tied up to the Vancouver dockside, Kerimov listened to Sven repeat the story about the tug incident Finn had already called him about. Then Sven went back over all the details of the careful preparations he had been making to protect against further problems, as though to mollify Kerimov as to his own innocence in all this mess. But the question in Kerimov's mind was whether it was really possible to protect against any further problems. *What else could there be?* he wondered. *Well*, he thought, *there is myself to protect.* He didn't really care about the Danes.

He doubled security onboard, put a diver on call to check the underside of *Ice Man II* every four hours, and set up underwater lighting focused on the aft, where the propellors and rudders were located. In addition, he increased illumination on the dock, set up control gates on both sides of the gangway, and brought in two ferocious-looking German shepherds with handlers to watch the comings and goings along the wharf and the dock to which the boat was secured.

Everyone who might need access to Kerimov had to have security clearance before coming through control. Every member of the crew was issued fingerprint access only to those cabins they needed to enter, and each cabin was equipped with additional cameras and voice monitors with a complete overview of everything both on the bridge as well as in Kerimov's private quarters on the owner's deck.

Kerimov knew he should be secure, but he still felt vulnerable for some unknown reason. Call it a sense or a real threat. His usual caution was the consequence of his many years floating from port to port, rarely going ashore, and always feeling as though his enemies were just out of reach of him… but, in this case, he seemed to feel a chill as he imagined ORB closing in on him, and he was now of the opinion it must have something to do with Hope Brook.

Of course, there was the obvious: the scam he and the Danes were pulling off. But there were so many reasons to hunt Kerimov down and, to him, Hope Brook was just a small one of them. Frankly, he considered it an innocuous one compared to the many extremes he had gone through over the years to illegitimately increase his wealth and hold on to power. Perhaps the interest in Hope Brook was the tip of some iceberg he hadn't yet seen—but ORB had.

* * *

It was two a.m. when Emma left the sanctuary of Matthew's apartment and headed north on foot across the peninsula to her own place. She loved these quiet times, particularly in this part of the city, where there were still single homes. As she walked by, she could peep through the ground-floor windows to the rooms still lit. She could stare up at the moon on a clear night and mentally note the constellations she thought she recognized and name them, while at the same time, she could keep walking, knowing she likely wouldn't bump into anyone on the deserted streets.

Regardless of the hour, it wasn't unusual for Emma to go back to her apartment after spending some intimate time with Matthew. They would get caught up with the project with him to begin with, open a second bottle of cold pinot grigio to lubricate their thinking and strategize their next move, and then revel in pleasure afterwards. In fact, she really liked it that way. This comfortable part of her life involved a person with whom to share her thoughts, to release some passion and pent-up excitement, and then to savor the after-moment of having some space to think. She could then wake up in her own bed and get ready for the next day at her own pace with her own things around her.

Matthew was her best friend, and more, but their lives were complicated by the work they did, and their personal space was important to each of them. Emma often thought about the prospect of some of their targets catching up to one or the other, maybe both, but the fact was Matthew was always the point man in the field and, therefore, the most likely target of some adversary. As such, he was more likely to be the first to attract the wrong attention and likely the only one. Call it callous. Call it selfish. But in a way, Emma was subconsciously trying to isolate herself from overexposure to danger by not totally succumbing to the temptation of being with Matthew for every moment, even if that was possible. But, regardless of how safe she felt in Vancouver when she was by herself, she always looked over her shoulder while walking at night, just in case.

The south side of the peninsula was naturally darker than the north at night. It was older and more established, with low-pressure sodium street lighting throwing a yellowy-orange glow and lampposts farther apart than in more modern areas. Sidewalks were mostly sheltered by overgrown trees badly in need of pruning. While Emma was accustomed to the spookier nature of the walk back to her place, she still always quickened her pace until she got into the brightness of the city lights on the north side.

* * *

The two ORB agents had scrambled down to the ground floor of the apartment building they had been occupying while maintaining a watch over Matthew and Emma. They had seen Emma leave the building opposite and start walking up the hill away from them. She disappeared from their view, but they noticed two shadows run across the road after her and slow down as they turned the corner to follow her up the hill.

One of the ORB agents called Matthew. "It seems as though Emma has company. The same two big crewcut guys from the coffee shop," the agent whispered into his phone.

"Okay, follow them, but don't interfere—unless you have to. My guess is it will be the Russian's people, and they'll be there to take Emma back to his boat over on the North Shore. Just get confirmation, and if it doesn't happen like that, then take them out and get Emma back." Matthew cut the call short and picked up his two-way radio.

"Emma," he whispered into her earpiece just as she stepped over a curb and onto the grass verge, "two suspects following you. Our people are behind them. Play dumb, get taken, and don't get hurt. Can't give the game away just yet. Hang tight, and you should end up on *Ice Man II*. Contact me from there if you can. If not, I'll have someone there within four hours." It was all Matthew could say before Emma spoke.

"They're here…" The line went dead as Emma caught the strong smell of the chloroform.

A figure stepped out of the shadows behind her, and a strong hand tried to cover her mouth. Her natural reaction was to squirm in multiple directions, push her arms straight out in front of her and up quickly, as she had been taught, then bend as low forward as she could and spring up and back to hit whoever was behind her in the nose with her head.

It was enough of a surprise and shock for the alien hand to release her as she spun around, only to be grabbed from behind again by a second attacker. As she kicked the first person in front of her sharply in the solar plexus with the tip of her ankle-booted foot and saw his shadow collapse backward onto the grass verge, the second attacker pressed his hand firmly over her mouth and wrapped the other hand around her neck from behind. She tried kicking backward but, by then, the first attacker had clamped her legs together as he stretched out from his otherwise prone position, and they all ended up on the ground.

They stayed that way for nearly five minutes, with Emma struggling and the goons hanging on, before the chloroform finally did its work, and Emma succumbed to drowsiness followed by sedation.

One of the ORB agents stood behind bushes just twenty feet away and watched as Emma was drugged and carried by her two attackers to a waiting car. The second ORB agent had already collected their car and moved in close to the bush for the other agent to get in. Both cars headed over toward North Vancouver, just as Matthew thought they would.

* * *

ORB's contacts with military and policing authorities at the highest levels were numerous and powerful. Their tentacles reached into major jurisdictions around the world. Matthew had put a call in to his ORB contact with the police brass in Vancouver and so the message got passed up the chain. The man at the top confirmed with Stockman and the order came back down the chain to the local for them to comply with any requests from Matthew. ORB needed help immediately to identify where one of their agents had been taken and what bodies were in the immediate vicinity. Matthew had described *Ice Man II* to Rudy, the desk sergeant on duty at the station in Vancouver, where the boat was located, and what information he needed from the drone they were planning on launching.

Ed Sleeman was sound asleep when his cell phone woke him with the sound of a police siren—Ed's amusing setting to alert him to who the caller was—in this case, his boss. He felt for the sound, pushed the cell phone around before he managed to grab it, pressed "Talk," and mumbled into the mouthpiece, "Ed."

"You need to get up right away, Ed. Duty calls." It was Rudy, Ed's sergeant, over at the city station. Clearly, Rudy needed his full attention immediately.

Ed pushed his side of the bedcovers off himself gently and rolled out of bed. He ignored the sleepy question from his wife, who asked if everything was okay. He didn't bother answering, expecting her to just fall back to sleep. It was just a natural reaction of hers, born out of a fleeting interest as his movement disturbed her. He made his way to the living room, where he could talk openly.

Rudy had his orders from the brass and Ed needed to get over to the marina and launch drone as soon as possible.

"Right now, Rudy? It's two thirty in the morning, for Chrissake. Can't this wait?" Ed whined, as most would when woken from a sleep where one had all the prospects of continuing a good dream.

"Nah, Ed. Some exec on the top floor somewhere wants action right away. Sounds like it could be a kidnapping. They didn't tell me much, but you need to get eyes on that Russian billionaire's boat sitting over at the Weyerhaeuser wharf in North Vancouver. Thoughts are he could be involved. We have to take a look and advise on body count onboard and in the vicinity. That body count has to also include any warm signals from inside the boat. Can you do that?" Rudy was a good cop. Mostly on night duty in the city, but he had been through his fair share of odd requests, and this was just another.

"Wow, I'll get right on it, Rudy. Gimme thirty minutes to get set up. Call you back when I'm ready to go up, and yeah, I can pick up hot spots inside that boat. Thin walls on boats, you know." Ed was referring to the ability of his baby, the top-of-the-line drone mostly used by the armed forces and police. Some police have dogs. Ed had a drone. It was one of the best on the market for what the police generally needed, including a thermal imaging camera so they could make out the movement of warm bodies inside buildings—and boats. It also had a range of close to ten miles, and a battery flight time of fifty-five minutes—better than most.

Ed had been one of the first to take a drone flight training program to qualify to operate the unit. The law had changed two years ago, and anyone who wanted to operate a drone over a particular size had to have FAA certification. Ed's drone was pretty big, and he knew the regulations inside-out for what he needed to do. There were only three major drone operators attached to the Vancouver police department, and he was the first, although that number was clearly going to grow rapidly over the next few years. It was a relatively small investment with major payoffs for policing.

Ed took his equipment to the helipad on the south side of the harbor, where it was open ground with a clear view across to the other side of the harbor. The drone batteries were always charged. He could see *Ice Man II* lit up across the water about a mile away. The fourteen-pound drone was equipped with a single night vision camera unit with a zoom, night vision wide lens, and a tele-infrared thermal device hooked up in the gimbal under the belly. Ed liked to keep the drone's ceiling height less than fifteen thousand feet, just for safety reasons, although he could go up to about twenty-two thousand feet with a small payload—say, one less battery. The unit was quiet, fast, and extremely versatile.

"Ready," he announced to Rudy over his cell. "Clear night. I should be able to get down as low as a thousand feet without being seen or heard, but with all lighting turned off. The closer I can get, the better penetration I get through walls." Ed sounded proud and enthusiastic about his job. He loved it.

"Great. I've got nothing else for you, Ed. Transmit directly to the station, and I'll let you know if the images are clear. Over and out." Rudy went back to his front office duties while Ed operated the control panel slung around his neck. The camera was operating, and the images he was receiving were excellent. He pushed the drone vertically to a thousand feet before setting off horizontally over to *Ice Man II*.

Rudy put a call in to his chief, who relayed the message to Matthew: "The drone is in the air."

Ed stood merrily controlling his drone out over the harbor toward *Ice Man II* and watched his own screen as the video performed as expected, and his unit transmitted the details to Rudy and on to Matthew. *Ice Man II* was five stories high, with each ascending deck smaller in area than the one above it. It was impossible for the drone to establish on which deck the bodies were located, but it did show there to be several warm spots on various decks, several on the dock, and what looked to be two in a small boat close to the stern side. Some of the bodies were clearly active, but others seemed to be inactive or likely sleeping at this hour or walking the perimeters. There seemed to be a small group of four bodies at midship, deck unknown, and Matthew assumed this was where they were holding Emma. It was likely the main deck.

Matthew wasn't a hundred percent sure why Kerimov had grabbed Emma but guessed he suspected ORB of being involved in his latest scheme, and holding Emma gave him some leverage in the event he needed to make a deal. He was right. It would give him leverage, except Matthew knew exactly where she was, and he could see where the weak spots were in the defenses of *Ice Man II*. Provided Kerimov's men had not stripped Emma of her personal effects, the transponder, which Emma always carried with her hidden in the cap of her lipstick, signaled her position.

* * *

"Stockman. How pleasant to talk to you again." Kerimov put on his smoothest voice. *Ice Man II* was already at sea, doing eighteen knots as she raced toward the southern tip of Vancouver Island.

One of his pilots had told him about the AIS and the likelihood of it being the device giving their position away. He instructed them to go dark by turning the system off and doing anything else they needed to do to cloak *Ice Man II* and keep it away from prying eyes—including any deck lights that weren't needed. By the time he put the call in to Stockman, they were coming up to a waypoint that would move the boat to a more westerly direction, toward the open ocean.

"Kerimov, I assume," Stockman responded, knowing full well Kerimov had kidnapped his daughter.

"Ah, you recognize my voice. How perceptive of you after all these years." Kerimov was truly impressed.

"I never forget the voice of a criminal, and that Russian accent. It gives it all away," Stockman commented glibly. "Now, why don't you tell me why you've called? But, before you do that, I'm sure you know I'm quite aware you have kidnapped my daughter, Emma, and I'm quite sure you have her on your little boat." Of course, Stockman knew *Ice Man II* had left its mooring and had almost a two-hour lead on any boat he could commandeer that might try to chase it. It had also meant any chance to storm the vessel from land was now impossible and could only be made from the air, or by a fast coast guard cutter.

Kerimov's chief engineer had told him the fastest coast guard boat in these waters was the Cape class vessel capable of twenty-five knots, with a range of two hundred miles, which carried only four people. Kerimov calculated it would take another hour or more to mobilize that size of a lifeboat, but it would need a few extra hands onboard if they were to be effective. By the time a coast guard boat was ready to move, *Ice Man II* would be almost four hours away, or some eighty miles. Even at top speed, the coast guard would not be able to intercept *Ice Man II* until twelve hours had passed since *Ice Man II* had left its mooring, even if the coast guard knew her position, which they wouldn't without the AIS operating. If luck was with them, and they managed to somehow follow her, the coast guard boat would have run out of time and range after almost eleven hours and would have to return to base. Their quarry would be long gone.

Kerimov was a little shocked at Stockman's response, although he shouldn't have been at all surprised to discover Stockman knew about Emma. After all, not only was ORB at his service, but he also had a number of other powerful groups at his disposal—and they all had the electronic, mechanical, and manual means to overpower Kerimov at some point in the chase.

He had already suspected they knew Emma was on *Ice Man II* and worried they would have surrounded it and not let it leave port until Emma was released. In fact, he thought they would have stormed the boat had they stayed tied up to the wharf, but then doubted such strong-arm means would be taken against such a high-powered figure associated with Russia. But he wasn't a hundred percent sure. Rather than enter into a protracted negotiation based on what was likely to become a lost cause, *Ice Man II* left port and headed out to sea with Emma still aboard. She was now, after all, Kerimov's only solid prospect of freeing himself from the whole mess.

Kerimov stayed cool with Stockman on the other end of the line. They both went quiet for a moment. Stockman worried about Emma and whether ORB was really able to free her unharmed while this madman was in control.

Kerimov worried whether he could get away with this ruse and be able to regain access to his bank accounts without seriously aggravating the situation more. He knew ORB would have the muscle with its allies, and he had little protection here in a foreign country.

"My dear Stockman. Your daughter is my guest." Kerimov played it cool again. "We met when she visited Puerto Banús, didn't you know? We became, how can I say this… close. You understand." Kerimov smiled sadistically and felt the engines of *Ice Man II* rumble as the boat sped forward. He was becoming more confident as he mentally calculated how far away he would be by the time ORB could do anything.

"Kerimov. Still the rogue playing with fire." Stockman was taunting him with sharp points, striking at Kerimov's pride. Words like "rogue" and "playing" were incendiary ones to a person like him.

"My dear friend, perhaps you will understand if I totally ignore your provocations and come straight to the point." Kerimov had that smile on his face again and refused to be baited by Stockman.

"Please do, but make it quick, would you, old boy? I have things to do, and talking to you any more than I really have to makes me, shall we say… nauseous?" It was Stockman's turn to smile, but in a cynical way.

"I see. Why are you no comfort to your daughter? You have not thought of her being in danger? No possibility you could get the fuck off my back if I set her free?" Kerimov was getting annoyed as his attempt at negotiation seemed about to hit the rocks. He couldn't help it. He was used to getting his way, and this *idyot* was getting in his way.

"You do what you have to do, Kerimov. Just another notch of stupidity on your belt. There must be many by now. Aren't you getting tired of being treated with so much disrespect around the world?" Stockman didn't mince words and while he had no proof of what he was telling Kerimov, he knew it would make the Russian think more seriously about his next move.

"You are full of bullshit, Stockman. They are just words. They mean nothing to me. I want you to agree to back away from me or there will be consequences."

Apart from not knowing if *Ice Man II* was still being watched, Kerimov had no knowledge of the underwater charges clamped to the propellor housings.

While tied up at the Weyerhaeuser dock, ORB agents, concealed on the fuel pontoon a hundred feet away from *Ice Man II*, watched the Russian's frogmen in their small boat as they prepared to dive for another four-hourly hull inspection. The agents wore wetsuits and waited for word from Matthew before they went into action. Timing of the operation was imperative. If the mines were clamped on too early, the frogmen might find them on their next dive. They needed to be installed in the hours before *Ice Man II* left its mooring. That was a judgment call that Matthew would need to make.

With Emma aboard *Ice Man II*, Matthew was sure it would leave with minimal delay. Perhaps even within an hour, by the time all was ready. As he was leaving his apartment to follow the two crewcuts who had taken Emma, he called his agents on the fuel pontoon and gave them the go-ahead to set the mines.

It was almost three a.m. when the frogmen surfaced after one of their four-hourly checks on the hull. The ORB agents watched through night vision scopes and wasted no time slipping off the pontoon and swimming silently toward the port side of *Ice Man II*, away from where the frogmen had surfaced. Each carried a remote detonation clam mine to be attached to the two propellor housings, with one transmitter to continually monitor the location of the boat in the event Kerimov deactivated the AIS.

After they finished their job, the agents surfaced on the port side of the boat, gave each other a thumbs-up sign, took a quick look around to get their bearings, and smoothly submerged again to swim back to the fuel pontoon. They were picked up by a waiting police dinghy, with no running lights, and purred off to their base, farther up Coal Harbour near the container wharves.

A message of success was transmitted to Matthew and on to Stockman after Matthew had explained the situation in more detail to his boss. Both of them had gambled on Kerimov making a run for it in short order as soon as Emma had been ensconced on the boat.

It had taken only forty-five minutes after Emma had been brought aboard for the engines of *Ice Man II* to rumble awake and pull away from its mooring. It stayed to the five-knot restriction until it reached the Lions Gate Bridge, when the rumble turned to a roar, and the wake rose to four feet above the stern as the luxury yacht went into overdrive and plowed its way on a direct heading south to the tip of Vancouver Island with a course plotted to two hundred and fifty miles west of that point before it intended to turn south. No final destination was plotted at this point.

* * *

Emma blinked, turned her head slowly to take in what she could of her surroundings and enough to see there was someone sitting opposite, reading a magazine. She twisted her head in the opposite direction and saw another person sitting near an open door to what appeared to be a bathroom. He was playing with his cell phone, and neither of them seemed to show any interest in her having come awake.

She could hear the thrum of boat engines and could tell from the torque noise they were operating at speed, although there seemed to be barely a rise and fall as the boat thrust through the water.

Emma regained consciousness from the chloroform, although her head pounded from the after-effects, and the feeling of nausea almost overcame her. But she managed to prop herself up on one arm before one of the goons helped put some cushions behind her head so she could at least half-sit. She slowly turned her head from side to side, taking in the whole room. It was well appointed; with everything one might need to spend a relaxing evening at home. Only this wasn't home, and she wasn't relaxing. She reached out for her handbag, which had been tossed on the bed beside her. It was a small comfort.

"Where am I?" she asked as she looked from guard to guard. Neither one looked up at her, and neither of them spoke.

Emma's memory came flooding back. She remembered the last words from Matthew and knew he would be champing at the bit to rescue her. But how?

* * *

Matthew boarded a Bell twin-engine Air 5 helicopter operated by the federally regulated Royal Canadian Mounted Police. It had a cruising speed of about a hundred and twenty-five miles per hour and reached the location of *Ice Man II*, from its base in Vancouver in an hour, as it neared the end of Georgia Strait. It was about to pass through the narrow channel separating Canada from the United States, leading to the open ocean. Some action needed to be taken while the boat was still on the Canadian side of the border with the US and before it reached international waters.

It was here Matthew remotely detonated the first of the clam mines. It was not meant to be powerful enough to blast a hole through the hull of *Ice Man II*, as they had done on the tug. This one took out one of the propellers and sent the blades flying backward through the water. *Ice Man II* lurched as half of its thrust collapsed, and with it, its speed. Ten minutes later, Matthew detonated the second clam mine and propellor number two splintered, taking a good part of its shroud with it.

Ice Man II totally lost thrust, and only the forward momentum allowed it to move. But within two hundred feet, all momentum was lost, and Matthew could see bodies running in all directions on the deck. It was only the autopilot that managed to continue to control the rudder and keep the heading toward the narrows—just where Matthew wanted them.

* * *

As *Ice Man II* jolted abruptly to half speed the first time, and the first propellor was destroyed, the two thugs watching over Emma exchanged glances of panic, grabbed their guns from their underarm holsters, and bolted through the door; one thug headed aft, the other forward.

Emma was stunned as she fell sideways from her half-sitting position but regained control and leaped off the bed, grabbed her bag, and raced awkwardly through the door. She had no idea which end of the boat was which until she glanced out of the window and saw which direction *Ice Man II* was traveling. As she mentally rationalized which way to go, the second blast happened, and the second propeller blew its casing.

Ice Man II came to a sudden and sharp slowdown, tipping Emma over onto the carpeted hallway and rolling her back into the room she had just come from. Her head knocked on the door jamb as she seemed to have been sucked in, and it was only her legs that saved her from crashing into the wall opposite. Gradually, the boat just moved forward under its own momentum. Although the engines were still operating at high speed, without propellors, it was going nowhere fast.

There seemed to be more panic about her as bodies flew past, heading to the stern. In the group was one of the thugs who had been guarding her and had initially run toward the bow of the boat. That made her mind up for her as she crawled forward to lever herself upright. The bow seemed to be the obvious choice for her now, and she hurried forward, cautiously watching for any bodies that might get in her way. There were none, and it seemed they had all gone aft, where the sound of the blasts had come from.

It suddenly dawned on Emma what was happening. ORB had concocted a plan to demobilize *Ice Man II* before it reached the open waters of the Pacific.

"I could kiss you, Matthew Black," Emma whispered loudly as she stumbled forward.

A plan was materializing in her head. She would make her way up as far as the upper sun deck, where there would very likely be no one around. It was still dark outside, and everyone would be occupied in the pilothouse, the engine room, or at the stern. She would take off her white blouse, and wave it as frantically as she could, to attract attention. Even in all this mess, she had guessed help could only come from the sky or the water, and most likely the sky—a chopper, yes, a chopper.

She smiled and pushed a door open onto the port-side gangway. One look out over the railing told her she was on the third deck, which meant there were at least two decks above her. Emma reached one of the outside escape ladders, climbed to the fourth deck, and peeped over the railing before climbing over. She headed to the next ladder and climbed as fast as she could. There were no human sounds anywhere close, but she could just make out the bodies in the distance on the stern of *Ice Man II* as they ran in all directions. A helicopter was hovering over them, and she could barely hear someone with a loudspeaker, but she couldn't make out the words.

Emma made it up to the sun deck only to be met by another helicopter only fifty feet above her. There was no need to wave a blouse; Matthew stood in the doorway and waved to her. He used a megaphone.

"Where have you been, darling?"

* * *

Within an hour, the Canadian coast guard had a rescue boat arrive at the scene and throw a tow line onto *Ice Man II*. The crew had little choice but to fasten it to the two anchor housings, one on each side of the bow. A tug arrived, and the mega yacht was on her way back to the wharf in North Vancouver.

Two hours later, it was secured to the dock and guarded to prevent any of the crew from leaving, including Kerimov, who was still stomping up and down in his stateroom, absolutely livid at Stockman, ORB, Canada, and anything else he could think of that might have anything to do with his current state—including the disappearance of Emma, his hostage. His phone rang.

"Hello, old boy. All well with you?" It was Stockman, and his voice sounded chipper.

"You can't do this, you bastard. Get me out of here. I'm an important person. A Russian, and we will not tolerate this nonsense," Kerimov shouted into the phone.

"Oh, we can do this, Kerimov. You kidnapped a Canadian citizen on Canadian soil and held her against her will. I'm afraid you're going to have to stay where you are for a while—not that you have any choice without propellors, mind you. Feel free to ask for anything you need while you are here, and we'll review whether we will supply it or not. In the meantime, your outgoing communications will be immediately stopped—so no calling Moscow, I'm afraid."

Stockman was smirking just as Lucy handed him a note from her discussion on the other phone. "All communications ready to be terminated in fifteen seconds."

"You bastard. When I find you, Stockman, you will feel my anger and the anger of our government—now let me go..."

Communications were cut off, and all went quiet. Stockman smiled and called Matthew.

"Well done, Matthew. How's my daughter?"

"Oh, I think we may have to replace the jacket she left behind, but other than that, a little wine will help, I think." Matthew smiled, and Stockman laughed as they ended the call.

Matthew rolled back over to Emma, pushed his arm around her shoulders, and pulled her to him.

"Mission accomplished; don't you think?" Matthew smiled at her and kissed her forehead.

"Oh, I love that position." Emma chuckled and slid under the sheets, with Matthew following.

* * *

Poor Danes

One of the many sad things about Finn and Erik was that they had left a trail of suspicious activities behind them that were really quite easy for an organization like ORB to get their teeth into and put the vice grips on this pair if it ever became necessary. It was necessary now, and Stockman knew he would thoroughly enjoy watching these two criminals squirm. While their Hope Brook project was clearly going under water, Stockman decided to execute a coup de grâce and make the Danes suffer a little extra for their sins.

It brought a smile to his face as he described what he was thinking and planning to Lucy, while they sat comfortably in over-stuffed armchairs on either side of a log fire in their home away from home in Hope Cove. A storm thundered overhead and the rain beat against the windows as they read, listened to their quietly playing favorite music, and sipped G&Ts to while away the time. Naturally, Stockman was not totally satisfied with so much idle time, and the thought of compromising the Danes further flexed his brain, making better use of some downtime rather than doing nothing constructive.

"Sounds lovely, dear," Lucy commented after Stockman had finished describing how he intended to bring justice to the Danes. She generally didn't elaborate on her thoughts unless asked and just went back to her book.

"What do you think?" Stockman couldn't help himself and looked across at his wife of thirty-five years.

"Oh." Lucy looked up, surprised. "I think it's an absolutely wonderful idea." She was genuinely enthusiastic as she returned Stockman's stare. "Let's face it, those rogues have been lucky to have stayed ahead of the law all this time. They really need to be punished heavily for their misdeeds, and while this isn't in your manifesto, it would be good to get a little something more out of this." She chuckled, sat back, and looked over the top of her book to the wood burning and spitting on the hearth.

"Those rogues," she whispered harshly, and looked serious. "Unless they end up in jail, I think we agree they would only dream up some other scheme, and away we go again. Do it, dear. Just do it. They need to be put away." Lucy looked away from the fire with a bemused smile that made Stockman chuckle.

"You're quite the woman," Stockman murmured to himself, quite happy he had Lucy's support.

As it had happened, Stockman had discovered during his research that before their latest underground mining trickery, the Danes had actually been up to similar shenanigans by using their nefarious influence, and deviousness, with a medium-sized Norwegian mining company they had bullied into controlling.

Once they were in the driver's seat, they convinced the majority of shareholders to relinquish their stock and put it up for sale through their broker in an attempt to raise finances sufficient to develop their properties. When the shareholders agreed, they all transferred their stock to the broker Finn and Erik had enlisted, with guarantees that they, the sellers, would benefit from any stock price increase if the stock was bought from their broker at a higher price. Unbeknownst to the shareholders, the broker was owned and operated by Finn and Erik, who used a front man for the transactions.

As it turned out, the Finn and Erik actually bought the shares, through the broker, on behalf of a Russian company, owned by Kerimov, without the knowledge of the mining company shareholders. Now, having bought the shares from the broker, the Russian company had no obligation to disclose the transaction, but they did pay the Danes a "transaction" fee for their trouble. Nor were the original shareholders compensated with the share price premium when the stock price suddenly increased overnight on the news of the involvement of the Russian and his reputation of success.

The original shareholders never knew Kerimov was really the buyer, and the Danes never offered the details at the time. They were just in it for the fee and by the time the original shareholders discovered what was going on, it was too late. Kerimov and his company, which was originally expected to mount a hostile takeover, now had a sufficient controlling interest in the mining company to avoid the difficulties and expenses of such a move. They just owned it by share majority.

There was little the original shareholders felt they could do to reconcile the situation at the time. They had, it appeared, agreed to sell their shares, although they had not known it was going to be to the same company planning a takeover. The Danes were clearly complicit but, to date, had walked away free of charges, having dodged from one country to the next, frustrating the authorities and avoiding receipt of subpoenas and subsequently ignoring indictments. That was all to end now.

Stockman had come to know all this from his contacts at Økokrim in Oslo. Økokrim was the National Authority for Investigation of Economic and Environmental Crime in Norway and was both a police unit and a prosecution authority. They were looking to bring justice to the situation by litigating gross fraud, subsidiary financial loyalty, and market manipulation against Finn and Erik, but weren't entirely prepared with an iron-clad case.

They needed to apprehend the Danes. Then someone suggested they look to ORB to help them solve their problem. The senior investigator at Økokrim contacted Stockman for help. It was clear they needed to go outside the box of what the government authorities could do—and ORB had been touted as the perfect fit. Stockman had resisted at the time, before the Hope Brook situation, on the basis that the injustice was not critical or large enough to warrant ORB's subversive intervention with the support of just one government. Stockman had filed the case away in the back of his head in the event he ever needed to recall it.

Now was the time he needed it. With several high-level parties being interested in seeking justice for the Danes for a variety of reasons, including original shareholders in the Norwegian stock fiasco, Stockman knew ORB would be well supported in their endeavor to go after Finn and Erik for criminal charges.

Stockman connected with Tony, ORB's lawyer, to raise a legal red flag with Økokrim in Oslo. This was the largest single case they had ever managed with a value in the order of twenty million US dollars for the initial fraud—the original value of the shares scammed from the shareholders that became over two hundred million once the company was bought out.

* * *

By now, money from the accounts of both the Russian and the Danes was flowing back and forth and diminishing the accounts of each party with each pass. The banks claimed ignorance. All procedures were being followed, and all passwords and account numbers were exactly right. No one could figure out the reason for what was happening—except for Plato and Colin.

Then the ultimate happened to the Danes. Their bank accounts were flagged red by the Norwegians and frozen—their money suspected of being the proceeds of illegal activities. No transactions would be allowed until the Norwegians released their flag—and that could take some considerable time, depending on how fast the legal system moved in Norway. Fortunately, ORB had already transferred all the money they needed for reparation to injured parties, as well as their fees.

The Danes were at their wits' end. They had no idea why the red flag had been issued—although they knew it could be for any number of nefarious reasons, but none had appeared to have surfaced sufficient to cause this action, as far as they were aware, although there was a nagging thought at the back of Finn's mind about the stunt he and Erik had pulled on that Norwegian mining company. It was the first time they had met Kerimov and somehow, for some reason, they had just clicked, and it was a forgone conclusion they would work together again at some point. But that would have nothing to do with the Norwegian red flag—would it? Finn wondered.

Finn and Erik started to lose focus on the Hope Brook project as they became completely absorbed by their financial woes. No money. Zero. Nothing coming in and bills still to pay. How the hell had this all happened? Fortunately, they both had another account hidden through surrogate corporations, but with limited funds, just enough to pay for *Viking I* and a steak dinner now and again. It was totally depressing.

Finn called Kerimov. No answer. He had gone dark, or so Finn thought. Little could he have known Kerimov was isolated, guarded, and incommunicado in Vancouver. There seemed to be no way they could consult with each other. Finn wondered if Kerimov's accounts had also been frozen. There was that darned link with the Norwegian mining company, but then he thought he was overthinking the situation. Why would Kerimov be red-flagged for something like that? As far as the authorities would be concerned, Kerimov's purchase of those shares was perfectly legitimate for him. It wasn't Kerimov who was in trouble over the share purchase. It was them.

"Okay, so what the hell is going on?" Finn was at a loss and shouted his frustration to the room around him. But only Erik was there.

"Maybe they know about Hope Brook?" It was Erik. "And Greenland?" He flashed a look at Finn that said it all. "Maybe they know about the others as well?" Erik got lost in his thoughts. There were so many possibilities.

"Fuck. You're right." Finn was red in the face. "Some bastard's been tagging us…" Finn stopped, and Erik could almost see the wheels turning in his friend's brain. "Fuuuuuuuck! Fuck! Fuck!" Finn hissed and banged his fists on the table. The glasses rattled, a cigar butt jumped out of the ashtray, and his cell phone bounced a few times before sliding onto the floor.

"It's got to be those ORB bastards Kerimov warned us about. Didn't he tell us that bitch, Emma, told Big Jim about some associates of hers visiting Greenland? Fuck. I never really thought about it before. But that's got to be it!" Finn fell back in his chair and cradled his head in his hands as Erik calmly watched from the other sofa. Calm he may have appeared, but shaken he definitely was.

* * *

The withholding of the financing from PCW had the desired effect on the Hope Brook operations. All work stopped. The barges that were en route to Aviles stayed unloaded when they reached the Spanish port and tied up to the wharf. Big Jim's contract was abandoned without notice and all his equipment and supplies were loaded on the three leased barges, not filled with ore, and taken back to St. John's, where it was all unloaded and sat in the marshaling area until CanMine could pay for transport back west.

The leased barges were retrieved by their owner—bills unpaid. The camp units were shuttered and left in place to be recovered by CanMine another day. The barge landing, with its ancillary facilities, was left to bear the brunt of the weather. Hope Brook became deserted, with even more waste piles draining onto the landscape than there were before. The CanMine facilities in St. John's were abandoned, supplies remained on the wharf or in storage, and bills were left unpaid.

Kerimov had no idea of what was happening, and neither did he have access to his banking, but there would be no way he would have subsidized the project once the principal lender had pulled out. Had he been able to communicate with the Danes, he would have pulled the plug on the operation himself.

Finn and Erik had little choice but to stand by and watch as the project unraveled while they were totally embroiled in their more personal financial problems with the Norwegians. They had no idea as to the whereabouts of Kerimov, how to locate him, who the financial sponsor was, or why the flow of money had stopped so suddenly. It was like looking into a black hole with no bottom.

James reported back to Matthew from Newfoundland before he left for Toronto, where he would catch a flight back home to the UK. No one suspected James throughout the venture. He had managed to keep a low profile while communicating with Matthew, helping the geologists do their work to "redirect" the miners and blow the tug.

Until the next time, James thought as he relaxed in his seat on the first leg of his journey back home.

* * *

Plato and Colin had been removing money from the accounts of the Danes and Kerimov for some time now. It seemed odd to them neither target had established alternative accounts to replace those being hacked. But then, there had been no reason for either to suspect foul play and it was more likely they would have put the matter down to banking errors that would eventually be corrected—although the accounts contained millions of dollars that would have been well worth the added safety. As the manager at Hambros Bank had assured Finn and Erik, they would "get to the bottom of this immediately." They never did. Kerimov was even less fortunate since his bank could not communicate with him at all. In the end, they left the matter alone, anticipating it was Kerimov just being Kerimov—secretive, unpredictable, and still very, very wealthy.

* * *

The Sinking of *Viking I*

The sense of frustration and anger Finn and Erik felt was palpable to anyone who came close to them. Aside from the money and ever-worsening Hope Brook project issues, it was impossible to get a berth in the Puerto Banús marina now that their credit facilities had been terminated. If they wanted to remain close to the town, they had no choice but to anchor outside the protective harbor walls sheltering those pampered mega-yachters who, unlike them, could still afford the mooring fees.

Still, at least *Viking I* remained in their hands, and they fully intended to continue to enjoy the luxury and pleasures of living and working at sea. They gave almost no consideration to the potential impending doom with the Norwegian courts—if the law could ever catch them, that is—nor did they think for one second another scam could not be invented in short order to help them out of their current dilemma. It was just a matter of time before something materialized on which to use their well-honed skills to bully, cheat, and lie their way through to the next venture.

In the meantime, to hell with Kerimov, to hell with Økokrim, to hell with the mining industry, oh—and to hell with gold—perhaps. After all, gold did have its allure, and it was fun playing in the same sandbox as all those corporate leeches who had no clue as to how to make a vast amount of easy money quickly from the fortune in their ground. All they did was to reap some mediocre pocket money from an occasional press release to up-tick their company share price by fifty cents so they could cash some of their own shares in for a meager profit. Then they would wait for the next convenient board meeting to vote themselves more shares for the hard work they were not doing. There were so many of those kinds of desperate hopefuls in the mining industry to choose from that it was like shooting fish in a barrel for

Finn and Erik. They just had to wait for the right one to come by.

Finn and Erik perked up at the prospect of fishing for another venture. So much so, they hosted a select group of mining people, staying at the Ocean Club Marbella, to enjoy an evening of food, wine, and dancing aboard *Viking I*.

The idea was a couple of weeks in the planning as Finn and Erik scouted the local Marbella news for upcoming events and discovered that executives of a number of mid-size mining companies from North and South America were meeting at the club for a few days to talk about interacting and common goals—probably just an excuse for a booze-up in a chic resort with their girlfriends or wives—all on company time and money.

Finn came up with the idea of suggesting an evening on *Viking I* might be something the club could offer, for a small fee for themselves, of course, at a cost of only five hundred dollars per person. It could even involve a trip around the bay if the weather was good and the seas were friendly. The club loved the idea. The maximum permitted number of thirty couples signed up.

By ten p.m. on the night of the event, the music in the sky lounge of *Viking I* was loud, the drinks were flowing, people were laughing and dancing to the small, loud three-piece band that had been brought in especially for the event. Finn and Erik were in their element, wining and dining their "guests."

Most of the rest of the boat was available for folks to wander around, although the master stateroom, the lower crew deck, and several other rooms were locked. Guests could visit the bridge, where a couple of the crew members had stationed themselves to keep prying fingers away from the controls but at the same time patiently and politely pointed out some of the interesting and salient features of such a boat. The stern deck, off the main, was also open for those who wanted to enjoy the fresh sea air and peacefulness away from the noise of the sky lounge, but the small pool and jacuzzi were shut down and covered.

There were only two people down on the stern deck. A younger couple, quite drunk, a little frisky, and very impressed by their surroundings, had wandered toward the ladders hanging down to the water surface from the deck. They sat with their legs dangling over the edge and spoke softly and lovingly to each other, he with an arm around her shoulders and a martini in the other hand, she with a tall drink and an arm around his waist. The sky was clear, the moon bright, and the mesmerizing lights of Puerto Banús in the distance spelled a beautiful romantic evening for the two of them.

As the young couple let their faces get closer to each other, their noses tipped together, and as their tongues started to poke through their lips in anticipation, the female noticed a light at the corner of her eye. It was coming from the water. She pulled away from her partner and pointed down silently, her mouth open as though to say something. Her partner's head turned and spotted the light, and within seconds, they were both mesmerized by lights coming up toward them from under the surface of the water. Suddenly, they were grabbed by the feet and pulled down into the water with a soft splash.

Their glasses fell to the deck, one rolled overboard, and the female tried to cry out as they both bobbed to the surface, spluttered with seawater pouring out of their mouths, and managed to grab the swim ladder.

The man put a handout and grabbed his company and pulled her up to the rung below him. She held on and tried to scream, but it was dampened by the water still coming out of her mouth as she kept spluttering. They were in shock. Woken from a drunken haze by the cold seawater engulfing them, they pulled themselves up to the deck and lay face down, gasping and wondering what the fuck just happened.

Matthew and Emma climbed onto the stern deck, lifted their face masks off, and removed their flippers while the pair of lovers were struggling in the water. They slipped quickly over to the engine-room door, hidden from any eyes that might be watching from the upper decks by the overhang of the second floor. It took Matthew less than a minute to pick the lock and let both of them into the fluorescent-lit room. The two engines, one on each side, had no hint of oil, grease, or even dust on them. The place was spotless, with every piece of equipment, every run of pipe, and every instrument tagged with a number and a name. Clearly, maintenance was taken very seriously on this vessel.

They stood together and looked around. There was no need for flashlights as both stepped cautiously toward the first engine. Neither was operating at this point and the vessel utilities were operating from diesel generator power supplied by a unit in a separate enclosure located in next door. They could hear it, but they couldn't see it.

Like most mega yachts, *Viking I* used a combination of fresh water and seawater to cool the engines and ancillary equipment to maintain them at a normal temperature of about two hundred degrees Fahrenheit. The seawater was a secondary system, automatically activated when the temperature of the engines started to run over the norm. That happened all the time when *Viking I* reached open water, past the harbor restrictions, and Finn or Erik would want the throttles opened up. They liked to travel at least five knots over cruising speed and, more often than not, ten over.

Matthew identified the high-capacity centrifugal pumps that would suck the seawater from below the boat through a strainer and into the cooling systems. Each incoming seawater strainer was bolted to a six-inch diameter section of pipe flange mounted on a reinforcing plate attached to the bottom of the hull. A bolted-in check valve, only allowing flow in one direction, was set in the open position under the strainer to always allow seawater entry when called for by the cooling system heat sensors.

Matthew temporarily closed the valve on the inlet to the first strainer, leaving only a residual amount of seawater in the system. He followed the discharge piping from the pump, through the exchanger and out the other end, through another check valve and a six-inch diameter through-hull fitting in the side of the vessel, allowing the water to escape to the sea again. Each discharge line had an isolation valve installed to stop the flow when needed for cooling system maintenance.

Matthew used a monkey wrench to remove the downstream valve where the seawater would be pumped back outside and replaced it with a dummy section of pipe with a third of its wall removed, like a slot. He made sure the slot faced the side of the boat so it would remain hidden, should one of the crew pass a casual eye over the equipment and spot the modified pipe section and missing valve. Returning to the inlet valve, he chained it in the open position so it couldn't be easily closed to prevent seawater from entering the system.

He repeated the process on the other engine cooling system.

Next, Matthew disarmed the four high-level water alarms so the bridge would be without warning signals when the engine room started to flood and the bilge pumps couldn't energize. In fact, there would never be an automatic alarm triggered at all, unless the water could make it through to the lower decks, where there were other alarms and bilge pumps. That was very unlikely since the engine room was essentially a sealed container with only one way out—the one Matthew had used to get in.

The floodwater would not be discovered until someone spotted it coming through the ventilation grates installed two feet above the bottom of the engine-room entry doors, were six steps up from the floor. That would mean the seawater would have to accumulate eight feet above the bottom of the hull before anyone could spot the flood. By that time, it would be too late. Even if the bilge pumps could be operated when the flood was discovered, they would never have the capacity to draw the level of the flood water down as well as keep up with the centrifugal pumps continuing to bring seawater aboard—until their motors were flooded and they stopped operating. By that time, *Viking I* would be sinking stern first under the weight of flood water and the engines. Once the centrifugal suction pumps stopped and the boat started to sink, the downward action would cause seawater to pour in through the exit holes in the sides of the boat and the mega yacht would continue to take on seawater as it sank.

Emma cautiously opened the engine-room door, listened for noises, and peeped around to make sure no one was down on the lower deck. She gave Matthew the thumbs-up sign before they both made a silent run to the stern ladder. The young lovers had left and taken their distress with them. Who would listen to their tale of lights coming up out of the water? Just another alcohol-fueled mirage, and everyone would laugh.

Matthew and Emma sat on the edge of the deck, put their flippers and goggles back on, and slipped into the water. Their ride back to shore was just fifty strokes away—a black rubber dinghy with no running lights—tied to one of the marina channel buoys. They rowed their way a hundred feet farther from *Viking I* before pressing the starter button on the outboard and slowly made their way back to the beach east of Puerto Banús, hidden by rocks piled to protect the shoreline from littoral drift.

* * *

Finn and Erik were pleased with their efforts at the party. They had managed to circulate while extolling their virtues as professional financial consultants well versed in "alternative" ways to raise funds for prospective ventures with proven resources and ready for development.

They hooked a few fish that evening who were interested in following up, often through their flirting rather than through the offer of a professional portfolio. Some of the guests claimed to know them by reputation. Others claimed to have done business with them before or even said they were currently working with them on a deal of some kind. But the truth was, these claims were all made away from the company of Finn and Erik as more of a means of impressing others. The fact was, no one had heard of either of them. But that didn't matter. They must be successful at whatever they did. After all, they had an expensive mega yacht and a membership at the Ocean Club Marbella, and they talked the talk—it just felt right.

Yes, Finn and Erik were very close to being back in business and would reinvent themselves as experts in something. They just had to discover the weakness of whoever needed them.

* * *

It was two days after the *Viking I* party when Finn got a call. It was a "John Winters," reminding him of the wonderful evening they had spent on *Viking I* and the fine impression both Finn and Erik had made on him and his wife, Cindy, who was also the corporate secretary of his relatively small gold mining company, and a member of the board. Finn couldn't remember either of them, but Winters was anxious to meet at the earliest possible time to discuss a project his company had in mind. All they needed was financing and were somewhat cash-strapped right now to deliver it any other way than the "alternative" ways Finn had suggested he and Erik might be able to organize. Winters mentioned the potential of selling all their gold forward to the market at a rate that would be somewhere around ten percent below the prescribed London standard.

Finn was intrigued. "Let me think on this and get back to you over the next few days, Mr. Winters. What's the name of your company again?"

"Oh, please call me John, but I don't think I can wait very long with the wolves at our doors. I would prefer not to deal with them, you know. Same old, same old. Once they get a grip on you, they don't let go, and before you know it, they'll control everything. What d'you say? Can you get over here right away? We're visiting just along the coast from where you are—in Cartagena. Can you make it over tomorrow sometime? I think you'll like what I'm offering."

Clearly, Mr. Winters was not divulging the name of his company just yet. Finn thought it could be just for confidential reasons at this point and shrugged it off. He wanted to mull things over with Erik, but his accomplice was in town on some personal business.

As he quickly reflected on what was happening, he didn't see a reason not to go and visit Winters, and Erik wasn't likely to disagree, other than for the cost of travel. But then, one had to spend some to get some, so Finn dismissed the issue as being a necessary expense. What else could he do?

"Sure." Finn had paused to think long enough. He needed to respond to Winters. "It's about six to eight hours away by boat, I think. We'll come up and get a berth at the marina. Let's say, arrival time about three tomorrow afternoon?"

"That's great. I'll send a message to let you know how to contact me and we'll meet you there. I think we can find a nice place to sit and chat for a while."

"We can do that on *Viking I*, John!" Finn sounded enthusiastic.

"Of course we can." Winters was also enthused. "Until tomorrow, then." He rang off.

Winters never did provide Finn the name of his company.

* * *

Viking I pulled anchor just after seven a.m., the morning after the call from Winters, and set a course northeast at their top speed of eighteen knots. There was always room for a little more when the ocean was calm with no wind, as it was this day, but for now, they didn't over-challenge the engines for the eight hours or so it would take to get to Cartagena. They stayed close to the shoreline but far enough away from the smattering of sailboats seen occasionally leaving the various marinas along their route.

The temperature of the engines started to climb above normal after thirty minutes. The centrifugal pumps activated and sucked the seawater into the secondary cooling system and through the exchangers as they should. The outflow water found its way through the slots in the six-inch pup pipe sections, where the exit valves should have been, and ended up on the engine-room floor instead of going back into the sea.

It took less than an hour for the seawater to reach a depth of twenty-four inches with nowhere to go, and still no one aboard had any idea of what was happening. None of the instruments on the bridge indicated a problem. No one noticed *Viking I* starting to ride lower in the water until the depth of the flood in the engine room reached three, then four feet, when the speed showed a marked decrease to fifteen, then eleven knots, and suddenly one of the engines stopped working altogether. The second engine quit a few minutes later, and panic broke out on the bridge.

Finn and Erik, who had been relaxing over a leisurely breakfast in the aft cabin, listened as both engines stopped and were further alerted by the sudden pandemonium as crew members thumped their way down the passageways toward the stern. Finn and Erik exchanged looks of shock, then panic as they pushed themselves up out of their seats with plates of food flying, coffee cups spilling, and chairs thrown to the deck. They joined the running group while asking what the hell was happening.

"Looks like we're takin' on water, chief," a crew member shouted over his shoulder as he carried on running.

"What?" they both exclaimed at the same time and raced to the lower stern deck with the crew.

By the time Finn and Erik reached the stern, *Viking I* was starting to take on water over the swim platform as it slowly sank. Two crew members, having opened the engine-room doors, were washed overboard by the sea water rushing out. Their crewmates threw buoys to them and hauled them back onboard. The water poured through the sliding glass doors over the main deck and in through the salon. As the boat sank further, seawater poured over the sides until the crew quarters on the lower deck were completely submerged, with the main deck following quickly.

Three of the crew members reached the upper deck, where two sizable life rafts were mounted on davits. With an enormous effort, they released them from their clamps, ripped off the covers, and lowered them into the water three stories below. No one had to shout, "Man the lifeboats!" It was an automatic reaction to the obvious—they were definitely sinking.

Finn and Erik jumped from the main deck into the water next to the first raft, not realizing they had none of their personal effects with them—including passports. Their raft moved away from *Viking I* with two of the eight crew rowing, while the second raft was being loaded with the remainder, including the captain. Everyone seemed to be accounted for, although neither Finn nor Erik were particularly interested, and just managed to squeeze out an "oh, good" when told.

The engine of the first life raft spluttered alive at the press of a button on the outboard and they set off toward shore. As Finn and Erik looked back, *Viking I* was sinking at a shallow angle, stern first. The second raft was on its way.

* * *

"Mr. Winters? Hello. Are you there?" Finn called from shore into his cell phone, which still worked despite its contact with water. Regardless of the trauma, he needed to contact Winters in Cartagena to let him know what had happened and assure him of their continued interest. By this time, he knew it was a desperate situation that called for desperate measures. Winters seemed to be their only lifeline—Finn had to make it work.

There were already police and ambulances on the beach awaiting the arrival of the survivors from *Viking I*. A police speedboat and helicopter were heading over to where the mega yacht's communications mast was just visible—the only part of the boat above water—at least for a few more minutes.

There were no survivors to pick up. All had made it to safety. The sea was strewn with remnants of the boat floating in with the tide to the beach. There were clothes, and loungers, papers and bottles, hats and floating devices, paintings and food, toiletries and filters, and all manner of other floating debris. Little of it was salvageable and the Danes never looked. What was important to them was in the safe, and that had gone down with *Viking* I. It would have to be attended to later with a diver.

"Are you there, for Chrissake? Winters!" Finn shouted at his cell phone, but there was no response. He tried again, and then again. There wasn't even the sound of a phone ringing at the other end. There was no other way to contact Winters, and it was then that Finn had a flash. "That fucking ORB." He threw his phone down onto the sand twenty feet away and Erik picked it up for his friend. It was the only thing they had left between them, apart from the money belt Erik always had attached around his waist—just in case. His friend never did plan for the worst.

* * *

Poor Roman

Knowing it was highly unlikely he would ever get the money back from Kerimov, unless ORB came through, Partwick shifted into full cover-your-ass mode and went on a PCW spending binge. He wanted to finance as many potential operations as he could in an effort to mask the visibility of the Hope Brook fiasco with others in the company. Hopefully, it would buy him a little time to figure things out, and perhaps by then ORB would bring him good news with the return of PCW's lost investment. Wishful thinking—but he had to have hope.

While Partwick was a senior partner, he had, like all the others, a fiduciary responsibility to report on the projects he was responsible for investing in on behalf of the company. He managed to build his portfolio of small prospects quickly to fourteen, containing the good, the bad, and the ugly. It would be difficult for his colleagues to delve too deeply into that many when they had enough on their own plates. Of course, they trusted Partwick—he was their mentor and guiding light.

Partwick was temporarily satisfied he had adequately dealt with his immediate concerns while he waited for ORB. Perhaps they really would come through, and while their fee was extortionate at thirty-three percent of the recovered amount, Partwick considered the remaining sixty-seven percent as being better than losing everything. Still… he wondered what more he could do to mitigate the financial damage. After all, his reputation had been attacked. He had been made a fool of. Partwick wasn't used to being the butt end of someone else's joke. He thought hard.

A few days later, Partwick had PCW lawyers contact a global service provider that handled cross-border legal matters and had them file an international lien against *Ice Man II*. It was common knowledge Kerimov's yacht was worth over five hundred million dollars, but ownership was typically unclear when it came to the assets of oligarchs. Regardless, Partwick was adamant the yacht would eventually be proved to be the property of Kerimov or his personal company. Since a lien claim did not have to go to court immediately, he hoped time would be on his side to investigate and establish ownership.

Tracking down a superyacht's true owner requires more than a Google search. It can be extremely difficult to unravel who owns these vessels. Ownership is often hidden behind shell companies and trusts, and registered in countries where information is tightly controlled—not something the US or the UK can always readily access. But nothing could stop Partwick from his mission. He employed the best investigators—ex-Lloyd's insurance fraud experts—to interview sources with knowledge of the boat's finances and had them scour bank statements and corporate records whenever they could be found.

The lien stayed on *Ice Man II* without Kerimov's knowledge. There was no need to advise him unless he intended to sell the boat, in which case the lien would prevent him until it was cleared, or Partwick executed the lien with the international court when he was ready with sufficient evidence of ownership. Of course, it was simple enough to prove the loans made to Kerimov by PCW were real, but based on fraudulent applications, and with ORB's help, he would be able to prove his claim.

The first thing his lawyers had to do was to establish which country *Ice Man II* was registered. Once that was done, the lien would be placed and immediately executed. Partwick had no intention of waiting and wanted his revenge, and his money as soon as he could get it.

It wasn't as difficult as Partwick had thought. *Ice Man II* was discovered to be registered in Malta, a law-abiding country, while at the same time a haven for corrupt money. His lawyer filed the lien and wasted no time in issuing a writ of summons together with an affidavit signed by Partwick, on behalf of PCW, against Kerimov and the bogus company he used to purchase and register the boat.

The gloves were off. Now all Partwick needed was to locate Kerimov and have the papers served and pressure the authorities to impound *Ice Man II* while the legal case was sorted out. The problem was, no one knew where Kerimov was, other than ORB.

* * *

Meanwhile, Kerimov had raided his safe onboard *Ice Man II* and confirmed the value of money he was holding there, including ten gold bars, each weighing one kilogram, worth about six hundred thousand dollars, and ten stacks of a hundred one-hundred-dollar bills. He also had a "spare" passport and two unlimited credit cards, all in the name of Boris Ivanof, his mother's maiden name and his father's first name, as a part of his backup strategy. He had been tied to the dock in North Vancouver now for almost two weeks, with no outside communications.

"My dear Stockman," Kerimov answered a call using a phone tossed to him by a guard on the quay. "How nice to hear from you, my friend."

"I'm sure it is," Stockman responded sourly. "Ready to go home?" he asked.

"At once, of course. But first I have to repair the damage to my boat, which you are responsible for. I have to replace both propellors, repair and repaint the hull, repair the other damage caused by your sabotage, and then pay the moorage fees before I can leave port." Kerimov sighed heavily down the phone, as though looking for sympathy. "It could cost me half a million. Are you willing to help with this?"

"Only by letting you go, but you're going to have to pay for the repairs yourself. Or perhaps you would rather go on trial for kidnapping?" Stockman waited for the response.

"We will meet again one day, Stockman, and perhaps our roles will be reversed."

"I doubt it, Kerimov. I don't travel in your circles unless I'm hunting." Stockman allowed himself a smile.

"Well, I will need access to my bank accounts if I am to pay." Kerimov was angry but held his temper in case he was penalized more than he had already been.

"I think you have enough in that safe of yours—or shall I say, you did—the last time we looked." With that, Stockman ended the call.

Kerimov was shocked and let the phone just dangle in his hand as he thought about his safe.

"That bitch," he said out loud to no one in particular. It could only have been Emma when she was on *Ice Man II* with Big Jim in Puerto Banús. She had certainly been out of his sight for a while, but he had assumed she was in the room next to where he was meeting the whole time.

* * *

The ORB guards disappeared from the dock as quickly as they had appeared. There was a cardboard box sitting at the bottom of the stern gangway. It contained phones, passports, keys to *Ice Man II*, and a few other small things removed from Kerimov and his men before they were quarantined. The phones worked, and the communications were back up and running. Kerimov was back in business, except his bank account had been substantially depleted by at least the amount PCW had transferred to him.

* * *

"You're in luck, my friend." Stockman had called Partwick and gotten through to him immediately. Clearly, the word had gone out that he must have immediate access.

"Oh, hi, Stockman. Any news?" Partwick sounded chirpy, given he was in the hole for over four hundred million dollars.

"I'd say so. We managed to recover your money, Partwick. What do you say to that?" Stockman was just as chirpy.

"Christ, you're joking. You must be." Partwick was lost for words.

"No joke. We have it safely stashed away and will wire it to you if you can give me the instructions—and the exact amount." Stockman was smiling.

Partwick was dumbfounded. "I'll send the information over to you. What a relief. I can't thank you enough."

"I'd say a hundred and thirty million was enough of a thank you—wouldn't you?" Stockman chuckled; Partwick didn't.

"Do you know what happened to Kerimov?" Partwick asked.

"Yes, of course. We held him up for a while in Vancouver. Why? Did you need to contact him for something?" Stockman was a little wary at the question. He wondered if there was some off-to-the-side arrangement between Partwick and Kerimov.

"Oh—yes. You see, we're going to place a lien against his yacht," Partwick said it quite distractedly, as though it was nothing in particular.

"What? You can't be serious." Stockman laughed out loud. "I'll be damned. Good luck to you, old boy. I'll give you his number and exact location—will that do?"

"That would be great. Just trying to recover everything we lost, you know. A hundred and thirty million is a hundred and thirty million. May as well have a go at getting it back as well."

"I'd say so—good luck. I'll send that information over right away. Let me know how it all goes, would you?" Stockman was still laughing.

"You bet. And thanks again, Stockman." Partwick chuckled as the call ended.

* * *

It was just after nine in the morning when the writ was issued directly to Kerimov as he was having breakfast in the aft salon on the main deck of *Ice Man II*. It was still tied up at the Weyerhaeuser wharf, waiting for the repairs to begin.

The person serving the papers was nervous but had been warned about the potential for intimidation and had brought company to bolster his confidence. That company stationed himself at the top end of the gangway so he could photograph the events. He waited patiently for his associate to emerge from the sliding glass doors and started shooting video as soon as he identified Kerimov standing up from his chair.

Kerimov had snatched the papers, read the first few lines, strode through the sliding doors, and ripped the writ in half, throwing the torn pieces of paper up into the air. There was no wind, and the pieces of paper landed on various parts of the open stern deck. A crew member picked them up and stuffed them behind his back. He knew the boss was going to ask for them later, but right now was the time to keep them hidden, whatever they were.

* * *

Time for Truth

Spurred along by additional information provided by ORB, indictments were issued by the Norwegian government against both Finn and Erik for their part in the illegality of brokering a deal using shares fraudulently solicited from the shareholders of the Norwegian mining company. All this while they were encumbered with the failure of their Hope Brook project, the loss of their revenue stream, the disappearance of their money, and the sinking of their special prize—*Viking I*. And where the hell was Kerimov?

Subpoenas to appear before Økokrim's committee hearing in Norway had been delivered to Finn and Erik as they sat licking their wounds in a bar in Puerto Banús and staring at someone else's beautiful mega yacht tied up in "their" mooring spot. That was where the Spanish police arrested and detained them until they received the extradition papers from the Norwegian embassy in Madrid.

Finn and Erik were sentenced to prison for five years by both the regional and appeals courts of Norway. The Supreme Court agreed with those decisions. They were required to pay restitution of five hundred and fifty million dollars to the original shareholders of the mining company they had scammed. That was the current value of those shares, which had multiplied by almost thirty times since the sale to Kerimov's company.

It was satisfying to both Matthew and Stockman to know the Danes had to pay their dues in prison for at least the shareholders scam, if not for their Greenland and Hope Brook capers. At least there was something illegal that could be proven against them now. After all, a scam is just a scam, but isn't necessarily illegal, and while one could certainly call their activities immoral, they were not quite up to prosecution in a court of law—too bad, but such is life.

* * *

The court reacted swiftly to the writ of summons served on Kerimov and had *Ice Man II* impounded where it was as a consequence of the international lien—it was still at the Weyerhaeuser wharf. The lines were secured by chains to the cleats, both on the dock and the boat. It wasn't going anywhere until the law decided what to do—complicated by it being in Canadian waters, but registered in Malta, and owned by a Maltese-registered corporation. At least everyone spoke English in Malta, and the Canadian and Maltese governments shared excellent relationships.

* * *

Kerimov had little choice but to make his way back to his homeland by air and land. His best friend, *Ice Man II*, was gone, his money had been drawn down to repay PWC, and he had no idea where Finn and Erik were, and neither had they tried contacting him through all this. All in all, it was a very sad situation, but it hadn't destroyed his hate of Stockman and ORB. He was bound to retaliate but, for now, he needed to recover.

* * *

Until the Next Time

"Of course, Henri." Stockman was on a call with a client at the World Bank headquarters in Washington. "I am extremely happy you all got your money back—minus our fee, of course, and we would love to see you whenever we get an opportunity." Stockman looked over at Lucy, who just raised her shoulders and eyebrows as if to say, "When? Where? Why?" but she knew better than to interrupt Stockman while he was on a call.

"Will do. Yes, you never know. You have my number, so just call if you run into more problems like this one." There was a pause as Henri thanked Stockman again and said his goodbyes. "You, too, my friend. Take care." Stockman put the receiver back in its cradle and reached for his Plymouth gin and tonic, a welcome thirst quencher after his discussion. "

"Well, he was certainly happy." Stockman looked over the top of his glasses at Lucy.

"I should think so, dear." Lucy put her magazine down and glanced over at him. "The World Bank collected their lost investment in Greenland and watched as those scoundrels were sent packing to jail. I'm sure Henri will want to get you involved if this kind of thing happens again. The only problem is if he asks you to get involved in everything that goes wrong for them. I'm guessing that that would be far too much for you to manage."

"Ah, I don't think I'm going to be jumping too high if they get themselves in the usual problems. They're going to have to sort those kinds of things out for themselves. But if they get tangled up in the type of skulduggery we've seen with these Danes and that Russian, I'm sure we'll make room for them."

They both went back to their reading and keeping one eye on the view outside. The wind was blowing up again. It seemed to hurtle in spasms over the top of the cliffs, almost bowling the casual walkers over as they made their way to either Thurlestone in the distance, or to Hope Cove just down the hill below them.

Suddenly, the curtains fluttered, the glasses rattled, paper flew around, and a draft rushed across the floor of the house as an outer door banged closed and Matthew and Emma appeared at the living room door after their walk over the cliffs. Their cheeks were flushed pink from the wind, their hair tousled in all directions, and they laughed for reasons only they knew.

"Sorry, Mum. Sorry, Dad. That wind caught the door before we had a chance to close it. It's wild out there. Beautiful but wild. I love it." Emma looked the picture of health.

Matthew followed her, rubbing his hands together to get the circulation going again. He smoothed his hair down as best he could. "Ahh, I'd love one of those." He pointed at the glass Stockman had just put down.

"Help yourself, Matthew. Get one for Emma if she would like something. It won't warm you up as much as a Scotch, but it'll keep the red in your cheeks." Stockman smiled.

This was the first time Emma or Matthew had stayed with Stockman and Lucy in their home away from home, tucked into the English countryside by the sea.

"That was enough fresh air to last a lifetime." Matthew poured a couple of gin and tonics over lumps of ice, dropped a fresh slice of lime into each glass, passed one to Emma, who had plonked down in one corner of the sofa, and sat himself next to her.

It had been several weeks since they wrapped up the case against the Danes and had Kerimov followed back to Russia. He had not been welcomed in the style he was accustomed to when faced by some of his oligarch friends and high-placed political figures at home, not least of whom was Putin. In fact, his future was in serious jeopardy now that everyone knew some of the secrets of his past and what he had been doing on the side while he was president of Polygold. Their respectability in the industry had been seriously tainted by the antics of Kerimov, and their board had wasted no time voting him out as president and off the board.

After that, he became little more than an employee and, as such, lost much of the power that so fueled him. But he was still wealthy and still a threat who would rekindle his need for illicit power—just not right away.

Stockman, Lucy, Emma, and Matthew sat around, twisting their glasses, talking about the Hope Brook escapade, and laughing at the demise of the Danes in particular, who had become more and more despondent, followed by recklessness, each time something happened to them. First, it was the money, and the four of them laughed mercilessly as they pictured the Danes scrambling around while Kerimov threatened them, and they had absolutely no idea what was happening.

Then, just as the Danes started to think the mining was faring well, they lost the direction of the gold, the barges started to sink, and the rudders of the tug blew out of the water. Kerimov had become more crazy mad as more money went missing and only partially reappeared with no explanation. The final straw that stopped the rape of the Hope Brook property by the Danes was the loss of the gold vein direction for the second time and waste ore just kept piling up. There seemed to be no end to their problems. By then, they were focusing more on their money disappearing faster than a trickle from their bank accounts; it couldn't be stopped.

It was Kerimov who really took everything to the next level, and Matthew and Emma laughed as they remembered the clumsiness of her kidnapping by Kerimov's agents, and her eventual rescue.

"I have to admit, I was worried there for a while, Matthew." Stockman glanced at Lucy as though he had already been berated by his wife for allowing Emma to be captured. Whether she believed him when he said he didn't know was still a question mark. But Stockman and Matthew knew he knew and had actually been a part of the caper.

"I had to do something." Matthew looked the picture of innocence as he spread his palms out. "My gut told me Kerimov wasn't coming to Vancouver just for meetings. He never came to Canada if he could avoid it. It's just too far, and there's no business big enough there for him to take an interest. So, it had to be something else, and I just knew from Emma's first meeting with him, when he planted that tracker on her and hid the spyware in her apartment, he was likely to use her for leverage if the time came—and it did."

"Well, I'm glad you didn't tell me what you were up to, Matthew. I may have put a stop to it rather than risk my daughter to who knows what."

Stockman looked serious as he lied to avoid the wrath of Lucy. "But it's all over, and we can look forward to the next one."

"Uh oh. My guess is you already know what it is." Matthew laughed and looked at Emma, who seemed to be struck dumb at this moment.

Lucy laughed. "Oh, come on, Murray. Out with it. What are you getting yourself into this time?"

"Did I ever tell you about…?"

THE END

www.ingramcontent.com/pod-product-compliance
Lightning Source LLC
LaVergne TN
LVHW020405211224
799577LV00007B/155